For Rosie Cheetham

Readers of *Salt of the Earth* and *Up Our Street* will instantly recognise Norton and Buckworth as the real-life town of Northwich and the village of Marston. So why change the names for *A Picnic in Eden*? The answer is that this book is set closer to the present, with the consequent danger that my readers might think, for example, that the two candidates described as standing in the 1966 Norton election correspond, in some way, to the two who actually stood in the 1966 *Northwich* election. Nothing could be further from the truth. All my characters are, as always, products of my imagination.

'. . . it is not only our fate but our business to lose innocence, and once we have lost that, it is futile to attempt a picnic in Eden.'

Elizabeth Bowen.

L'amour est aveugle; l'amitié ferme les yeux.
Love is blind; friendship closes its eyes.

Anon.

It was bitterly cold, even for March, and the gravestones were covered with a sheen of glittering hoar-frost. The sun was no more than a pale, watery spot in the sky. The birds perched in black, skeletal trees ruffled their feathers, but were otherwise still. The only noise to disturb the frozen silence came from human onlookers, who shuffled their feet and exchanged semi-reverential whispers as they strained against the police cordon for a better view of the grave.

The church door creaked and necks stretched to watch the cortège, led by a mahogany coffin carried on the shoulders of four men. This was not a common sight anymore. Trolleys were used nowadays to convey the casket to its last resting place, their rubber wheels gliding smoothly, effortlessly, over the worn paving stones. But the two front pall-bearers had insisted on the old way. They wanted to carry, not guide – to take the weight of the relationship in death as they had done in life.

It was almost too much for them that they were forced to share the load with others, men who had liked the deceased and been liked in return, but had never been close to him. He had only ever had two real friends, and as the box pressed down on their shoulders, the rear pall-bearers felt like intruders on a private grief.

The crisp, biting air buzzed with excitement. The crowd began to push and the policemen had to strain to hold them back.

There would have been a large turn-out under any circumstances. The deceased had been a famous son of Norton. A local hero – at least to some. But the suddenness – the unexpectedness – of his death, had turned the event into street theatre. And already the rumours were flying.

'I've got a cousin in the police force and he says something's not quite right.'
'Drunk? At that time of day? You're not telling me . . .'

The celebrities had caused a stir too, arriving in their big cars all the way from London. It was worth getting cold just to see the rich and famous standing there, almost within touching distance. Was that *her*? Didn't she look different on the telly? Wasn't that tall chap the one who . . . you know?

The three plainclothes policemen positioned strategically away from the crowd watched the scene with unflinching intensity. The eldest, a Chief Inspector in his early forties, wore a heavy tweed overcoat and a worried expression. He had donned a black armband, but his eyes were focused not on the coffin itself but on one of its bearers. His business was with the quick, not the dead.

The cortège reached the grave. The hard ground had been hacked rather than dug, and wicked, jagged spikes of petrified earth stuck out from the edges.

The chief mourners reluctantly surrendered the casket to the grave-diggers, and stood solemnly while it was lowered into the hole. As it bumped to the bottom, a heavy grey cloud drifted in front of the sun, and it was suddenly darker, colder.

The vicar, prayer book held in hands that were almost numb, began to read the service.

'In the midst of life we are in death,' he intoned.

Three days earlier, the man in the coffin had been fit and active, with the prospect of a golden future before him. Now he was just a lifeless slab of meat and bone.

> *'For as much as it hath pleased Almighty God of his great mercy to take unto himself the soul of our dear brother here departed, we therefore commit his body to the ground, ashes to ashes, dust to dust . . .'*

It was difficult to see all this as the result of divine providence, one of the chief mourners thought. Not when you knew how and why he had died. And yet . . . and yet, perhaps there *was* a celestial logic behind it. If they were not God's puppets, then they were certainly fate's. Because none of this would have happened but for that meeting in the playground over twenty years ago. The seeds of the funeral had been planted then and had been growing, invisibly, ever since.

The vicar closed his prayer book and retreated, leaving the stage free for the dead man's two friends. They stepped forward together and their fingers tugged and clawed at the frozen earth until each had managed to prise free a chunk. They stood at the side of the grave, looking down at the shining box but seeing beyond it, to the man they had known and the destiny they had shared. They did not move for almost a minute. Then, on an unspoken signal, they opened their hands simultaneously and let the earth fall.

The solid clods hit the coffin with the crash of a hammer striking a skull and bounced back into the air. They landed again, with less force this time, rolled a little along the mahogany, and were still.

The two mourners saw none of that. They had turned their backs and were walking away. The ceremony was over – at least for them.

From a distance, the Chief Inspector watched them uneasily. It was possible, with this crowd, for his man to make an escape, and though they would catch him eventually, it would look bad. Even if he didn't run he might resist arrest, and nobody wanted any trouble at a funeral.

The suspect saw the Chief Inspector's anxiety and gestured discreetly that there was no need for it. He would not cause problems, neither now nor later. He turned to his companion, and gave him a thin, wan smile.

'You'll come with me, won't you?' he asked.

It was not really a question. Signalling to the policemen to follow, they walked together towards the lych-gate, their minds no longer in the graveyard but roaming the playground of their childhoods on that first day of school . . .

PART ONE

The Secret Camp

Chapter One

During the long, sweet summer holiday, the children had forgotten what it was like to be cooped up in a classroom. When playtime finally came, they erupted, skipping higher than ever before, pursuing furious games of tag under the warm September sun. They shouted, they screamed, they laughed. All except the infants.

The new children stood with their hands in their pockets and watched the others play, or else wandered aimlessly up and down the playground. Just yesterday, they had joined in the big kids' games, but that had been in the village street – familiar territory. Now the solid, redbrick school loomed over them, its slated gables gazing down like disapproving eyes. And they felt lonely and afraid.

Some of the children had cried when their mothers left; a few had even tried to follow and been restrained by Miss Gladstone. But not the two squatting by the fence, looking at the ground; not the two that Jimmy Bradley, new to the village as well as to the school, was studying.

One of them, David, was a stocky child, and it was possible even then to see that he would be a powerful figure when he grew up. He had just gazed blankly as his mother walked away, as if he had never expected anything but desertion. The other, Paul, the slight pale one, had *wanted* to cry, but bit his lip and held back the tears.

Jimmy wondered whether or not to approach – but only for a second. There was something about the other two that made him feel he would be welcomed.

As he got closer to them, he could see what they were doing. In the dirt at the edge of the playground, they had scraped a hole into which they had herded several ants. The sides of the hole were not steep, but when one of the creatures reached the top, Paul would lift a twig and flick it back down. Try as they might, the ants could not escape, and their tiny minds coped with this frustration by adopting an even more frantic pace.

Jimmy's shadow fell across the hole – and across the two small boys. They looked up, sharply, expecting trouble. Then, seeing that he was new too, they relaxed again.

'What are you doin'?' Jimmy asked.

'Playin' a game,' Paul said.

'What's it called?'

Paul shrugged his thin shoulders.

'It's not got no name. It's just a game. You've got to stop the ants gettin' out of the hole.'

Jimmy watched as another one scrambled up the slope. Just as it reached the top, Paul poked with his stick, and the insect rolled backwards, stopping only when it reached the bottom.

'It's scared,' Jimmy said. 'Why don't you let it go?'

'Because!' Paul said, somewhat snappily.

This tall blond stranger had no right to ask questions.

And then Paul discovered that he wanted to tell him because, in some peculiar way, explaining the game to the new boy would be explaining it to himself.

'It doesn't matter if it's scared,' he said, and then added, with sudden, fierce emphasis, 'It shouldn't want to get out. It should want to stay with its pals.'

Jimmy took it as a cue.

'I'm Jimmy. Shall *we* be pals?'

He saw the serious expression on the faces of the crouching boys as they stared at him, examined him. Their assessment seemed to take for ever.

'If we're goin' to be pals,' Paul said finally, 'we've got to be *real* pals.'

David said nothing, just pointed down to the ground. Jimmy's gaze followed his finger. While the boys' attention had been distracted, one of the ants had succeeded in climbing over the lip of the hole and was scurrying away.

'Real pals,' David said, repeating Paul's words. 'Not like them.'

'I won't leave you in no hole,' Jimmy promised. 'Never. Cross me heart an' hope to die.'

Paul looked at David, David looked at Paul and slowly their eyes widened and smiles spread across their faces. They clambered to their feet and each put a hand on one of Jimmy's shoulders.

'We'll be a gang,' Paul said. 'A proper one.'

And though they could not have articulated it, each felt as if a force had surrounded them, locked them together, welding their destinies – and excluded everyone else in the entire world.

For an infant, the playground is as fraught with hazards as any jungle, and it was only three days later that they met their first, in the form of Barney Jenkins. Barney was a big dull lad, and he was all of nine. Most of the other children called him 'Barmy' Jenkins, though never to his face. He had misbehaved just before playtime, and Miss Howard made him stay behind for ten minutes, so that by the time he reached the milk crate there was none left. He looked around and saw David, just pushing his thumb through the foil-top of a fresh bottle.

'You've pinched me milk,' Barney said. 'You've had yours and now you're pinchin' mine.'

'That's not true,' David replied. 'Honest. This is the only one I've had.'

But he knew there was no point; the bully did not want an argument, he wanted the milk.

Barney reached across and grabbed at the bottle. All his experience told him that the smaller child would relinquish it and then run off somewhere to have a private cry. But David was gripping the milk tightly.

'Give it here,' Barney said threateningly. 'It's mine.'

'No, it's not,' countered two small, squeaky voices behind him.

He turned and found himself confronted by Paul Wright and the new boy. Barney knew the rules. Individual big boys bullied individual small ones; that was the way it had always been, that was the way it would stay. Somebody had to be taught a lesson, probably the kid with yeller hair, because Barney hated people with yeller hair. He made a fist and punched him in the face, as hard as he could. It must have hurt because the yeller-haired kid started to cry. But he didn't move. Well, if he had to hit him again . . .

He felt a pressure on his back as two small arms locked about his neck and two small feet started kicking him just below his knees. He lost his balance and fell backwards, landing heavily on David. In an instant, the other two boys were on him, pulling him away from their friend, beating at him with tiny, angry fists. He fought back furiously, sensing that this was more important than an ordinary fight, that a fundamental law of playground life was being challenged.

He grabbed Paul's hair and yanked as hard as he could. The younger boy was pulled to the ground and Barney did not release his grip until Paul's head hit the asphalt. He turned on the new kid – he'd show the little bugger. But before he could get to his feet, David was on him again, his arms tightly around his neck, and

Jimmy was punching at him, oblivious to his own pain. Then Paul was back, sobbing but fighting.

The four children rolled around the playground, kicking, biting, gouging and punching for all they were worth. By the time Miss Gladstone arrived on the scene and broke it up, all were battered and bleeding.

'It was just incredible,' she told Miss Howard later. 'I've never seen such a vicious fight in this school. And little children don't gang up on bigger ones. I mean, it just doesn't happen.'

For Miss Howard, the post-fight interview followed the normal course for such occasions. Barney blubbered and said that he was sorry, Miss, and he would be a good boy in future. For Miss Gladstone, it was quite different. As she sat at her teacher's table, she found herself looking across at three bruised but firmly unrepentant infants.

'I'm ashamed of you,' she said. 'Children from my class, fighting like that! Aren't you ashamed of *yourselves*?'

'We didn't start it,' David said stubbornly.

'We didn't start it – what?' Miss Gladstone demanded.

'We didn't start it, *Miss*. He wanted my milk.'

'Maybe he did, David. But we don't solve anything by fighting, do we?'

There should have been nods of the heads and murmurs of agreement. There was nothing but a wall of silence.

'What do we do when this sort of thing happens, David?' Miss Gladstone asked firmly.

David said nothing, but she was prepared to wait. She had twenty-five years' experience of dealing with children and was noted for her ability to enforce strict discipline when she chose. She was certainly not going to be faced down by a five-year-old. Soon there would be tears, then apologies for letting their teacher down. Possibly one of the boys might wet himself – that had happened before now.

The old-fashioned clock on the wall ticked away loudly. The boys stood there, uncomfortable but determined. Miss Gladstone felt her eyes wandering from them to the nature table and from that to the Toyland wall display. This would not do at all.

'Well?' she asked – breaking both the silence and her own rule.

'We tell a teacher,' David said finally.

'And why didn't you tell a teacher this time?'

It was Jimmy who answered.

'If we tell a teacher, the big boy will only get us back later.'

It was true; she knew it was true, but that was the way things were. It was all part of the painful process of growing up.

'Barney Jenkins won't get us back,' Jimmy continued. 'He won't dare.'

'Nobody will,' Paul added. 'Cos now they know we'll stick together.'

Miss Gladstone gasped. Little children lived from minute to minute. They didn't think long-term, they certainly didn't *plan* long-term. For the first time in many years, she had no idea how to handle the situation. Because she knew that they were right, this mutual-aid society would give them better protection than a teacher ever could.

The Bradleys had moved to Buckworth because Mrs Bradley wanted a house of her own, not something rented from the Council. The village was in many ways no better than a council estate – in some respects it was a lot worse.

It was not a pretty place. There was no green surrounded by thatched cottages, no pond on which sleepy ducks bobbed contentedly. Instead, the rows of terraced houses, their slate roofs turned grey by wind and weather, squatted disconsolately along the sides of the Norton-Warrington road. There was only one other street, which bisected the village and was called, prosaically, Cross Street. It was not a community which had grown organically. It was nothing more than a series of dormitory units, thrown up to meet the needs of rock-salt miners a century earlier. And though on the very edge of the countryside, the houses had only small front gardens and poky back yards.

The salt works, with its two tall chimneys, dominated the place. When they were firing up, the chimneys would belch out clouds of soot, which fell like tiny black locusts on the clean sheets that Mrs Bradley had boiled and dollied furiously before hanging them out to dry.

If the Bradleys had had a council house, they would have had an inside lavatory, not a brick structure at the bottom of the yard, a narrow, cramped place without electricity, where in winter they huddled over the hole and froze. Nor, with a proper water closet, would Mrs Bradley have had to undergo the indignity once a week of knowing that the sanitary wagon, 'the shit cart' as it was called locally, was pulling up behind the house and the night-soil collectors sliding the large pan from underneath the lavatory, exposing their private 'business' of the previous week to the whole world.

Yet the house was theirs, and when she was scrubbing the front step, *her* front step, or applying a coat of Woolworths' bright yellow paint over the damp patch in the kitchen, she knew it was worth it.

She was a slim, pretty woman of twenty-five, blonde like her son. When she was a girl just starting at the shoe factory, she had hoped that she would marry some rich handsome man who would whisk her off to a large house in Manchester. The years went by, the rich man never appeared, and in the end she had to settle for Tom.

Tom was a good husband, a hard worker and a steady provider within his limitations, and she supposed that she loved him. But she had never got used to the sex thing, his body lying heavily on top of hers while he grunted and strained. And when she saw him setting off for work in the morning, his trousers tucked in by bicycle clips, his baggin tin hanging from a strap round his waist, she felt vaguely ashamed, and could not help wishing that he had a job that was more fitting.

Jimmy would never follow in his father's footsteps. He would be important and go to work in a place where you didn't have to turn up until nine o'clock and could wear a jacket and tie all day. She had a burning ambition to see her only child do well and, young as he was, she thought she detected ambition in Jimmy too. That was enough to make her happy. Her own future, and Tom's future, were not really important; it was Jimmy who mattered.

There were no skateboards, Walkmans or video games in the far-off days of 1957, the year Jimmy, David and Paul turned eight. Even television was a luxury. David's father, who worked long hours at the scrap yard, had recently bought a KB seventeen-inch model. It had cost, David told his friends, seventy-five guineas. They were astonished; none of them had realised there was that much money in the whole world.

When it first arrived, they had all sat in David's kitchen, mesmerized by the flickering screen, while Mrs Harrison rattled pots in the background, or stoked up the fire so that the oven would be hot enough to bake a pie for her husband's tea. They cheered Sir Lancelot and laughed at Lucille Ball. Even the adverts – *Washday White Without Washday Red* – seemed thrilling. But television did not hold them in its power for long. Their natural playground was the outdoors, and as long as the weather was fine, they were rarely found inside.

There was the canal that skirted the edge of the village. It was crossed, close to the salt works, by a hump-backed bridge on the outside of which ran a wide pipe. The boys would crawl along the pipe, knees gripping, arms pulling, until they were suspended twenty feet over the green water. From there, unseen by adults, they watched the narrow boats pass below, long thin craft, most of their length given over to their salt cargo which was protected from the weather by a triangular, green-canvas frame. They marvelled at the tiny cabins at the backs of the boats, painted with bright, exotic designs almost like gipsy caravans, and they wished that they could live in one.

There was the railway spur which ran right up to the salt works. The guard would sometimes let them travel in his van and by sticking their heads out of the window as the train rounded a curve, they could catch a glimpse of the puffing, chugging monster that was pulling them.

But best of all, there were the woods, thick and dense – dazzling green in late Spring, azure when the bluebells came out, black and mysterious in the winter. It was there that they created the Secret Camp.

It was Paul's idea. Paul was always the inventive one, the originator of exciting schemes, the wizard who could take an ordinary scene and invest it with mysterious qualities. He came across a large elderberry bush growing down a slope, and immediately saw its possibilities.

'If we cut some of it down from the inside,' he said, 'we could have a camp, and nobody would know it was there. It'd be a secret camp.'

They worked for two days under David's direction. That was the thing about David: he never said much. When there was an argument, which was rare, it was usually between Paul and Jimmy. But in practical matters David seemed to know exactly what to do. He told them which branches to break, which roots to dig up with the tools they had smuggled out of their homes. They struggled and sweated, and in the end it was just as Paul had visualised it, a hollow in the green foliage, undetectable from the outside.

'We can be like real bandits here,' Paul said. 'We can hide, and nobody will know where we are.'

But it was not enough for Jimmy.

'We need to put some things in it,' Jimmy said. 'To make it look like a real hideout.'

Paul looked at him, puzzled. He didn't see the need for anything else. They had their Camp, their secret place. It was enough to

13

squat on the floor and be Davy Crockett and his men hiding from the River Pirates or Long John Silver's crew on some tropical island. But he didn't argue – it didn't seem worth it.

So they brought a few objects from home: a broken chair from Jimmy's which David managed to fix, some pictures of football teams cut out from magazines, an old kettle and tin mugs, and some bricks.

'If we can get some tea, we can make a brew here,' Jimmy explained enthusiastically as he heaped the bricks into a small circle and put the kettle on top.

In some ways, all these additions spoiled the Camp for Paul. The things were tatty; he could have imagined them much better. But it didn't really bother him. It was not what was in the Camp that was important, not even the Camp itself. It was the *idea* of the Camp that mattered, a secret place that was *theirs*, for just the three of them. He was perfectly happy with what they had.

But Jimmy was not. He could see what possibilities the Camp offered, and in an effort to exploit them, he broke one of the gang's big, unspoken rules.

Jimmy had seemed content at first just to come to the Camp, to sit on the chair and drink cups of strong black tea – or hot water when they had nothing else. But as the days passed, he became more and more restless. Finally, he could bear the pressure no longer, and one lazy, sunny afternoon, when they were just lying there, he looked up and said casually, 'With a camp like this, we could have a gang.'

Paul felt as he had when he was down with the 'flu – one second sweating, the next terribly cold. His head thundered and pounded.

'We don't want a gang,' he said. 'We've got one.'

Jimmy realised that he was treading on dangerous ground.

'We'd still have us,' he said carefully, 'but we'd have a bigger gang as well. A lot of kids would join a gang that had a camp like this.'

They both looked across at David for support.

'I don't care,' he said, shrugging.

'It wouldn't be the same,' Paul said firmly.

'Course it would,' Jimmy urged.

He struggled for the right words, the magical words that would convince Paul.

'We'd be a little gang,' he said, 'the three of us – but we'd have a bigger gang to boss around!'

Paul's eyes were hot; he could feel the tears forming. He jumped to his feet and rushed out, searching for a place where he could be alone with his sorrow. When he reached the big oak tree, half a mile from the Camp, he stopped, and huddling down at its base, began to sob uncontrollably. His chest heaved, battering his cheek against the thick, gnarled roots, but he did not even notice the pain this caused him. It was all over. They had been together for ever, and now it was all over.

Jimmy told David to stay in the Camp, and went searching for Paul. It was half an hour before he found the other boy, a minute figure sitting against the trunk of a huge tree. Paul got up when he heard his friend approaching. Jimmy stopped, several feet away from him, and the two boys stood in silence for a while, neither knowing quite what to say.

'Comin' back to the Camp?' Jimmy asked finally.

'No,' Paul said. 'I'm a bit fed up with it. I think I'll go an' play somewhere else, on me own.'

'It was only a joke,' Jimmy said reassuringly. 'I don't *really* want anybody else to join our gang.'

He saw relief flood through Paul. He should have left it at that, thrown his arm around his friend's shoulder and led him back to the elderberry bush. He couldn't do it!

'But if we *did* want a bigger gang,' he continued, 'it wouldn't make any difference to us. We'd still be best pals.'

It happened one day in August, near the end of the summer holidays. The moment the Camp came into sight they could sense that something was wrong, even though the elderberry bush, its green leaves gleaming in the sunlight, looked as undisturbed as usual. Inside the hollow they had so diligently constructed, there was chaos. The chair had been smashed to pieces, the pictures torn. Bricks had been dropped on the kettle and someone had shat in the corner.

They stood for a while, dazed, surveying the wreckage. David recovered first, and picked up the chair.

'The chair's no good,' he said. 'I can't mend it.'

If David couldn't, nobody could.

They set to work, shifting the excreta with sticks, trying to knock the dents out of the kettle.

And as they laboured, Paul asked himself why anyone would do this. It didn't make sense to smash up somebody else's camp. Why didn't they build a camp of their own instead? But it bothered him more that people had been there at all.

He looked across at David and Jimmy. The stocky boy was

methodically tidying up the mess, but though his tall, slim companion was working too, Paul could tell that his mind was not really on the job.

When they had done the best they could, they all sat down, cross-legged in the dirt. Paul was weary and dispirited, but a light blazed brightly in young Jimmy's eyes.

'They've got to be punished!' Jimmy said.

Paul had never considered that.

'We don't even know who they are,' he said.

'That doesn't matter,' Jimmy replied confidently. 'They'll be back.'

Sometimes Jimmy exasperated Paul. He seemed so sure of things that were far from obvious. Yet he was often right.

'How do you know?' Paul asked.

Jimmy looked around the shattered Camp.

'They liked doin' this,' he said. 'They'd like to do it again. They'll come back to see if we've fixed it.'

They waited for two days, hidden in the bushes. They arrived early in the morning and did not leave until dusk. Jimmy said they were not to talk, so they just lay there, gazing at the Camp. Occasionally, Paul would glance at David, lying with his thick elbows on the ground, perfectly placid and content, waiting patiently for the wreckers to come. Then he would turn his head and look at Jimmy, who was always coiled, tense, his eyes never once leaving the elderberry bush. It would make Paul feel a little guilty and he would turn back to the Camp, soon to retreat into his own thoughts.

He made up stories as he lay there, embroidering on adventures he had seen on the television. Some were about knights in armour, others were westerns, but wherever they were set, the hero was always the same, a grown-up version of himself, bigger, stronger, with shoulders ten times the width of his narrow ones. There would always be a girl, too, a pretty girl in trouble. The hero would dispose of the villains, often against tremendous odds; the girl, once free, would put her arms around him and kiss him – and the story would be over.

But even for someone with Paul's fertile mind, it was still indescribably boring waiting there, and he would have given up after the first hour but for Jimmy's insistence. Jimmy made an issue of it, a test of friendship, and Paul had no choice but to go along with him.

On the third day, the boys came. There were two of them and they looked about seven. They were new faces, not from the village. One was wearing a ragged girl's cardigan, the other had on an old corduroy jacket. The one with the cardigan kept wiping his nose on his sleeve, and Paul could see that his hands were dirty, and not just from today – the muck was deep in his skin.

The boys glanced around furtively, to make sure that they were not being observed, then disappeared into the bush that housed the camp. Jimmy signalled silently that the gang should follow.

'They've not fixed it up properly again,' they heard one of the boys say.

'No,' said the other. He sounded disappointed. 'Let's go and watch the narrer boats.'

The gang stepped into the bush and the new boys saw them for the first time.

'What are you doin' in our camp?' Jimmy demanded.

There was a coldness in his voice that Paul had never heard before.

'We can go where we like,' said one of the boys, defiantly. 'It's a free country, innit?'

'You were the ones that wrecked it, weren't you?'

It was clear that they had been judged and found guilty. There were three in the gang, and they were bigger and older. The smaller boys turned and fled down the slope with David and Jimmy in pursuit. They slipped and skidded and the one in the cardigan went into an uncontrolled roll, only stopping when his left leg banged against a tree stump. His companion hesitated for a second, then ran off into the woods. David and Jimmy let him go and stood, towering, over the fallen boy.

'I've hurt me knee,' the child on the ground said piteously.

'Get him up!' Jimmy ordered.

David pulled the boy to his feet.

'Take him back to the Camp.'

The boy started to struggle. David put his arm in a hammerlock and forced him to climb back up the slope.

They re-entered the small clearing and Jimmy gestured to David to stop. He walked to the other edge of the Camp, so that he was as far away from David and the boy as possible and stood with his back to them for what seemed to Paul like hours. Then suddenly, he whirled round.

'You were the ones that wrecked it,' he shouted. 'Weren't you?'

Paul looked at the small, frightened boy, bent forward by the hold David had on him, his knee grazed and bleeding. He wasn't looked after at home, you could tell. Maybe that was why he broke other people's things. Maybe it wasn't really his fault.

'Why don't we let him go?' he asked himself. 'Why are we doin' this?'

The boy was silent. Jimmy nodded his head to David, and the latter increased the pressure on the boy's arms.

'Ow . . . stop . . . yer breakin' me arm,' the boy said, and then, realising there would be no mercy until he had confessed said, 'Yes . . . yes . . . it was us, but Brian did most of it.'

'Was it Brian who did his business in the corner?'

'Yes, yes. It was Brian.'

'I don't believe you,' Jimmy said contemptuously. 'You're the one that did it. You're the shitter.'

Jimmy reached under his jersey and pulled something out. It was a bread-knife! He must have brought it from home. He held it up to let the terrified younger boy see it and assess its significance.

'D'you know what I'm goin' to do with this?' he asked.

The boy shook his head, half to answer the question, half as a gesture of blind, unreasoning fear.

'I'm goin' to cut your willie off,' Jimmy said.

The boy struggled frantically, but the more he pulled, the more his arm hurt.

Paul was frozen to the spot, unable to speak, unable to act.

'He means it,' he thought. 'He's goin' to do it.'

And what should he, Paul, one of the Secret Camp Gang, do? Stand there and watch it? Or try to stop Jimmy – betray one of his best friends? He was the smallest and the weakest of the three, and if David stuck with Jimmy, he could not stop them. Yet he knew he would have to try, even if he lost both of them, because there were some things that you just couldn't let happen, even if it meant, even if it meant . . .

The boy shrieked hysterically, begging for mercy, saying he was sorry, promising he'd never do it again.

'Are you really sorry?' Jimmy asked, and suddenly his voice was different, more reasonable, more forgiving.

'He was just playin',' Paul thought joyously. 'It was all a game. He wasn't really going to do it.'

But he had fooled Paul as well as the boy, and Paul wondered if he had fooled David too. Would David have done it, if Jimmy had wanted him to?

The boy had picked up the change in tone. He stopped crying and nodded his head mutely.

'If you're really sorry,' Jimmy said, 'you'll prove it. You'll crawl across here on your tummy and lick my shoes.'

David relaxed his grip, and the boy sank to the ground. He lay there moaning for a while then, seeing there was no alternative, did as Jimmy had told him. Jimmy's shoes were caked in mud, but he showed no compassion.

'Lick 'em properly,' he said. 'I want to see your tongue.'

And even when he had finished this, the boy was not off the hook. Jimmy pointed to Paul.

'Now I want you to crawl over there and lick his,' he said.

'No!' Paul wanted to shout. 'I don't want him to! I don't! I don't!'

But he knew he would be letting Jimmy down, so he stood there, ashamed and humiliated, as the boy performed his abject task.

'You can get up now,' Jimmy said finally.

The boy climbed shakily to his feet. He was near the entrance to the Camp and he could have made a dash for it. Instead, he just stood there, head bent, saliva and filth around his mouth, mucus running freely from his nostrils.

'Get out of our camp and don't come back,' Jimmy said.

The boy moved slowly, hesitantly, as if he was reluctant to go. It was not until he was some way from the elderberry that he broke into a half-hearted trot.

'Did we have to do that?' Paul demanded later. 'Couldn't we just have bashed him up a bit?'

'No,' Jimmy said. 'If we'd thumped him, we'd only have made him angry. He'd have come back and wrecked the camp later. He won't be back now!'

Paul believed him. He could still see the boy, looking down at his feet, utterly defeated – all the fight, all the spirit, knocked out of him. He would probably avoid this part of the woods for the rest of his life.

'It was your fault I had to do it,' Jimmy continued harshly. 'You wouldn't let us have a bigger gang. If there'd been more of us, somebody would have been on guard, and the camp wouldn't have got wrecked.'

If there'd been more of them it wouldn't have mattered if the camp *had* got wrecked, Paul thought, because it wouldn't have been *their* camp any more.

'But there's only three of us,' Jimmy continued, 'so we've got to have another way to look after what's ours.'

Even if it meant doing terrible, terrible things like they had just done to that poor boy? Paul lowered his head. He was almost crying. Jimmy put his arm around his friend's shoulder.

'You have to fight for what you want,' he said, slowly, kindly, like an adult explaining something difficult to a very young child. 'You have to fight any way you can.'

Chapter Two

The Secret Camp Gang inhabited a world that was ordered and understandable, that had never changed and would never change. Calendar months had no meaning for them. Time was not to be measured by dates, but by the seasons – the rhythms of nature – and what went on in them.

After the summer, there was the autumn – and conkers. They tramped the woods looking for horse chestnut trees, and threw sticks and stones at the heavily laden branches with all the strength in their small arms. They hurried home with their prizes and sat in front of the fire, splitting the green spiky balls to discover the nut that just might be better than the ones all the other kids had. Jimmy and Paul would scoop up the first four or five they had opened and rush off to soak them in vinegar, bake them in the oven – apply whatever the latest magic formula was. David would open the rest and examine them all critically, sometimes taking hours to select one.

Then followed the weeks of competition in which a conker's reputation rose or fell by its own prowess and the strength of its owner's propaganda.

'This conker's a thirtier.'

'You said yesterday it was a tenner. Anyway, that little thing's never smashed thirty conkers.'

'I never said it 'ad. It was a tenner, then it smashed Billy's, and Billy's was a twentier.'

'Billy's wasn't a twentier . . .'

But talk is cheap. Nuts cracked under opponents' blows or were so weakened in combat that they fell apart later. New conkers, virgin conkers, were introduced. By the end of the season, only one veteran remained, the nut that David had selected after the first chestnut hunt.

In the winter there were snowmen and skating on the ice. The classrooms had to be re-arranged, the rows of neatly marshalled desks crammed together, leaving the part of room furthest from the fire completely bare. The children became mountaineers, scaling desks, leaving their footprints on other kids' work, risking life and limb to get to the teacher's table. Everything became temporary. Children moved desks several times a day in order to be closer to, or further away from, the blazing coals.

'I'm burnin', Miss.'

'All right, change places with Jennifer.'

'Can I change as well, Miss? It's freezin' here.'

'I'll deal with you in a minute. Jimmy Bradley, why are you turning round?'

'Cos this side of me's too hot, Miss, and this side's too cold.'

It was an inevitable chaos which teachers looked forward to with dread and the children exploited for all it was worth.

Spring brought expeditions into the woods, bird-nesting.

'And remember,' the teachers always told them, 'only take one egg. Leave the poor little mother something to hatch out.'

They all did as they were told, except for Freddie Mather who took the lot, and once actually bit the heads off a clutch of new-born chicks, blind and with their mouths wide open for the anticipated worm. He was Bird-eater Mather after that and would probably be call Birdie until his dying day, even by those who had no idea how he came by the name.

Summer returned, and brought with it the glorious holidays, weeks and weeks to play in the woods. They built new Secret Camps, each more elaborate than its predecessor, but they never returned to the original one.

And suddenly the years had melted away, and they were in Mr Giles' class – the Gaffer's class. The tall, big-nosed man who smoked a pipe and pronounced from on high at every full assembly, was *their* teacher. What privileges that conferred! It was the senior children who took it in turns to walk around the school ringing the heavy brass hand-bell that announced the start of playtime. It was their duty too to pour the dregs from the milk bottles into one big jug for the caretaker's cat, a chore which was always rewarded with a piece of cake or biscuits.

When it froze, they sat impatiently through their lessons until Mr Giles said, 'Well, I think the swans could use our help again.'

They trooped excitedly down to the pond just beyond the school and broke the ice around its edges. They did not mind that the work was hard, or that their hands were numb with cold. As they toiled, they knew that the younger children in the playground were watching and envying, as they themselves had done in previous years.

'That should do it,' Mr Giles said, finally.

'Can we stay for a bit, sir?'

'Yes, but keep well back. A swan's wing could break *my* arm, so goodness knows what it would do to you.'

They stepped back through the frozen bullrushes, and the swans, their webbed feet slapping against the ice, waddled over to the channel they had created. The children looked on, and felt proud.

As Christmas approached, their minds turned to the Nativity Play. For five years they had served as vocal background or crowd fodder. Now, at last, they had the chance of a starring role.

'What do you want to be?' Paul asked Jimmy one morning, as the three boys stood throwing stones across the ice.

'The Angel Gabriel,' Jimmy said in that casual tone that told Paul that he wanted it very much.

'Don't talk daft,' Paul said. 'The Angel Gabriel's a girl!'

Jimmy gave a superior smile.

'Well he isn't, Clever. I've got an uncle called Gabriel!'

'Then why do they always have a girl playin' him?'

'Because they're tall.' Jimmy stood on tip-toe. 'But I'm tall too.'

He was the tallest boy in the class, and the handsomest, Paul thought. He wished his own body could be as slim and elegant, that his own pale skin would acquire some of Jimmy's golden glow. He looked at David, flicking his stones methodically across the pond, adjusting his technique after each throw. He didn't have to be like Jimmy, he would have settled for David's thick, muscular frame and healthy redness – anything rather than what he was.

'Why do you want to be Gabriel anyway?' he asked.

'He's the one that brings the news. The one that tells everybody else where to go and that.'

'Well, I bet you don't get it, anyway,' Paul said. 'Betty Thomas is much taller than you.'

It was true. She was a toothy, spotty girl. She had none of Jimmy's angelic looks – but she was head and shoulders above anyone else in the class.

Jimmy stood for a while, hands in pockets, kicking the ground. Paul saw the disappointment gradually ebb away, to be replaced by a thoughtful look. Jimmy never wasted his time going after what he couldn't get.

'Well if I can't be Gabriel,' the blond boy said, brightening, 'I want to be a King.'

'The one who brings gold?' Paul asked. 'Because he comes in first, because he's like the boss?'

It was an attack, even if it was a joking one. But that was allowed. It was not the same as making fun of Jimmy to an outsider.

Jimmy looked a little shamefaced. He threw a stone and watched as it bounced across the frozen pond.

'It's not because of that,' he said, and Paul could see that he was groping for another reason. 'It's the hat. He wears a lampshade. I like it better than the other hats.'

Jimmy looked at Paul's smiling face, full of amused disbelief, and decided to take the offensive.

'Well, what do you want to be?'

It was Paul's turn to look uncomfortable.

'Joseph,' he said.

'What for?'

'I don't know, really.'

But he did. If Jimmy wanted to be First King, he would certainly be First King, and he was Jimmy's friend, not his follower. Besides, there was something appealing about Joseph. He didn't just bring Mary and the baby Jesus gifts and then go away – he stayed and looked after them.

They realised that David had been quiet, even for David.

'What do you want to be?' they asked, simultaneously.

'Nothin'!'

'Nothin'?'

They couldn't believe it.

'It's all show, isn't it?' David said. 'It's not real. It doesn't mean anythin'.'

They got the parts they wanted, and when the great day came, Jimmy carried it off brilliantly, as Paul had known he would. He walked through the hall of doting parents with a truly regal gait. For the first time in living memory, the lampshade looked as if it were really some exotic oriental crown.

Paul was reasonable; his own misgivings about his acting ability fitted well with the part of a concerned Joseph, shepherding his heavily-pregnant wife into the inadequate stable.

David, unimpressed by the whole thing, sat on the choir bench as he had for the last four years, opening and closing his mouth at appropriate moments and producing very little noise.

Mrs Bradley, making her way back home to polish the grate, was torn by mixed emotions. She was proud of Jimmy, he had outshone all the others in the play. But she was angry with him too, because when it was all over he went straight off with those two mates of his, instead of coming to her and letting people see that she was the mother of this wonderful child.

She didn't really like David and Paul, but then she wouldn't have approved of any of the friendships Jimmy could have formed in the village. He was far too good for any of them, and next year, when he had his place at the grammar school, he would meet a better class of boy, and could leave all these ragamuffins behind.

Jimmy knew all about his mother's attitudes and beliefs. They had been his only bedtime stories ever since he was old enough to understand. In some ways, he thought, she was right. He would go to the grammar school, and he would get on in the world – you were daft not to. But he saw no reason why, as he moved on and up, David and Paul couldn't go with him.

He rarely spoke to his father, unconsciously taking his lead from his mother. Tom was someone who was there in the evenings, who said little and was consulted on nothing, who seemed to have no aspirations or secret desires. His mother treated his father the way she treated the dog, with kindness and condescension.

Jimmy never thought it strange that his mother ruled the roost. It was exactly the same at Paul's. He had stood in the back kitchen of the Wright house many a Thursday evening and watched Mr Wright hand over his pay packet, unopened, to his wife. The ritual never varied. Mrs Wright, tall and angular, her already greying hair pulled in a tight bun, ran a bony finger along the edge of the cellophane so that her nail tore through the seal. She tipped the money onto the table, being careful to catch the clattering coins before they rolled away. Next, she examined the pay slip and carefully counted the money.

Occasionally, she would address a comment to her husband – 'Not much overtime this week,' or 'Coal's goin' up again,' – but Wright rarely answered. He would just stand there, if not patiently then at least with resignation.

Only when she had checked the money twice would Mrs Wright separate the household expenses from her husband's pocket money. Her share of the spoils went into a battered leather purse, notes in the front, silver in one compartment, copper in the other. Mr Wright's money was left on the table, just out of his reach, so that he had to move round to pick it up. After he'd put the money in his overall pocket, he would invariably jangle the coins for a second, then say, 'Well, I think I'll just go out for a quick pint.'

Jimmy wasn't sure whether Mrs Wright ever heard him, because by that time she was sitting in front of the fire, a bowl of vegetables balanced on her knee, or else mending a tear in Paul's second best shirt.

Yet though both men played second fiddle in the home, Mr Wright had something that his own father was denied, or else never sought. Tom Bradley's world outside work was bounded by his home, The George and Dragon and the pigeon lofts. Mr Wright, shorter than his wife, with straight sandy hair and a sort of craggy handsomeness, wandered free, visiting pubs in Norton, going off fishing at weekends. There was the other thing as well, the thing that Jimmy had not told anyone about – not even Paul.

He had been coming back from the Secret Camp one evening when he had seen Mr Wright walking through the woods. He was on the point of saying hello when he noticed that the man was not alone. He was holding hands with a big girl called Annie Ashton. Annie was lagging behind a bit and Mr Wright was sort of tugging her.

Even though Annie was little more than a child herself, just out of the secondary mod, Jimmy sensed that what was going on was something grown-up, and that his presence would not be welcomed. He ducked down behind the bushes.

Mr Wright stopped by a moss patch, looked around, and smiled.

'Well, here we are, Annie,' he said.

He held her close to him and started kissing her. It was not the sort of kiss that mums and dads exchanged, it was more like what the older kids did, down by the lake on summer Sundays. Jimmy felt his heart beating faster, though he didn't know why.

Annie Ashton squirmed a bit, then kissed back just as hard.

'Shall we lie down then?' Mr Wright asked.

'I don't know. I'm not sure.'

'Come on, Annie!' Impatient. Irritated. 'That's what we're here for.'

'Well, all right,' the girl said reluctantly. 'But only for a bit.'

Mr Wright held on to her as if he thought she might try to run away, and slowly lowered her, until her knees were resting on the green, springy moss. He eased her backwards, and she was forced to stretch out her legs.

She was wearing a long Shetland sweater that came almost down to her knees and a black, pleated skirt. As she moved her body, the skirt rode up, and Jimmy could see the point where her stockings ended and her white flesh began.

Mr Wright lay down next to Annie – just lay at first – whispering in her ear so quietly that Jimmy could not hear the words. Then he began kissing her again and Jimmy saw his hand move down,

down, to the bottom of her sweater, under it, and up again – inside! The smell of wild crocuses filled Jimmy's nostrils and his fingers dug into the rich black earth.

Mr Wright's hand had climbed right up Annie's body, and was resting on her left titty, making it stick up much more than the other one. He began rubbing, in a circle, like he was cleaning the windows. Annie was making funny noises, almost as if Mr Wright was hurting her. Jimmy's fingers gouged the ground, cutting a series of small channels.

Mr Wright's other hand moved up Annie's skirt, and Jimmy could see her knickers, not navy blue, like the girls' at school, but white, with little butterflies on them. Jimmy felt his little willie go hard – it was the first time it had ever happened.

'We'd better stop now,' Annie said. 'We've gone far enough.'

'You know you like it.' And Mr Wright put his hand inside Annie's knickers.

'Oh, I do,' Annie moaned. 'Oh God, I do.'

Now Mr Wright was using both hands, first unfastening Annie's stockings and then pulling down her pants. As Annie arched her back, to make it easier for him, Jimmy realised that his own hands were fumbling with his fly buttons. Mr Wright stuck his head between Annie's legs, and seemed to shake it about. Jimmy began to stroke himself, gently at first, back and forth.

Mr Wright stood up, unfastened his trousers, let them drop around his ankles and pulled down his underpants. He stood perfectly still for a few seconds, while the setting sun cast an orange glow on him. Annie looked up at him from the ground. And Jimmy stared too. He had never imagined that anybody's willie could be as big as that.

Mr Wright lay down again, this time on top of Annie, with his legs between hers. All the smutty comments Jimmy had heard in the playground, all the dirty jokes he had laughed at but not understood, suddenly began to make sense. Mr Wright was *shagging* her!

Mr Wright's bare white bum rose in the air, fell and rose again. Annie, beneath him, wriggled furiously and Jimmy tugged at himself as hard as he could. Annie cried out, even louder than before and just at that moment Jimmy felt the hot sticky liquid gush into the palm of his hand.

Jimmy watched as they pulled their clothes back into place and walked away. Mr Wright didn't hold Annie's hand now. He moved quickly, as if he were alone in the woods, and just wanted to get home. But Annie, running slightly, stayed as close to him as she could, and kept talking, chattering. Jimmy didn't know what she was saying, but he could tell that Annie wanted to please Mr Wright, to make him like her.

Jimmy lay back, his thing now safely restored to his pants, and watched the sky gradually darken. He could see the pale yellow moon and hear the evening chorus of the birds in the trees. He held his hand to his nose, and sniffed it.

He knew now what the kids from the big school meant when they said his thing wasn't just for pissing through. It had been a wonderful moment when his willie had seemed as if it must burst, and then the milky liquid had shot out. But there was more to it than just pleasure. Mr Wright had used his thing to give him power over Annie, to control her. Jimmy touched his fly buttons. He had discovered a marvellous weapon.

Time increased Miss Gladstone's fascination with the threesome, if only because they were becoming more and more unreachable. They were so mutually-absorbed, so self-sufficient. It wasn't that they didn't have individual personalities. They did – very strong ones. But each personality seemed to be there to contribute to the whole, to the entity that was the Secret Camp Gang. The three boys fitted together like interlocking Chinese rings, and nobody had found a way to slip one away from the others.

She followed their career from a distance, talking to their teachers, watching them in the playground. They weren't like other children, she was told, wanting to sit by their friends. They didn't care where they were placed. It was as if they had managed to draw a distinction between the classroom and the rest of their lives.

Miss Gladstone watched them, but she rarely spoke to them. She remembered the day when, as new infants, they had faced her down. She wasn't frightened of them. It would be stupid to be frightened of children. Nevertheless, she was, she supposed, a little wary of them.

It was in early January that she noticed a change in the three boys. While every other child was running around to keep warm, they stood huddled against the fence, books clumsily held in mittened hands. From their gestures, it was obvious that they were talking seriously. Studying? Children from posh prep schools might do it outside lesson time, but it was unheard of in that school. She was half-way across the playground when she checked herself. Better, far better, to wait until she could catch one of them alone, rather than find herself banging against the solid wall of their collective resistance.

She got her chance at the end of afternoon school, when she found Paul waiting outside the Infants' cloakroom for his younger sister.

'I saw you had books in the yard at playtime,' she said severely. 'You know we're not allowed to take our books out of school, don't you?'

Paul nodded miserably.

'And why aren't we?' the teacher asked.

'Because we might get them dirty. But we didn't, honest, Miss.'

It really was easier to deal with them separately. On his own, Paul was almost like any other child.

'Why did you take the books anyway?'

Paul hung his head then said to the ground, 'We've been workin' – for the 11-plus.'

'All three of you?' Miss Gladstone asked.

Paul twitched and reddened under her gaze and she knew that she had caught him out in a lie.

'Well, we're not all workin',' he admitted. 'David is. And we're helpin' him.'

He looked confused, wondering whether to proceed.

'Go on,' Miss Gladstone said, trying to sound kindly and encouraging, but realising that her voice had that aggressive-defensive edge that it always had when she was talking to the gang.

'Jimmy and me – Jimmy and I – want us to go to the Grammar,' Paul explained, 'and David's a bit behind, so we thought we'd give him extra lessons. I'm doin' English and Jimmy's doin' Arithmetic.'

'Does David want to go to the Grammar?'

'He says he doesn't mind.'

'But you want him to go with you because he's your friend.' Maybe underneath it all, they were just like all the other children. 'Isn't that nice?'

'That's not why,' Paul said. 'We don't need to be together at school.'

Miss Gladstone realised that this was one of the rare occasions when, by inadvertently asking the right question, she had tapped into a line in the Secret Camp mentality. She felt the thrill of an explorer, though like all successful adventurers she knew she could be stepping into dangerous territory.

'So why do you want David to pass?' she asked.

'The teachers think that because David doesn't say much, he's stupid. An' you've got him believin' it as well, because you're the grown-ups. But you're wrong!' Paul was almost shouting now, and waving his hands about wildly. He suddenly remembered where he was, and who he was talking to. He reddened even more and his arms dropped limply by his sides. When he spoke again, his voice was almost a whisper. 'He isn't clever like me, but he's clever in a different way. He's got great pot . . . pot . . .'

'Potential?' Miss Gladstone supplied.

'Potential. And he *ought* to go to the Grammar.'

'Dear God,' Miss Gladstone thought to herself, trying to reconcile the words with the thin child who had spoken them.

Aloud, she said, 'Well I think it's very nice of you to help your friend. Whatever the reason.'

She patted him on the head. She didn't know why she did it, unless it was to convince herself that he was just a child, to re-affirm the big teacher-little kid relationship.

Paul's sister appeared in the doorway.

'All right, Paul,' Miss Gladstone said. 'You can go.'

'Thank you, Miss.'

She watched his narrow back retreating towards the playground fence until it was swallowed up by the mass of home-going children.

'If he talks like that now,' she pondered, 'if he *acts* like that now, what will he be like when he's twenty? He'll want to change the whole world.'

But he would fail to do it, of course, just as he would fail with David. Competition for the Grammar was very stiff and it was still a middle class institution with an entrance examination that reflected its cultural bias. Some very bright working class children got through despite it all, but there was usually only one a year from Buckworth. And that year it would be Paul. It was just possible that Jimmy would pass as well, though such success was unprecedented. But David? Not a chance.

That Spring there were some great pictures on. There was *Around the World in Eighty Days* which was all about this feller who had a bet, see, and he had to go round the world on a train an' on an elephant an' in a balloon an' . . . There was *The Vikings* with this fantastic fight on this castle roof between Tony Curtis and Kirk Douglas, an' they were always nearly fallin' off, an' . . .

But the three boys did not exercise their recently-won right to go to the Saturday matinée without parents, to stand in the excited queue clutching their sweets tightly in their hands, to cheer loudly when the doors were finally opened and join in the rush to capture the back seats.

There was no bird-nesting either, no trips to the woods at the weekend. Last year's Secret Camp decayed, and a new one was never built. All through the months leading up to the examination, Paul and Jimmy used every spare minute to drill David in grammar and long division, vocabulary and multiplication.

It was an unexceptional May morning when the identical brown envelopes were delivered to the homes of every child in the senior class. The letter that arrived at David's house was addressed to Mr and Mrs E. Harrison, but David's mother didn't even think of opening it, and instead placed it on the mantelpiece to await her husband's arrival.

Despite himself, the boy found his eyes were glued to the envelope. He hadn't seriously thought of the grammar school as a possibility until Paul had brought it up. And even then, he had only begun studying because his friends had wanted him to. But gradually, over the months, he had begun to feel that he could do it, and had realised that he wanted to – very much. He didn't intend to end up in the scrap yard like his dad, using only his muscle. He would never do as well as Paul, but he was good with his hands and he might get a chance to learn to use them properly – become an engineer. The clock ticked on, the envelope remained untouched on the mantelpiece.

Finally, he heard his father's heavy clump on the stairs and then Harrison was standing in the doorway, broad, red-faced, his braces still hanging down from his trousers.

'Mornin', Dad,' the children said in unison.

'There's a letter come,' Mrs Harrison squeaked, 'about our David's schoolin'.'

'Oh, has there?' Harrison replied, passing his braces over his shoulders and fastening them with his thick, stubby fingers. 'Well, you don't mind if I have me breakfast first, do you, our David?'

It was not a question.

'No, Dad,' David said.

As his father ate his way through three eggs, sausages and fried bread, David suffered agonies.

'Dad needs his food,' he told himself. 'He works very hard.'

Still, as his father mopped up his egg yolk and took deep swigs from his mug of tea, it was difficult to sit still and maintain the silence that was expected in his father's presence.

When he had eaten the last piece of egg and drained the last drop of tea, Harrison rose and picked up the envelope. It looked tiny in his hand – tiny and yet so important. Harrison ripped it clumsily open; he was not used to such delicate work. David could see that he had torn the corner of the letter. His father walked over to the window, where the light was better, and read the letter slowly, moving his lips as he did so. David tried to make out the words that were being formed on his mouth.

'It's from the Council,' Harrison said unnecessarily. 'It's about what school they're sendin' you to next year. Do you want to know what it sez?'

Suddenly, David realised that it was very important to his father that he appear not to care, one way or the other.

'Might as well tell me,' he said, as casually as he could manage.

'The tests have determined which school is app-rop-riate to you,' Harrison said slowly. 'Now what the bloody hell does app-rop-riate mean?'

As the Secret Camp Gang passed the pond, they saw a group of children, almost a procession, coming towards them from the school. It was the senior class, their class. They had read their own results and gone in to school early to find out how the others had done. In front was Terry Keenan, the leader of the school gang, that loose organisation that exists in every primary school – the gang that David, Paul and Jimmy had never joined. In his hands, Terry carried an old cricket bat.

The caravan stopped just short of the threesome and Terry stepped forward.

'Well, you've done it, haven't you?' he demanded. 'Just stand there while you get thumped.'

He lifted the bat, swung it fiercely through the air, and brought it down on Paul's head, pulling it at the last moment so the impact was light. Then he repeated the ritual with the other two boys. Everyone was grinning. Even though the other kids envied them, and perhaps even hated them a little, they were generous enough to join in their triumph.

Mr Giles ordered a special assembly for the whole school and after the recorders and tambourines had battled against the piano in a version of *All Things Bright and Beautiful*, the bright, beautiful successes were marched out onto the small stage.

While the headmaster extolled their virtues, the three stood there, legs spread, hands clenched behind their backs, the correct stance for anyone on public display.

Miss Gladstone, in between shushing her new infants and

stopping them from fidgeting, took one of her last opportunities to study her three old pupils. There was Paul, still so slight that it would have been a gross exaggeration to call him wiry, a broad smile on his face. He had known he should pass, Miss Gladstone thought, but he'd never been sure. Boys like him always expected things to go wrong for them – and very often they did.

Next to him was David. He looked huge in comparison, almost a perfect replica of his father, with that square jaw, that big nose that seemed to have been hacked out of stone. She couldn't say that he was ugly, not exactly, but there was something far too physical, too animal, about him. How had he ever got through the examination?

On the end was Jimmy, beautiful Jimmy, with a lick of blond hair falling into his eye, accepting all this as if it were his due. Miss Gladstone was scrupulous about not having favourites, but there were some children with whom she had a closer relationship, and Jimmy could have been one of them – if he'd been willing.

She saw them at close hand only once more, when as part of the end of term ceremonials the senior children went around individually, or in groups, and thanked their old teachers for what they'd done.

'Well, good luck,' the teachers would say. 'And I hope you'll come back and visit us sometime.'

'Oh yes, Miss.'

'Most of them will,' Miss Gladstone thought. 'At least for a little while. They'll sit in their old classroom and run around at playtime, re-living their childhoods.'

But not those three. Even as they stood in front of her, she could tell they were looking to the future.

It had been an interesting six years. But in a way, she was relieved that they were finally leaving. It had been like studying wild animals in captivity. They looked tame enough – but you could never be sure.

'Yes,' she whispered to herself, as she watched them turn their backs on the school after the final bell and head for the village without even once glancing over their shoulders. 'Yes, I'm glad they're going.'

PART TWO

Odd Man Out

Chapter Three

In later years, as they sat in a pub somewhere and discussed the past over a pint, they would talk about it as an easy, peaceful time, a golden age. But, it wasn't that easy or that peaceful. There were battles to fight, battles which, to their eleven-year-old minds, seemed matters of life or death. There were failures to endure, bitter crushing failures, the depths of which an adult could never comprehend. And yet, in relative terms, it *was* a golden age, and unlike most golden ages, could be dated exactly. It began on the fifth of September 1960, when they entered the Lord Fairfax Grammar School, and it ended, abruptly and tragically, five weeks before the end of the Summer term of 1964.

The gang's territory expanded as they grew themselves. Trips to the woods became rarer. Instead, they rode their bikes into Norton and loitered outside the chippie, making sarcastic comments to passing girls. When they turned twelve, they were allowed to go out to the flicks – *in the evening* – and saw *Samson and Delilah* or *Hercules Unchained*. After the film they ran wildly through the streets, imagining they were smashing up whole armies with only the jaw-bone of an ass or tearing through steel links with their bare hands.

At twelve, they back-combed their hair and whistled *Livin' Doll*; at fourteen they grew mop-heads and sang *She loves you, yeah, yeah, yeah,* in ragged harmony. Biblical epics no longer interested them. They lied about their ages and went to see *La Dolce Vita* and *Only Two Can Play*, sniggering on the back row over the fact that you could actually see the naked bum of the woman Peter Sellers was having it off with.

They graduated from looking for kindly understanding women in off-licences who would sell them bottles of brown ale – 'for me dad' – and chanced their arms in the pubs. With David's size and Jimmy's confidence, they usually got away with it. A couple of pints downed, they would stand outside the Drill Hall, watching the older teenagers through the big glass windows, wishing they could be inside too, hoping to catch a glimpse of the famous group appearing that night.

The new Pullman train could go at ninety miles an hour and have them in London in an incredible three hours and thirteen minutes, but aside from occasional holidays in Blackpool, they had never left Norton, nor wanted to – not yet. First they had to finish grammar school, and that was far in the future. For now, their predictable, planned existence suited them. They were content to wait patiently for the big, dramatic changes, but Fate, as is so often the case, was not.

There was nothing unusual about the eleventh of June, 1964. The weather was mild, as it normally was at that time of year. It had been drizzling slightly at seven o'clock that morning, but that was to be expected too. The only event slightly out of the ordinary, as far as the gang was concerned, was that the eleventh of June was the day David turned fifteen.

His brothers and sisters sang a loud 'Happy birthday, Our David' to him over the breakfast table, his mother pecked him drily on the cheek. When his father came downstairs, the customary hush fell over the room. Harrison did not wish David Happy Birthday, but the boy was neither surprised nor disappointed. His father hardly ever seemed aware of his wife and children – his was a sweaty masculine world, a place where you shifted heavy weights and swung big hammers.

It came as a shock when after he had wiped his plate clean, Harrison said, 'Step into the back yard for a minute, will yer, lad?'

Smaller brothers and sisters looked up questioningly at David, then risked a quick glance at their dad. Harrison didn't look angry, but if he was ordering David outside . . . David rose heavily to his feet and opened the kitchen door.

'Right,' his father said, 'stand up against that wash house wall.'

Almost in a trance, David did as he was told. He could feel the rough bricks pressing through his thin shirt. His father stood several paces away, looking him up and down as if there was something wrong. The inspection seemed interminable, but finally Harrison smiled and shook his head.

'Aye, you're a big bugger and no mistake about it.' He walked over and stood shoulder to shoulder with his son. 'You almost top me.'

Apparently satisfied, he moved away again.

'So yer fifteen today, are yer?' He put his hand in his pocket and pulled out some pound notes. 'Here y'are. Get yourself summat.'

'Me mam's already got me a present,' David said stumblingly.

'This isn't a present from yer mam,' Harrison said. 'This is a present from me. How are you set for a few pints tonight?'

David nodded dumbly.

'Good lad,' his father said, slapping his hand heartily on David's shoulder with just slightly less impact than a sledge hammer. 'Be ready about eight.'

David broke the news to Paul and Jimmy on the way to school.

'I know we said we'd go out together,' he said uncomfortably, 'but it's me dad, you see, an' . . .'

'Don't worry about it, old mate,' Jimmy said, wishing that his father had the style to invite his under-age son out for a drink.

'Don't give it a second thought; there's always tomorrow,' Paul added, knowing that his father would have the style, but probably wouldn't waste the honour on him.

David had expected to go somewhere local, but when his father arrived home for his tea, he had brought the scrap-yard van with him.

'Fred said I could borrow it for the night. Give us a bit more freedom, eh?'

To David's amazement, his father gave him a broad adult wink.

'Where are we going, dad?' David asked, as they drove out of the village.

The older man smiled, his wide mouth open, showing all his teeth.

'I thought we'd go to Stockport,' he said.

He reached into his pocket and pulled out a packet of Player's. 'Fancy a fag?'

David shook his head, confused. Yesterday, he had been a boy, running down to the post-office for his father's cigarettes – now he was being offered one.

Much of the sixteen-mile drive was dual-carriageway, and Harrison, a fast, capable driver, made good time. Once or twice he turned his head towards David as if he wanted to say something but kept changing his mind at the last second.

Their final destination turned out to be a tall brick building with a brightly lit sign spelling out the words *The Diamond Theatre Club*. More significant was the coloured poster which announced that it was stag night.

'Ever been to one of these places before?' his father asked.

David shook his head.

'Aye, well, it's time you started,' said Mr Harrison, as he pulled out his membership card and a wad of pound notes.

The club was a huge barn of a place, but it was crammed with formica-topped tables between which white-coated waiters rushed with trays of best bitter. David and his father were shown to a table very close to the stage.

'Slipped him a quid,' Harrison explained when their waiter had left them. 'After all, this is a special do.'

The worn mock-velvet blue curtains were open, and at the back of the stage a four piece group was performing an uninspired instrumental version of one of the current hits. It was all a little seedy but to David it seemed wonderful, not so much that he should be there, but that his father had chosen to take him.

The compère walked on stage to the accompaniment of a half-hearted drum roll. His dinner jacket and tie looked in about the same condition as the curtains.

'Ladies and Gentlemen,' he pretended to scan the audience, 'not that I can see many fuckin' ladies in here tonight, welcome to the Diamond Theatre Club Stag Night. We have some beautiful girls to entertain you this evening, and will you give a big hand for the first one – all the way from Rotherham – Miss Lindy Danvers.'

The band broke into a tinny rendition of *World Without Love* and Miss Lindy Danvers – all the way from Rotherham – strutted onto the stage. She was a tall brunette and her hair spilled down over her shoulders. Her glittery dress hugged her curves. David reached absentmindedly across for his pint and took a swallow.

The girl danced around the stage for a while, then turned her back on the audience so that they could see the zip that ran from her neck to her buttocks. She reached up with one hand and pulled the zip down a couple of inches, immediately raising it again. She repeated the action several times and on each occasion the zip travelled a little further, revealing first her bra strap, then the small of her back and finally the top of her panties. She raised her hands to her shoulders and eased the dress over them, wriggling as it slithered down her body, over her sequinned bra, garter-belt and panties, stopping only when it was around her ankles.

Suddenly, unfairly, *World Without Love* came to an end and the girl bowed. There was clapping and whistling from the audience.

'Is that it?' David asked, disappointed.

Harrison smiled at him. He was enjoying showing his son a bit of the world, explaining things to him.

'No, that's not it,' he said. 'They all tek three songs to get their clothes off. Pad it out a bit, don't they? Means they need less girls.'

The dancer picked up her dress, folded it neatly and placed it over the back of the wooden chair. She nodded to the drummer and he began pounding out the beat of the next number. The girl started to gyrate her hips so that her pelvis swung back and to, hypnotically, before David's eyes. Her breasts bounced furiously against the constraints of her bra.

'Take it off!' David pleaded silently. 'Take it off!'

The stripper stopped dancing and stepped out of her shoes. She lifted one leg and placed her foot on the chair. Her hands reached up to her suspenders, and her stocking was released. Slowly, the red-nailed hand peeled the stocking down, revealing more and more white flesh. She repeated the process with the other leg, then removed her garter-belt. Her hands snaked up her body, caressing it, stroking it, as they went, then disappeared behind her back. She was unfastening her bra.

It was really happening, David thought. Any minute now he would see a pair of real live female tits. His heart was beating faster, he seemed to have trouble breathing. He was frightened that something would go wrong at the last second, that the compère would walk on stage and announce that the show could not continue until David Harrison, a minor, had left the room. He wished the woman would get on with it – quickly – before the tragedy occurred.

With her back to the audience again, Lindy removed her bra and dropped it on to the chair. When she turned around, she had her hands crossed, covering her breasts, but David could still see the edges, round and smooth and white. The song ended, the stripper stood still.

David looked across at his father. He seemed calm and relaxed. There were none of the beads of perspiration on *his* brow that David knew had formed on his own.

'You enjoyin' yerself, lad?'

David nodded.

'Aye, you're like me,' Harrison said. 'Not a great one for words.'

The final number came, the one in which, his father had confidently predicted, all would be revealed. The stripper stood facing the back of the stage, her arms held high in the air. She was close to the curtain, and as she did a number of knee-bends, her lovely, gorgeous boobs must have rubbed against the material. Those people sitting at the sides were already getting a glimpse of her bust. David wished his father had not got them such good seats.

The girl turned round, and there it all was! Her nipples were brown and the size of pennies. Her breasts drooped a little more than David had expected, but that didn't matter, they were his first and however many more he saw, he would always treasure them.

The stripper sat on the chair and pulled down her panties. Now all she had on was an emerald green G-string. When she turned her back and waggled her bottom, it was like she had nothing on at all. David gazed, almost afraid to blink. As she pranced around the stage, her breasts swung to and fro, almost independent of the rest of her body. Then, as the number reached its close, she stood completely still, and her hands went up to her G-string. One second it was there, the next it was gone. David's eyes, and a thousand other pairs, feasted on the small black patch of pubic hair.

There was a clash of cymbals, and it went dark. David could hear the chair scrape and then the click of retreating heels. When the lights came on again, the girl and her clothes had gone. David could hardly believe that he had seen her, that she existed at all.

The compère was back on stage. He had taken off his bow tie and was holding a cigarette in his hand.

'It's all right for you lot,' he said. 'You've only got to look at the girls.' He lit the cigarette and inhaled deeply. 'When the show's over, we 'ave to shag 'em all.' There was some laughter. 'Talkin' of shaggin', have you 'eard the one about the pie-maker and the sausage-slicer? Well, this pie-maker starts a new job, see, and on 'is first day 'e gets an irresistible urge to stick 'is thing in the sausage-slicer . . .'

David was far away. Part of him was trying to absorb what he had just seen – the girl's face was a blur now, but he would never forget the body. The other part of his mind was wondering why his father had bothered to bring *him* here, and for the first time in his life it occurred to him that perhaps Harrison *loved* him.

' "And what about the sausage-slicer?"
"Oh, they gave her the sack as well!" '

The compère's patter continued for about five minutes before the second stripper came on. Her breasts were not as big as Lindy's, but David thought they were nicer in some ways, more rounded and delicate. He had seen two naked women in his life and he was already a connoisseur.

There was one more set of jokes from the compère, one more dancer, and it was the interval. David felt very hot – and a little drunk. His father had kept ordering pints and he, totally absorbed in the spectacle on stage, had been knocking them back.

'By bloody hell,' Harrison said, 'when that tart Lindy was doin' her stuff I thought your eyes were going to pop out of your head. An' I swear if I'd moved me foot, I'd have stepped on yer tongue.'

David smiled happily. It would be the first of many nights like this. Him an' his dad together, havin' a good time. He didn't even feel guilty that his friends were not with him, because what he shared with them was different from what he had discovered he could share with his father.

'It's about time we had a talk, lad,' Mr Harrison said, signalling the waiter for more drinks. 'I've never interfered much at home. Well, it wasn't my place. That's yer mother's job, and damn good at it she is too. But I've always seen you've wanted for nowt, haven't I?'

David nodded. His father worked harder than any man he knew, and apart from his beer money, everything went into the family coffers.

'It's like when you wanted to go to the grammar. It cost a lot more, what with that expensive blazer and fancy games kit. It meant a good few more hours at the scrap, but I never begrudged it you.'

It was true. Never once had David heard his father complain about the cost of anything.

'Anyway,' Harrison continued, 'you're fifteen now. Old enough to be workin'. And by God, you're strong enough for any job.'

David could detect the pride in his father's voice, but at the same time a sick panic welled up inside him. He wanted to be a civil engineer: he had wanted it desperately ever since the day his father opened that brown envelope and told him he had won a place in the grammar school. He had visions of himself, in a safety helmet and boots, standing in the mud and looking at piles of bricks and metal girders that would one day be a bridge – a bridge that he would help build. And now his dad wanted him to leave school and if his dad wanted it, it would happen. He could throw his ideas of a Higher National Certificate out of the window. He would have to settle for an apprenticeship. He would still be creating things, but it would not be the same.

'You'll get used to it,' he told himself.

It was just that it had come as a shock on top of everything else that had happened that night – the strippers, the drink, the first real contact with his father.

'Aye,' Harrison plunged on, 'you're ready for a man-sized job. I don't want to raise yer hopes too much, but I think I can get Fred Rathbone at the scrapyard to take you on. How about that! Me an' you workin' together, havin' your old feller teachin' you the ropes, knockin' off at dinner time and goin' out for a pint – just the two of us.'

So he was not even to become a craftsman. He would be a destroyer, a wrecker, a disposer of the worn-out endeavours of others. Until that morning, his father had been an unapproachable presence, now he was almost a pal. David desperately wanted to keep his friendship, but if working in the scrapyard was the price, then he knew he couldn't pay it.

'I want to stay on at school for a bit, dad,' he said timidly. 'I want to learn a skill.'

It took a while for the idea to sink in. When it did, Harrison's expression changed from beery benevolence to sorrow of a depth and intensity that David had never seen before. His head bowed, his broad chest seemed to shrink. David willed himself to say that he had only been joking, but the words would not come.

Harrison lifted his head and looked at his son. His eyes were red.

'So my job's not good enough for you,' he said in a quiet, cracked voice. '*I'm* not good enough for you. Not now you've been to the grammar. It's them fancy friends of yours what's done this.'

'Dad, please understand . . . it's just that . . . listen, I didn't mean . . .'

Sorrow did not sit well on Harrison's shoulders, it was simply not part of his emotional make-up, and as he listened to his son's halting attempts to make everything all right again, there was a new feeling rising in him – blind red rage.

'You ungrateful little bastard!' he shouted.

Though the air around them was abuzz with animated conversation, Harrison's roar cut through it. The surrounding tables fell silent and heads turned in their direction.

'Fifteen years I've kept you,' Harrison continued, 'clothed you, fed you. And now, when I ask you to pull your weight, you don't want to.'

From the corner of his eye, David could see the bouncers moving in on them.

'Dad!' he hissed. 'Please!'

'Don't you tell me to be quiet,' Harrison said, raising his voice even more. Then he, too, noticed the men in dinner jackets. 'Don't worry, lads,' he slurred. 'There'll be no trouble. We're just leavin'. I don't want to be seen in public with this little shit.'

As David followed his father's winding path to the exit, he realised that the older man was even drunker than he was. They crossed the car park in silence. While Harrison struggled to get the key into the lock, David stood by the passenger side and wondered if he could ever make things right again. Harrison slid the door open and then looked across at David.

'Oh no,' he said. 'I don't want *you* riding with *me*.'

He staggered round to the back of the van and opened the double doors.

'Get in there – with the rest of the rubbish.'

Totally miserable, David climbed into the back, struggling over the remains of a consignment of builder's rubble. It was ruining his only suit, his pride and joy, but at that moment it was of little consequence to him.

In Stockport, Harrison kept more or less within the speed limit, but once out on the open road, he put his foot down. The old van began to groan and rattle in protest, but the driver would not let up. The faster they went, the angrier Harrison seemed to become. He had started muttering to himself in the town, but on the dual carriageway his voice rose to the level it had reached in the club. What he was saying, David didn't know. Harrison's words were drowned by the engine.

David just sat there in the back, elbows on knees, head in hands – swaying with the van and wishing he was dead.

'And I'll tell you something else, you selfish, stuck-up, little sod . . .' his father said – quite clearly this time.

David looked up and saw that Harrison had twisted his head round so that he was facing his son. And beyond his father, through the front window, he saw a lorry. It was not moving, and the man standing next to it was waving frantically.

'Dad!' David screamed. 'Look out!'

Harrison turned and saw the lorry. He swung the wheel violently in an attempt to get the van off the road, and at the same time slammed on his brakes.

The lorry was still looming up at them, but now it did not seem directly in front as before.

'We're going to make it,' David thought. 'Thank God! It's going to be all right.'

He felt a jolt and heard the sickening crunch as the offside of the van ploughed into the parked vehicle.

Harrison was thrown through the windscreen, but he could not go far. Before half his body was clear of the van, his head hit the back of the truck with a loud crack and his legs slumped back down around the steering column.

The van juddered, rocked, tilted and finally toppled, turning over twice as it rolled down the slight embankment. David, hurled

43

around in the back, caught fleeting horrifying glimpses of his father falling one way and then the other.

By the time the driver of the broken-down lorry reached the wreckage, David had pulled Harrison clear and was kneeling next to him.

'Are you all right, dad? Are you all right?' he was asking the bloody pulp of muscle and bone which had once been his father's head.

The doctor in the emergency unit said that David was very lucky to come out of it with just a few scratches and bruises. If he had been in the front with his father, he would almost certainly have been killed.

David wished he could have turned the clock back to the time in the club. Given that second chance, he would have said, 'Yes. Dad. Certainly I'll work with you. Thank you for liking me enough to *want* me to work with you; thank you for approving of me as a son.'

If time wouldn't go back that far, if it would only bend a little, then he would at least have wanted to be sitting next to his father when they hit the lorry.

Chapter Four

The sofa and table had to be moved against the walls of the parlour, and the closed coffin was laid on three chairs in the middle of the room. In death, as in life, Harrison dominated the house.

David stood at the front door, normally only open on Christmas Day, and received those who had come to pay their last respects. His mother sat in the kitchen, whimpering quietly, and did her best, with a great deal of sewing and sponging, to make David's suit look respectable for the funeral.

At two o'clock on a grey June afternoon, the casket was carried out, placed in the hearse and driven slowly up the village street. The curtained windows of all the houses gazed down on the cortège like blind, dead eyes.

The cortège drove by the salt works and crossed the hump-backed bridge the boys had played on when they were younger. They moved along the side of the pond with its tranquil, regal swans and passed the school yard, where the small children stood silent for a moment before returning to their games.

It started to drizzle lightly during the graveside service. The grave-diggers strained under the weight as they lowered the coffin. For a second it looked as if the rope was slipping out of their hands, but they grasped tightly, grunting, and the box settled with only a slight bump on the bottom of the grave.

When it was all over, when the diggers had finished heaping shovel after shovel of dirt, when it was finally clear that Harrison was not coming back – ever – the damp mourners trudged to David's house for the funeral tea.

There was whisky for the men and port for the women. Jimmy and Paul had worked hard all morning, inexpertly making potted meat sandwiches, laying out cakes on blue willow-pattern plates. They'd had to do it, Mrs Harrison was no good for anything. Even now, she stood in the corner of the parlour, children clutching her dress. She looked lost, defeated, terrified.

'You'll be OK, Mrs Harrison,' Paul said comfortingly. 'It looks black now, but it'll all work out.'

The woman stared at him with wild, frightened eyes.

'How can it be OK, Paul? We've no savings, none at all. We've always spent everything. If we ever needed any extra money, Ted just put in a few more hours at the scrap.'

The children encircled her tighter, though whether to comfort themselves or to protect her, Paul wasn't sure. He could see that she was shaking and that the motion was becoming more violent every second that passed. He searched for some words of solace, the *right* words that would calm her down, stop her running shrieking from the room. Suddenly he was aware that Jimmy was standing next to him.

'It *will* be OK, Mrs Harrison,' Jimmy said. 'Things will work out. Believe me.'

Paul saw some of the tension drain away from the woman's face.

'Do you really think so, Jimmy?' she asked, hopefully.

The mourners gradually drifted away, offering platitudes to Mrs Harrison and firm handshakes to David. When they had gone, the young men cleared away the plates, cups and glasses and re-arranged the furniture until the parlour looked like a best room again, to be left unused until the next significant event.

The boys stepped across the road to The George. They had never been in there before, the landlord was too well aware that they were under age. Today they did not bother with such considerations and the landlord himself made no protest – they were entitled to a drink.

The three took their pints into the tap room and sat down, not speaking. David gazed vacantly at the cream and brown walls, Paul drew patterns with his finger in the puddle of beer that dropped off the bottom of his glass, Jimmy began delicately whittling the edge off a beer mat. Finally, it was Paul who broke the silence.

'What will happen now?'

'We can't manage on a widow's pension,' David said. 'I'll have to leave school and get a job.' He laughed, bitterly. 'Just like my dad wanted me to.'

'But you can't! It would be such a waste of talent.' Paul groped for a solution. 'Look, if the three of us did Saturday jobs – and maybe a paper round during the week – we could probably get together enough money to keep your family going.'

Jimmy ripped his beer mat down the middle, crumpled it into a ball and flung it furiously across the room.

'For Christ's sake, be realistic, Paul,' he said. 'You're talking like an idiot. We're not characters in one of your stories.'

Paul was startled, not just at the anger, but by the fact that Jimmy was prepared to use the stories, about which he was so unsure and secretive, as a weapon against him.

'Look,' Jimmy continued, 'how much can we earn between the three of us? Nothing like enough – and nothing like what David could make full-time. And how long do you think we could keep it up? It'll be all right at first, but we're coming up to examination year. And even if we manage it this year, what about next? If David goes on an engineering course, it'll be another *seven years* before he's earning what he could be pulling tomorrow in an unskilled job.'

He stopped talking to Paul and addressed himself to David.

'I'm sorry, kid,' he said. 'I'd give my life for you, but I'm not prepared to do it for your family. They were never part of the deal.'

Jimmy was right, of course. Paul knew his own ideas were impractical. David would have to find a job, he had no choice. Yet it shouldn't be like that. Harold Macmillan said that people had never had it so good – and that was true. But did they have it good *enough*? It only took a twist of fate like the wage-earner's death, and they were back at the bottom of the heap.

There had to be a way of ensuring that what had happened to David didn't keep on happening. And suddenly, all his old vague feelings – feelings that made him sorry for the under-privileged kids who had destroyed the Secret Camp, feelings that had pushed him to force David to study hard for the grammar school – crystallised. Real change could only come through political action. The Tories had been in power for thirteen years. The country needed a new government, an idealistic government, concerned with the well-being of *all* the people. He would put his faith in the Socialists.

David saw that Jimmy was right too. His friends couldn't shoulder the burden – and why should they even try? It was his fault that his father was dead.

'I'll see you lads later,' he said, getting to his feet.

They both knew where he was going, but neither tried to stop him.

David walked briskly up the cinder track, known locally as the Cart Road, though carts had not passed along it for thirty years. There were no fields sprouting golden wheat, no animals grazing peacefully – only scrub and the odd clump of trees. To his left was

47

the embankment on top of which flowed the canal. He could see none of the narrow boats of his childhood, road transport had taken their business from them. To his right ran the old railway track which had once connected with now-abandoned salt pits. Occasionally he came across small areas enclosed by solid, wooden fences. Large red notices nailed to the cross-pieces screamed a single word – Danger! Here, the ground had begun to subside. It was slowly slipping into the shafts and tunnels where miners had hacked away at walls of salt, and small, blind pit ponies had struggled with heavy trucks. The village, like his father, was finished, only it was taking a longer time to die.

He got to his first view of the scrap yard, as he had known he would, when the track skirted a copse of silver birches. The rusty corrugated-iron walls loomed up twenty feet high, and along the top of them ran strands of barbed wire glinting wickedly in the pale evening sun. Around the edge grew bushes, pale stunted things, denied their share of natural light by this human abomination. From within, a ferocious dog barked, warning of David's approach.

'It looks like a prison,' he thought, and if he was successful in his quest, that was exactly what it would be for him.

He pushed open the heavy, creaking gate and entered. The land trapped inside the oppressive walls must have been at least an acre. Some grass grew, but not much. Most of the ground had been conquered by junk – a mountain of wood spars, a huge mound of old boilers, cookers and mangles waiting to be melted down, a heap of lead, a stack of warped doors and even three or four battered cars. There seemed to be no order, no plan. It was as if some race of giant consumers had dropped its rubbish from the air, letting it fall where it would.

The dog that David had heard earlier, a huge Alsatian, was straining at the rope around its neck. Its teeth were bared and the sound of its snarls reverberated off the walls.

In the very centre of the graveyard of twisted, mutilated objects, was a dilapidated garden shed. David picked his way through the debris and knocked at the door.

Fred Rathbone had changed out of his funeral clothes and was in his working gear – old trousers, thick boots and innumerable layers of cardigans. He had been making a brew on the Primus stove when David entered. He looked questioningly at the young man, standing earnestly in front of him, still dressed in his suit.

'I'm sorry about your dad,' he said. 'He was a right good worker, the best I ever had. What can I do for you, lad?' When David

48

hesitated, he reached into his pocket. 'If you need a few bob to tide you over . . .'

David shook his head.

'I want a job, Mr Rathbone.'

Rathbone didn't reply immediately. He was sixty-seven years old, and had been in scrap all his life – except when he was a lad, they called it rag-and-bone. He was tall and broad and looked almost as powerful as he had ever been.

But he was weary of work. His bungalow was all paid for, and he had a fair amount in the bank. The prospect of retiring was very appealing, especially now that Ted was gone. He rubbed his balding head with his gnarled right hand.

'I don't know, David,' he said. 'I really need a driver – if I need anybody at all.'

'You do all the drivin', Mr Rathbone, and I'll do all the humpin' work that you and me dad used to do between you.'

It was ridiculous, of course. David was big, but not as big as his father had been – and Fred himself was no slouch when it came to hard work. Yet there was something about David's calm intensity that, even flying in the face of common sense, was convincing.

'I'll tell you what I'll do, lad,' Rathbone said, after a pause for thought. 'I'll take you on, but I'll make no promises, mind. While you're learning, I can't pay you much, but if you turn out all right, if you do the work your father did, I'll pay you what I paid him. I'm not offering you a job for life, like, only until your family gets back on its feet. When can you start?'

David stripped off his jacket.

'Right now,' he said. 'Them boilers need sortin' out.'

'You can't work in yer best suit, lad,' Rathbone protested. 'You'll ruin it.'

'You only need a suit when you're goin' out,' David said. 'There'll be no money for that for the next few years – no time neither.'

He walked over to the pile, assessed his task, then put his thick arms around one of the larger boilers and heaved it clear.

'You'll not regret takin' me on, Mr Rathbone,' he shouted over his shoulder.

'No, lad,' Rathbone said softly, almost to himself. 'No, I don't think I will.'

On the first day of the school summer holidays, David took Jimmy and Paul to the yard.

49

'These are me mates,' David explained. 'They want to help me get the yard ship-shape.'

'You cheeky young bugger,' Rathbone said gruffly – but not unkindly. 'There's nothin' wrong with the place as it is.'

'There is, Mr Rathbone,' David said earnestly.

Rathbone looked down the yard. Young David might be right. Maybe he had let it get a bit disorganized over the last few years. But these two lads wouldn't be much help. The fair-haired one looked as if he thought manual labour was beneath him. And as for the other, the scrawny one – well, he couldn't punch his way out of a paper bag.

'I can't afford to pay 'em owt, you know?' he said.

'That's all right,' Paul answered. 'We don't want any money, we just want to help David.'

'Aye, well, you'd better get on with it,' the scrap dealer said, shaking his head and walking away. He'd give them till dinner time, then they'd get bored and drift away. David could take hard graft, but the other two were a different kettle of fish.

They re-arranged the junk so that the piles of metal were all close to the smelter. They sorted the wood into different stacks – hard-wood, soft-wood, re-useable timber, material only suitable for pulp. They made it so that it was possible to get at anything without having to move something else first. They even wanted to shift the shed.

'It's been there for fifteen years,' Rathbone protested.

'An' as long as it stays there,' David argued, 'we'll never be able to get a lorry into that left-hand corner. Think of how much time we could save if we loaded direct instead of havin' to hump the stuff across the yard.'

It made sense, Rathbone thought, right good sense.

'Move it if you bloody want to,' he said. 'I can't be bothered arguing with yer.'

He'd been wrong about the other two, he admitted to himself. They might not have David's strength, but they gave the job all their effort. He had never seen anything like it. They were there as soon as he opened and they did not leave until dark.

On Friday, Rathbone broke his lifetime rule of never paying more than he needed to for anything, and offered Jimmy and Paul a couple of pounds each. They shook their heads.

'It's only fair, lads,' Rathbone said, realizing with astonishment that he was trying to argue himself out of money. 'Between the three of you, you've done the work of at least two men. Tek it! Go and buy yourselves a few pints; you deserve 'em.'

'Give it to David,' Jimmy said.

They never did slacken off. Throughout the whole holiday, all six weeks of it, the two boys were there every day, working side-by-side with their friend.

It was still possible, during that long hot summer, to see life in simple terms. The enemy of one was undoubtedly in the wrong, and became the enemy of all. The problems of one would be taken on the shoulders of the others. They were united – the Secret Camp Gang against the world.

They would work together again in the future, but it would never again be so easy. New forces would pull at them, demanding their loyalties. They would all have to walk a tight-rope between their old friendship and the different directions their lives were taking.

Of the three, only Jimmy could see it coming, and it did not worry him. He was a mental and emotional acrobat. He would not fall himself, he thought, and he would guide his friends along the narrow wire to the safety of the other side.

Chapter Five

The Conservative Government had lost its impetus and for a year had been on the edge of collapse. Fate was not kind to it. Rocked by its failure to take Britain into the Common Market, it tottered under the news that Secretary of State John Profumo had been seeing call-girls who were also servicing the naval attaché at the Russian Embassy. Finally, when Harold Macmillan resigned – ostensibly due to ill health – the administration, like the autumn leaves, curled up and died.

The new conversative leader, Sir Alec Douglas-Home, was largely unknown. Only a few weeks earlier, he had been an earl. The popular press ran pictures of him on his Scottish estate, dressed in plus-fours, shotgun in hand. When he spoke, he seemed superior, aloof, out of place in post-war Britain.

His opponent, Harold Wilson, wore a functional, efficient, Gannex mac. He smoked a pipe – which told people that he was a deep thinker. He was the grandson of a railway man and had gone to grammar rather than public school. When he talked of a better future for the country based on British skills and technology, his voice still bore traces of flat Northern vowels. Wilson seemed to emanate confidence both in himself and in the country.

The polls indicated that it would be a close-run thing, but for the first time since Paul was a baby, it looked like there was a real chance of a Labour Government.

The Conservative Party was housed in a solid, dignified building on the High Street, Labour made do with a converted terraced house in an area scheduled for re-development. Harold Wilson might be projecting a shining new image for Labour, but it hadn't reached Norton yet.

Paul had to knock four times, at first timorously, then loudly, before he was admitted. The girl who opened the door couldn't have been more than eighteen or nineteen.

'Yes, love?' she said.

'I'd like to see Mr Yarwood,' Paul said, adding unnecessarily, 'the constituency agent.'

'Is it a message from someone, love?'

'No,' Paul said firmly. 'I want to work for Labour.'

'Well, isn't that sweet of you, love?'

'Could I see him, please?'

The girl tittered.

'I'll see if he's available.'

As she walked down the corridor, Paul watched her backside, swaying yet firmly held in her tight black skirt. She didn't see him as a man at all, he thought sadly, just as a kid. Jimmy wouldn't have got this kind of reception – and it wasn't just because he was taller.

The girl returned, and this time he could see her breasts bobbing under her blouse.

'Mr Yarwood can spare you a minute,' she said, 'but you mustn't keep him longer than that. He's a very busy man, you know.'

All thoughts of sex disappeared from Paul's mind as he entered the agent's office. Yarwood was sitting behind a battered metal desk. Though he was still in early middle age, his hair was white and his moustache was stained brown with nicotine. The room itself was untidy and a little seedy. Political pamphlets were heaped in one corner, placards were propped untidily against the wall. The place smelt of dampness and Woodbines.

None of that mattered. Paul knew, objectively, that Yarwood was only a small fish, that Harold Wilson had probably never heard of him, yet at the same time he was conscious of the fact that he was meeting a real political presence in Norton – and he was overawed.

'My secretary tells me you want to help us,' Yarwood said.

Paul nodded, not trusting himself to speak, afraid that if he did his voice would come out as a childish squeak.

'You're a bit young for politics, aren't you, lad?' the agent said, smiling indulgently, almost laughing.

All Paul's nervousness vanished in a sudden spasm of anger.

'My dad daren't go sick because we couldn't manage without his overtime,' Paul said. 'I've got a pal who's had to throw up his chance of being an engineer because he had a family to feed. People in my village have worked hard all their lives and are still strugglin' to make the HP payments. And yet outside the Roebuck Hotel, there's any number of big cars parked, while the owners eat their two-hour dinners. It's not how old you are, it's what you've seen. Isn't it?'

It was Paul's first political speech, and it was a success. The look of patronising amusement disappeared from the agent's face, and he began to fiddle with his waistcoat.

'Aye, you're probably right, lad,' he said, when he had checked all the buttons and found none missing. 'No, dammit, you *are* right. But,' he added with regret, 'I can't use you.'

'You still think I'm too young,' Paul said disappointedly. 'You think I'm not ready to join the party yet.'

The agent chuckled.

'Oh, you're ready for the party, all right,' he said. 'It's just that I'm not sure the party's ready for you. Be patient, lad. Give it a few years, until they're prepared to take you seriously, and you'll really shake the buggers up.'

Paul didn't want to wait and in an agony of frustration he threw himself into the only outlet available, the school mock election. He lobbied his classmates, stayed up late into the night producing posters, stood for hours in the playground making speeches.

Labour lost the school, Labour lost Norton, but it won the country – and Paul was happy. 'Give it a few years,' the agent had told him, 'and you'll really shake the buggers up.' He would, and in the meantime, while others were creating a technological utopia, he'd have to be content with preparing himself for the task, attaining an enviable academic record, studying every book of political theory and practice he could lay his hands on.

Jimmy, like Paul, accepted that this was a waiting time, a quiet period before he burst on the unsuspecting world. Yet both the schoolboys were slightly envious of David. The scrap yard might be a dead end, but at least David was out in the real world, doing a real job for Fred Rathbone.

Rathbone had started his working life with a horse and cart, going from door to door, but he had given that up long ago. Now he dealt mainly with demolition firms, buying iron railings and lead roof lining by the hundredweight – or even the ton. At first he did all the negotiating himself with David as a passive observer. And that was how it would have stayed if he hadn't been struck down by a bout of flu just after he had heard about a nice consignment of copper pipes that was up for grabs.

'The money's on the dressing table,' he croaked from his sick bed. 'Don't give 'em more than a hundred quid or I'll stop it out of yer wages!'

The young man just nodded and left. Rathbone knew that if he had been conducting the deal, he'd have got the copper for ninety, but with the lad doing it . . .

David was back an hour later.

'How did you get on?' Rathbone asked.

'Pretty well,' David said. 'I got 'em to throw in a set of doors – good ones. I think I know who we can sell 'em to. Should be worth at least a tenner.'

Rathbone narrowed his eyes. If they had given David something for nothing, they must have been well satisfied with the price they got for the copper. He should never have sent the lad.

'I told you no more than a hundred,' he said. 'Is that what you give 'em?'

'No,' David said.

'Well,' the scrap man thought, 'I suppose it serves me right. You learn by your mistakes.'

'So how much did you have to pay 'em?' he said aloud.

David put his hand in his pocket, pulled out some notes and laid them on the bed-spread. Fivers – four of them.

'They seemed happy with eighty,' he said.

So David discovered, as much to his own surprise as anyone else's, that he had a good head for business. It might have been that he said so little and thought long and hard before he spoke at all; it could have been that he gave off the air of one who had worked hard for his money and knew the value of it. Whatever the reason, contractors usually found themselves selling him scrap for much less than they intended.

But where did that leave him? He had worked for Rathbone for nearly two years, putting in all the overtime he could and saving nearly everything that he didn't hand over to his mother. And all he had was fifty-seven pounds, fourteen shillings and four pence in his Post Office account. He couldn't start up any kind of business on that amount of capital, and at this rate he would *never* have enough.

It was a casual remark of Fred Rathbone's that gave David his idea. It had been a painful experience walking to work that early Spring morning. All around him, nature was bursting out. The trees had green, sticky buds, the birds were building new nests. Everything was full of life, full of hope, and for him there was only a dead junk yard with its sad, useless relics. But that was how it was. How it had to be.

Rathbone was not there when he arrived, and David looked around for something to do. His eyes fell on a grey Morris Minor which had been waiting for two weeks to be reduced to smelter-sized pieces.

It wouldn't be easy, he thought. Although it was old, it would still have been on the road had it not come off second in an argument with a lamp-post. He picked up his oxyacetylene torch, selected his starting point and began to cut.

Fred arrived ten minutes later. He parked his new Hillman Imp in its usual spot, but instead of going straight into the shed, he leant against the vehicle and watched David work. It was bloody marvellous the way the kid did it, poetry in motion. Even so, it was hardly worth bothering with the price they would get for the metal. And it was a pity to see such a piece of engineering being destroyed.

'Bloody shame,' he said. 'The finest car ever made, the Morris Minor. We'll not see its like again. Look at this!' He hammered his palm down on the roof of the Imp and seemed to gain pessimistic satisfaction from the sound it made. 'A bloody tin can. I was readin' in the paper that they're workin' now on somethin' called the principle of built-in obsolescence. That means they're buildin' the buggers to fall apart.'

David took two weeks to mull the idea over before deciding he was right. The number of cars on the road would go up, he was sure of it. They were building motorways everywhere. The one that ran through Cheshire even had a café on it, a sign that the planners were expecting more and more long distance drivers. And the previous year, for the first time, the *Norton Chronicle* had run a big section on the Motor Show.

Soon, everybody would want a car, would regard it almost as a necessity. Not everybody, however, could afford five hundred and twenty-seven pounds for a new Vauxhall Viva, not even if they got it on the HP. Most would have to settle for second hand.

If only he could get Fred Rathbone to go into partnership with him!

The scrap dealer was not enthusiastic.

'Stick to what you know, lad,' he said. 'Stick to what you know.'

Then he remembered that this was just the advice his own father had given him – and if he'd followed it, he'd never have got rid of the horse and cart. Even so, he was too old to start a new venture.

'It's a good idea,' he admitted. 'And if you'd mentioned it to me a few years ago . . .'

David was crushed, his faint glimmer of hope extinguished.

Though he towered over Rathbone, he felt like a small boy who has been told he can't go to the seaside after all.

It was a shame, the older man thought. The lad had worked damned hard – he deserved a break.

'I'll tell you what,' he said. 'I'll give you the space and let you run it yourself.' The look on David's face made him feel like Father Christmas. 'But on your own time, mind,' he added, not wishing to sound soft.

David's advertisement went into the *Norton Chronicle* the following Thursday.

'*Old cars towed away free!!*' it read. '*Contact Harrison Enterprises, c/o Rathbone's Scrapyard, Buckworth.*'

There were a number of enquiries, but David hit problems almost immediately. Only the owners of complete wrecks were prepared to give them away free. The rest required what was usually phrased as 'a few bob' as well.

'After all, son,' said one of them pointing to his Hillman Minx, 'they'd give me fifty quid for that in part exchange for a new one.'

Though David knew that this was true, fifty pounds was most of his capital and he could not afford to pay that much for one car. So he had to make do with wrecks.

'You agreed to do it on yer own time,' Fred grunted cheerfully as they struggled to get a battered A40 up the tailboard of the lorry. 'An' you are. But you never mentioned nothin' about me doin' it on *my* own time as well.'

David grinned and strained as the car rolled back slightly.

'When I've made a few sales, I'll be able to pay for a driver.'

Fred heaved and the back wheels were finally on the lorry.

'You always were a cocky young bugger,' he said. 'I hope you've not been *too* cocky on this one.'

As a result of his – and Fred's – efforts, David had acquired eight cars, a mixture of Morrises, Fords, Vauxhalls and Hillmans. They would all be of some use, but he still needed a few in slightly better condition to start him off. And so he did what he had been hoping to avoid all along – he went down to the Post Office and made a withdrawal.

'You're taking out all the money you've got,' the clerk said. 'Are you sure you're doing the right thing?'

No. He wasn't sure – but he knew he had to try anyway.

When he left the Post Office, he made a tour of the used car salesrooms.

'I'll do you a favour, son,' one of the dealers said, pointing to the Ford Popular David was interested in. 'I won't sell it to you. I had to take it in part-exchange though God knows how its last owner even managed to drive it here – I doubt if you'd get it back home.'

It might not be in great condition, but it was better than anything David had back at the yard.

'I'll tow it if I have to,' he said.

'You young lads are all the same,' said the salesman, shaking his head sadly. 'You've got a few quid in your pockets and you think you can buy some banger and fix it up. You'll not get this road-worthy for less than fifty or sixty pounds. Now over there I've got an Anglia. A really nice little runner. Of course, it'll cost you a bit more, but you'll have transport immediately, and it'll be paid for before you know it.'

'I want the Pop,' David said stubbornly. 'Will you take ten pounds down and the rest on the never-never?'

The salesman shrugged.

'Why not, if you're fool enough to buy it. Only you'll have to get your dad to sign the papers.'

'Me mam,' David said. 'Me dad's dead.'

The other man looked uncomfortable.

'Aye . . . well . . . your mam will do just as well.'

The next day, Thursday, David led his mother round four separate car salesrooms and got her to sign the HP agreements for the four cars he had agreed to buy. Then he took her to the market café for a pot of tea – she was badly in need of it.

'But however will you meet all the payments, our David?' she asked.

'I'll be doin' business soon and then I'll have plenty of money to pay off the HP,' David said. 'My advert's gone into today's *Chronicle*.'

It had, and it had cost the remainder of his capital. The few coins in his pocket would just about cover the cost of the tea.

'But you've only got until this time next week,' his mother protested.

'That's plenty of time,' David said – and prayed to God it was.

No one came in answer to the advertisement on Friday – nor on Saturday. By Sunday afternoon, four days after it had appeared, David felt miserable and defeated. He sat in the hut, his head in his hands, and thought about what would happen. He was ruined. The HP companies would take the cars back and he would lose all the money he had paid in deposits – the money it had taken him two years to save. If they found out that he had bought four cars at the same time, with no chance of paying them off, they might even send him to prison. He wondered what kind of prison they had for boys who had not quite turned seventeen.

But worse than all that, far worse, he didn't think he'd ever have the nerve to start up a business again. When Fred retired, he'd go and work for another scrap-man, and would end his days as a semi-skilled labourer.

His flood of black thoughts was interrupted by the coughing, spluttering sound of an A40 pulling up at the gate. David was out of the shed and standing by the car before the owner had opened the door.

He was a middle-aged man with thinning hair, a duffle-coat and National Health spectacles. The sort of bloke, David reckoned, who lagged his own cock-loft and had plans to build an extension on to the back of his kitchen.

'Is this Harrison Enterprises?'

David said that it was.

'So where's your spare parts shop?' the man asked, looking vaguely around the yard. 'I need a new carburettor. I reckon this one's just about knackered.'

'No shop,' David said. 'There's an A40 over there. Take the carburettor from that.'

'You want me to tek it out meself?' the man asked, surprised.

'What'd you rather do? Take it out yourself and get it cheap, or have me do it and pay more. And who's goin' to put it in *your* car? A mechanic?'

'No, meself,' the man said. He thought for a second. 'You're dead right. If I can put it in, I can tek it out in the first place. I've got more time on me hands than I have brass.' He stripped off his duffle-coat. 'Got any tools?'

'They're in the shed.'

The man removed the carburettor, then fitted it in his own vehicle. He switched on the engine and listened while it ticked over.

'Very good,' he said. 'How much do I owe yer?'

It was so tempting to take the money, but it would not have been enough to pay off the next week's HP debts. And now that the A40 had lost its carburettor, David couldn't even return it to the finance company.

'D'you have any mates with old cars?' he asked.

The man grinned.

'Too bloody right. We're not all shift workers with big pay packets, you know.'

'I'll tell you what, then,' David said. 'You get four or five of them to come and buy parts from me by next Thursday, and I'll let you have the carburettor for nothin'.'

That would be a doddle, the man thought.

'You've got a deal, son,' he said, pulling on his duffle-coat.

Saturdays and Sundays, when the yard used to be closed, became David's busiest days. As the cash accumulated, he was able to buy a wider range of cars and attract more customers. Other scrap dealers in the district caught on to the idea, but David had a head start. It was Harrison's that most people called when they had an old car that the dealers wouldn't take, and it was to Harrison's that most motorists went to get their replacement parts.

In no time at all, David was able to fulfil his promise to Rathbone and advertise in the *Chronicle* for a part-time driver. He didn't have to wait long. Two hours after the paper appeared on the streets, there was a knock on the hut door and David found himself facing a tall, broad, red-faced man of about forty-five.

'The name's O'Malley,' he said. 'Oi'm lookin' for a feller called Harrison.'

'That's me,' David said.

O'Malley smiled.

'Oi think it must be your dad Oi want, the one that needs a droiver.'

'I'm the one that needs a driver,' David said.

The Irishman looked him up and down. Though he was big, he was still a kid. O'Malley wondered if this was a joke, taking the piss out of the thick Paddy.

David had already assessed the man, with much the same skill and calculation he used to weigh up job-lots of scrap metal. He was a drinker, that was obvious from his cheeks, but he seemed like the kind who could keep off the ale until after the job was finished. He looked intelligent too, a worker who could use his own initiative.

'I can offer you ten hours a week,' he said crisply, 'whenever it suits you best. It'll be a cash business, so the tax man doesn't need to see a thing. I'll pay you fifty per cent more an hour than you're getting in your regular job, and if you find any old cars that are worth me buyin', you'll get ten per cent commission on the purchase price.'

He risked a glance at O'Malley. The other man's face registered both interest and surprise.

'I'll pay you a Christmas bonus based on turnover,' he continued, adding, as coldly and deliberately as he could, 'but if I ever think you're swingin' the lead or tryin' to fiddle me, you're out.'

He put his hand in his pocket and took out a wad of notes.

'You'll probably need a sub. Who doesn't these days?' He peeled off the top two blue notes, and held them out. 'Will ten quid do you?'

O'Malley stepped forward and took the money.

'Ten quid will be just foine, Mr Harrison,' he said.

Nobody had ever called David 'Mr' before. He rather liked the sound of it.

It was a long-established tradition at the Lord Fairfax Grammar School that the headmaster himself interviewed every pupil entering the Upper Sixth about his long-term plans. That year the process took the entire day, and when it was all over Mr Pike, helping himself to a stiff Scotch, found it hard to say which boy had disconcerted him most – Wright or Bradley.

'We think you're Oxbridge material, Wright,' he'd said to the thin boy sitting uncomfortably in front of him.

He'd been expecting a response along the lines of, 'Do you really think so, sir? Do I have a chance?'

Paul simply said, 'Yes, sir, I think I am too.'

'And . . . er . . . would your parents object if you stayed on an extra year to take the entrance examinations?'

'I don't want to take three years. I want to do them this Christmas.'

Really, there was such a contrast between this boy's lack of social poise and his confidence in his academic ability.

'You can't just take the Oxbridge exams. There's a lot of preparation involved.'

'I know,' Paul said. 'I did some of it during the Summer holidays.'

'I see. And I suppose you've already picked out a course and a college for yourself,' Pike said, with a mixture of sarcasm and admiration.

'Yes, sir. PPE at Balliol.'

'Any particular reason for your choice?'

Because Balliol turned out Prime Ministers like a baker turns out bread. Paul wanted to be a journalist, but not for long. By the time he was twenty-five, the Party would be looking for bright young men.

'Because it has a fine academic record, sir.'

'Yes, yes, indeed it does. Very well, Wright. See your form teacher. Get his opinion. That will be all for now.'

Pike saw Jimmy half an hour later. Unlike his friend, the tall, blond boy leant back in the interview chair, crossed his legs and placed his long slim hands over one knee. Perfectly at ease!

'I suppose *you've* already got plans,' Pike said.

'Yes, I want to study accountancy – at Seahaven University.'

'Accountancy's a very sound choice. But Seahaven? Are you sure? It's a long way away and it's not really an *established* university yet. Wouldn't you feel more at home in Manchester or Liverpool, somewhere where there'll be people like yourself? From what I've heard of Seahaven it's a bit of a . . .'

He groped for the right words.

'An upper middle class club?' Jimmy supplied. 'A sort of academic finishing school?'

'Well, yes, I suppose you could put it like that.'

'I'll feel right at home there,' Jimmy said confidently.

In the middle of a grey, miserable morning in early March 1967, Fred Rathbone shouted across the yard to David to stop what he was doing and come into the office. He had been calling the shed 'the office' – only partly sarcastically – ever since David had had a phone installed.

'Shall I make us a brew, Fred?' David asked.

'No, lad. You sit yerself down. I'll do it for once.'

David sank into the old armchair and thought how unusual it was to have the boss waiting on him. Rathbone boiled the kettle and two minutes later they both had steaming mugs cupped in their hands.

'It's bloody cold today, David,' Rathbone said. 'Bloody cold. But a few years ago, it wouldn't have bothered me.'

So that was what all this was about.

'Me old bones can't take it no more. I'm going to be seventy next birthday, and I think it's time I jacked it in.'

David had always known that the old man wouldn't go on for ever, but it still came as a shock. Fred had given him his first chance and had helped him start his business. How would he fare without Fred? Would the new owner rent him a space in the yard, or would he have to persuade some other dealer to take him in? What if none of them would?

'I'm going to give you first option on the place,' Fred said.

David's mouth fell open. Working under Fred's wing was one

thing but . . . the idea scared him. Then he thought about how much Rathbone would be asking for the business – and relaxed.

'I can't afford it, Fred,' he said. 'I've got a few hundred in the bank but the good-will alone must be worth a thousand pounds. Then there's the lorry and the van and all the equipment.'

'I know you can't pay me all in one go,' Rathbone continued. 'And I don't need the money, not right now. What we'll do is, I'll rent it to you, then when you've got enough cash together, you can buy me out. And we'll take the rent you've paid off the purchase price – sorta like that lend-lease we had from the Yanks durin' the war.'

It all sounded so easy when Fred said it.

'You can do it,' Fred insisted. 'You're as good with scrap as what I am. An' anyway, how much of the business *is* scrap? More than half the turnover comes from Harrison Enterprises.' He chuckled. 'You've bin so busy you haven't noticed how far you've come. You've got two full-grown men workin' for you part-time, and when I bugger off you can probably take 'em on permanent.'

It wasn't that simple, David told himself. It wasn't that simple. It wasn't that simple.

The phone rang, and David picked it up.

'Harrison Enterpri . . .'

He looked across at Rathbone and saw that he was smiling broadly. David grinned back. He dealt with the caller quickly and efficiently and replaced the receiver on its cradle.

'You knew it was for you,' Rathbone said. 'It nearly always is. So what do you say, lad?'

The whole idea still frightened David, but if he *was* going to do it, he was going to do it *properly*. He didn't want charity, he didn't want favours.

'No lend-lease. I'll pay you a fair rent, and if I can't manage that and still save up enough money to buy the yard off you in a year or two, then I shouldn't be in this business at all. Agreed?'

'Whatever you say, David,' Rathbone replied. 'You're the boss now.'

On the first of June, while Jimmy and Paul were sweating over their 'A' Levels, worrying about who exactly got what from the Treaty of Westphalia, David nailed up a painted sign to the yard's double gates. It was hand-painted and had cost him five pounds.

He stepped back so that he could see it properly. The background was a pale blue, the lettering – solid but elegant – was in black.

'Harrison Enterprises,' he read to himself. 'Proprietor D. Harrison.'

After three years of destruction, here was something new and beautiful. And while he had not created it himself, it would never have been created without him.

Chapter Six

In the middle of June they made their annual pilgrimage to the Norton Carnival. It was one of those days that occur so rarely in late Spring and early Summer, but which when they do are uniquely, gloriously English. The sun shone in a cloudless sky, but there was a gentle breeze and the air seemed to caress them. They all felt good. Paul had not only got into Oxford but had been awarded an Exhibition; David was his own master at last; Jimmy was looking forward to conquering Seahaven. They had always enjoyed the Carnival and they were determined that this one, this last one before Paul and Jimmy went away, would be the best of the lot.

Things seemed to go wrong from the start. They stood on a corner of the High Street, watching the procession go past, and felt nothing but disappointment. They had always known that the floats were made of hardboard and papier mâché, yet even as they had laughed at them, they had enjoyed the spectacle. This year, the whole thing merely looked tatty, the pathetic attempt of a small provincial town to infuse some colour into its drab life.

Though they all shared the same feeling, none of them was willing to express it to the others. So they all waited, embarrassed and uncomfortable, while the floats filled with smiling, waving children rolled by. Then, as they had always done, they cut through the side streets to beat the procession to the park, where the Carnival Queen was to be crowned.

The Corporation Park had been built as a public works project in the 1920s. The north end of it was flat and bare and only used for the Carnival and visiting circuses. From there, the land sloped down and there were a number of walks – through the small wood, past the ornamental duck pond, along the side of the rose garden – until all the paths converged at the south side of the park, just near the Drill Hall.

The field was packed, but the police had kept a narrow avenue open for the Carnival Queen and the visiting celebrity. The Queen's float arrived first and she and her hand-maidens stepped daintily onto the platform. She was a pretty seventeen-year-old. Her white dress was long and flowing, but it left her shoulders tantalizingly bare and emphasised her firm breasts and slim waist.

'I wouldn't mind giving *her* one,' Jimmy whispered to Paul as they watched the hand-maidens re-arrange her robes. 'Or any of her little mates, for that matter.'

An expectant hush fell over the audience, especially the girls. The guest of honour was one of the hottest new pop stars.

When he finally appeared, standing in an open car as it made its slow regal way to the platform, the female fans screamed, pressed their clenched fists hard against their foreheads and pushed with all their might against the police line. The star simply smiled and waved calmly, as if all this was his due.

He stepped out of the car and climbed the steps, and the hysteria increased. He placed the crown on the Queen's head, spouted the required phrases, and the ceremony was over. He posed for photographs standing by the Queen's throne, his arm around her, his hand resting on her soft white shoulder as casually as if she were a piece of furniture.

The Queen gazed up at him with adoration in her eyes. Yet he wasn't particularly handsome: his nose was too big, his eyes too close together and his shoulder-length hair greasy and uncared for.

'He could have her,' Jimmy thought angrily. 'He could have half the silly bitches here today. Just by clicking his fingers.'

He sensed that his friends shared his frustration. They were living in the Permissive Society, the Swinging Sixties. Everyone, everywhere, seemed to be into free love. But apart from a few girls wearing beads and kaftans or walking around barefoot, the revolution had hardly reached Norton, and all three of them – much to their chagrin – were still virgins. Yet here was this ugly bloke on stage who could get all he wanted, just because he was a pop star. It wasn't right. Where was their share?

After the crowning, they made a tour of the fairground. They were surrounded by an animation that none of them could really be part of. Little children rushed around excitedly, clutching toffee apples and candy floss. Bigger kids sat on the roundabouts, their knees tightly gripping the sides of their horses, proving that *they* could ride without having to clutch on to the central pole. Barkers shouted out to them to try their luck at shooting moving ducks or knocking down coconuts.

And coming from every side, there was music – the hurdy-gurdy noise of the organs – the heavy thudding of the latest pop songs.

I may win on the merry-go-round, then I lose on the swings, Sandie Shaw sang. '*In or out, there is never a doubt, just who's pulling the strings.*'

Paul and Jimmy had a couple of rides on the dodgems. In their individual cars they would home in on pairs of girls crammed into one vehicle. The girls shouted and waved their hands in the air, begging for mercy, but when the ride was over they would giggle, link arms and walk away, as if there had been no contact at all. They couldn't stay long on the cars, hoping their luck would improve, because ever since his accident David had refused to go near the track and always wandered off on his own.

They drifted over to the Octopus and stood, heads in the air, looking up the skirts of the girl riders. Even that palled after a while, and they went in search of alcohol.

The beer tent was crowded and they had to queue for ever to get their drinks. When they had finally secured three bottles of Newcastle Brown, Paul said, 'Don't let's drink it here. We'll have people knocking into us all the time.'

'Where do you want to go, then?'

Paul pointed to a patch of woodland about a hundred yards from the fairground. As they walked towards it, the Sandie Shaw record was playing yet again:

Are you leading me on? Tomorrow will you be gone?
I wonder if some day that you'll say that you care,
If you say you love me madly, I'll gladly be there,
Like a puppet on a string . . . like a puppet on a . . . string.

They lay on the grass, sipping their beers and watching the Big Wheel slowly turning round in the distance. They had no real desire to move, though they were not really happy where they were. It was a clump of trees, but it wasn't really a wood, not in the sense that they used the word. This place would never swallow them up, hide them from the rest of the world. It could never have been a pirate island or a jungle. It was far too civilised, too close to mundane reality.

'So what shall we do?' Jimmy asked, finishing his beer and throwing the bottle over his shoulder.

If they went home, the day would be a complete washout – their last carnival would have flopped.

'We haven't been all round the fairground yet,' Paul said. 'Shall we see what's going on the other side of the Big Wheel?'

There was little enthusiasm in his voice, nor did the others seem enthralled. Still, it was better than doing nothing, so they pulled themselves to their feet.

The side-shows were located on the rim of the ground, close to Winnick Road. The boys paid their money and visited an exhibition billed as *The Wonders of the World*. It contained a dirty, three-legged sheep, a dog with two heads and various other mutant animals. The creatures moved listlessly around their cramped pens, displaying no interest in the people who had come to gawp at them.

'Well, that was a waste of time and money,' Jimmy said once they were outside. He filled his lungs with fresh – if slightly diesel-tainted – air, ridding his body of the fetid smell of the trapped, uncared-for animals. 'Look, there's another freak show.'

The tent he was pointing to was covered with cheap cloth hangings, painted with stylized, brightly coloured pictures of nude women with wide smiles and enormous breasts.

'Step up, step up,' the barker was calling. 'The most exciting show outside gay Paree. Lovely ladies inside. A show not to be missed – adults only. See it now before the Watch Committee closes us down. Lots of lovely ladies inside. The show is starting right now . . .'

There wouldn't be lots of lovely ladies inside. At best, there would be two or three tired, bored women with sagging boobs and slack stomachs. Yet though they knew the reality would fall far short of the promise, they stood for a while, each waiting for one of the others to suggest that they might as well see it, that it could be 'a laugh'.

In the end, it was Jimmy who said, 'Do you fancy this then? It's only two bob each.'

The moment the words were out of Jimmy's mouth, David knew he couldn't – just couldn't. His heart was racing. His head felt hot. His hands were deathly cold. It had been three years since he had seen anything like this and . . .

He searched around desperately for a diversion, an excuse, something that would at least buy him time, and his eye fell on the boxing and wrestling marquee.

'Let's go and see that,' he said quickly. 'It's just startin'. We can take a look at the strippers later.'

And since neither Jimmy nor Paul wanted to be classed with the seedy, middle-aged men who could scarcely disguise their eagerness as they queued, they hid their disappointment and followed David.

There were no seats, just a ring. The marquee was nearly full, but with a minimum of good-natured elbowing the boys managed to get next to the ropes.

The sun beat down on the canvas, giving everything a slightly green tinge. It was hot and stuffy, and the smell of a hundred sweating men rose and hung in the air.

The MC/referee was already in the ring. He was dressed in a threadbare dinner jacket and had greasy, slick-backed hair.

'Gentlemen,' he called over the buzz of conversation, 'a big hand for our professional wrestler – the Middlesbrough Crusher!'

The Crusher entered from the back of the tent. He wore a black hood with holes cut in it for his eyes, nose and mouth. He was tall and broad. He must once have been powerful, but now his belly spilled over the elastic top of his tights and his biceps wobbled. He pushed his way roughly through the crowd, snarling and cursing and then climbed into the ring.

'Is there any sportsman in the audience willing to take on the mighty Crusher?' the MC asked,

Almost immediately a stocky, bearded man, wearing jeans and a floral shirt, stepped through the ropes.

'What's your name, sir?' the MC asked.

'Tom,' the man replied.

'Tom what?'

'Just Tom,' with a modest shrug of his shoulders.

'A big hand for Tom,' the MC called. 'A boy who helps to keep the town clean.'

The Crusher seemed determined to win by any means, fair or foul. He stamped his heavy boot down on Tom's stockinged feet, he stuck his fingers in Tom's eyes when he was on the blind side of the referee. Yet however vicious and underhand the blows, the bearded man was never quite laid out.

Two minutes into the fight, the Crusher landed a kick in Tom's stomach, and the man went down. The spectators roared that it was unfair, but the referee, apparently, hadn't seen it. The Crusher threw himself against the ropes in order to get up momentum for a final assault. As he was flung back across the ring, Tom was on his feet. He bent low and thrust his shoulder into the Crusher's stomach. The hooded man somersaulted over him, hitting the canvas with a heavy thud. Now Tom had the upper hand. He tossed the Crusher around the ring for thirty seconds, and it was all over. The professional crawled through the ropes and Tom stood in the centre of the ring, his hand held by the MC, acknowledging the applause.

'That's how life should be,' Paul thought. 'Good and evil clearly defined, and the good guy always winning.'

But he was coming to realise that this was rarely the case. Labour had been in power for three years now, and there had been no signs of a coming socialist millennium.

Perhaps he was being naive, he told himself. It was easy for good to triumph in a wrestling match. 'Just Tom' was probably a plant, always intended to win. The fight was fixed.

But what if life was, too?

When Just Tom had left the ring, the MC turned to the audience again.

'The next event on the programme is boxing,' he said. 'Will you please give a big hand to the champion – the Everton Kid!'

The atmosphere in the tent changed. Though the crowd had enjoyed the wrestling, it had only been a game, a bit of fun. The boxing would be for real, with punches that hurt, noses that bled. Less entertaining perhaps than the wrestling, but infinitely more exciting.

The Crusher had barged his way through to the ring, pushing spectators roughly out of the way. The Everton Kid's progress was much less impressive. He was small and thin. At first people weren't aware that he was there at all and it was only when they noticed his cheap, imitation silk dressing gown that they moved aside and let him pass.

'I will pay five pounds, five crisp, one pound notes,' said the MC, taking the notes out of his pocket and holding them up, 'to any sportsman in the audience who can stay in the ring for three minutes with the Kid.'

As the boxer was pulling himself up by the ropes, his foot slipped and caught David's head a glancing blow. He stopped and turned to see what had happened. He was young, only the gang's senior by a couple of years, but his face bore the signs of poverty, and he would be an old man by the time he was thirty. He saw that David was rubbing his head.

'Sorry about dat, ar kid,' he said, smiling. 'Why don't yer come up 'ere and put the gloves on? A knock like dat could earn yer five quid.'

'Is there *any* sporting gentleman who will take on the Kid?' the MC said.

'Aye,' came a voice from somewhere in the centre of the tent. 'Me.'

The volunteer stepped forward. Many of the audience recognised him. He was one of a gang who, despite marriages, mortgages and kids, still clung to the fashion of their youth – the Norton Teddy Boys.

He had a Tony Curtis haircut, and was over six feet tall. Once in the ring, he stripped off his velvet jacket, string tie and white shirt. He had a muscular build that was only just turning to fat. He draped the discarded clothes neatly on the ropes and started to put on the gloves.

'And what is your name, sir?' the MC asked.

'Dennis – just Dennis,' said the ted, in clear imitation of the wrestler he followed.

'A big hand for Dennis,' shouted the MC. 'A boy who helps to keep the town clean.'

The Everton Kid had taken off his dressing gown. His pale body looked as if it had never seen the sun and his ribs stuck out over tightly stretched flesh. He and Dennis advanced to the centre of the ring and touched gloves. The Kid was a good five inches shorter than the ted, and his arms, with the brown gloves on the ends, were like safety matches.

'Please take your corners, gentlemen,' the MC said, 'and when the bell rings, come out fighting.'

The ted swaggered back to his corner, his lip curled in imitation of Elvis Presley. He had been in enough fights to know how to handle himself, and he didn't see any problems with this little runt. It was money for jam.

The bell rang.

'Come on then, "Champ",' Dennis shouted. 'Let's be havin' yer.' The two fighters danced into the middle of the ring. There was some initial sparring, while they sized each other up, and then the bigger man began his attack, raining a series of rapid punches on the Everton Kid.

'One minute gone,' the MC called out.

The Everton Kid was landing the occasional blow but if the round had been decided on points, it would have been the big man's.

'Two minutes!'

Paul knew nothing about boxing. Even so, it seemed to him that the professional wasn't really taking much punishment. He was light on his feet and most of the punches were either glancing or else were landing where he, not his opponent, wanted them to.

'Two and a half minutes,' the MC shouted. 'Can this young man survive three minutes with the Everton Kid and win the five pounds?'

The young fighter stopped dancing around the ring and went for the ted. A number of blows landed so swiftly that his thin arms were a blur and suddenly the cocksure Dennis was gasping for breath, his nose and mouth both bloody. He staggered backwards against the ropes, shaking his head and holding up his hands to indicate that he had had enough. He turned, slowly and painfully, so that he could lean over the ropes. Both his eyes were already beginning to puff up.

'Fuckin' little bastard,' he said to no one in particular.

He spat out a tooth and a bubble of blood formed on his lips.

'In two minutes and forty-five seconds,' the MC said behind him, 'a victory for the Everton Kid!'

He stood in the middle of the ring, holding the pale young man's arm up in the air. The Kid's pinched features showed no sign of triumph, no pride in beating a much larger opponent. Even though it hadn't been fixed, as the wrestling had, the result had. been certain from the start.

'And a big hand for the gallant loser,' the MC continued, walking towards Dennis to help him to the centre of the ring. But Dennis shook his head. He wasn't going back there for anything. He climbed groggily through the ropes.

'If the Everton Kid is willing,' the MC said, looking at the boxer, 'there is just time for him to take on one more challenger.'

The Kid nodded to show that it was all right.

This was just part of the show. The hicks had seen what happened when a local hard-case came up against a professional fighter. There would be no takers.

'Come along, gentlemen. Doesn't anybody want to win five pounds?'

Nobody moved a muscle – it was as if they were at an auction and a slight nod of the head or twitch of the nose could result in their buying a place in the ring.

'Come on, gentlemen,' the MC said. 'I'll tell you what. I'll make it ten pounds instead of five. Now I can't say fairer than that, can I?'

Something had been happening to David while he watched the fight. He couldn't define it, but it was tied up with being unable to force himself to go and see the strip show. It was to do with his father too – and not living up to his expectations. He had been puzzling about it and had got nowhere, so he acted on his instinct instead.

'I'll take him on,' he said, in a loud, clear voice.

The audience gasped.

'Don't be an idiot,' Jimmy whispered urgently, 'he'll murder you!'

The MC appeared disconcerted too.

'Ah . . . a . . . er . . . true sporting gent,' he said. 'Are you sure you wish to fight the Everton Kid?'

'Yes,' said David.

Paul was tugging at David's jacket even as he climbed into the ring.

'Forget it,' he said desperately. 'Let's go and have a few pints, see the strip show – anything!'

But the strip show, in some peculiar way, was why David was standing in the ring now.

Paul and Jimmy watched with horrified fascination as the fight followed the pattern of the previous one. David seemed to be doing better than the last challenger; he wasn't any faster, but he was stronger and the punches that the kid allowed him to land seemed to be having more effect. It would make no difference in the end. They dreaded the moment when the MC would give the signal and the boxer would move in to pulverize their friend.

'Two and a half minutes. Can this young man survive three minutes with the Kid?'

The Kid began to batter his opponent. As if on a spring, David's head rocked to and fro under a succession of blows that came first from the left, then the right, then the left again. He didn't retreat – not an inch. The Kid's gloves struck and retracted, struck and retracted, like ruthless, lethal pistons. David had already taken much more than the last challenger – already his face was a bloody mess. Still he would not move.

'We've got to stop this,' Paul screamed. 'He'll kill him!'

The two boys were on the point of climbing into the ring when David collapsed.

His knees went first, then his whole body fell to the side and he was sprawled out on the canvas. The MC bent over him and lifted one arm into the air.

'A-one,' he counted, bringing the arm down, 'a-two, a-three . . .'

David groaned and began to move.

'A-four, a-five . . .'

He put his hand on the floor and began to lift himself up.

His pals breathed a sigh of relief. He was hurt, but he was tough – and he would be all right.

'A-six, a-seven . . .'

David was half-up, his left foot and right knee were on the floor.

'Don't get up,' Paul willed him. 'Don't get up. There's only a few seconds left. Stay where you are.'

'A-eight, a-nine . . .'

David's face was bloody and his left eye was beginning to puff out, but he was standing. He made his way groggily towards the centre of the ring, towards the Everton Kid.

The time must be up. The half minute must have gone.

'The bell!' Jimmy shouted. 'Ring the bell!'

The MC put his hand nervously in his pocket and felt the pound notes. The Everton Kid was about to launch another attack.

The rest of the audience joined in the shouting.

'The bell!'

'He's had more than three minutes!'

'Play fair!'

'Time, gentlemen please!'

The Everton Kid punched once, twice, three times. David staggered and swayed but did not fall. Then, finally, the bell rang.

'Gentleman, a gallant sportsman and a brave fighter,' said the MC, making the most of a bad job.

He held up the two five pound notes.

'And here is your money, young sir.'

He tucked it in the waist-band of David's trousers.

'Thank you, gentleman. There will be another show in half an . . .'

For David, it wasn't enough. His face ached, his ribs felt bruised, but the feeling that had forced him into the ring in the first place had not gone away.

'I'm not beaten,' he said. 'I want another round.'

The MC ran his tongue along the edge of his upper lip and fiddled with the lapels of his jacket.

'Look here, son,' he hissed. 'Why don't you call it a day? You'll get no more money out of me, and you can't go another three minutes without gettin' really hurt.'

'I don't want any more money,' David said. 'I just want another round. I'm not beaten yet.'

Most of the audience hadn't heard the MC's words, but David's reply came over loud and clear.

'Give the lad a chance!' somebody shouted out.

'He's a real sport. Let 'im 'ave a go.'

'What's the matter? You scared he'll beat the Kid?'

The MC looked at the faces below him. Their shouts were good natured. The men were not angry – not yet.

'OK, son,' he whispered. 'Just don't say I didn't warn you.' He turned to the audience. 'For the first time in the history of this show, not only has a contender survived a round with the Champion, but wishes to go another. Give him a big hand!'

Paul looked at Jimmy appealingly and moved to grab the rope to pull himself into the ring. Jimmy placed a restraining hand on his arm.

'We can't help him,' Jimmy said. 'Not when he doesn't want to help himself.'

'Why is he doing this?' Paul asked.

'I don't know, but I know he's got to.'

Paul shrugged helplessly. Both young men felt a hot prickling in their eyes – for the first time in years they were on the point of crying.

The bell rang and the second round began. It didn't last long. The Everton Kid came in swinging and misjudged, leaving his mid-riff exposed. David planted his big fist in the middle of it, and the Kid froze. David hit him there twice more and he began to fold. A blow to the jaw, and he was on the canvas. There was a loud, excited roar from the crowd.

The MC walked over to his fallen fighter. He looked troubled and concerned, but – above all – surprised.

'Count 'im out!' someone shouted.

'A-one, a-two,' the MC began, 'a-three, a-four . . .'

Feet were stamped, hands were clapped in time and most of the crowd joined in the ritual chant.

'A-five, a-six, a-seven, a-eight . . .'

The Everton Kid put his hands on the canvas and attempted to pull himself up. It was too great an effort and he collapsed again.

'A-nine, a-ten. Out!'

The MC lifted David's hand high above his head. The cheers and whistles were almost deafening. Paul and Jimmy were bursting with pride. Moments before, they had been expecting tragedy and now their friend had triumphed. Their last carnival, which had looked like being a failure, had been rescued by David's strength and courage. What a glorious event to remember the day by, David taking on a professional boxer and coming out on top.

They went to the beer tent to celebrate. It was not so full now, there were even a few spare tables.

'You look like you've been in the wars, love,' the barmaid said as she handed David his pint.

'This man,' Jimmy said, 'this man has just taken on a real full-time boxer and beaten him.'

'Have you, love?' the barmaid asked, impressed.

'No,' David said. 'I haven't.'

The good humour left the barmaid's face.

'I don't know which one of you is tryin' to be funny,' she said, 'but I don't see the joke.'

They went and sat at a rickety table in the corner.

'Now what the hell was all that about?' Paul demanded.

'I didn't beat him,' David said.

'What d'you mean?' Jimmy asked. 'Everybody saw you knock the vicious little bastard out.'

'He wasn't vicious, any more than the Crusher was vicious. They were both just doin' their jobs. And I didn't knock him out! You saw him in the first round. He massacred me.'

'But then you got him in the second,' said Jimmy, punching the air and adopting a sports commentator's voice in an attempt to lighten the atmosphere. 'A blow to the stomach, the Kid looks dazed. Slugger Harrison follows through, and again, and the Kid's down!'

David didn't smile.

'He could have had me down any time he wanted,' he said.

'Then why didn't he?' Paul asked sceptically.

'In the first round, he had to try and beat me to protect the owner's money. In the second round there was nothin' at stake – for him. He knew I wouldn't stop till I was down. An' he knew it would hurt me a lot.'

'So?' Paul asked.

'So he took a dive.' David's puffy eyes were moist and the glass in his hand shook, spilling beer over the table. 'I think he's the gentlest person I've ever met.'

Chapter Seven

The fairground was suddenly a depressing place again. They drank their pints quickly and headed back into town. All the pubs had afternoon extensions and the High Street was packed with young revellers, shouting and singing.

They stopped in at The Cock and met some lads from Buckworth.

'What the bloody hell's happened to your face, David?' one of them asked.

'Got into a fight,' David replied.

'You should have seen the other feller,' Paul added. Whatever David felt about it, *he* wanted people to know that his friend had defeated the boxer, but cracking an old joke was as far as he dared go.

They moved on to The Ring o' Bells and then The Wheatsheaf, passing the time with the boys they knew from school or had met at dances. When they were alone, they mostly sat in silence. What conversation they did have was concerned with old times – the fight they got into in primary school over the free milk, the Secret Camp, that summer they had all worked together in the scrap yard.

'Is that the only bond we've got left?' Paul asked himself. 'Memories? Don't we mean more to each other than that?'

They had had enough to drink. They walked along the river, past Blackthorne's Engineering, then sat on the bank and watched the green water slowly flow by. At half past six, they went and bought some fish and chips.

They probably wouldn't have made the effort to go to the dance at the Drill Hall if they hadn't already bought the tickets. As it was, they nearly didn't get in.

'Bin fightin', lad?' one of the bouncers asked David.

'It wasn't his fault,' Jimmy said quickly. 'A gang of rockers picked on him.'

The bouncer stood for a while, weighing them up.

'All right,' he said finally, 'you can go in. But think on, we don't want no trouble.'

When they were inside, they wondered why they had bothered. They looked around the rectangular room with its big picture windows and heavy grey curtains. Chairs ran the length of the wall and most of the people who were already there were sitting down. The only activity came from a few girls, handbags at their feet, doing the latest steps they had seen on *Ready, Steady, Go* under the glare of the pseudo-psychedelic lights.

They could see the younger kids through the window, standing on the ledge, noses pressed to the glass. They had done that too, in the days when this had seemed a wonderful, glamorous place – before they had seen it for what it really was, a shoddy dance hall, vaguely tarted up with a few coloured lights.

When the supporting group came on, Jimmy and Paul got up and asked a couple of girls to dance. Paul's girl was not as attractive as Jimmy's – she had a sharp nose and a bit of a squint. Still, she was better than nothing, and as they danced he tried to be witty and interesting, shouting his words into her ear over the noise of the group. She mostly replied monosyllabically, and when the number was over, she said, 'I 'ave to go back to me friend.'

The other girl was standing close to Jimmy and laughing at something he was saying. Paul watched as his own partner went over to her and dragged her away. It was probably for the best, he told himself. They didn't want to abandon David, not that night.

The musicians performed a string of songs – The Stones' *Paint It Black*, Georgie Fame's *Get Away*, The Four Tops' *Reach Out, I'll Be There*. Most of the audience paid them no attention. All they wanted was a beat to dance to, and records would have done just as well. It would be different for the main attraction, the greasy-haired, big-nosed lout who had laid his paw on the Carnival Queen that afternoon. When he appeared, the girls would all crowd around the stage, and scream.

'What time's "Mr Big-Shot" on?' Jimmy asked.

'Dunno,' Paul replied. 'Half ten? Eleven?'

'Let's get out of here before then, shall we?'

The others nodded in agreement. At that moment, they felt the singer's whole mission in life was to humiliate them, to rub it in that he could have all the women he wanted and they hadn't even got one between them.

Then Jimmy noticed the girl, standing alone, with her back to them. He pointed her out to his mates. She had blonde, shoulder-length hair which had been curled and back-combed, and was wearing a white shirt and an A-line black skirt. Her hem-line was a good three inches above her knees and her legs looked all right.

She turned round, and they realized that they knew her. Maggie Boroughs. She had been three years above them in Buckworth Primary and worked in the village sub-post office.

She looked nice from the front too, Paul thought. Her hair was cut in a fringe and almost touched her big blue eyes. Her nose was slightly hooked and she had laughter lines around the edges of her wide, generous mouth. Not a stunner, but pleasant enough. Definitely a step up from the girl he had tried to get off with earlier. And underneath her button-down collar and knotted scarf was a lovely pair of boobs, just straining to get out.

'I think I'll go and have a word with Maggie,' Jimmy said. 'She looks like she needs cheering up.'

Before David or Paul could say anything, he was gone.

' 'lo, Maggie,' Jimmy said. 'Anything wrong?'

She had been staring at her shoes. She looked up, and seeing a familiar face, smiled weakly.

'I'm a bit fed up,' she admitted. 'I've just had a row with me date and he's walked out on me.'

'He must be off his head,' Jimmy said. 'Anyone I know?'

She shook her head.

'Don't think so. It wasn't serious anyway, I only met him last week. It's just that I feel such a fool, left on me own in the middle of a dance.'

'Never mind, love,' Jimmy said. 'Let me buy you a drink.'

He could see the hesitation in her eyes. He was a good-looking lad, but he was only eighteen, and she didn't want to be accused of cradle-snatching.

'Just a quick drink,' Jimmy said, 'that's all. Me and my mates are pushing off in a few minutes anyway.'

Maggie smiled again, an amused, grateful smile this time.

'That's very thoughtful of you, Jimmy,' she said. 'Thank you very much.'

Paul and David watched Jimmy's retreating back. His arm was already draped loosely over the girl's shoulder.

'Lucky bugger!' Paul said enviously.

'Jimmy makes his own luck,' David said.

Paul supposed that was true enough. They had all seen the girl standing there, but only Jimmy had had the confidence to approach her.

'Anyway,' he said, 'that's the last we'll see of him tonight.'

He was wrong. Jimmy was back less than half an hour later.

'I've run out of money,' he said urgently. 'Slip us a couple of quid, will you?'

'Typical!' Paul said. 'You pick up some woman, bugger off with her, and then expect us to pay for your fun.'

He said it as lightly as he could. He was annoyed with Jimmy, but he knew he had no right to be.

Jimmy winked at him.

'Don't be a prat,' he said. 'I'm doing this for all of us.'

'How do you mean? For all of us?'

'Maggie was already a bit gone when I met her and I've bought her three drinks myself. By the time she's had a few more, she'll be well away. Then we'll take her for a walk and give her one!'

'You're talking stupid,' said Paul. 'She's not going to let all three of us slip her a length, is she?'

Yet he could feel the butterflies in his stomach even at the possibility.

'Course she is!' Jimmy held his hand out for the money. 'She's had more pricks in her than a second-hand dart board. She's twenty-one for God's sake! She doesn't think she's getting all these drinks for nothing. She knows what's happening as well as I do – only if you don't give me the cash soon, she'll go off the boil.'

David reached into his pocket and pulled out the money he had won at the boxing.

'Take this,' he said. 'I don't want it.'

'I don't need that much. She's only on Babychams.'

'Take it!' David said fiercely. 'I don't want to see any of it – ever again.'

Jimmy smoothed out the notes and folded them neatly in his wallet.

'Come and join us in about another half hour,' Jimmy said as he left, 'and – for Christ's sake – try to act natural.'

The group was performing their own version of *A Whiter Shade of Pale*, the vocalist straining his voice to imitate the deep throaty sound of the original.

But David and Paul were not listening to the strange, hypnotic lyrics. Instead each was wrapped up in his own private thoughts.

Paul didn't want to arrive in Oxford a virgin. He felt sure people could tell if you'd 'had it'. It shone through and made you seem more like a man worthy of serious consideration, not only in social situations but in political and intellectual ones too. The aura of experience would go a long way to compensate for his narrow frame and thin arms. There was the rub; with his thin frame and arms, however would he get a woman – a real woman – to let him do it in the first place? And it would be awful if Jimmy had slept with a girl and he hadn't.

David's mind roved freely and confusedly over the day's events. He hadn't wanted to see the strip show, and though it had something to do with the memory of his father, he sensed that in some undefined way he had let his dad down by not going in. He had let him down again in the fight, not because he didn't take the punishment well, but because there was something *in* him that had caused the Everton Kid to pull his punches at the end. Even in the business, he was turning into a disappointment in his dad's terms, using less brawn and more brain. If he could screw a girl, it might make him feel better – he would have achieved something at least that his father would have been proud of.

The bar was as cheap and nasty as the dance hall. Groups of youths in their best Saturday jackets sat hunched over tables, smoking Embassy Tipped and speculating drunkenly on their chances of scoring. Young men who had girl friends waited impatiently for them to return from the toilet, where they had gone to renew their make-up and have a natter.

Jimmy and Maggie were sitting on stools at the black plastic-covered bar. Jimmy was gesturing with his long, slim hands, and Paul knew that this meant that he was in the middle of an anecdote. As he got closer, he heard Maggie laugh loudly.

'Here's David and Paul,' Jimmy said slowly, as if he were speaking to a retarded child. 'Say hello to them, Maggie.'

' 'lo David, 'lo Paul,' she said, carefully and dutifully. 'Jimmy's been very good. He's been cheerin' me up with his funny stories. Only,' she gazed at them blearily, 'I can't remember any of them.'

There was a pause and David and Paul stood there, self-consciously, their arms drooping by their sides.

Then Jimmy said, 'It's very hot in here. Why don't we go and get some fresh air?'

'Yer what?'

'I said it's very hot in here. Why don't we go for a walk?'

'Yes. 's awful hot. *Let's* go for a walk.'

Jimmy took her arm, and Maggie got shakily off the stool.

'David an' Paul comin' too?'

'Yes, they're hot as well.'

'S'all go for a walk.'

Jimmy was still holding her right arm, and he signalled for David to take the other. Paul walked behind them.

The bouncer at the door, the one who had warned them that he wanted no trouble, watched the party leave.

'You with them?' he asked and when Paul nodded he leered and said, 'Well, have a good time. And give her one for me.'

Paul felt his face glow red.

David and Jimmy were half-carrying the girl, but she didn't seem to object. Paul caught them up.

'Where are we taking her?'

'The Park. Where else?'

They took the quickest path, past the fountain. A few teenagers were sitting round it, singing to the accompaniment of a badly tuned acoustic guitar, but they showed no interest in either the boys or the young woman with them. The gang reached the edge of the small wood and were swallowed up by it.

Paul gazed across to the fairground. It looked better, not so tatty, now that all the lights were on. The Big Wheel was turning, the Octopus flew through the sky. He could hear the strains of several songs as they mixed together in the warm evening air and could smell the aroma of hot dogs wafting across. For a moment, he almost suggested that they forget all this, and just take Maggie for a ride. Then he grinned, ironically. Having a ride with Maggie was exactly why they'd come here. He kicked something with his foot, and looking down could just make out that it was the bottle Jimmy had thrown over his shoulder that afternoon.

'This'll do,' Jimmy said.

'What'll do?' Maggie asked.

David moved away on cue, and Jimmy took Maggie in his arms and kissed her. It was a long, passionate kiss, and though she struggled at first, she soon began to respond. After what seemed to Paul like hours, Jimmy broke off the embrace, though he still held on to the girl.

'Wasn't that nice?' he asked.

'You are naughty, Jimmy Bradley. You promised there'd be no funny business. Whatever will people say? You're only a kid, and I'm twenty-one.' She started to sing. 'I've got the key to the door.' She fumbled with the catch of her handbag. 'I have! It's in here somewhere.'

'And now you've given me a kiss, you should give Paul one as well,' Jimmy said, coaxingly. 'He's been buying you drinks too, so it's only fair.'

'Has he?'

Jimmy led Maggie across to where Paul was standing, and draped her arms over his neck. Paul clasped his own arms around her waist to steady her. He could feel her legs against his, her breasts pressing on his rib-cage.

'Yes,' Jimmy said. 'Paul's spent a lot of money on you tonight, so it's only fair you give him a kiss.'

Maggie just stood there for a while, then she seemed to come to a decision.

' 's only fair,' she said.

She missed Paul's mouth at first, planting a wet, clumsy, baby-kiss on his cheek. At the second attempt, their lips came together and Paul could feel her hot breath – and her tongue, probing his mouth. He had never been so excited in his life, but at the same time he felt that what they were doing was terribly, terribly wrong.

Jimmy let the kiss continue for a while longer then gently pulled Maggie away.

'David's been buying you drinks too,' he said. 'Give him a kiss. It's only fair.'

'Don' wan' to kiss anybody else. Don' wan' to. Kissed enough people.'

'That's all right then,' Jimmy said soothingly. 'You don't have to kiss anyone you don't want to. Why don't you just lie down instead?'

He pressed lightly on Maggie's shoulders and she sank to her knees. He lowered her further and she was lying on her side on the grass, legs bent. Kneeling beside her, he turned her onto her back, and straightened her legs. He stepped back to examine his handiwork.

'Like an undertaker laying out a corpse,' Paul thought.

'We've got to stop,' he hissed at Jimmy. 'We've gone far enough.'

He could just see, in the moonlight, that his friend was smiling.

'We haven't even started yet,' Jimmy whispered.

'It's not right. She's drunk.'

'Drunk or sober, do you think it would make any difference to her sort? Anyway, I'm going to do it, and from the look of it I'd say David is too. So if you don't want to – you can just fuck off.'

And if he did? David and Jimmy would have shared something and he would be an outsider. He looked across at the fairground again, as if it would give him inspiration, but all that would come into his mind were the lyrics of *Puppet on a String*.

'I haven't got any French letters,' he said. He had. They were sitting snugly in his wallet in their shiny tin-foil, as virginal as he was. 'Have you got any?'

'We don't need them,' Jimmy said. 'Do you know the odds

83

against her getting pregnant? Some married couples have to try for years.'

'But what if she's got VD?'

Jimmy sighed in exasperation.

'The trouble with you, Paul, is that you're never prepared to take chances. She might have the clap for all I know, but right now I'm more worried about missing a good shag than I am about catching it. So are you with us or not?'

'I'm with you,' Paul said miserably.

He could not even produce the rubbers from his wallet now – that would be as good as admitting that he had tried to chicken out.

Maggie had not moved. Jimmy bent down and began massaging her breasts. She groaned.

'Here, what's goin' on? What do you think you're . . .' then she relapsed into silence again.

Jimmy put his hand up her skirt.

'She's wearing tights,' he said angrily. 'It should have been stockings – like the other girl, that time in the woods.'

Paul did not understand what he meant. There had been no time in the woods.

'Help me get them off,' Jimmy ordered David.

David knelt and together they lifted Maggie's bottom off the ground and eased down her undergarments until they were around her ankles.

Her skirt had ridden up around her waist and the moonlight fell on the pale patch of pubic hair between her legs, making it look golden.

'Well, at least she's a natural blonde,' Jimmy said.

Paul had often imagined the moment he would first make love to a woman – she would be beautiful and willing and they would do it in a huge bed with clean, crisp sheets. He had never dreamed it would be like this – a drunken slag in a public park.

'Well, who's going first?' Jimmy asked.

Paul looked at David, who gestured towards Jimmy.

'I don't mind,' Jimmy said. 'I might as well have her while she's fresh.'

He unbuckled his belt, dropped his trousers and underpants to his knees, and lowered himself onto the supine girl. When he thrust, he seemed to be having difficulty penetrating and Maggie groaned as if she found the whole thing slightly uncomfortable.

'No juices,' Paul thought. 'She's not worked up at all. She'll be as dry as a bone.'

Jimmy let out a small gasp and Paul knew that he had entered her. He watched as Jimmy's pale backside moved up and down, up and down. Despite all the circumstances, he felt his own excitement mounting.

Jimmy sighed again and stopped moving. He lay there for a short time, rubbing his body against Maggie's like a contented cat, and then got to his feet.

'Your turn, David,' he said.

There was no need for that, Paul thought. He had had his share and he should have let them decide who went next. Was Jimmy punishing him for being unwilling, for trying to talk him out of it?

David was on top of the girl now. He wasn't much taller than Jimmy, but he was broader and he seemed to swamp Maggie. Her torso was entirely covered by his, her head must have been buried somewhere in the middle of his chest. If it had not been for her slim legs, spread either side of David's thick, trunk-like ones, it would have been possible to imagine that there was no girl there at all. David grunted and strained and displayed none of the elegance that Jimmy had shown. He was finished quicker too.

Finally, it was Paul's turn. He didn't want to do it. Even if Maggie was as randy as a bitch on heat, this was not right. It was degrading for her. And it was degrading for him as well. But there was no backing out now.

He did not dwarf her as his friends had done. He was scarcely taller than her. His cheek pressed against hers and he could feel her soft, irregular breathing on his face. He had no difficulty entering her, David and Jimmy had seen to that. Her vaginal wall enclosed his penis – and he felt nothing. It was like wanking off into a milk bottle. He raised himself onto his elbows and began the rhythmic movement that he had fantasized about so often. And still he felt no glow of achievement, no great gush of joy. He only hoped that his mates thought he was doing all right.

He looked across at the fairground again, and wished that he was there instead of here. The candy-floss was closing, the fair was the preserve of the big kids now, and he could just make out a group of them crowded around the shooting gallery, probably showing off.

He wished that he could hear one clear tune instead of a jumble. It might help him to get his rhythm right. He started to mentally hum the one that had been haunting him all day.

'I . . . won . . . da . . . if one day that . . . you'll say that . . . you care,
If you say you love me mad . . . ly, I'll glad . . . ly . . . be there,
Like a pupp . . . et on a string, like a pupp . . . et on a string.'

It seemed to work. Occasionally, he was aware of minor irritations – a wisp of the girl's hair getting up his nose, the stickiness at the tops of her legs, where the cum of the others had been spilled – but most of the time he shafted and shafted as his primitive urges dictated, until there was a muscular spasm, a rapid ejaculation, and it was all over.

Paul pulled himself to his feet, twisting away from Maggie as he did so. His trousers were still round his ankles, and the action almost caused him to lose his balance. He clawed at his clothes and dragged them up to waist level. With shaking hands, he tucked in his shirt, fastened his zip and buckled his belt.

He had an absurd hope that once he was dressed again, it would be as if it had never happened. But it had. His penis, the thing he had once called his little willie – and which was now capable of doing such terrible degrading things – was still so sensitive that it sent little charges of electricity through his body as it brushed against his Bri-nylon underpants. And the girl was still lying there, where he had violated her.

Jimmy clapped him heartily on the shoulder.

'Well, you took your time,' he said. 'You were longer than either of us. You virile little bastard, you.'

So Jimmy had forgiven him and was assuming that his lack of passion was nothing more than strong, masculine, sexual self-control. Despite his self-disgust – the shame was still there – there was another small part of him that was rejoicing. There had been a moment earlier when Paul had felt in danger of losing David and Jimmy. After what they had done together, he could wake up in the morning in the happy certainty that they were still the same old gang, their bond closer than ever. Whatever else happened, friendship mattered above all.

But there was still tonight to deal with first – still the girl.

'What are we going to do about Maggie?' he asked, panicking. 'We can't just leave her here.'

'Of course we can't. We'll do the gentlemanly thing and see her home,' Jimmy said. He leant over the girl. 'Come on Maggie, love. Time to go home.'

Maggie didn't move.

'I think she's passed out,' Jimmy said.

When had she passed out, Paul wondered. When Jimmy laid her on the ground? After he had screwed her? After David? How much had she known of what was going on?

'We'll have to walk her around a bit,' David said, 'until she's sobered up.'

David and Jimmy plucked at the tights and panties, pulling them up Maggie's legs, over her pubic mound and around her hips. It was more difficult to get them on again than it had been to get them off, and when they had finished it still didn't look right.

'She can fix them herself when she comes to,' Jimmy said.

They kept to the small paths, away from the public gaze. At first, Jimmy and David supported the girl entirely, but after a while her legs began to work and she took slow, painful steps.

'She must be sore, after three of us,' Paul thought.

'What you need, Maggie, is a strong black coffee,' Jimmy said. 'That'll make you feel better.'

Maggie said nothing so Jimmy took that as assent.

Mario's cafeteria had plate-glass windows running around the front and side. Even from a distance, the boys could see that it was crowded, but it was the only place open at that time of night. They negotiated between the tightly packed tables to the remaining empty one which was close to the bamboo pole divider at the other end of the room from the juke box.

Paul went to order the coffees and Jimmy pulled out a chair for Maggie. When Paul returned, the only seat available was opposite the girl. He placed the drinks on the table and sat down. He had spilled some coffee in the saucers, but nobody commented on it. Nobody said anything.

Paul looked up at the notice on the wall. '*To all teenagers,*' he read. '*You are kindly requested not to comb your hair in the cafeteria, put your feet on the chairs or sit there all night with only one drink.*' The last nine words were underlined. At the bottom, it said, '*By order. The management.*'

He read the notice five or six times. Finally, reluctantly, he turned to look at Maggie. She had drunk some of her coffee and was sitting with her elbows on the table and her head in her hands. The hair, which had seemed so clean and shiny earlier in the evening, now looked greasy and bedraggled. Her mascara had run and her lipstick was smudged. Pieces of dry grass clung to her blouse, and Paul had to check an instinct to reach across and pluck them off.

The minutes ticked by and still no-one spoke. Paul tried to concentrate on the music blaring out of the juke box, and when that failed, on the noisy conversations that were going on around him. But his gaze was, inevitably, dragged back to the girl.

Her eyes had registered little at first except a kind of numbed shock, but slowly they came back to life and Paul read in them a misery and shame that matched his own.

'Do you want another coffee, Maggie?' Jimmy asked, though she had hardly touched her first.

Maggie ignored him and looked directly at Paul.

'I want to go home,' she said.

They phoned for a taxi to take them the three miles back to Buckworth. When it arrived, it turned out to be a Mini.

'Didn't know there'd be four of you,' the driver said. 'How we doin' it? One of you lads next to me, the others in the back with the lady?'

'She can sit in the front,' Jimmy said quickly.

The cabbie was dubious.

'Be a bit of a squeeze.'

'We'll manage.'

None of them wanted to sit next to Maggie.

There was not a light on in the village, and the squat terraced houses brooded in gloomy silence. As they passed The George, Maggie turned round.

'Tell him to drop me here,' she said urgently. 'I don't want him to take me all the way home.'

'I'm not totally deaf to women's voices,' the cabbie said crossly. 'I can hear you when you talk direct, like.'

He pulled in at the side of the curb and Maggie had her hand on the door even before he had stopped.

'Easy, love. Don't be in such a hurry!'

She was already out of the taxi. Paul flung his own door open.

'I'll see her home. It's dark.'

He had to run to catch up, and when he reached her she gave no sign that she knew he was there. It had started to rain and as they walked down the street – two people side by side but not together – their feet made slop, slop sounds on the pavement.

At her door, Maggie opened her handbag and rummaged for her key.

'Can I . . . ?' Paul asked, reaching out o help her.

Maggie swung the bag away from him. 'I can manage,' she said and he could tell she was crying. She found the key and tried to fit it in the lock, but her hands were trembling too much. Paul gently took it from her and inserted it himself.

'Are you sure you're all right, Maggie?' he asked.

He was about to ask if there was anything else he could do – but he had done enough already.

Maggie turned to him, her face contorted with pain and tears.

88

'I wish I was dead,' she said.

She opened the door and rushed into the house.

Paul let himself in through the back door. His mother and sister would have been in bed long ago, but they had stoked up the fire – which burned summer and winter alike – and he was greeted by rosy, glowing coals. He was glad of it, for he was cold now. He sat down, legs spread and felt the warmth spread along them and through to his body. He looked into the embers and made the burning lumps of carbon resemble animals and objects, as he had done as a child. One was a camel, another looked like a house.

He picked up the poker and stuck it into the fire, and all the shapes were gone. He sighed heavily and got to his feet. He was desperately tired, but there was something he must do before he went to bed.

The moon had retreated behind heavy clouds, but he knew his way well enough. As he walked towards the wash-house, drops of rain trickled down his neck. God alone knew where his father was. It had turned into a filthy night, but once Jack Wright got the smell of sex in his nostrils, it would take more than weather to keep him in.

'And am I any better?' Paul asked himself.

He groped for the wash-house tap and held the kettle under it, judging how much had gone in by the sound the water made. When it was nearly full, he returned to the house.

While the water heated up, he brought the other things he needed. He placed an enamel bowl on the floor in front of the fire, and then poured half a bottle of disinfectant into it. When the kettle boiled, he added the steaming water, which mixed with the Dettol to form a pale yellow liquid. It was hot, and it would sting, but he wanted to both cleanse and punish himself.

He stripped off his trousers and underpants and knelt down by the bowl. It was only then that he saw that the sticky substance which had been at the top of Maggie's legs, which had clung to him and irritated him ever since, was not cum at all. Sperm was colourless – this was crimson. It took him a second to understand, and then he leant over the bowl and vomited until his stomach was empty.

Chapter Eight

Paul ambled along the canal bank, stopping now and again to pick up a flat stone and skim it across the water. The early July air was fresh and mild. He could smell the honeysuckle and wild roses, and in the distance the birds were singing their final chorus of the day. In just a few weeks, it wouldn't be a canal he would be strolling next to, it would be the River Isis. He might even be punting along it, while some girl, a bright, committed under-graduate like himself, smiled up at him in between mouthfuls of strawberries and cream.

He would be sorry to leave the village in some ways. It had been the scene of his childhood adventures, the backcloth against which he had struggled, against all odds, to win his place at Oxford. Most of all, he would miss his two best mates. Still, they could come down and visit him, be his guest at the Union when he stood up to speak on some burning political issue and managed to combine ready wit with a serious point.

His one regret was that he had not been able to do anything to make it up to Maggie Boroughs. But what could he have done? What could he even *say* to her? For the first few days after the fair, he had been weighed down with guilt. He had looked away when he saw her in the street. He still could not bring himself to go into the post office. But gradually his conscience had eased, and it now only pricked him intermittently. Anyway, he told himself, she hadn't come to any physical harm – she was going about the village as if nothing had happened. The memory would fade for her, just as it was doing for him.

He reached The Pack Horse, a pub which had once served thirsty bargemen and now, with its leaded windows and dark oak beams, was a favourite haunt of townees out for a drive. He glanced at the watch his mother had given him when his results came through. He was late. It didn't matter. It was to be a long, lazy summer, a respite before the real work began. Time had no meaning.

Jimmy and David were sitting in the corner, fresh pints in front of them. One look at their faces was enough to tell Paul there was trouble. David was looking grave and pensive. Jimmy, on the other hand, was smiling, and apart from his left fist, which was clenched tightly, he looked perfectly relaxed. And that bothered Paul more than David's sombre expression, *because* he knew that smile well. From their early childhood when he suggested crawling along the pipe over the canal, right up to the night in the park when he said he was prepared to risk VD, that smile had appeared on Jimmy's face whenever there was danger. It was a gambler's smile – a smile Paul hated and his legs wobbled as he walked across the room to join his friends.

Jimmy would have spun the tale out, making the most of its dramatic possibilities, but it was David's story, and he simply said, 'Maggie Boroughs came to see me at the scrap-yard this afternoon.'

Immediately, Paul knew what it was all about.

'What are we going to do?' he asked.

'She wants the kid,' David said. 'But she doesn't want it to be illegitimate.'

'How can we be sure one of us is the father?' Paul almost asked.

But he already knew the answer. From the moment he had seen the sticky blood clinging to his legs, right through the puking and the frantic scrubbing, only one thought had been pounding through his head. Maggie had not had as many pricks in her as a second-hand dart board, she was not the village bike that everyone had had a ride on. Until the second Jimmy thrust himself into her, she had been a virgin.

'Which one of us does she want to marry?' he asked

Jimmy was handsome, David was big and strong. He was nothing – she couldn't want him.

'She doesn't *want* to marry any of us,' David said. 'Would you *want* to marry somebody who'd treated you like that? But she's no choice, she *has* to get married. And it doesn't really matter which one of us it is.'

'We got her into this mess,' Jimmy said, speaking for the first time, 'and we'll have to get her out. But it's not something we can all do together. The other two will help support Maggie and the child – but only one of us can marry her.'

'How will we decide?' Paul asked.

Jimmy smiled again.

'Any volunteers?'

Neither of the others spoke. Paul found his eyes were being

drawn hypnotically to Jimmy's clenched fist, which had not moved all the time they had been talking. He did not know what it contained, but he sensed it held Jimmy's answer.

'Right then,' Jimmy said, 'there's only one thing for it.' He opened his hand. It contained three halfpennies. 'Odd man out.'

'But that's a beer game,' Paul protested. 'We're not deciding who buys a round of drinks. We're settling who gets a life sentence.'

'Can you think of a better way?' Jimmy asked.

Yes he could. It was Jimmy who had planned the whole thing, Jimmy who had robbed Maggie of her virginity. Let him marry her. Or David. David was rich enough to support her. David had no plans to leave the village. He wasn't going to Oxford, he didn't want to be Prime Minister.

He felt ashamed of himself. They had done it together, as they had always done everything. They were equal partners and they all had to take the same chance. He held out his palm and Jimmy dropped a ha'penny into it.

Paul closed his hands around the coin. It felt huge. He was amazed that he could hold anything so massive. It was hot, too, burning into his skin, branding him on one palm with *The Golden Hind* and on the other with the Queen's head. And it was so heavy that it was making his arms ache.

Jimmy gave David the second coin and kept the last for himself. 'Best out of three?' he asked. 'Or the first one to lose?'

It would be awful to decide the future on one turn of the coin. But if they played 'best out of three' it could run to eight games. Jimmy would enjoy that, the tension, the drama of it all, but Paul knew he couldn't stand it.

'First one to lose,' he said.

They shook their cupped hands vigorously and on the third beat they pulled their right ones away at the same time as they slammed down their lefts, trapping the coins on the table. Several of the older customers turned round to see what the noise was, and smiled indulgently when they saw what game was in progress.

There was a time-honoured way to play the game and they did not deviate from it now, when the stakes were so high and ritual seemed to invest the occasion with the appropriate solemnity. Jimmy raised his hand first and revealed a head. David followed – another profile of Elizabeth II stared at Paul. His would be a tail. He would have to marry Maggie. Why, oh why, hadn't he chosen to play 'Best out of three'? He felt that if he could keep his hand there for ever, on the table, then nothing more need happen – they could forget all about the problem of the girl. But the others were looking at him – waiting. He lifted his hand slowly – and revealed a head.

What an incredible fluke! Well, that was it. Clearly the gods of chance didn't want any of them to marry Maggie – they might as well just finish their pints and go home.

'Again!' Jimmy said.

They picked up their coins and shook. Thud! went their hands on the table. It was David's turn to start – tails. Paul had tails too. The chances against Jimmy having tails were astronomical, especially after the last game. So Jimmy would have to marry Maggie. He would cope, he always coped. Paul felt his chest-muscles relax, and realised that for several minutes he had hardly been breathing.

He fixed his gaze on Jimmy's hand. In a moment he would remove it, show them the head, and it would be all over. The hand seemed to float into the air in one smooth movement. There was no hurry about it and the long slim fingers did not tremble. Paul wanted to fling his head onto the table, so that he could see the coin before Jimmy's hand was clear, so that he wouldn't have to wait the extra, precious, microsecond before he was sure.

While Jimmy used the hand to brush back his sleek blond hair, Paul looked down at the coin. A tail. The constriction was back in his chest.

'If that happens again, I'll be sick,' he thought. 'I know I will.'

They cupped their hands once more.

'Bloody hell, lads,' a voice called from across the room, 'by the time you've decided who's gettin' the ale, it'll be gone closin'.'

It was Paul's turn to start on the third round. A head. Maybe that was a good omen, heads always seemed to come up more than tails. Jimmy went next. It was a tail. So it would be decided this time. There was no way it couldn't be. Either David would have a head and Jimmy would take Maggie on, or it would be tails and . . .

David did not prolong the agony. He lifted his hand quickly, glanced at the coin, then got to his feet and marched over to the bar.

'Three double whiskies, Terry.'

'Bells' do you, David?'

'Anythin' – as long as it's quick.'

Paul's body hadn't exactly frozen, he could still twist his neck from side to side and see Jimmy watching him, but he couldn't bend it, even a little bit, so that he could examine the ha'penny.

Jimmy hadn't looked yet either, yet his face was totally calm –
except for the eyes, which blazed with excitement.

'Well, old mate, it's you or me,' he said.

He took a long relaxed swig of his pint. Grinning at Paul, he
turned and looked at the coin.

'You'd better see for yourself,' Jimmy said.

Neither his expression nor his voice told Paul anything.

Paul willed his body to obey him and could feel his muscles
resist, creakingly protest, and then give way. On David's coin was
The Golden Hind, out on an open sea, and away with it sailed all
Paul's hopes and aspirations.

It was almost dark when Paul got back to Buckworth. He was half-
way down the alley that separated the Boroughs' house from their
neighbours' when he saw the pale light being cast over the fence.
The kitchen light. Someone was in. Oh God, why did someone
have to be in? He retreated back up the passageway, onto the main
street and began pacing the stretch between the post office and
The George.

What would he say if one of Maggie's parents answered the
door?

'Good evening, Mr Boroughs. I've come to propose to your
daughter, who's three years older than me and not the right kind of
girl at all. I've got to. She's pregnant, you see, and I'm one of three
possible fathers who lost the game of Odd Man Out.'

Wouldn't it be better to leave it until tomorrow, catch Maggie as
she was leaving the post office? No, the street was not the proper
place, and Maggie had a right to know what had been decided as
soon as possible. Besides, if he left it any longer, he was sure his
nerve would crack. He re-traced his steps down the alley, opened
the creaky yard gate and knocked hesitantly on the kitchen door.

It was Maggie who answered it. She was wearing a nylon floral
housecoat and old carpet slippers with the backs trodden down.
Her hair, which had looked so smooth and silky in the Drill Hall,
was a greasy mess. Her face was puffy and her eyes were red, as
though she had been crying. He wondered if he should have
brought some flowers or something. But it was a bit late for
courtship now.

'Mum and Dad are at the pub,' she said, dully. 'You'd better
come in, I suppose.'

She led him into the kitchen. The drying rack had been lowered
from the ceiling. It and the ironing board took up most of the
available space.

94

'Even in the midst of tragedy – or farce – normal life has to go on,' Paul thought.

Somehow it made him feel a little better.

'We'd better use the front room,' Maggie said, and led the way.

It was exactly the same size and shape as the one in his parents' house, and like theirs it would only be used on special occasions. Important occasions – Paul corrected himself – like funerals and shot-gun weddings. The ornaments on the mantelshelf were recently dusted, the lino was spotlessly clean, but it was a cold, impersonal place, and it smelt musty.

Maggie pointed to the dark brown imitation-leather sofa. He sat down obediently, perched awkwardly on the edge, his hands clasped nervously over his knees. Maggie switched on the electric fire. The artificial coals glowed and a red light flickered with mock flames. It made the room feel a little more cheerful – but not much.

Paul wondered if he should kneel down and formally propose. He wished he had thought it all out before he arrived, but it had taken all his effort – all his willpower – to get him there at all.

'So it's to be you, is it?' Maggie asked bluntly.

Paul looked up at the three plaster ducks on the wall, all of different sizes, but all flying – flying – and nodded miserably.

'How did they decide on you?' Maggie asked bitterly. 'Did they bully you into it?'

So that was how low her opinion was of him. She actually thought that he could be pushed into a lifetime with a woman he didn't love by his bigger tougher friends. And she thought that *his* friends would try to do that.

'No,' he said angrily. 'David and Jimmy aren't like that. It was all decided fairly.'

He couldn't tell her about the ha'pennies. She had been cheapened enough already, without making it worse. But it was all going wrong! If they started off like this, how would they be in five years – ten years? Dislike – and lack of respect – would sour and soon turn to hatred.

'Look, Maggie,' he said. 'I don't want to marry you, and I'm sure you don't want to marry me. I know what you think of me – and Paul and David. I don't blame you, either. But we aren't marrying for ourselves, we're marrying because you're pregnant, so shouldn't we try and make the best of it – at least for the child's sake? It didn't ask to be born, but it's entitled to a decent life. And if we can't give it one, who can?'

Maggie picked a shepherdess off the mantelpiece. She held it for a while, running her finger up and down the edges, then put it back. When she looked at him again, she was smiling, and he could see some of the prettiness that had been so evident in the Drill Hall.

'You're right, Paul,' she said. 'We have to think of the baby.' She sighed, her lips forming a wistful curve. 'And maybe, if we can squeeze it in, we could think a little of us, too.'

She knelt by his side, put her arms around his neck, and kissed him on the lips. It was not a hot kiss like the one in the park, it was slower, gentler, more affectionate, yet strangely asexual.

She drew away again.

'Thank you, Paul,' she said. 'I'm not sure the others would have done it.'

They agreed they'd each tell their own parents at exactly the same time the following day. Paul's father, predictably, was out, so he had to make do with just his mother who, also predictably, went into hysterics.

'The shame, the disgrace,' she screamed, clenching her fists and pressing them to her cheeks, so that her bony elbows pointed outwards. 'Think of your poor little sister. How can she ever hold her head up in the street again, after what you've done?'

Paul said nothing. He'd had eighteen years of his mother's tantrums, and whether they were about something of importance or merely the result of a minor irritation, the intensity never varied. It was best just to stand passively and let her emotions run their course.

'You want a damn good hidin'.'

Mrs Wright reached behind the clock and pulled out a number of papers. She rifled through them, discarding electricity bills and rate demands on the kitchen table, until she came to the telegram from Oxford. She picked it up, and waved it in Paul's face.

'And this is out, you know! You can't go to college. Not now!'

He didn't need her to tell him that. He could not afford to keep a wife and child on a grant and whatever Jimmy and David could spare him – not and pay accommodation as well.

Mrs Wright rushed out of the room, but she was not away long. When she returned she was carrying a bowl of water and some Brussels sprouts. She sat down by the fire, balancing the bowl on her knees.

'You've had your chances,' she ranted. 'You've had every chance in the world.'

As if Oxford had just fallen into his lap without night after night of eye-straining, back-breaking toil. Would he never get credit for what he had achieved? Would everybody outside the gang always assume that if he could do something it must be easy?

'Oh yes,' his mother continued. 'You've had your chances and you've thrown 'em all away. And why? Because you're just like your father.'

She sliced viciously through the base of a sprout and yanked at the leaves, stripping them all off until nothing was left but the pale yellow stalk.

'You're pigs, the pair of you. You just can't keep away from women. Well, you've made your bed and now you must lie on it. You're *just* like him!'

He was *nothing* like his calm, stocky, handsome father, Paul thought. He was angular and nervous, like his mother. His dad was the kind of man who would always get away with having his women, and he was the sort who was destined to get caught first time.

He looked up and saw his father standing in the doorway. He wondered whether he had heard, and if he cared if he had.

Mrs Wright noticed her husband too.

'You know what your son's gone and done?' she demanded, tailing another sprout and clawing at the leaves. 'He's only gone and got Maggie Boroughs pregnant, that's all. Not that I blame the lad entirely. She must have led him on. It stands to reason. She's older than him. And she's always bin a bit of a slut.'

This was one barb of his mother's that Paul could not take. He broke a life-time habit and fought back.

'You're talking about my future wife,' he said coldly, 'and you'll speak of her with respect.'

His mother looked up from her task, surprised and confused. The peeling knife fell from her hand and the water slopped around in the bowl.

'*You're* his father,' she said, all the force gone from her voice. 'You speak to him.'

'So, you've put Maggie Boroughs in the club,' Wright said.

'Yes,' Paul replied – defiant, ready to go for his father just as he had gone for his mother.

'Well, then, we'd better go and have a pint.'

It was the first time his father had ever invited him out for a drink, and as Wright was ordering at the bar, Paul sat in the empty best room and thought about how envious he had been that night three years earlier, when David's dad had done the same with him.

Wright returned, placed the pints on the table, and sat down.

'Now the first thing to get straight,' he said, 'is – are you the father? There's many a young lad bin caught out before now. You don't want to spend the rest of your life payin' for some other bugger's kid.'

'I'm the father,' Paul said. 'She was a virgin.'

It wasn't fair to Maggie to say what had really happened. And he could not bring himself to admit that while all three of them had done it, he was the one who had to pay the price.

'A virgin, by God!' Wright said. 'Well, lad, you've got more about yer than I thought you had.'

He had already downed most of his pint, though Paul had scarcely touched the one in front of him.

'She's a good lookin' lass, Maggie Boroughs. You could have done a lot worse for yerself. Course, you've bin unlucky, havin' to get married before you've really had a chance to play the field. But never mind. Bein' wed doesn't have to tie you down.' He winked. 'It's never stopped me havin' a bit of fun on the side.'

He swallowed the dregs of his beer.

'Sup up, lad, and I'll get us another pint.'

'I'm not quite ready yet,' Paul admitted.

He couldn't drink at his father's pace. He couldn't do anything at his father's pace.

'Work on it while I'm gettin' the next round in,' Wright said, standing up and slapping him on the shoulder.

At the door, he stopped and stood looking at Paul. There was an expression on his face that the boy had never seen before.

'I'm proud of you, son,' Wright said, then he turned quickly and disappeared into the bar.

His father was proud of him! His commitment to socialism and justice had left Wright unimpressed. Winning a place at Oxford had meant nothing. But now, his father was proud of him! He was beginning to think that life was nothing more than a cruel joke, and that he was the butt.

It was to be a Register Office wedding, on a special licence. Maggie was still showing no signs that she was carrying, but the sooner it was done, her mother said sniffing, the more difficult it would be for folks to count up once the baby was born.

There were guest lists to be drawn up, invitations to be sent, bookings to be made. Paul was rushed off his feet and was glad of it. All the petty details helped to keep his mind off the enormity of the step he was taking.

A few days before the wedding, David and Jimmy came to see him.

'He's in the back bedroom,' his mother said, 're-decoratin' it ready for that Maggie.'

The bedroom smelt of paint and flour-paste. Two of the walls were bare, except for a few slivers of paper that had stubbornly resisted the scraper. The other two had already been covered with a cheap yet cheerful floral design that Maggie had selected on her day off. The double bed, bought on the never-never, was due to arrive any day, and once Paul had finished papering the walls he intended to sand down the heavy, mahogany-veneered dressing table and paint it a pale blue.

'It'll look nice when it's finished,' David said, gazing out of he window on to the back yard.

But it wouldn't be like rooms in Balliol with a view over the quad.

'We were wondering,' Jimmy said, 'where you're planning to go for your honeymoon.'

Paul gestured around the room.

'Here,' he said. 'Buckworth-off-sea. We can't afford anything else.'

Jimmy put his hand in his pocket, extracted a buff-coloured envelope and placed it on a dry bit of the pasting table.

'It's not much,' he said, 'but it's all we could scrape together. It'll just about run you to a week in Blackpool.'

By the window, David shifted uncomfortably.

'David *could* have put a bit more in a pot,' Jimmy added, 'but I wouldn't let him. I wanted to pay half.'

That was just how it should be, Paul thought. If it had been a head instead of a tail, Jimmy instead of him, he would have wanted to pay his share too.

Yet there was a nagging question gnawing away at him. Would it ever have been Jimmy? Or David? He remembered Maggie's words that night, a million years ago, in her parents' front room.

'Thank you, Paul. I'm not sure the others would have done it.'

Would they? If either of them had been the odd man out, would they have laughed it off and said now that the joke was over, what were they *really* going to do about Maggie Boroughs?

He had to believe that they had been sincere, not only since that made *him* seem less of a fool, but also because, otherwise, they were not the friends he thought they were. And this friendship, this bond, was the most important thing in his life – especially now.

Chapter Nine

It was the sound of water, gushing and gurgling down the drain pipe into the yard below, that woke Paul up. He looked at the cheap alarm clock and saw that it was only a quarter past six. His mouth felt furry and his head was beating out a tattoo in competition with the rhythm of the rain on the slate roof.

He had spent his stag night – his 'night out with the lads' – in the back room of The George with David and Jimmy. It had not been a joyous occasion, rather it reminded him of the condemned man and his warders on the night before the hanging. He had got drunk and felt better for it, but now he wished he hadn't. He pulled the chamber pot from under the bed and urinated some of the poison out of his system. A little improvement. He reached for the packet of Embassy on the dressing table and lit one. It tasted foul but the infusion of nicotine was welcome. As he took a second drag, he examined himself in the mirror. The way he held the cigarette, the expression on his face as he inhaled, all looked wrong. He was not really an adult smoking, he was a child with a chocolate cigarette. And his wedding was not real either; it was only an extension of the game of doctors and nurses, mothers and fathers.

He opened the wardrobe and examined his new suit. Blue, formal, Burton's best, bought on the never-never. The never-never! That was a laugh. The trouble with life was that it was always-always.

He put on the suit and went back to the mirror, looking for signs of strength and maturity now he was at least dressed as an adult. He despaired at the image reflected back – a callow youth with a pale sensitive face and a jaw that looked as if it would wobble with self-pity at any moment.

He leant forward and examined the moustache he had been cultivating for over three weeks.

'Bum fluff!' he said in disgust.

It would have to come off, it only made him look ridiculous. How could anyone believe that the owner of such a wispy, pale effort had fathered a child?

He picked up his wallet. It was thick with the pound notes David and Jimmy had given him. It was not a fortune, but it would be a start. He balanced it in his hand for a moment, then pocketed it.

He did not switch on the landing light for fear of disturbing his parents. As he groped his way quietly down the narrow staircase, he could hear his father's lusty snores, like the snorting of a bull.

The kitchen seemed a lonely place. Paul sat in front of the smouldering fire, backed up with slack the night before. He poked it, and a few sparks flew up, but there were no large glowing cinders for his imagination to transform into magical figures, only tiny islands of redness surrounded by a sea of black. He took his white shortie mac off the peg, slipped it on, and stepped out into the yard.

The street was as quiet as the house. Only the rain falling on the pavement told him that there were any sounds in the world apart from his own breathing, his footsteps, the rustle of his clothing.

He walked past The George and Dragon, past Maggie's house and the post office where she worked. Already his hair was soaking wet. Tiny droplets of water clung to the ends of it tenaciously, then lost their grip and plopped down his back. He lit another cigarette, but the merciless rain dive-bombed it, turning the white paper into a dirty grey. He threw it into the gutter and watched as it revolved, got picked up by the current and was pulled irresistibly towards the grid.

He had reached the edge of the village, where the buses for Norton stopped. There would not be one for another hour, but that didn't matter. He could walk to town; he had done it often enough in the past. And from there, a train to Manchester, connecting with one bound for London. He would live off the social security and odd jobs while he wrote his masterpiece. It would be hard; he would be hungry and cold, but at least there'd be some hope, not like the death-within-life which was all he had to look forward to in Buckworth.

Maybe he could even prostitute his art a little, and write for television.

'That's Paul Wright,' he imagined people saying in fashionable Soho restaurants. 'Have you seen his stuff on the box? Really powerful. Could have gone to Oxford, you know.'

'And who's the gorgous girl with him?'

'Star of that new West End show.'

'Is she his regular girl?'

'Doesn't have a regular, not him. Likes to play the field.'

He could do it. He knew he could. He could leave all this behind, the grime, the struggle on the very edge of poverty, the narrow-mindedness – and Maggie. He could leave her to face one final humiliation.

A shift worker, riding a bike, his head low against the buffeting wind, drew level.

'Now then, young Paul,' he shouted good-naturedly. 'Not doin' a bunk, are we?'

'No,' Paul called to his retreating back, 'just givin' me new suit an airin'.'

Mrs Wright was in the kitchen when he got back, ironing her daughter's dress.

'Where've you bin?' she demanded. 'Just look at the state of you! Them trousers are wet through. They're ruined, absolutely ruined. Tek 'em off an' I'll see what I can do. My God, I don't know what's got inta yer, walkin' in the rain like that. An' yer wedding day as well.'

Paul took off the trousers and handed them to his mother. As she ran the iron over them, drying out the damp patches and muttering to herself, he sat silently and stared at the wall. There was no turning back now.

It was still raining when the taxi arrived, and the wind blew sheets of water onto them. Paul sat in the back, next to his mother, and looked out at the bedraggled white ribbon stretched across the bonnet. The car smelt of dampness, and his new shoes were splashed with mud.

There was no difficulty parking near Norton Register Office, the weather had kept most of the usual shoppers off the High Street and it was virtually deserted. As his taxi pulled up, Paul could see Maggie, surrounded by a vanguard of umbrellas, climbing out of hers.

They stood in the ante-room, looking at each other, not knowing what to say. Maggie seemed so pure and virginal in her long white dress, Paul thought. No one would ever guess she was pregnant. But when the baby arrived, people would be able to count up easily enough.

'Mr Wright. Miss Boroughs.'

For a moment, Paul thought the Assistant Registrar was calling for his father, then he took a clumsy hold on Maggie's elbow and led her into the office.

The Registrar, a balding man with pinched features, was sitting behind the desk. His glasses were perched on the end of his nose, his pen gripped firmly between his fingers. Paul wondered if he should hold out his hand, but the man appeared too absorbed in the papers in front of him to have any interest in the normal courtesies.

Paul and Maggie stood awkwardly by the desk while as many friends and relatives as there was room for crowded in behind them. When the door to the ante-room had been closed, the Registrar lifted his head.

'Mr Paul Wright?' he asked, as if it were a test.

'Yes.'

He sniffed and looked down at his papers.

'Miss Margaret . . . sniff . . . Elizabeth Boroughs?'

'Yes.'

More sniffing, more scrutiny. Apparently satisfied, he took a large white handkerchief out of his pocket, blew his nose loudly, and looked up at them again.

'You've chosen . . . sniff . . . a rum day for it,' he said.

This was terrible, Paul thought, and his heart went out to Maggie. She looked so pretty in her wedding dress. Even though this marriage wasn't what she would have chosen, even though he wasn't the man of her dreams, it was still her day and she deserved better than this awful man who was treating the whole thing like the signing of an HP agreement.

He looked at Maggie, and saw that she was looking back at him. Her eyes were serious, almost tearful, then, suddenly, they twinkled and she began to giggle. And Paul found himself chuckling too. The joke was the first thing they had ever really shared.

'Yes . . . sniff . . . well, when you're quite ready,' the Registrar said sternly over the sound of their laughter, 'we can make a start.'

The reception was held in the upstairs of the Norton Liberal Club, a large room with a bar at one end and a small stage at the other. Three big tables formed a square U so that everyone could see the cake, the bride and the groom. Paul shook hands with the sixty-odd people who had been invited to the sit-down tea, Maggie's lot and his own – long-lost cousins, almost-forgotten aunts – who had travelled by bus and by train to celebrate this day with him.

They sat. The food was served by waitresses in black dresses and white aprons. Then came the glasses and the bottles of sparkling wine, and Jimmy, the best man, was on his feet. There was something about the way he was standing and the look in his eye that made Paul uneasy. Jimmy was about to pull a stunt, and he didn't know what.

'Ladies and Gentlemen,' Jimmy began, 'it is the duty of the best man to praise his friend. After all, if he doesn't – and excuse my language, ladies – who the bloody hell will?'

Most of the guests chuckled good-naturedly. Paul relaxed. Jimmy was just putting on a show, playing the role of working-class best man and loving every minute of it.

'Now I'm not going to do what best men always do,' he continued. 'Instead, I'm going to ask you two questions.' He looked around the room for a butt, and his eye fell on Maggie's mother who was fiddling with her handbag. 'Don't worry, Mrs Boroughs, you don't have to write anything down.'

There were more smiles as the bride's mother opened her bag, closed it again, and finally, looking flustered and confused, laid it on the floor.

'The first question is, why should a lovely girl like Maggie – and I'm sure you all agree she does look particularly lovely today – why should a lovely girl like Maggie marry my friend Paul?'

Paul felt a stabbing pain in his stomach.

'Oh, dear God,' he thought. 'What's he doing? Is he pissed? Is he going to tell them about the Odd Man Out?'

It would just be too much. Not only would he be saddled with Maggie for the rest of his life, but everyone would know that he had been the fool, the one who had had to pay. And poor, poor Maggie. Her lips had gone white. Paul reached under the table, took her hand and found that she was trembling.

'I mean, even if he is one of my best friends,' Jimmy went on cheerfully, 'I have to admit he doesn't exactly look like the catch of the year.'

There was some nervous laughter, but most people sat in embarrassed silence, playing with their food or looking at the floor. And they just imagined that Jimmy was showing bad taste in being rude about his friend. They didn't even know about the park – not yet!

'No one know the answer?' Jimmy asked, sweeping the tables with his eyes. 'OK, I'll give you time to think about it and come back to it later. Now my second question is this. Why do I like Maggie so much?'

'Because you had her first?' a voice screamed in Paul's head. 'Because you don't have to marry her?'

He gazed frantically around the room. His mother's face was twitching, Maggie's father was going red. He wondered if he should jump to his feet and hit Jimmy with a wine bottle before he could say any more. Then he saw his other friend, looking calmly on. David shook his head slightly, and instantly, Paul felt better. The gesture told him so much. It said that David knew what he'd been planning, and it wasn't necessary. It said that if it *had* been necessary, David would have done it already.

'It's not a very difficult quiz, this one,' Jimmy said. 'It's not like *Take a Letter* or *Double Your Money*. Both questions have got the same answer. It's because Maggie can see that underneath that unprepossessing exterior is a really wonderful feller.'

There were audible sighs, and not just of relief – looking round Paul saw a few female eyes glistening with tears. The speech had worked out brilliantly, leaving everyone with the impression that it was a true love match – Beauty and the Beast. But like so many things that Jimmy enjoyed, for a while it had teetered on the edge of disaster.

Paul thought his own speech sounded awful; dull and flat. He had a way with words, just as Jimmy had, but only if he were sure of his arguments, convinced of the rightness of his cause. He could have made a powerful speech on the dangers of youthful randiness or the evils of seeing a woman not as a woman at all – but as a vagina to masturbate in. He could have held them spellbound with a lecture on the random malevolence of fate which had caused him to be here today. Instead, he thanked all the guests for coming and said that he and his wife (his wife!) hoped they had enjoyed themselves. The presents were much appreciated and would be very useful in the coming years.

Paul and Maggie cut the cake, the flash bulbs popped, the guests applauded. The formalities were finally over. The men put down the wine glasses which had sat uncomfortably in their work-hardened hands and went to the bar to order pints, loosening their ties on the way. The women, some of them pulling knitting out of their bags, formed chatty little groups to discuss this wedding and the prospect of future ones.

The waitresses began taking away the plates and Paul watched, half-amused, half-saddened, as some of the female guests followed the movements of the workers with their eyes.

'They're dying to help,' he said to himself. 'They're not used to sitting still. They need to be there in the kitchen, scraping the plates, washing up, drying – doing something.'

The male guests suffered from the same disease. Waving away

the waitresses' protests that it was their job, the men began to move the tables and chairs back against the wall.

'They don't know how to handle leisure, any of them,' Paul thought. 'But it's not really surprising. What with normal shifts and overtime and doing their own decorating and repairs to save money, they've no bloody experience of free time.'

All that would change when the Socialist Utopia came. People would learn to develop interests outside work. They would live, rather than just exist. And perhaps in his new role, the role of trainee teacher, which had been thrust upon him, he could help. It wouldn't be the same as going to Oxford but . . .

The Les Hale Trio (organ, drums and double bass) had set up their equipment and Les Hale signalled to Jimmy. The best man stepped up to the platform and took the microphone in his hands.

'Ladies and Gentlemen, the first dance will be for the bride and groom only. Give 'em a bit of space, will you? I thank you.'

The guests formed a semi-circle and the young couple walked into the centre. This was at least one thing that Paul could do with conviction – he was a good dancer, and Maggie wasn't. He led her around the floor with style and confidence. It felt good, holding a woman close against you, guiding her through the movements.

As the afternoon wore on into the early evening, great aunts felt the need to go home for a rest, cousins had to leave to catch their buses. By six o'clock, when the drink was beginning to bite and the dancing was becoming less inhibited, there was only a hard core of forty people left. The function had successfully completed the transition from wedding tea to party.

Paul, chatting half-heartedly to Maggie's uncle, looked around to see what his friends were doing. David was at the bar, his pint pot looking tiny in his massive hand. Paul knew from the expression on his face that he was talking business. He never missed a chance.

Jimmy was in the corner, right palm resting against the wall, left leg bent, chatting to a pretty little brunette, one of Maggie's cousins. When the girl had had a few more Cherry Bs, Jimmy would probably say that it was getting hot and suggest they go for a walk – only this time he wouldn't be taking his mates along.

Paul and Maggie left at half-past six, under a shower of confetti, but the party carried on. New people, who had nothing to do with the wedding, arrived from the bar downstairs. Nobody minded – the band was already paid for and they were buying their own drinks.

It was around ten o'clock that Jimmy and David ran into each other at the bar.

'Enjoying yourself?' David asked.

'Not as much as I'm going to.' Jimmy flicked his thumb at Maggie's cousin who was disappearing into the toilet. 'Only seventeen, but a lovely little body. And just about ready for it. What are your plans?'

'I think I'll make an early night of it,' David said. 'I've got a lot to do in the yard tomorrer.'

They ordered more drinks and stood with their backs to the bar, watching the dancing. There had been something on David's mind all the way through the ceremony and the reception and now he felt the need to voice it. He glanced around to see if anyone was listening, then asked, 'Would you have done it?'

'Yes,' Jimmy said, without hesitation. 'Would you?'

David nodded.

'I think she's got more chance of bein' happy with Paul than she would ever have had with me,' he said. 'But if the coins had gone different, I would have married her.'

Maggie's Uncle Harry was on the stage, swaying in front of the microphone.

'I wanna shing you a shong,' he said. 'Itsh one you all know, sho I wan' you to join in. Ish called *King of the Road*.'

The double bass began the intro, and Harry came in only a few beats too soon.

'Is he drunk,' Jimmy asked, 'or has he just taken his false teeth out?'

David grinned.

'Could be either.'

He was still bothered by Jimmy's answer. It seemed too glib, too unqualified, so unlikely from the complex person Jimmy was becoming.

'Wouldn't it have buggered up all your plans for the future if you'd married her?' he asked.

'Yes,' said Jimmy, 'just as it's buggered up Paul's.'

David thought back to the game of Odd Man Out, when he had turned over his coin in the last decisive round. Paul hadn't been able to look – that had been fear. Yet Jimmy had been remarkably calm, taking a long swig of his pint before he examined the coin.

'And could you have stood that?' he persisted.

'No,' Jimmy said. 'No, I couldn't.'

Some of the guests were joining in with the singing, others took the opportunity for a little harmless adultery as they smooched around the floor.

'We're all very different, us three,' Jimmy continued. 'Paul wanted to go to Oxford, to be a success, but once he gets used to his new life, he'll settle down. I don't say he'll be happy, but at least he'll be content. I could never be just content, David. I've got to be a success, I've got to make my mark in the world. It's all or nothing with me.'

'You say we're different. What about me?'

Jimmy paused for a while then said, 'You want it *in vino veritas*?'

'What does that mean?'

'It means I'm pissed and I'll tell you what I really think if you want me to.'

David shivered, as if someone had walked over his grave. The conversation was out of control. He didn't want to know what Jimmy thought, he wanted to back away, yet he couldn't force himself to do so.

'Tell me,' he said.

'I don't know how I will end up, but I know about you. You'll be a success – fuck it, you're a success already. But I don't think you're meant to be happy or even content – at least, not for long. There's something hanging over you, a sort of black cloud.'

David put down his glass. Imagination was not his strong point, but now that Jimmy had spoken he could feel the hand of fate hovering above his head, pressing down on his broad shoulders, buckling his powerful knees.

'Aw, forget it,' Jimmy said. '*In vino crappus*. Let's have another drink.'

David didn't want another drink. Jimmy had said that he would have married Maggie. Jimmy had said that he couldn't have stood it. Jimmy had found a way to cheat fate, and David wanted to know what it was.

'So what would you have done after you'd married Maggie?' he demanded.

'I would have waited until the child was born,' Jimmy said, 'then I'd have taken out a large accident insurance policy in its name – then I'd have had a fatal accident.'

'You can't mean that.'

'Oh yes,' Jimmy said. 'I couldn't have endured the sort of life Paul will have. I'd have killed myself.'

They were too late for supper but the landlady made them

sandwiches, showed them up to their room, and tactfully with-drew. Maggie rapidly and efficiently unpacked the cases and hung the clothes in the wardrobe.

Paul just stood there, feeling useless. When everything was neatly put away, Maggie said, 'What shall we do now?'

Paul looked at his watch. It was still only five to ten.

'We might as well go for a drink before we turn in,' he said.

Even as he spoke, the words struck him as ludicrous. Turn in! Not 'sleep together', not 'make love', not even 'have it off'. Turn in – as if they were an old married couple with their hot water bottles and bedsocks. Marriage made you old – instantly and for ever.

'If that's what you want, luv,' Maggie said.

Her voice seemed sad, regretful. She wasn't thick, Paul thought to himself.

They walked along the promenade. The sea lapped against the shore, the air was tangy with the smell of salt. In the distance, they could see the Tower.

A tram rattled by. Paul remembered a previous holiday, a trip to the Illuminations, when the trams, decked with coloured lights, had been magic carpets, wafting him through Fairyland. Black-pool was not Fairyland now. It was only the embarkation point for a long journey that he and Maggie would take together – slow, creaking, unexciting and a little uncomfortable – a tram ride with death a terminus.

He realised that neither of them had spoken for some time. The last few weeks had been hectic: breaking the news, making all the arrangements for the wedding, filling in application forms and attending interviews at the training college. All their conversations had been confined to practical details. Even on the train, they had been able to talk about how the wedding had gone and to laugh about the registrar and the rain. They had exhausted that subject now, and there they were, alone together. Two comparative strangers, with a week to fill with words and no script to work from.

The pub was called The Crown. It was a huge barn of a place, packed to capacity with holiday-makers wearing 'Kiss-me-quick' cowboy hats and talking loudly and happily.

'A week or two of escape,' Paul thought, 'of mindless oblivion, and then they'll all be back to the grind, with only Christmas to look forward to.'

These people were entitled to more, even if they did not realise how much they were missing out on, how they were being cheated of what was rightfully theirs. He felt as he had done when David had to leave school. He would fight for them. He had screwed up his own life, he could no longer bring about the great changes he had once hoped for, but he could have some impact.

The waiter was middle-aged. He wore a green jacket and his collar was flecked with dandruff. He looked Paul up and down critically.

'Oh God,' Paul thought. 'He's going to ask me how old I am.'

The final humiliation.

The waiter didn't ask. His face indicated that Paul had passed his inspection, at least well enough for a crowded Saturday night.

Paul ordered the drinks and looked at Maggie. Her head was bent and she was examining her nails with far greater concentration than they merited.

'What do you want it to be?' he asked.

'What!'

His voice had startled her.

'The baby,' Paul said. 'What do you want it to be?'

'I don't mind,' Maggie said, 'as long as it's fit and healthy. What do you want it to be?'

'Mine!' Paul felt like screaming, 'I want it to be mine!'

Instead, he reached across and stroked her hand.

'I don't mind either,' he said.

The first painful topic had been dealt with, but there were many more still left to discuss. Bravely, Maggie brought one of them up. 'I know you're upset that you can't go to university,' she said. 'I know you didn't want to be a teacher. But you'll be a wonderful one, Paul. I'm sure you will.'

Looking into her eyes, he believed it; or at least believed that she believed it.

'Thank you, luv,' he said. 'That means a lot to me.'

The landlady had put her hair in curlers and was wearing a heavy blue dressing gown and fluffy carpet slippers.

'You know where everything is,' she said. 'Toilet at the end of the corridor, breakfast at half past eight. You shouldn't need anything else.'

She smiled at Paul. It was intended to be encouraging, but she'd already taken out her teeth and the gaping grin made him think of the leers of condemned souls in hell.

The house was quiet, and though they tried to tread softly, their footsteps seemed to reverberate through the whole building. The key scraped in the lock and the door creaked as it swung open. Paul felt like a guilty schoolboy creeping into a place that was out of bounds.

The room was square. The wall-paper was geometric and just beginning to peel away at the joins. The bed, wardrobe and dressing table were all of the same heavy, dark wood, with machine-carved mouldings fastened to them by invisible nails. On the walls were cheap prints of an older, more elegant Blackpool, the resort as it had been at the end of the last century, when women in long, billowing dresses and men with top hats and canes sauntered up and down the prom.

Paul looked at the single straight-backed chair, then sat down on the bed. The springs groaned in protest.

'Well, here we are then,' Maggie said.

'Yes,' he replied, 'here we are.'

What happened next?

Maggie turned awkwardly, so that her back was to him and began to unbutton her going-away dress. Paul, his hands clutching his knees, counted – one . . . two . . . three. There were seven buttons and when she had undone them all, Maggie slipped out of the dress, folded it neatly over a hanger and put in the wardrobe, smoothing down her blonde hair as she did so.

She was wearing just a bra and panties in matching, blushing pink. Paul had never seen her nearly naked before. She stood in front of the dressing table and unhooked her bra. Paul could see her breasts reflected in the mirror. They were nice, really nice: milky white with small, pointed, pink nipples. She lowered her panties and revealed a patch of pale pubic hair – and Paul felt himself hardening.

'Maggie,' he said, hesitantly, 'would you mind if I . . . if I made love to you?'

Maggie turned slowly. It was her body that his eyes were drawn to first, no longer just a reflection but real, there, in front of him – beautifully, superbly naked. Then he looked up at her face. Her mouth was curved in a smile that suggested both shyness and amusement.

'Of course I don't mind,' she said. 'We are married, you know.'

As he kissed her breasts and ran his trembling hands up and down her rib cage, Maggie's tongue snaked in and out of his ear. When he rolled on top of her, she locked her legs tightly around his buttocks. He knew that although she was nervous and inexperienced, she was trying, really trying, to make him happy. And he was happy. He had never known that such a level of sexual excitement was possible. His nerve ends tingled, his body ached for release.

He entered her, and the moment he felt her muscles tighten around him, he had a vision of Corporation Park. It was so vivid it was as if he were actually there. He could smell the grass. He could hear the music from the fairground. And he could see it all, the whole horrendous evening, acted out before his eyes – Jimmy, his backside pale in the moonlight, thrusting with style and confidence – David, his thick legs rooted to the ground, simply ploughing away. And it was her they were doing it to, Maggie, this woman lying beneath him, who should have been his but wasn't – because she had already been shared out. He felt his organ go limp and he drew away from her.

He had failed, even in *that*. He lay on his side, staring at the wallpaper, while Maggie gently stroked his head.

'It doesn't matter,' she said. 'Don't worry. It will be all right in time.'

Paul wondered if it ever would be, wondered if he could wipe the images of David and Jimmy out of his mind.

'Paul,' said Maggie, her voice still sympathetic, but now intense and urgent too. 'Paul! Look at me!'

He didn't want to look at her. He didn't want to see the expression in her eyes, the resignation, the stoic acceptance of a bad bargain.

Maggie eased him onto his back, then cupped his face in her hands.

'Look at me, Paul,' she said again. 'I'm glad it was you and not one of the others. Honest I am.'

PART THREE

Goats and Monkeys

Chapter Ten

Jimmy was the only passenger waiting to get off the green Corporation bus at the University stop. Most of the other students, he guessed, would have their own transport, or at least have been driven down by daddy. His own father was busy that day – on the two-ten shift. Anyway, he would have looked silly balanced on the cross-bar of a push-bike.

He pulled his case from under the stairs and stepped on to the pavement. The gears of the old Leyland crunched and the bus pulled off, giving him a clear view of the collection of glass and concrete buildings which constituted Seahaven University.

The porter's lodge – the porter's blockhouse, more like – was located near the main gate. The man on duty was elderly and balding. He snapped his head up from his *Daily Express* when Jimmy tapped on the window, rapidly assessed the importance of the young man, and lowered his eyes again to finish the article he had been reading.

Jimmy waited patiently.

'Yes?' the porter growled finally.

'I'm looking for Sutton Hall.'

'The Alderman Sutton Hall of Residence, do you mean?'

'That's right.'

'Straight up till you come to the library, then turn left.'

The directions had been delivered indifferently, the man had not even bothered to point.

Jimmy let it all wash over him. There were times for confrontations and this was not one of them. It would only give the porter pleasure if he became annoyed. Besides, it was unnecessary. In a couple of years, the man would be calling him 'Mr Bradley, *sir,*' without any prompting.

The students wandering up and down the paths or sitting under the trees, were dressed casually. Ah, Jimmy thought, but what effort and expense had gone into achieving that casualness. Their jeans were Levis, imported from America. Their shirts had never seen the inside of a Marks and Sparks. Even their flip-flops were leather, rather than plastic. He glanced at a bunch of girls, stripped down to their expensive bikinis, lying in the sun. No doubt adding an extra layer to their South of France summer tans.

Paul had not understood why he wanted to come to Seahaven, but he supposed that was one step up on his mother, who couldn't see why he was going to university at all.

'With all your qualifications,' she'd said, 'you could get a job as a trainee manager at Lipton's just like that.' She'd clicked her fingers and when there was no response from Jimmy, had added, 'And if you don't want to work in a shop, I'm sure you could get somethin' in Blackthorne's office.'

'I want to study accountancy, Mum.'

'Isn't that like book-keepin'?'

'Sort of.'

'Well I don't see the point. We had a book-keeper at the shoe factory. Mr Grimes, he was called. He wore an old mac I wouldn't have given to a tramp. And his suit? My God, it was as shiny as a mirror.'

Jimmy only smiled.

'An' he lived in a council house,' his mother had said, triumphantly, as if she had produced the final, unanswerable argument. 'What's the point in all that studyin' if you're only goin' to end up like Mr Grimes? Why don't you see if they're takin' anybody on at the Town Hall?'

He had long ago given up trying to explain things to her. He knew that she would only really understand that he had chosen the right path when he could show her the tangible signs of it – good clothes, a car, a house. If he could manage to buy a poky little semi on one of the new estates, she would be overawed, her life's work complete.

He skirted the library, a large hexagonal building with tinted glass windows, long study tables and very few students. Seahaven was weak on academic excellence and serious research; its strength lay in the areas of rugby and horse-riding, late-night champagne parties and ducking passers-by in the fountains.

Ahead of him lay Sutton Hall, a bastion of privilege that looked like a stunted block of council flats. He picked up his key from the desk and went up to his room.

It was exactly what he had expected – a formica and wood veneer cell. He had no intention of staying there for the whole year.

The Conservative Society held its recruitment social early one evening in Fresher Week. It was still daylight, but the pearly-grey curtains had been drawn as if to exclude the outside world. Jimmy looked around the room. Young men in blazers with rowing or rugby club badges on the breast pockets, stood chatting to young women in expensive Laura Ashley copies of cheap hippy dresses; parties of giggling girls congregated around the table of dainty nibbles; groups of over-grown boys blocked the way to the drinks table and brayed excessively. They were all completely at home, perfectly at ease. If they didn't know each other from school or house parties, then they at least recognised those around them as belonging to the same club.

Only Jimmy stood out. No one came across to talk to him, no one suggested that he should go to the desk by the door and join the Society. They wanted members, but they were particular and he was clearly not their type. It was the jacket that did it. He felt the tweed between his thumb and finger. Buying it had been a calculated decision. He could never pass himself off as one of this lot, nor did he wish to. Instead, he had opted for another image – prosperous but different.

He looked around the room again, and selected his target. She was one of those fairly stocky girls, slightly bow-legged, with a ruddy complexion and a loud voice; the sort who, in middle age, naturally slip into a twin-set. She was explaining something to a bored-looking youth whom she'd probably been brought up with.

Jimmy waited until the young man had found some excuse to slip away before he approached her.

'Jimmy Bradley,' he said. 'Can I get you another drink?'

It was his accent she noticed first, flat, Northern, not even properly educated. Jimmy had thought of getting rid of it, but though it might create initial difficulties, it was one of the best long-term assets he had. So it stayed – he even played it up a little.

A flicker of distaste crossed the girl's face. She had no wish to be seen talking to an oik.

'I mean,' Jimmy continued quickly, 'I don't want to intrude or anything. I'll just get you a drink and then go away – if that's what you want.'

He gave her his broadest winning smile, a smile that said he was attracted to her, that paradise for him would lie between her sturdy thighs.

'I don't think . . .' she began in haughty tones, faltering as the chemistry started to work. 'I mean . . . cider would be super.'

Her name was Veronica, but most of her friends called her Ronnie, which was a bit of a scream really, because, you see, that was a boy's name.

He spent the rest of the evening letting her talk at him. She told him all about Mummy and Daddy and the house in Suffolk, what she and her chums had done during the holidays, and all about the sweet little ways of her horse. He listened, recorded for future use, and made appropriate noises at the right moments. At the end of the social he saw her back to her room and judged that the time was right for a single kiss, a fairly intimate one promising further excitement to come. He squired her around for the rest of Fresher Week, each meeting terminating in just a little more sexual contact. On Sunday, he bedded her. She was a virgin, but very willing to give up that status. It wasn't quite as unpleasant as he'd expected.

Paul spent much of his week's honeymoon thinking about Oxford. He had only been there once – for the interview – yet the image of it was indelibly stamped on his mind. Blackpool did nothing to wipe the memory out: the Tower mocked the dreaming spires, the promenade parodied the path that ran along the river to the boat houses, the cowboy hats were a grotesque reminder of straw boaters.

He did the financial calculations again and again, and always came up with the same result. He could not afford it – they needed Maggie's wages, and Maggie could not work unless she was living close enough to home for her mother to mind the baby. But still his heart ached when he thought of the Oxford Union, the Sheldonian and Magdalen Bridge.

When the honeymoon was over, they returned to Buckworth to set up home in the back bedroom of Paul's parents' house. That, at least, would not last for ever. After Christmas, when the baby was born, there would be a little money coming in from David and Jimmy and with what Paul could earn himself working part-time, they should be able to rent a place of their own.

Although Paul's mother had given them a roof over their heads ('You have to, when it's yer own children'), she saw no need to go further than that. She was merely sullen at first, and it was not until the end of the first week that things really came to a head.

Paul was sitting in the kitchen, scanning the classified ads for a job. His mother was preparing the food, as nervously and noisily as she always did. When the clock on the mantelpiece struck six, she sniffed.

'I wonder if your father'll be home for his tea tonight,' she said. 'One thing you have to say for that slut you married, at least she's usually on time.'

She had called Maggie names before, when he told her about their wedding plans. Twice was too much! Paul felt himself experiencing an emotion that was entirely new to him – blind rage! He slammed his fist down on the table.

'What did you call my wife?' he demanded.

Mrs Wright had got so used to meeting only passive resistance over the years that for a second she didn't know how to react.

'What did you call my wife?' Paul said again.

'Don't you speak to me like that!' Mrs Wright shouted. 'I'm yer mother!'

'And she's my wife. And that's a hell of a lot closer,' Paul said. 'Don't you *ever* call her that again!'

He rose to his feet and tugged impatiently at his jacket which was hanging on the hook.

'And where are you goin' now?' his mother asked.

'Out!'

'But yer tea's nearly ready.'

'Bugger my tea,' Paul said, slamming the door behind him.

It was drizzling slightly as he stood outside the post office, waiting for Maggie to leave off work.

'What's up?' she asked, as soon as she saw him.

As they walked up the street, he told her about the row with his mother. They had reached the top of the hump-backed bridge over the canal by the time he had finished.

'Why did you tell me?' Maggie asked.

'Because we're married. Because I don't want to keep any secrets from you.'

'Even if you know they'll hurt me?'

She *sounded* hurt.

Paul looked over the parapet at the green canal. A few feet below, out of sight, was the pipe that he, David and Jimmy had crawled along when they were boys, daring each other to go on until they were right in the middle, twenty feet above the cold water.

'Even if it hurts you,' he said. 'That's the way I am. That's the way it's got to be.'

'I suppose it is,' Maggie said, laughing lightly. 'So what do we do now, luv?'

'We can't stay there, we can't possibly stay there. Not after what she said.'

'Oh, luv, you do talk daft sometimes,' Maggie said. 'What else can we do? Would it be any easier at my mother's?'

Paul shook his head miserably.

'You're goin' to have to apologise,' Maggie said firmly.

'I'd rather die.'

'Maybe you would, luv, but we've got the baby to think of as well.' She kissed him lightly on the cheek. 'Besides, you can't really blame her, can you? I mean, I am older than you, aren't I? She's bound to think I led you on.'

Paul looked at her with amazement. Not only could she see his mother's point of view, but she could mention getting pregnant as if the park had never happened, as if it had been something that had just occurred between the two of them.

Paul turned to go back. Maggie grabbed his arm.

'Not yet,' she said. 'Let's play The Game first.'

It was a game she had invented in Blackpool. Now was not the time to play it. If he had to crawl to his mother, it was best to get it over with.

'It's a good idea,' Maggie insisted.

She was probably right. Paul scanned the immediate area. He could see fishermen around the pond by the school, saltworkers pushing a heavy cart down to the store, a few people ambling towards The George.

'Who?' he asked.

'The feller that's comin' up the bridge.'

She pointed discreetly to a middle-aged man on a bike, struggling against the steep gradient.

'Where does he . . .' Paul began.

'Wait till he's gone,' Maggie laughed, punching him in the ribs.

The cyclist reached the crown of the bridge, said, 'Evenin',' to them and free-wheeled down the other side.

'Where does he keep his false teeth?' Paul asked.

'In the goldfish bowl. Well, it gives the fish something to play with. What's his favourite food?'

'Fish and chips – wrapped in newspaper. Only they've never tasted the same since they closed down *The Daily Herald*. Where would he *really* like to go for his holidays . . .'

They continued for ten minutes until it was deemed by both of them, judged on a scoring system neither could explain, that Maggie had won. Paul felt much better, though he couldn't have said why.

They got back to the house to find Mrs Wright sitting in front of the fire, head first, hands dabbing her eyes with her pinny, bony elbows sticking out at all angles.

'Where've you bin?' she sobbed. 'Yer tea's ruined, absolutely ruined.'

Paul opened his mouth to make the bitter apology he had been practising all the way down the hill. Maggie shook her head, bent down in front of the oven and took out the plates containing the blackened remains of her mother-in-law's afternoon labours.

'Does look a bit over-done,' she said. 'Never mind. I'll make us all some bacon and eggs. Won't take a jiffy. Would you like a cup of tea first, Mrs Wright?'

Paul's mother dabbed her eyes again.

'Thank you, Maggie,' she said between sniffs. 'You are a good girl. But I wish you'd call me "Mum".'

When they went to bed, they made love, as they had done every night since the first failure in Blackpool. The second time had been better. Once more, Paul had felt the rising sexual excitement, and once more had visions of the park the moment he entered his wife. Only by an effort of will, by concentrating on abstract, unemotional subjects, had he managed to maintain his erection long enough for Maggie to have her orgasm and for his body to give way to the physical sensation of his penis being stimulated and thus eject its sperm.

'I came,' Maggie had said when it was all over. 'The first time. That was really losing my virginity. The rest doesn't matter.'

It did matter to Paul. He enjoyed the foreplay, but every single time he penetrated Maggie he had to force himself to become cold, detached and clinical. He couldn't afford to be there on top of Maggie, because if he was, the park was there also. Maggie told him he was a marvellous lover, that she had never dreamt that sex could be like this – and he went through with it because he felt he owed it to her.

Only David was alone that autumn of 1967. He didn't look for new friends, that was not his way. Instead, he started making solo visits to local rock clubs. He never danced, he never spoke to anyone except the barmen. He became, without intending it, something of a local character, the tall, broad shouldered, solitary figure who would stand in one corner of the room and knock back pint after pint with mechanical precision and no apparent pleasure.

He went for the music. In the daytime, when he was working at the yard, operating the metal-press or swinging the crane, he had plenty of noise to distract him. But the night-time was quiet, so he sought some substitute, a loud pounding in which he could lose himself, obviating the necessity to focus his mind on anything else.

He expected nothing more, that night in early October when he went to Maxie's Club to see The Sharks. They were a Norton group with a local following, capable of thrashing out gutsy rock at a sufficiently high level to suit David's needs. There was another group on before The Sharks called, David noted with disgust, Barry and the Aces. What would they be like? Watered-down Fleetwood Mac or diluted Rolling Stones? Perhaps they would be into flower power, the summer craze, and sing about peace and love in San Francisco. You certainly couldn't expect much from a group with a name like that.

The group shambled on to the stage, four young men with the standard line-up of three guitars and a set of drums. They were all wearing jeans and tie-and-dye shirts, and had their hair down over their shoulders. There was no official announcement of their arrival – they were only there to create background until The Sharks came on. They set up their equipment and tuned their guitars. The lead guitarist, a skinny boy with a bum-fluff moustache under his sharply pointed nose, went up to the microphone.

'One . . . two . . . three,' he said.

He grimaced slightly, hearing the echo bounce back at him.

'Four . . . five . . .'

The microphone whistled wildly.

'Oh, fuck it!' he said. 'Let's start anyway.'

He was talking to the group, but his voice carried loudly over the speaker system.

'*Now* it fuckin' works,' he said, unembarrassed and unrepentant.

There was a strident guitar opening, and then the young vocalist began singing.

'Battlin' my Cadillac along the south-west freeway,
There's a red-neck fat-slob cop who won't give me no leeway,'

The quality of their equipment was appalling, the sound seemed as if it were being forced through electrified tin cans.

'Grindin' at the gears as I try to overtake him,
If he don't get out my way, I'm goin' to have to break him,'

Though he hadn't heard the song before, David was impressed. Maybe it was the harsh, earthy lyrics or the pounding rhythm. Perhaps it was just the raw energy, the total commitment of the young singer. Something made it special. Other members of the audience were realising it too. Conversations were stopping and heads were turning towards the stage.

'Pigs have got the road blocked now, want to see me stoppin'
Man, I'm high, my brain is spaced, I feel my eye-balls poppin','

The driving guitars and the incessant thud of the drums conjured up the screech of tyres, the whine of the engine, the whoosh of the wind.

'I can slow down right this second, just one more surrender,
'Stead o' that, acceleration, crash into their fender,'

The guitars built up into a frenzy, and David, closing his eyes, could see the picture they painted; the high-speed crash, the impact of metal on metal – bending, crunching, as the van ploughed into the back of the lorry and his father shot through the windscreen.

The youth's hair hung in damp rat-tails. There were beads of sweat on his brow. He drew a deep breath and almost spat out the last verse.

'Now I'm in the wreckage of that policeman-pigshit's cruiser,
Might be dyin', but by Christ, I've proved I'm not a loser.'

After they had finished their set, the group sat on their own, morosely sipping at rum and Coca-Colas. David walked over to their table.

'Mind if I join you?' he asked.

They all looked up at him, then their vocalist, presumably Barry, said, 'Fuck off!'

It wasn't really aggressive, just weary. On stage, he had been powerful and forceful. Now the performance was over, he looked vulnerable and tired.

'I'm a big fan,' David said, smiling. 'I was thinkin' of buyin' you all a few drinks to show my appreciation.'

Barry smiled back at him. He had a nice smile, it seemed to soften the lines on his angular features and suggest that there was perhaps a third level hidden below the aggression and weariness.

'Sit down, Big Fan,' he said. 'We're all on Bacardi and Coke.'

The waiter came, and David ordered.

'You from round here?' he asked Barry.

The young singer picked up his drink and held it against the flashing light show, as if looking for an answer to the question in the bubbles.

'Yeah,' he said. 'Refton Village.'

'Funny I haven't seen you play before,' David said. 'I know most of the local groups.'

'We don't get many gigs,' Barry said. 'There's not a lot of club work, and most of the pubs want you to play Tom Jones, The Tremoloes – shit like that. We won't do it,' he concluded, with a hint of pride in his voice.

'*I* liked your set,' David said. 'Where d'you get the number about the Cadillac?'

'Wrote it,' Barry said, as if he couldn't imagine where else songs came from.

'Got a manager?' David asked casually.

Barry was not fooled. His stage-aggression was back on the surface.

'Wherever we play,' he said, 'it doesn't matter if the fuckin' audience fuckin' hates us, there's always some twat who comes along and asks us if we've got a manager, some smart-arse who thinks he'd like to run a group – even if it's a crap group. Yeah, we've got a manager.'

'It doesn't look as if he's doing you much good,' David said.

For a moment, Barry's body tensed, and David thought he was about to get a drink thrown in his face. Then the young singer relaxed again.

'Listen,' he said, 'do you know how much we make on a gig? By the time we've paid the bus fares and bought our drinks, it's probably costin' *us* money. So we can't afford a proper manager. So my dad does it for us, because he's willin' to give up his time, sort of help us out like. Would you do it for nothin'? 'Cos that's all we could afford to pay you.'

'If I was your manager,' David said, 'you'd soon be able to pay me a lot.'

David's confidence was having an effect on the other three members of the group. He could see that they were itching to ask him questions.

'How d'you know we're goin' to make money?' Barry asked.

'Because you're good,' David said. 'Fuckin' good. It's just that you've got things workin' against you at the moment. Your equipment stinks. Norton isn't big enough for you – there's not enough clubs, and they're not the right kinds of clubs anyway. You need to go to Liverpool, Manchester, maybe even Birmingham. If you do well on the circuit, I can get you a record contract.'

'*You* know record producers?' Barry asked sceptically.

'One or two,' David lied.

Barry was still not convinced. Perhaps if he'd been older, wearing a sober suit, the vocalist might have believed him; dressed as he was, he looked like any nineteen- or twenty-year-old punter.

David stuck his hand in his pocket and brought out a fist full of notes, the scrap-dealer's basic float. He counted out fifty and laid them on the table.

'Put this down as a deposit on some good amps,' he said. 'I'll meet the HP payments. You can pay me back when we hit the big time.'

The group looked at the money with greedy eyes, but without a sign from Barry, none of them dared moved.

'I've got a van,' David said. 'No more humping equipment on corporation buses.'

Barry smiled again.

'You're on,' he said.

Afterwards, David wondered why he'd made the offer. He was doing a lot of that these days – wondering why he'd done things. The group was good, the best local talent he'd ever seen, but he'd never been tempted to manage a group before. And he sincerely believed that they would make money – but they would take a lot of his time too, and he was doing all right with the scrap-yard as it was. In a strange way, it was all connected with that first song, and with Barry – and somewhere in there, in his mind, floating about and almost translucent, was the face of the Everton Kid.

Chapter Eleven

The party was typical of the ones Ronnie had been taking Jimmy to since Fresher Week. The light bulbs were covered with coloured cellophane, the expensive hi-fi blasted out Jimi Hendrix, incense burned in a pottery jar on the coffee table. The girls were in flowered dresses; the boys mostly wore suits – with paisley shirts to show that the Swinging Sixties were not passing *them* by.

Jimmy looked at the pimply youths gyrating their bodies in a clumsy mating dance. He liked these parties, enjoyed watching the smug, superior sons and daughters of the landed gentry make complete bloody fools of themselves. It gave his confidence a boost, reminded him that however formidable the obstacles in front of him, they *were* surmountable – because the people who had erected them were only older versions of the idiots in that room.

The drinks were in the kitchen, and he had the door half-open when he heard Ronnie's voice inside.

'Can't stand here chatting all night,' she said in her lazy drawl. 'Got to get back to Jimmy.'

'Whatever d' you see in him, my dear?' asked a voice that might have been Samantha or Olivia or any other of her look-alike, sound-alike friends. 'He's really a bit of rough, isn't he? I mean, I know he's handsome, distinguished-looking really – and he dresses *quite* well. But no one would ever mistake him for one of us, would they?'

Ronnie gave a throaty chuckle. She must have been practising it, Jimmy thought.

'He's awfully good in bed,' she said.

The others gasped and then giggled; shocked, virginal, revelling-in-it giggles.

'You don't mean you . . . oh, you are awful!' said Samantha or Olivia.

'Well,' said Ronnie, the only recently ex-virgin, 'I mean he does make a change from the sort of men one meets at hunt balls. He's got balls of a different kind.'

'Oh, Ronnie!' said Olivia or Samantha.

'He's a bit of an animal,' Ronnie continued. 'You'd expect it really, wouldn't you, coming from the sort of place he does?'

Jimmy smiled to himself and moved away from the door. So that was the line she was putting out, the rough Northern beast who exhausted even experienced Veronica. It helped to explain the changing attitude of some of Ronnie's girlfriends. He *was* handsome, he knew that, yet they would never have considered him while he was outside their group. But he wasn't an outsider any longer – Ronnie had brought him in and was boasting about him as if he were her new sports car. No wonder some of her bitchy little mates were starting to make a play for him – it must be insufferable for them to see the self-satisfied expression on dumpy little Ronnie's face.

It was on the upstairs corridor, heading for the loo, that Jimmy met the bulky, square-jawed man.

' 'ello Jimmy,' the man said, in an appalling imitation of a Northern accent. ' 'ow you doin'?'

Jimmy gave a wide grin as if the other man had said something terribly witty, because although Sebastian Woodley was a moron and a bore, he was also a leading light in the Conservative Association.

'Met a chap from up your way the other day,' Woodley continued.

Which could mean anywhere north of Watford.

'Oh yes?'

'Nasty little yob. Name of Ramsbottom or Higginbottom – or something like that. D'you know him?'

'Can't say that I do.'

Woodley belched and scratched his backside.

'That's better,' he said. 'Anyway, this oik claims to be a socialist. Beards me in the bar. Tells me my class is the enemy of the working man. Says we're trying to smash the unions so we can lower the wages and see our profits go up.'

'What did you tell him?'

'Told him not to be so bloody stupid. Asked if he'd care to step outside and settle it like a gentleman. Didn't, of course, his kind never will. Do they all think like that up there?'

'I know some workers,' Jimmy said. 'Not well, of course.'

'Course not,' Woodley chuckled.

'But the workers in my father's . . . where my father works, don't think like that. The unions, with their restrictive practices and unnecessary strikes, are holding them back – and they know it.

What they want is a government brave enough to tackle the bloated union bosses, so that the people with money will want to invest it again. That investment, and the workers' know-how, will soon put us back on top. A real partnership – and good for Britain.'

'Quite right,' Woodley said.

'Next time you see this Higginbottom chap,' Jimmy continued, 'don't offer to fight him. That's only sinking to his level. Tell him what I've just said.'

'A real partnership, Good for Britain,' Woodley echoed. He patted his pockets. 'I say, Jimmy, you couldn't lend me a couple of pounds, could you?'

Jimmy smiled.

'Speaking as the son of a poor working man . . .' he began, already reaching for his wallet.

'Stout fellow,' Woodley said, slapping him on the shoulder. 'Son of a poor working man. That'll be the day.'

He pocketed the notes and set off down the stairs. It would be the last he would see of the two pounds, Jimmy knew that, but it had been money well spent.

The party ended at two. Jimmy escorted Ronnie back to her flat and performed the usual service. She had barely finished groaning when he was out of bed and putting his clothes on.

'You're not going, are you?' Ronnie asked, sounding hurt.

'Got to get up early,' Jimmy said, pulling on his socks. 'I'm meeting some chaps from the local Constituency Association in the morning.'

He glanced at his watch. He was going to be late.

'Don't be beastly, Jimmy,' Ronnie said. 'You could get to your meeting just as quickly from here as you could from that grotty hall you live in.'

He didn't want a row with her – not yet.

'If I woke up in the morning and found you next to me, I would be late,' he said. 'I couldn't just leave without . . . you know.'

She giggled.

'Oh, all right. I forgive you. But I'll see you tomorrow night, won't I?'

'Of course you will, Ronnikins,' he said, barely able to keep the heaviness out of his voice.

He sprinted to his room, changed his clothes then dashed along the sea front towards the town. It was still dark, and the cold bit into him. He was going to be late, there was no way round it.

It was nearly five o'clock when he reached the Victorian red-brick building that could have been a school or a library – or a giant public convenience. The man with the clipboard was scowling.

'You're late, Bradley!'

'Sorry, Mr Stubbs.'

'There's plenty of others'd be glad of the job.'

At the slave wages he was paying?

'I know that, Mr Stubbs. I really am sorry. It won't happen again.'

'Well, it 'ad better not. Get started then – you've some catchin' up to do.'

Jimmy lifted a pile of heavy vegetable crates and hoisted them onto his shoulder. After the first day, he'd wondered whether he would ever walk again. He'd got used to it now, but it was still a strain. He half-ran, half-staggered across the market, and stacked the crates in their assigned place. One load shifted. He walked quickly back to the entrance and picked up a second. It was a bloody hard way to earn money, but he had little choice. Most of his wages he saved – for when the baby was born. The rest, he would probably end up 'lending' to bastards like Woodley.

David worked the group hard. He rented a church hall on Tuesdays and Thursdays and just to give them the feel of playing to a live audience, he advertised these rehearsals as free concerts. Within a month, they had developed a fair-sized local following, and the fans were actually queuing up to get in. He didn't interfere with the music, he didn't know enough about it. What he did understand was business.

'You have to sell yourselves,' he told Barry. 'You've got to value what you're offerin', because if you don't, no bugger else will. Don't just walk on stage. Make your arrival seem like an event. Leave a space between your numbers for the clappin'. You deserve it – and you'll get it if you wait long enough. And when you come off, don't sit in the bar as if you were punters; if you want a drink, go somewhere else for it. Every second you're in the club you should be the centre of attention.'

The young vocalist would sit quietly, his hand resting on his chin, listening to David's suggestions, and then go off and put them into effect. David never gave advice to the rest of the band – he knew Barry would resent it.

He spent money on their clothes, bizarre brash outfits that fitted their music. The name had to go too. David wanted something that suggested their raw, earthy quality. Paul came up with Urban Decay.

'I don't like it,' Barry said. 'An' I'm not fuckin' havin' it!'

'Why not?' David asked, reasonably.

'What's wrong with Barry and the Aces?'

'It doesn't fit in with the music.'

'Well, it fuckin' stays and if you don't fuckin' like it, you can fuck off.'

David looked at Barry's face and saw that the young man was almost in tears. He still had difficulty reconciling the tough, hard image that Barry projected on stage with the vulnerable, almost elfin character he was off it. And suddenly, he knew what Barry's problem was.

'How about if we call it Urban Decay – featuring Barry Crowther?' he asked. 'That way you'd have your whole name in the title.'

Barry thought about it.

'I'll do it, David,' he said finally, 'but only because it's you.'

It was the first real argument they'd had, and now it was over. David felt his heart lighten – but only a little, because he could see bigger, more bitter rows looming in the future. Barry had worked hard tightening up the group, and soon he would be demanding that David use his contacts to get them some bookings. If only he really did have contacts! But he didn't, so he spent his evenings visiting clubs in Manchester, playing the managers a tape of Urban Decay.

It was a thankless task – the real excitement of their music came from live performances, and the Grundig recorder he carried with him could never hope to do them justice. David tried everything he knew, including offering to waive the fee. Nothing did any good, and as he tramped the streets of Manchester, and later, Liverpool, he worried about how long he could keep the young guitarist's loyalty without delivering on his promises.

Norton College of Education was a sprawling, disorganized place. A series of brick buildings and pre-fabricated huts, thrown together under one administrative umbrella, it churned out teachers to meet the increased demand. Most of the students were local, female and lower middle-class. They were pre-occupied, Paul thought, with looking good and getting married as soon as possible – the former probably nothing more than a means of attaining the latter. They had plenty of time to devote to their interests – the demands of the course were laughably light.

It was just as well for Paul that they were. He had other things to do. In late September, he started a part-time job, stacking shelves at the local Tesco supermarket. In early October, he began his London University external degree, often staying up until the early hours of the morning to study sociology and economics.

But it was politics that took most of his energy and imagination, and if there was one tangible advantage he had gained from his being a married man with a baby on the way, it was that now people in the Labour Club were prepared to treat him like an adult.

Examining himself in the mirror Paul thought that marriage had changed his appearance, too. There were lines on the face which suggested, perhaps not worry, but at least the acceptance of normal adult responsibilities. And his body seemed stronger, more grown-up – his arms more solid, his jaw firmer and more forceful. Was he imagining it, or was he really filling out at last?

The weather turned cold in the middle of November. In the mornings, the bare trees glittered with a sheen of frost. The sun, when it appeared at all, was weak and watery. The bedrooms were freezing, even at mid-day, and life in the Wright house concentrated more and more around the kitchen fire.

To counter the darkening gloom, the shops in Norton put on bright displays of Christmas presents. Walmsley and Taylor's announced that Father Christmas would be coming soon and could be visited daily in the fairy grotto. Jimmy would be home too, Paul thought, back from the glamour of university life, to spend a boring, mundane Christmas with his parents and friends.

On the last Saturday of the month, when Mrs Wright was out shopping, and Mr Wright was just *out*, Maggie asked Paul if he could put down his books for a while and go with her into the front room.

He was surprised to see that she'd lit a fire.

'Well, it's not Christmas Day,' he said, 'so it must be a wedding or a funeral.'

Maggie did not share in the joke. Instead, she pointed to the best armchair and said, 'Sit down, luv.'

When Paul was seated to her satisfaction, she picked up a stool, placed it opposite him, and lowered her heavy body onto it.

'The baby's due in three months,' she said.

As if he needed to be told. Paul wondered where all this was leading.

'It'll be a boy,' she continued.

'How do you know?' Paul asked.

'I know,' Maggie said, enigmatically. 'It'll be a boy, and it'll need two godfathers.'

The names sprang immediately to Paul's mind and he realised they were treading on dangerous ground. Maggie had only seen David and Jimmy once since Paul had lost the Odd Man Out – at the wedding. She had virtually ignored them, and Paul hadn't blamed her: she had had to accept him, there was no need for her to go out of her way for the others.

'The godfathers?' he said, letting her be the one to lead them through the minefield.

'It should be David and Jimmy,' Maggie said in a rush.

It should be David and Jimmy! Paul looked at Maggie's face, serious and intent, glowing in the firelight. *David and Jimmy.* She couldn't stand them but . . . but it was the only way to be sure that the child's real father was present at the baptism. It was logical, and it was only fair to the baby. Yet Paul wished that Maggie had never thought of it, wished that she could wipe the night in the park out of her mind. Even though he never could.

He didn't want to ask the next question, but he knew he must. He had to make sure.

'You'd like them to be the baby's godfathers?' he said.

Maggie looked puzzled for a moment.

'No,' she said. 'I won't like it; I'll hate it, but it's right. If it was goin' to be a girl, I'd have my mates. But it isn't. It will be your son and it's only fair that your best friends should be with you at the christenin'.'

It will be your son! He leaned over and kissed her gently on the forehead. For a moment, he almost loved her.

The day before Jimmy was due to leave for Norton he got the note from Tony Hawsley – the ex-chairman of the University Conservative Association and still the power behind the throne – asking him round for drinks. Jimmy knew him vaguely from social gatherings when they had exchanged a word or two, but Hawsley was far too important to spend much time with first year students.

He was supposedly a student himself, doing research. In fact, he was really only filling in time until he was called to greater things. Though he was only twenty-four, the Party machine was already casting about for a safe seat in the next election.

Hawsley lived off-campus. He greeted Jimmy at the door and led him into his living room. Jimmy's eyes took in the furnishings – soft leather armchairs, expensive prints on the walls, Persian rugs scattered on the floor.

'One day,' he thought, 'one day.'

Hawsley matched his surroundings – tailored trousers, silk

shirt, cravat. He looked completely self-assured, convinced that Jimmy would be overawed.

'Sherry?' he asked.

'Yes, please.'

'I'm afraid I don't have any sweet.'

'You bastard,' Jimmy thought.

He could almost see the bottle of Cyprus Cream on his parents' sideboard, ready for the Christmas visitors. He remembered the British sherry he had dispensed to guests at David's father's funeral.

'I said, I'm sorry, I don't have any sweet.'

'That's all right,' Jimmy said. 'I'll have a Moriles.'

Hawsley frowned and examined his selection of bottles.

'I'm afraid I don't seem to have . . . I don't think I've ever tasted it.'

Neither had Jimmy – but he did have a book on foreign wines.

'Never mind,' he said, cheerfully. 'If you've got a decent Amontillado that'll do almost as well.'

Hawsley was temporarily knocked off-balance, but he had recovered by the time he sat down.

'I've been following your progress, Bradley,' he said. 'Getting good reports on you. You're a smart lad.'

The last sentence slipped inelegantly from his lips. Was he being deliberately patronising, or had he seen too many of those grainy black and white films about Northern life? It didn't matter, Jimmy expected to eat a lot of shit on the way up.

'I'm a very smart lad,' he said. 'I'm the sort of lad the Party's going to need in a few years' time.'

For a second time, Hawsley was a little taken aback. The standard response, Jimmy guessed, was to become flustered under praise.

This interview was vitally important to Jimmy. Hawsley could make or break him with the University Conservative Association. Even so, he wasn't planning to ingratiate himself, to pour out all the stale old platitudes. That road led only to plodding mediocrity, and if he was going to rise, it would be as a shooting star.

'Why should the Party need you . . . er . . . James?' Hawsley asked.

'Call me Jimmy. For a start, the voters are changing. Macmillan won elections on the slogan, "You've never had it so good", but he was talking to a population that lived through the deprivations of war. Now the working class and the lower middle class are looking around and saying to themselves, "There's a lot of people who are having it better than we are." They want a bigger share.'

Hawsley sat silent, his fingers running up and down his cravat.

'Labour promised them a bigger share,' Jimmy continued, 'and that's why they won. And the Conservatives are going to have to do the same if *they* ever want to get back in.'

'Equal shares for all,' Hawsley said coldly. 'If you feel like that, I suggest you join the socialists.'

'I'm not talking about equal shares. I'm talking about bigger shares.'

'Increasing the size of the national pie?' Hawsley sneered.

'No; Labour tried that, technological socialism increasing the size of the gross national product – and it hasn't worked. And even if it had, the pie wouldn't have been big enough. It never is.'

Hawsley stood up and walked across to the window. He gazed out over Seahaven, the new executive estate close to the marina, the rows of back-to-back terraced houses huddled around the railway station.

'If you don't increase the size of the pie then you're robbing the rich to feed the poor,' he said. 'I thought you were a smart lad. I'm beginning to change my mind.'

He moved over to the door and rested his hand on the knob. In a second, he would turn it, and invite Jimmy to leave.

'You're being simplistic,' Jimmy said.

Hawsley's cheek muscles twitched. He was not used to being spoken to like this by anybody, not even people quite high up in the Party.

'Too simplistic, am I?' he asked.

He turned the knob and opened the door an inch or two.

'Yes,' Jimmy said. 'You're thinking in terms of bigger shares for whole classes: I mean bigger shares for individual members. The message we've got to get across is, "There's a lot out there that's up for grabs, and under the Conservatives there's nothing to stop you grabbing it".'

'Appeal to their greed,' Hawsley said.

Jimmy smiled ironically.

'Appeal to their meritocratic instincts. And it's no good having old gentlemen in tweed suits standing up at party conferences and saying that everybody has a fair chance. Nobody will believe them. You need lads like me to do it.'

Hawsley took his hand off the knob, and the door clicked gently to.

'Go on,' he said.

'The Party's started to realise it already. That's why we have *Mr* Heath now, instead of *Lord* Home. That doesn't mean we still haven't got a long way to go yet. I don't think that Heath will last.'

'You don't think what!'

It was almost sacrilege. Even though the Party had lost one election under him, Heath still looked strong. Besides, loyalty to the Leader was one of the cardinal virtues.

'Oh maybe he'll be around for a few more years,' Jimmy said. 'He might even win the next election. But if the Party's ever going to have another long run, like it did in the Fifties, they're going to have to ditch him. He's too close to the gentlemen politicians. He doesn't understand the voters.'

'Who does?' Hawsley asked.

'I don't know,' Jimmy admitted, 'but there'll be *somebody* in the party, a junior minister maybe, and when the time's right, he'll take over. Do you know George Bernard Shaw's *Arms and the Man*?'

'Certainly not,' Hawsley said. 'I read law.'

'There's a Swiss mercenary called Bluntschli in it. He's always one jump ahead of everyone else. And one of the other characters, an aristocrat, realises this and accuses him of having a "low, shop-keeping mind". That's what our next leader, whoever he is, will have – "a low, shop-keeping mind".'

Hawsley gave a wry grin.

'Another sherry, Jimmy?' he asked. 'I'll try to get a bottle of Moriles in for the next time you come round.'

He poured the drinks and sat down again.

'Are you really sincere, or just an opportunist?' he asked. 'Could you actually stand up at a Party Conference and make a speech about meritocracy and equality of opportunity, and really *believe* it?'

Jimmy smiled sardonically.

'If I ever get to stand there, at the Conservative Party Conference, and make a speech like that, I'll be the living proof myself. Won't I?'

He was in! He was sure of it. Now, finally, he could afford the luxury of dumping Ronnie. He could have sent her a note over the Christmas holiday telling her they were through, but that was not his way of doing things. He went straight from Hawsley's flat to hers.

Predictably, she made a scene, and equally predictably was outraged that he should ever consider breaking it off.

'How dare you!' she screamed. 'How could you after all I've done for you? I've introduced you to my friends, taken you to parties – I've even let you sleep with me.'

'I think you've got it the wrong way round,' Jimmy said. 'You've introduced me to your friends and taken me to parties *because* I was sleeping with you. Let's be honest, we've used *each other* and it's time to bring it to a close.'

Anger gave way to tears.

'What will I tell my friends,' she sobbed. 'They'll laugh at me.'

He wouldn't be surprised, not after the way she'd been flaunting him, rubbing their noses in the fact that she had him and they didn't.

'Tell them you got rid of me,' he said. 'I won't deny it.'

She stopped crying and looked at him.

'Oh, could I, Jimmy? Thank you!'

And why not? No one would believe her.

David was finding it more and more difficult to speak to club managers in Manchester and Liverpool. When he appeared, they retreated into their offices, and the bouncers told him firmly that they were not available. He was becoming a nuisance, yet he had to keep trying. Barry was pressing him constantly. When were they going to get a booking? What was the point of all that practice if they never played anywhere but a crummy church hall? Where were all the contacts that David had talked about when they had agreed to let him manage them?

He was almost on the point of despair when, ten days before Christmas, he got a call from The Swamp, one of the biggest venues in Manchester.

'That Harrison?' the manager growled.

He was very fat, David remembered, and had cigar ash all over his waistcoat. A man who couldn't have cared less about the music, as long as it sold tickets.

'Yes, David Harrison here,' – trying to sound as if he was answering from a plush office rather than a shed in a scrap-yard.

'This group of yours. Turban Decay, isn't it?'

'Urban Decay,' David said.

'Right. Urban Decay. They available to play a week tomorrow?'

David's hand started to tremble, but he managed to keep his voice from quivering.

'I'll just check.'

He counted slowly to thirty, then went back to the telephone.

'Yes, I think they are,' he said, 'or at least I think I can get them out of their other commit . . .'

The manager wasn't interested.

'Thing is, my opening group's let me down and I can't get anybody else so near Christmas. So your boys can do it?'

'Yes,' said David firmly.

'Oh – and didn't you say something about us not having to pay them?'

'Yes,' said David, abandoning his pretence that they were almost fully booked-up.

'OK, kid, don't let me down, now,' the manager said. 'And if your boys do it well, there might be other bookings,' he added, without conviction.

There was no time to include Urban Decay in the poster advertising, and The Swamp management wouldn't have bothered anyway. The audience was paying to see The Red Dogs, a band currently high in the charts – nobody gave a toss who the opening group were. So David did a little advertising of his own. His posters, expensively and hurriedly printed, were plastered all over Manchester, and featured Urban Decay as if they were the headliners.

On the night of the performance, the cellar club was packed. David stood by the bar, listening to the conversations around him.

'Who the fuck are Urban Decay?'

'Never heard of 'em till I saw the posters.'

'Is that them, setting up the equipment?'

'Search me.'

It wasn't the group. David had hired roadies for the night. It had cost, but everything had cost, and it would all be worth it in the end.

They were finally ready. The disc jockey got the signal and faded out the last record.

'And now, boys and girls, will you give a big hand for the first act of the evening – Urban Decay.'

There was little enthusiasm in his voice. He was used to introducing opening groups who only got a smattering of applause. That night was different. The group, dressed in shiny futuristic suits, walked onto the stage amid loud clapping and cheering.

'Bar-ry! Bar-ry! Bar-ry!'

The Norton fans. They sounded happy – and they should be. They were seeing their local heroes make good. Besides, they had travelled to the club for free, on double-decker buses David had hired from Norton Corporation. And the next day, when they handed in their used Swamp entrance tickets to Harrison Enterprises, they would get a complete refund.

The excitement spread from the two hundred and fifty supporters to the rest of the audience. This was obviously going to be something special.

Barry looked thin and helpless on stage, dwarfed by the equipment, intimidated by the bright lights that shone down on him. David prayed that it would go well, that he hadn't pushed the young vocalist too far, too soon. Barry waited until the applause had diminished but not died out, just as David had told him to. He walked over to the microphone and blew into it.

'This first song's one I wrote meself,' he said. His voice sound cracked and squeaky. 'An' it's about obeyin' the Highway Code.'

The opening chords cut their way through the air, and Barry began to sing.

Battlin' my Cadillac along the south-west freeway,
There's a red-neck, fat-slob cop who won't give me no leeway . . .

It was strong, raw and gutsy, and as the song progressed, Barry seemed to get bigger and bigger until he totally dominated the stage. At the end of the number the whole crowd went wild, and they were still screaming for more an hour and a half later, when Urban Decay finally left the stage to make way for The Red Dogs.

The Manager, complete with ash-stained waistcoat, was waiting for them by the door.

'Listen,' he said, 'I don't want to see you out of pocket on this. I'll give you a bit towards travel expenses. Say – thirty quid.'

'Thanks,' David said.

That wouldn't even cover the hire of the buses, but at least it was a start.

'An' . . . er . . . would your boys like to play here again?'

'As headliners?'

'Er . . . well . . . how about if they headline on weekdays and support on Saturdays?'

It was better than David had dared hope.

'I'm not sure,' he said. 'We've got a lot of . . .'

'I'll pay top rate,' the manager said. 'You'll not get a better offer anywhere in Manchester.'

David held out his hand.

'You've got a deal.'

*

On the way back, Barry sat in the front of the van next to David. The rest of the group sprawled in the back with the equipment, drinking Newcastle Brown, singing and shouting.

'Who's the fuckin' greatest?'

'We are!'

'What are we?'

'The fuckin' greatest!'

David drove slowly through the suburbs and onto the dual-carriageway. They had used the same route to get into Manchester, and it hadn't bothered him. But now they were returning home, duplicating the journey he and his father had made three years earlier.

He remembered it all. The strippers, the drink, the expression on his father's face, how the rubble felt against his legs as he sat in the back of the van, the whine of the engine . . . just as the engine was whining now.

He felt his foot press down on the accelerator, although he was sure that he hadn't willed it.

The other side of this bend was where it had happened.

'Look out, dad!'

The brakes screaming, the van slewing to one side, the jolt, the shattering glass, his father flying!

They rounded the bend and David saw the lorry! It was parked, not broken down as the other one had been, but it was on the same spot.

What had Jimmy told him at Paul's wedding? There was a black cloud hanging over him. He wasn't meant to be happy, at least not for long. He was happy at that moment. Ecstatically happy. So the only way to go from there was downhill.

He could see the lorry clearly now. Its canvas cover, its illuminated number plate, even the weight limited notice. He turned the wheel away from the crown of the road and pushed the accelerator right down to the floorboards.

'Who's the fuckin' greatest?' someone called.

'David is!' Barry shouted back.

David wrenched at the steering wheel and the van shot past the parked lorry. He slowed down a little. He didn't want to get booked for speeding.

He dropped the group off at their houses. Barry was the last. He opened his door to get out, then changed his mind.

'I mean it, David,' he said. 'You're the greatest. We'd never have done it without you.'

A car passed on the other side of the road, its headlights sweeping the van, and David saw that Barry was crying. They were not the tears of anger, frustration and ego he had seen before. They were soft drops of gratitude and affection. He put his arm around Barry's shoulder and pulled the thin young man's head to his strong chest.

'I didn't do anythin' really,' he said. 'It was all you. You're the one with the talent.'

'I'll never forget tonight as long as I live,' Barry sobbed, his voice muffled by David's jacket.

It was indeed a night to remember, the night Urban Decay took the first step on the road to the top, the night David and Barry became lovers.

Chapter Twelve

Paul saw the secretary enter by the side door and discreetly pass a note to the lecturer, but he didn't really pay it any mind. Rather than listen to the trite discourse on preparing teaching materials, he had been thinking back over the Christmas holidays.

David had seemed elated, happier than he had been for years. At first, Paul put it down to Urban Decay's appearance at The Swamp, but he was not so sure now. After all, Harrison Enterprises had known success before, and it had never affected David like that.

Jimmy was a mystery too. Paul imagined how *he* would have talked after his first term at university. He would probably have bored his mates senseless. But Jimmy seemed reluctant to say anything. Maybe he realised that he'd made a mistake in choosing non-academic, upper middle class Seahaven.

The lecturer read the note, finished his sentence on work cards, and then said, 'Do we have a Mr Wright, Paul Wright, with us today?'

Paul raised his hand, feeling like a schoolboy again.

'The Principal would like to see you, Mr Wright. Immediately.'

The air outside was extra-cold after the stuffy lecture room. The secretary ignored the 'Keep Off The Grass' signs and cut straight across the lawn, aiming directly for the Administration Building. She was moving so quickly that Paul had to take large strides to keep up with her.

'What's it all about?' he asked.

'I . . . there's been . . . the Principal had better tell you himself.'

Paul felt his stomach churn. It could only be illness – or death. His mother? His father? Maggie!

The secretary stepped back onto the paving stones and opened the door to Administration for him.

'Go straight up,' she said. 'He's waiting for you.'

It was one of those new, light, airy offices, all pale furniture and pot plants. The Principal, a grey-haired, harassed bureaucrat, jumped to his feet when Paul entered, walked rapidly round his desk, and put his hand awkwardly on the younger man's shoulder.

'We've just had a phone call from the Infirmary,' he said. 'Your wife was rushed in there about fifteen minutes ago. You'd better go immediately.'

There was a sudden pounding in Paul's head and the room swam before his eyes. He clutched the Principal's desk for support.

'What . . . how has she . . . is she?'

'I haven't got any details,' the Principal said, 'just that you were to get there as soon as you could.'

A car horn honked outside the window.

'I ordered a taxi,' the Principal said with evident relief. 'That will be it now.'

He rummaged in his pocket, found his wallet and pulled out a ten shilling note.

'Take this,' he said.

Paul shook his head like a man in a trance.

'No,' he said. 'No. It's all right. I've got money.'

He walked to the door slowly, heavily, as if his shoes were made of lead.

After the initial shock had worn off, Paul felt a great surge of energy course through his body. He tramped the sterilised corridors of the hospital, stopping occasionally and gazing at, without really seeing, notices on the importance of regular check-ups and eating a balanced diet. He could not sit still; it seemed very important to him that he keep covering these miles of tile-lined passageways.

'Your wife's had a fall,' the young doctor had told him, 'and it's induced premature contractions.'

'Is she going to be all right?' Paul demanded. 'Is the baby going to be all right?'

The doctor looked away.

'It was rather a *bad* fall,' he said carefully, 'especially for someone in an advanced state of pregnancy. We're doing all we can, of that I do assure you.'

We're doing all we can!

If Maggie died, or the baby died, he would be free. He could go to Oxford the following year – they would still have him. All the things he had dreamed of – punting bright young women from LMH down the Isis, engaging in passionate intellectual discussions right through the night – could all be his. No one would blame him. He had done his duty. If Maggie died, he could do as he wished. But what he wished most in the world was for Maggie and the child to live. A cloud of icy panic engulfed him, sending shudders down his entire body, making him want to scream until his lungs burst.

It was two hours before the nurse came to find him.

'The doctor will see you now,' she said.

Her face showed concern, but he couldn't tell whether it was for him – bedraggled and half-mad – or for Maggie.

'Is she . . . does she . . .'

'The doctor will explain it all,' the nurse said crisply.

She took his arm and led him back down the corridor.

Now the moment had come, he wanted to turn and run, keep on running. So that he need never find out the truth, need never learn what had gone on in the operating theatre.

He could see it all in his mind's eye. The swabs, the forceps, the bandages – the bright cutting instruments, their shiny surfaces sparkling under the dazzling ceiling lights, their blades thin and sharp, slicing through Maggie's flesh and muscle as a bread knife slices through a loaf.

He didn't run. Instead he allowed himself to be shepherded into one of the examination rooms. It was a different doctor this time, an older one. He was sitting on the couch, his head in his hands, his jaw slack, his eyes drooping. Paul knew instinctively that this was the one who had done it. He was wearing a clean white coat, but only minutes earlier he would have been dressed in a green gown – except for the crimson spots, except where it was obscenely stained with Maggie's blood. And he looked totally defeated, absorbed in the tight cocoon of his own failure.

The doctor became aware of his presence and lifted his head.

'Mr Wright?'

'I don't want to know!' a voice screamed, loudly, overpowering-ly, in Paul's head. 'If she's dead I don't want to know. You don't have to tell me!'

The doctor smiled tiredly and with all-engulfing joy Paul realised that what he had taken for defeat was merely exhaustion.

'Your wife's a little weak at the moment, but she's going to be all right.'

'And the baby?'

'He's under-weight – you'd expect that with him being prema-ture – and we'd like to keep him in for a couple of days, but he should be fine too.'

Paul flung his arms around the doctor and hugged him. He

realised what he was doing, moved rapidly backwards and stood shifting from one foot to the other, offending arms drooping loosely at his sides. The doctor smiled again, to show that he understood.

'Thank you, doctor,' Paul said. 'When can I see her?'

'Not for hours yet,' the doctor replied. 'If I were you, I'd go home and have a rest. You look like you could use one.'

Paul couldn't go home. He walked the town; down to the market, along the riverside to Blackthorne's Engineering, round the gasworks and up to the bus station. Only the park escaped his restless feet. He went back to the hospital every hour. Finally, when it had already gone dark outside, and the hospital lights were making great yellow patches on the lawn, he was allowed to visit Maggie.

Her face was drained of its colour, her eyes were hollow. She smiled bravely when she saw Paul and held out a shaking hand for him to hold.

'I told you it was going to be a boy,' she said.

Paul put his palm on her forehead. It felt like it was on fire.

'Are you pleased with me?' she asked.

'I'm very, very proud of you. I think you're wonderful.'

Her face clouded over and her lips trembled as she spoke again.

'Paul,' she said, 'I've talked to the doctor. We can't . . . have any more . . . children. I'm so sorry, luv.'

He stroked her neck softly.

'It doesn't matter,' he said softly, reassuringly. 'We've got our son. What do we want any more for?'

When it was time to leave Maggie to her rest, the nurse took Paul to see the child that she had borne. He was not allowed into the room. He was positioned next to a window nearly as big as the ones in shop-fronts. Inside, another nurse bent over a cot and held a tiny bundle up – to see if the customer wanted to buy. He did! He did!

The baby seemed so incredibly small and vulnerable. It was nearly bald and its head, big for the size of its body, was red and wrinkled, like a huge blood orange. Paul examined the face carefully, trying to see in the eyes, the nose, some resemblance to himself. Or Jimmy. Or David. But the baby just looked like a baby.

He felt a strange sensation; a contraction of the muscle around the heart, a slight tightening in the throat. Almost as if the infant were sending out telepathic messages to him, controlling his emotions. He waved at the baby, and the nurse picked up its tiny arm and made a waving gesture back.

And that was when Paul saw it!

After he left the hospital, he walked around the town again. By now his feet were aching and every step was agony, but he found the physical pain a blessed release. His emotions had been racked in a way he had never imagined possible. He still didn't love Maggie, he was sure of that, but the thought of life without her had been terrible.

He and Maggie would have no more children. This one *had* to be his! Yet he was far from sure that it was. He had seen the baby through a sheet of plate glass for perhaps half a minute. It had looked like no one he knew. Then there had been that moment when the nurse had waved its arm, and its head had been pointed in his direction. The child had seemed to look straight at him, and smile. He told himself he was being foolish, that infants only a few hours old didn't do that. Yet he had only to close his eyes to see the smile again, a smile of confidence and self-assurance that belonged exclusively to Jimmy.

In early February, there was a great deal of moving. Maggie came out of hospital and she, Paul and the baby – whom she had insisted on naming after her husband – settled into a rented house at the other end of the village. Jimmy left the hall of residence for the more luxurious surroundings of his new girl friend's flat. He was pleased with his choice. Even though Rosemary was hardly distinguishable in her outlook from dumpy little Ronnie, she was far more attractive – and had much better connections.

It was David who excited most comment. He had actually *bought* a house the previous autumn, and all through the winter months the neighbours watched with raised eyebrows as workmen knocked down walls, installed pipes and enlarged windows.

'There's no sense in it. It was a perfectly good house before.'

'He's havin' work done on his mother's as well.'

'Eee, the lad must be up to his neck in debt.'

David knew what he was doing, and what he wanted. His house was an act of creation. All the hours spent thinking and planning in those woodwork lessons so long ago were now realised in his own little palace.

Urban Decay were doing well. In a little over two months, they had become a phenomenon on the Manchester scene, drawing bigger crowds than some star groups from outside. Yet they were not moving fast enough for Barry. He had come a long way since the time when his main ambition had been to get a regular booking at one of the Norton clubs. And he deserved better, David admitted. Barry and his reputation had grown apace. His stage act had always been good, but he had developed into the most mesmerizing performer David had ever seen. He played his guitar with such an intensity and ferocity that it was almost possible to imagine blood dripping from his fingers.

Things were made worse by the fact that in February a Manchester group, Dave Dee, Dozy, Beaky, Mick and Tich, were actually Number One in the Hit Parade. If them, why not us, Barry seemed to demand with every look and gesture. Because Dave Dee had worked the Manchester club circuit for a long time, building up a name for himself; because the kind of soft pop that he played was more instantly accessible than the raunchy style of Urban Decay; because these things took time. Because . . . because . . . because, David explained. Why? why? why? Barry demanded.

There was no such conflict in his personal life. Barry, who was so aggressive and demanding as an artist, was gentle and giving as a lover. The hours they spent together, at first in the back of the van parked in a discreet woodland clearing and later in the new house, were the happiest of David's life. He had heard jokes and comments about homosexuals. He had even made them himself. Cock-suckers! Bum-boys! It wasn't like that at all. Sometimes David found the experience of making love so beautiful that he cried when it was over. His life was centred on Barry, and if Barry wanted to be a success, David would see to it that it happened. So in March, shortly after Barry finally agreed to move in with him, David packed his bags and went down to London in search of fresh opportunities.

It was like banging his head against a brick wall. The record companies simply didn't want to know. David had reasonably good tapes of the group's performances now, but even these could not capture the excitement of Barry's guitar work and vocals. Yet it was impossible to persuade any of the record company executives to travel up to Manchester to catch the act.

'Every week, son,' said one producer who at least took the time to talk to him, 'every week we get hundreds of managers convinced they've got the hottest thing since The Beatles. And most of them don't even belong on the stage at all! Take my tip and stick to what you know they can do. There's a good living to be made out of the clubs.'

Money was not the main consideration for David. He was

making enough out of the scrap-yard and he was hardly there now – O'Malley was handling everything. Money didn't matter to Barry either. He wanted acclaim, and he was looking to David to get it for him.

David made one last attempt. He took a minor executive from a minor label out to one of the smoother pubs, and plied him with drinks. Over the course of two hours, the man managed to knock back nine gin and tonics.

'I'll do my besht for you,' he said at the door on his way out. 'I'll get your little group – whashit called? Bourbon Sway? – I'll get them a contract just as shoon as there's a shpace in the catalogue.'

David loaded him into a taxi and went gloomily back to the bar for another drink. He was just ordering when he felt a tap on his shoulder. He swung round and found himself looking at a fat, greasy man in his late forties with a bulbous nose and a five o'clock shadow. He had bad breath, detectable even at a distance, and smelt heavily of cologne.

'I'm sorry,' the man said, 'but I couldn't help overhearing your conversation.' His voice was smooth and syrupy. 'The problem is that no one is interested in what's happening in the North any more. It's what goes on down here in the Smoke that matters. Now if your group could make a few appearances in a big London club, or perhaps do a spot on one of the London television programmes, well, they would have a much better chance of getting a record contract.'

'And how would they manage that?' David asked.

The fat man smiled. His bad breath came from bad teeth, a jagged, rotting picket fence suspended above a puffy purple lip.

'They'd have to know someone like me,' he said. 'I'm at Metropolitan TV. We've got a half hour programme called *Pop Spot* goes out every Thursday night at half past six, just when most people are eating.'

The breath, worse when he laughed, was like a mixture of bad eggs and sour cider.

'Let's have another drink,' the man said, signalling to the barman, 'and you can tell me all about this group of yours.'

David told him the whole story, how he had met them, how the act had changed, the impact they were making in Manchester.

'Very interesting,' the man said when David had finished. 'Yes, it should be possible to get them on the show.'

'Without even hearing them?' David asked, astonished.

The man leaned closer to David.

'I like the look of you,' he said. 'You're a young man who knows about music. If you say they're good, I'll take your word for it.'

He reached over and patted David's thigh. But it wasn't just a pat, his stubby fingers kneaded and massaged, caressed and fondled. It was all David could do not to vomit.

'Look,' the fat man said. 'This is no place to talk about business. Let's go somewhere more conducive.'

The fat man's name was Archie – 'like the ventriloquist's dummy, if you're old enough to remember him!' He took David to a succession of pubs and private drinking clubs, each one a little rougher, each one a little camper. Archie ran into chums everywhere – a simpering actor David remembered playing a macho role in a TV series; a scriptwriter who said he had just finished a wonderful play about two beautiful young men, though he doubted if the Great Unwashed were ready for it; a freelance producer with pink-rinsed hair who reminded Archie that they must get together sometime and discuss his exciting new project.

At midnight, Archie suggested that he and David go back to his flat for a nightcap. David had been expecting it all evening, but had not known how he would react. Now, when it came to the crunch, he forced himself to go through with it. He could not return to Norton without something to show for his efforts. Barry would not understand failure.

Archie had an attack of wind in the taxi, and burped and farted most of the way back to St John's Wood.

'Too much beer,' he explained by way of apology. 'Can't take it like I used to.'

David paid off the cabbie.

'Fakin' queers,' the driver said disgustedly, pocketing his tip without thanks. 'I fakin' hate them. Why don't you find yourself a nice girl?'

Even at the doorstep, as Archie was fiddling with his keys, David told himself that it was not too late. He could walk away – go back home empty-handed.

They both knew what they were there for, so the preliminaries didn't take long. When Archie kissed him, David thought he would faint. The breath was actually not as bad close to, but instead there was Archie's slimy tongue – darting, probing the corners of David's mouth. They undressed. Archie was all flab from his drooping breasts to his convex stomach. His legs were thin, his knees were knobbly and blue veins stood out like a map of the Underground.

As David lay on his stomach, his face buried in the pillow, with

Archie thrusting away on top of him, he tried to blank the other man out of his mind and imagine that it was Barry instead.

'Oh Barry, Barry, my love,' he thought. 'The things I do for you.'

It took three more trips to London to finalize the details of the television programme, and each time David spent the night at Archie's flat. It never got any better.

'How'd you manage it?' Barry asked when David told him about the *Pop Spot* booking.

'Luck really,' David lied. 'Plus the fact that the producer could recognise good music when he heard it.'

Barry was not taking it as he'd expected. The young man was excited enough, yet there was something missing. David thought back to the night of Urban Decay's first appearance. How had that been different? It was the way Barry looked at him, he decided. That night, there had been admiration in his eyes that bordered on hero worship. Now, the eyes were questioning, probing, as if he suspected that David had somehow cheapened himself in order to pull it off. Barry must never find out about Archie.

It was natural that the hero worship should fade, David told himself. Barry was growing, not just as an artist, but also physically. He had added two inches to his height since they met, and his muscles were becoming rounder and harder. As Barry got older, their relationship was bound to change. And that was a good thing. They would become equals, and out of that equality would grow an even deeper and more intense love.

He closed his eyes to the fact that Barry took everything he did for him for granted. He hid from himself the knowledge that Barry was regarding him not only with less awe, but with less respect.

Yet if respect decreased, Barry's possessiveness grew and grew. It reached a head when Jimmy came home for Easter, and the gang, as usual, arranged to go out for a drink. Barry wanted to go with them and was furious when David told him he couldn't.

They were sitting in the kitchen of David's new home – their new home. They faced each other across the table, David tense and concerned, Barry aggressive, his elbows planted firmly on the formica top.

'Don't you love me?' Barry demanded.

'Of course I do,' David protested. 'It's just that the three of us have always knocked around together. Paul doesn't take his missus with him, and she doesn't seem to mind. We're special friends, that's all.'

'Do you love *them?*' Barry asked, very angry now.

David wouldn't lie.

'Yes,' he said. 'I do. I love them deeply, nearly as much as I love you. But it's a different sort of love. I don't want to *make* love to them.'

'You mean you've got too much respect for them to want to stick your prick up their arses!' Barry screamed.

David felt as if he had been hit with a hammer. How could Barry talk like this? Their love-making was a world apart from the sordid little incidents with Archie. It was beautiful – pure.

'Barry,' he said, 'you don't understand. It's not . . .'

The young vocalist was already on his feet. He kicked his stool over and as he slammed the door angrily behind him, it rolled round the kitchen floor.

In early May, they had the recording session for *Pop Spot* and David and the group travelled down to London. It was a great success, as David had known it would be. Even in the fairly antiseptic atmosphere of a studio, the power and raw energy of Urban Decay came across.

Archie was waiting for him outside, holding on to a No Parking sign as if he could fall down without its support. His thinning hair was clean and fluffy and he was wearing a new suit. The sky above him was blue and the sun shone brightly on his puffy features. It only made him look more pathetic. People like him should never go out in the day time, David thought. They belonged in dark, seedy clubs under purple neon lighting.

'Did the recording go well?' Archie asked, his voice cracking as he spoke.

'Yes, fine.' David glanced at his watch. The group would be out in a minute, and he didn't want Barry to see him with this *thing*. 'Look, Archie, I've got to . . .'

'I suppose that's it, then,' Archie said. 'You've got what you wanted. There'll be no more visits to my flat.'

The tone of reproach in his voice made David angry.

'We both got what we wanted,' he said, 'so don't go tryin' to make me feel guilty.'

He saw tears in Archie's eyes and softened.

'I'm sorry, Archie,' he said. 'I didn't mean . . .'

'Don't say any more,' Archie interrupted. 'You're right. We *both* got what we wanted. I should have kept away from the studio today.' He looked down at his shoes and then up at David again. 'I wanted to see you just once more.'

He put his hand on David's shoulder. For the first time in their relationship, there was nothing sexual in the contact. Instead, the touch emanated compassion.

'You made me very happy for a while, David,' he said. 'I hope that when you get to my age someone will come along and do the same for you. Because one day, you *will* be like me – a lonely old queen.'

And he turned and walked away.

Chapter Thirteen

The interview had gone so beautifully that Jimmy splashed out on a taxi back to the university. He paid off the driver and stood for a moment, his back to the sea, looking at the campus.

It was incredible how far he'd come in a few short months. He would be elected Chairman of the Conservative Association in his third year. There was no doubt about that. And through Hawsley, he'd got to know a number of influential members of the Chamber of Commerce, all of whom had been impressed by his 'sensible' attitude. It was one of these businessmen who'd just offered him work over the long vac – a job which would not only pay more than most students could hope to earn, but would make him invaluable contacts as well.

There was a gap in the traffic and Jimmy sprinted across the road. He waved at the porter in the gate house. The man raised his own hand in return, and his fingers almost touched the peak of his cap, making the gesture less of a wave and more of a salute.

His domestic arrangements were very satisfactory too, Jimmy thought, as he strolled up the path. The flat he was living in with Rosemary belonged to her 'Daddy', so it was expensively furnished and rent-free. The girl herself had a lot to recommend her. She was inventive and uninhibited in bed, and had taken him home for a couple of weekends and introduced him to the county set.

Yes, Rosemary had been a very good choice. He saw no reason to trade her in for a while.

Everything was going as it should, the engine of his ambition was steaming smoothly along the rails and the first station was in sight.

And then he saw the girl.

She was sitting on the grass, under an oak tree, reading a book. The heavy branches, covered with bright green leaves, bent low, seeming to form a bower just for her. Shafts of sunlight highlighted her lustrous black hair and cast delicate shadows on her pale skin and long, aristocratic nose. She looked Italian – not full-blown like Sophia Loren, more the enigmatic Madonna of a

Renaissance painting. She was wearing a brown skirt and her legs, bent at the knee, were long and slender. There was just a hint, under her white peasant blouse, of round, firm breasts. She was beautiful, marvellous, and Jimmy wondered how he had managed to be there for nearly a year without at least sensing her presence.

He walked over, and sat down on the grass beside her. She didn't look up. All his opening lines, smoothly polished and refined, disappeared from his head – or else seemed too cheap and flashy.

'Hello!' he said, finally.

She raised her head, gave him an absent-minded smile, and returned to her reading.

More time passed. He must either speak again or walk away.

'What are you reading?' he asked.

He sounded adolescent, almost stuttering. He was not in control of the situation. It had been a long time since that had happened. She didn't answer. Was she ignoring him, he asked himself, or was she so absorbed in her book that she didn't notice?

He steeled himself to speak again.

'I . . . er . . . said, what are you reading?'

This time his voice must have penetrated.

'Sorry?'

'What are you reading?' he asked for a third time.

Instead of answering directly, she read aloud.

> *Thou liknest eek wommenes love to helle*
> *To bareyne lond, ther water may nat dwelle*
> *Thou liknest it also to wilde fyr*
> *The moore it brenneth, the moore it hath desir*
> *To consume every thyng that brent wole be.*

He didn't understand half the words, but was entranced by the sensuous way she rolled them around her mouth.

'Chaucer?'

'Yes.'

She seemed puzzled that he had ever needed to ask.

Many of the girls he knew were studying English, it was one of the 'in' subjects. They'd probably read Chaucer too – but not for *pleasure* and not with such total concentration.

In a second, she would return to her book, and he would lose her. He had to think of something else to say.

'Do you think poetry has any relevance in the modern world?' he asked.

Oh God, that sounded awful, pseud, the intellectual's equivalent of 'Haven't I seen you somewhere before?'

She chose to take the question seriously.

'All art has,' she said. 'Look at all this,' she swept her arm round to indicate the campus, its futuristic library, the almost structurally-impossible Arts Building. 'It's just camouflage, an attempt to run away from ourselves. True art strips away all pretence, smashes through the shield of civilised veneer and shows us our real selves – exposed, naked.'

Exposed. Naked.

'Read me some more,' Jimmy said.

She read for nearly an hour, and he got the impression that she'd have gone on reading even if he'd left. It was not so much that she liked the sound of her own voice as that she loved the sounds her voice could make. And so did he.

'Would you like a cup of coffee?' he asked when she had finished. 'I think you've earned it.'

'Yes,' she said.

She closed her book, tucked it under her arm, and stood up. Jimmy marvelled at the grace of her movements and the lines of her body.

The cafeteria was free of whimsy. There were no bamboo pole dividers or fisherman's nets hanging from the ceiling. Instead it had the minimalist decor of the new, clean technological Britain – white walls, stainless-steel counter, easy-wipe formica tables. Jimmy bought the coffees, and he and the girl sat down.

She told him her name was Claire and that her father farmed some land in Hampshire. Any other girl in his set would have embellished the subjects, telling him about the house, the acreage, her friends, her horse . . . Claire spoke in short, unadorned sentences, conveying information rather than a self-image. She was not curt, but she was certainly economical.

'So what do we talk about now?' Jimmy wondered as he sipped his coffee.

There was a poster on the wall just behind Claire's shoulder, advertising a new production by the Seahaven Theatre Company.

'I've got two tickets for *Othello* tomorrow night,' he said. 'I was going with my friend . . . er . . . Paul, only he can't make it. It would be a shame to waste the ticket. Would you like to come with me?'

'I can't.'

'Does that really mean you don't want to?' he asked, disappointedly.

'No. If I'd meant that, I would have said it. I can't. I'm going to a lecture.'

'Wait a minute,' Jimmy said, slapping his forehead. 'I've got my dates confused. I keep thinking today's Wednesday, and it's only Tuesday. It's Thursday night I've got the tickets for. Are you free then?'

She smiled a small quizzical smile, hardly moving her lips yet charging her face with light and energy.

'Are you sure you've got it right this time?' she asked. 'Thursday?'

'Thursday,' Jimmy said. 'Definitely Thursday.'

She nodded.

'All right.'

As soon as he had left her, Jimmy set off down to the theatre to buy the tickets. He ran. He had never run for a woman before.

Later that night, as he and Rosemary sat in their flat, drinking wine and getting gently drunk, he mentioned, casually, that he had met a girl called Claire.

'Not Claire Peel?' Rosemary said. 'Long black hair, big nose, looks like a gypsy?'

'I think we're talking about the same girl.'

'What did you make of her?'

There was no hint of suspicion or jealousy in her voice. Claire Peel wasn't a threat – she wasn't Jimmy's type.

'She was . . . interesting,' Jimmy said carefully.

'Weird would be closer to the mark,' Rosemary said offhandedly. 'I was at school with her, you know.' She laughed at an old memory. 'You should have seen her on the hockey pitch. I had to play her in my team once. Pathetic – she hardly knew one end of the stick from the other.'

'Were her friends the same?'

'Didn't have any. Pretty anti-social really. Spent all her time reading. Poetry usually! Oh, and painting – the strangest things you've ever seen, little green men all lined up. That kind of rubbish.'

'Is she interested in politics?' Jimmy asked.

'Interested in politics! I bet she doesn't even know who Mr Heath is!'

There was no greater condemnation than that.

*

The performance was due to begin at eight and they had agreed to meet at seven thirty. Jimmy turned up at ten past, the tickets in the pocket of his best jacket, a box of Swiss chocolates in his hand. He found it hard to stand still, and prowled from one end of the frontage to the other. By half past seven, the foyer was beginning to fill up. At twenty to eight, he started to worry. By five to eight, he was frantic. She had stood him up! It was a new experience – but it wasn't his pride that was hurt.

At one minute to eight, just after he had angrily stuffed the chocolates into the bus-stop bin, just before he set off to get blind drunk, she turned up. She was wearing a different blouse, a lush green one like the oak leaves, but she had the same skirt on as the last time he'd seen her. She wasn't wearing any make-up either.

'Sorry,' she said. 'Painting. Didn't notice the time.'

They were shown to their seats just as the curtain went up.

Jimmy studied the action carefully, aware that Claire would want to talk about it later and wishing to make some intelligent comments himself. To his surprise, he found that he enjoyed it. He admired the style and confidence with which Othello – a black, an outsider – stood before the Senate of Venice and defended his right to marry Brabantio's daughter Desdemona. He had grudging respect too for Iago, the arch-plotter, as he gradually turned Othello's mind against his wife, choosing exactly the right words to summon up gross images of her infidelity. It would be hard to prove the adultery, he explained, even if they had been 'as pride as goats, as hot as monkeys, As salt as wolves in pride.'

Slowly the poison began to work. Othello, the proud general, gave way to jealousy – the green-eyed monster. He ranted and raved. He foamed at the mouth and threw epileptic fits. He called his wife 'a cunning whore'. He screamed 'Goats and monkeys!' in the face of the Venetian ambassador. He killed his wife, strangling her as she protested her innocence. And finally, when he learned that she had been true to him, he stabbed himself, killing the beast inside him which had taken possession of his soul.

The pub across the road had framed playbills and signed photographs of visiting thespians on the walls. It was packed with theatre-goers. Jimmy fought his way to the bar, bought the drinks, and carried them back in triumph to Claire, who was guarding a small, round table with a beaten metal top.

'Did you enjoy it?' he asked.

'I always do. I like to see Othello change.'

He wondered if he had misunderstood the play. It was a tragedy. The noble Moor, consumed by jealousy, falling from his high eminence and becoming little more than an animal.

'You *like* it?'

'Yes,' Claire said. 'He's so artificial at the start, always there with the carefully balanced phrases. He's nothing but an actor playing at being a general. Later, all that melts away.'

'But he's in agony,' Jimmy said.

'At least he knows he's alive. It doesn't really matter *what* you feel, as long as you really feel *something*.'

She was a strange girl, Jimmy thought, and not only in her views. It was not vanity on his part to think that he was attractive. Whatever their age, whatever their background, every woman he met showed some degree of interest in him. Yet this one, on whom he was exercising his charm and scx appeal to the full, seemed totally unaware of his maleness.

When he went to the toilet, he took the opportunity to examine himself in the mirror, just to check that he hadn't suddenly grown ugly and repulsive. The face that confronted him was the one he'd expected. The blond hair, the clear blue eyes, the long straight nose and sensual mouth. He turned so that he could examine his figure. Tall and slim, elegant but well-muscled from his market portering. So what was wrong with him?

He walked her back to her flat. She took his arm, but did not use it as an excuse to get close to him. Nor did she fake a stumble so that he would have to throw his arms around her. She wasn't playing hard to get – she wasn't holding out any promise at all.

It was a mild night. A gentle breeze was blowing in off the sea, carrying with it the smell of tangy salt; somewhere a nightingale was singing. If he had been with any other girl, he would have said it was a waste of such a lovely evening not to go for a stroll in the park. Once there, he'd have led her into the trees, kissed her and gently lowered her to the ground, as he'd seen Paul's father do, all those years ago.

He didn't dare risk that with Claire. He had to play it softly, carefully, and hope that eventually she would come to feel for him what he already felt for her.

When they reached her front door, she kissed him chastely on both cheeks.

'Did you really enjoy yourself?' he asked.

'Yes, it was good.'

She didn't invite him up for a nightcap and was on the point of going in and closing the door behind her when Jimmy said, 'Can I see you again?'

She stood on the doorstep, her face made paler by the yellow moon, her forehead puckered in thought.

'Oh God,' Jimmy prayed, 'please make her say yes.'

'Mahler concert. Some time next week. In the Town Hall. Can you get tickets?'

'I'll go down tomorrow.'

'Right. See you then.'

She stopped inside and the door clicked behind her. Jimmy stayed perfectly still, listening to her footsteps as she climbed the stairs.

He walked back to Rosemary's flat feeling elated and yet knowing that he had no reason to be. Rosemary was curled up in a chair, a bottle of wine in the crook of her arm, watching the large colour television.

'Where've you been?' she asked.

She didn't usually question his movements; he was too good a catch to scare off – although he suspected that if they ever married she would soon try to impose a very different regime.

'I went to the theatre.'

She looked at him strangely, squinting.

'It must show,' he thought. 'It must be written all over my face.'

'Did you have a good time?' she asked.

'Yes, I enjoyed it.'

'And who did you go with?'

He knew she meant to sound light and casual, but it came out as harsh and inquisitorial. He could have lied and she would have believed him. She *wanted* to believe that everything was all right between them. He said nothing for a while, but looked around the flat: luxury that his mother, for all her petite bourgeoisie aspirations, would never have dreamed of.

'I was with Claire,' he said.

'Claire Peel?'

Although he had planned none of this beforehand, he knew what he needed to do now.

'I'll start looking for a flat tomorrow,' he said. 'As long as I'm here, I'll pay rent. And I'll sleep on the couch.'

Rosemary's eyes were wide with disbelief.

'Because of Claire!'

He found it incredible himself, but it was true. Claire was totally unsuited to play a part in the life he had mapped out for himself, but he didn't give a damn. If love had not derailed the engine of his ambition, it had at least diverted it into a siding.

Chapter Fourteen

There were days when Paul loved the baby so much that he was almost afraid to look at it in case the intensity of his gaze should burn a hole in the little pink head. But sometimes another mood would descend upon him, seeping into his bones and casting a dark shadow over his soul. Then he would see the child through cold objective eyes – like a butcher appraising a side of beef. As he rocked the infant in its pram, he would move first to one side and then to the other, examining the face in sun and shadow, looking to see if the nose had any of David's bluntness, if the eyes held a suggestion of Jimmy's quick brain. But the baby was just a baby. His conviction that first day at the infirmary that it was definitely Jimmy's gradually disappeared, leaving in its place a giant question mark.

As the child grew, it seemed to sense when Paul was in one of his clinical moods, and would gurgle or smile or make some other cute baby gesture which would melt the hardness in the watcher's heart and cause him to pick up the tiny bundle and hold it close.

David and Jimmy never visited the house before the baby was born, but after the christening it was understood, although never directly stated, that Maggie would allow them to come and see their godson. It was hard for her at first. Her skin crawled when they were near her, as if she could feel them touching her, as if she were naked in their presence and their eyes were running hungrily over her body. David sensed the feeling, and tried to keep as far away from her as possible. Jimmy seemed to be oblivious: he chatted and made jokes, turning on his charm with her as he did with every other woman he met.

In time, it all ceased to bother her. Jimmy and David became just two childhood friends of her husband's – one solid, taciturn and boring, the other flighty and superficial – whom she tolerated for Paul's sake. The park was just a bad nightmare which had had at least one good consequence – she had married a boy who had rapidly become a man; a man, moreover, who worked hard, treated her kindly and satisfied her in bed – a man she could love and respect.

For Paul too, the memory of the park had somewhat faded. There were occasions now, during their love-making, when he could afford to let himself relax, wipe thoughts of abstract subjects out of his mind, and concentrate on the sensation of being with his wife, being *in* his wife. And afterwards, as his head lay between her breasts, made more voluptuous by her pregnancy, he told himself that though Maggie was far from the ideal intellectual soul mate, and though he did not love her, he was lucky to have her.

If only he could have been sure about the baby!

He watched his friends playing with the child like indulgent uncles, rattling the plastic beads on the front of its pram, or chucking it under the chin – yet never looking at it closely.

'They don't want to see anything that reminds them of themselves,' Paul thought.

And neither did he. The greatest fear of Paul's life was that if it became clear that the baby was not his, his feelings towards one of his friends would turn to hatred.

Oh why, when they all wanted the same thing, couldn't it be true!

Paul had known of Ben Moore from the moment he first become interested in politics. The old man had been a town councillor since the war and had become the leader of the minority Labour Group in 1958. He looked like an evangelist. His wrinkled skin was almost as brown as a gypsy's. His long white hair crowned a face dominated by a large hooked nose and imposing eyes.

Back in the early halcyon days of the first Wilson administration, Paul had seen Moore as an anachronism, an old-style hard-liner who refused to see that the new prosperity would bring about Socialism far more efficiently than class warfare could. If anyone was going to break the Conservative hold on Norton, woo the farmers and engineering workers to the socialist cause, it would be a technologist, not a prophet.

But as the Sixties progressed, Paul's faith began to waver. Labour froze wages, raised purchase tax and re-introduced prescription charges. Public expenditure was reduced, the housing programme slashed back. The Prime Minister gave public support to American policy in Vietnam and seemed more interested in keeping the International Monetary Fund happy than helping the people who had put him in power. And Paul began to feel that the middle ground was not the way, that compromise led to betrayal.

He was introduced to Moore at a Labour Party Social, a drab seedy affair held in a wooden hut that had been a 'temporary' structure for at least twenty years. They talked politics energetically and enthusiastically for over an hour, then Moore said, 'It's not against your political principles to refuse a good single malt when it's offered to you, is it?'

'Don't think so,' Paul replied, 'but I've never had the chance to find out.'

'Right,' Moore said. 'I think I've done me duty here. Let's bugger off. I can't hear meself think with all this noise.'

He took Paul back to his home, an old but well-maintained terraced house.

'We'll use the front room,' he said, 'since you're a grammar school boy.'

It was different from any working class parlour that Paul had ever been in. Every available inch of wall space had a bookcase fixed to it, and every bookcase was crammed with political and economic texts.

'They were bloody hard goin',' Moore said, flicking his thumb in the direction of the books. 'All of 'em. I never had much education. Worked on the salt pans from the time I was twelve until I retired. 'Cept for me holiday in Spain.'

He poured two generous measures of malt. Paul sipped his cautiously and felt it burn the back of his throat.

'Holiday in Spain?' he gasped.

'The Spanish Civil War, lad. By, but it was a grand time to be alive.'

'Did you do much fighting?'

Moore shook his head.

'Too bloody old, even then. They kicked me out of the International Brigade and lent me to the Republicans as a night watchman. Well, I suppose it freed some bugger who *could* be of use in the fightin'.'

It was only after Ben's death that Paul, as his executor, first saw the medal awarded to the old man for the part he played in the Siege of Madrid. Ben had acted as a messenger in the notorious Shell Alley, and every day for nearly two years had run the gauntlet of Franco's bombardments.

'Anyway, let's not dwell on the past,' Moore continued. 'What about the future? Do you see any hope?'

'Not as long as we try to out-capitalist the capitalists,' Paul said.

'Not until we've really shaken the tree and made some of the fruit reach the bottom.'

'Got a way with words, haven't you, son,' Moore said, filling up his glass. 'You're bloody right, an' all.'

Because Ben was a widower, living on his own, Paul got into the habit of inviting him home for tea. Maggie liked the old man enormously. She knew nothing about politics and half the time she didn't even understand what they were talking about, but she saw a kindness and warmth in Moore to which she responded.

The relationship became stronger and stronger. Paul was in many ways what Moore would liked to have been: educated, intelligent and highly articulate. And Ben was what Paul wanted to become, a dedicated socialist who, after a lifetime of fighting, still had spirit. They had much to learn from each other, and to give in return. Age made no difference, and Ben was soon Paul's closest friend outside the gang.

But in those first few moments, during all their talks, Paul never even got an inkling of the plans Moore had for him.

The wallpaper was heavily embossed, the lighting subdued. The tables seemed further apart than was strictly necessary, and David would never have believed that one restaurant could employ so many waiters.

'How's it going, Michael?' the bald-headed, smooth-skinned man sitting opposite him called across the room. To David, he said, 'He comes here quite a lot. Not many people know that.'

He chuckled and drew on his thick cigar. David had been impressed by the flow of celebrities passing through the restaurant, but he knew, too, that Zeb Goldsmith had taken him there for precisely that purpose. He was suspicious of everything the other man said or did. Big London impresarios did not call managers of new groups unless it was to their own advantage, and David hadn't yet worked out what Goldsmith wanted. That, he told himself, was why he had slipped quietly away on his own, without mentioning anything to Barry.

It wasn't until the coffees and brandies arrived that Goldsmith's talk became anything more than show business gossip.

'Caught your boys on the box last week,' he said. 'Very impressive. How's the record coming along?'

David looked startled. Goldsmith grinned.

'There's not much I don't know. You've been signed up by

Alpha, you've already cut the track, and they're releasing it next Friday. And do you know what will happen to it?'

'No, Mr Goldsmith.'

'Please, David, call me Zeb.' He lit another cigar. The rings on his fingers and gold bracelet on his thick wrist twinkled in the flame. 'The record will sink without trace. You see, the reason Alpha have done everything so quickly is they're hoping people will buy it on the strength of one TV appearance. They won't. Do you know how many records are released every week and simply die?'

David didn't. Goldsmith told him. It was a depressing figure.

'What your group needs is national exposure,' he continued.

There was always one more hurdle. When the group was well-known in Manchester, it was important that they should make an appearance in London. Now they had done that, it was national exposure they were short of.

'Nobody bothers to tell you you've got a problem unless they're the people who can provide the answer,' David thought.

He sat back and waited.

'I'm putting a package together,' Goldsmith said. 'Just like I did in the early sixties. You remember how it used to be – five or six acts, plus a compère, 'stead of one group in concert like we've got now. It'll do all the big venues, Hammersmith Odeon, Manchester Free Trade, Colston Hall Bristol – a few nights at each. I'd like your boys to be in on it.'

'Who'll be playin'?' David asked.

Goldsmith told him.

'They're none of them that big any more,' David said.

Goldsmith beamed.

'Spot on, my boy. You're right, none of them could fill the Glasgow Apollo on their own. Together . . .' he waved his arms expansively '. . . it's possible. But I'd like to hedge my bets, see if I can come up with a big name.'

David began to wish he hadn't drunk the wine that Goldsmith had been pouring so freely into his glass. You knew where you were with pints, but this stuff crept up on you.

'Don't you have any big names on your books any more?' he asked.

'Sure I do, but why should they agree to it? They can pull in capacity crowds on their own. Besides, what if the tour flops? Failure sticks, especially when you're at the top and the only way to go is down.'

Goldsmith waved across the room at yet another celebrity.

'Where does Urban Decay come in?' David asked.

'I think they *could become* a big name. Look, you start in Brighton, the record sells in Brighton. I make sure all the local shops have enough copies and we even push them in the foyer of the theatre. They play in Birmingham, the same thing happens. By the time they're mid-way through the tour, Urban Decay have got a hit on their hands and tickets are going like hot cakes.'

'And what if the tour flops?'

'It's a gamble, but how much can you lose anyway? You can't damage a reputation you haven't got yet. And if it works out, you're laughing, aren't you?'

There was something else that bothered David.

'All the other groups are under your management, aren't they?' he said.

'Correct,' said Goldsmith, apparently unperturbed.

'Urban Decay's got a manager,' David said, suddenly angry. 'Me.'

Goldsmith reached across the table and patted David in an avuncular fashion.

'Don't worry, my boy,' he said. 'Don't worry.'

'I'd want a contract to say that the group is being managed by Harrison Enterprises and is only to be loaned to you for the tour.'

'Agreed,' Goldsmith replied. 'There's a standard form to cover that. We won't even need to waste money on lawyers.'

David didn't like it. It was all too pat, too logical, for real life. If Goldsmith had offered a ton of lead or a consignment of old Morrises, he wouldn't have bought, but then he knew more about scrap than he did about the world of entertainment. And already Barry was pressuring him for more. After each achievement – the Manchester club performance, the appearance on television, the record contract – the breathing space before Barry expected a new miracle was becoming shorter. David didn't know when he'd get a break like this again, and if Barry ever found out that he'd been offered it and turned it down . . . It was so difficult to think straight after so much drink.

He asked Goldsmith how much they would be paid. It was generous.

'And if the record is a hit while they're on tour, I want the money to go up,' David said.

He half-hoped that this would be too much, that the impresario would become angry and make a stormy exit. Goldsmith didn't lose his temper. Instead, he beamed again.

'You've got a good head on your shoulders, David, my boy,' he said. '25% if it's in the Top Twenty, 75% in the Top Ten and 100% if it hits Number One.'

David was defeated; it was too good a deal to turn down.

The tour had been organized before Goldsmith even spoke to David and there were only three weeks between the deal being signed and the group hitting the road.

Barry was ecstatic.

'You mean we're really going to be on tour with The Zoots?' he asked.

'Yes,' David said, laughing affectionately, 'but don't forget, they'll be at the top of the bill and you'll be at the bottom.'

Barry's enthusiasm refused to be dampened.

'Touring with The Zoots!' he kept saying over and over to himself.

Those weeks before the tour were wonderful. It seemed as if Barry had finally got what he wanted. There were no more demands, no more harsh words. He helped around the house. He complimented David on his inexpert cooking instead of merely wolfing it down without comment. He even suggested that David might like to go out on his own, with his friend Paul. And in bed, Barry was so sweet, so loving, that it felt as if they were one, as if nothing could ever separate them.

There were only two days before the tour began. Their suitcases were already half-packed and lying on the bed. David was peeling the potatoes over the sink, Barry was sitting at the table. It was wonderful to have Barry in the room, even if he couldn't see him, even if he was silent. When Barry did speak, what he said seemed louder than any explosion.

'David, I've bin thinkin'. I don't think you should come with us.'

There was a sudden burning pain above David's heart, as if he had been stabbed. He turned and looked at Barry, elbows resting on the table, an uncertain, embarrassed look on his face.

'But I've made all the arrangements,' David protested. 'O'Malley's goin' to run the yard and . . .'

'I don't want you to come,' Barry said, his voice quavering but stubborn.

I don't want you to come! What had he done to deserve this?

'I'm your manager.'

'We don't need a manager on this tour,' Barry persisted. 'All the bookin's are taken care of, rooms – everythin'. And we'll be usin' the same roadies as the other groups.'

David's mouth had gone dry. His hands were cold.

'Come an' sit down,' Barry said.

David lowered his weight onto the stool opposite his lover. The young vocalist looked so fragile. It would be easy to take Barry's head in his huge strong hands and squeeze and squeeze until . . . But the hands stayed where they were – flat on the table. Barry reached across and stroked one of them, and David felt the life returning to him, the madness easing.

'Look,' Barry said, 'the only reason you're needed on this tour is as my friend, my lover. And that's just why I *don't* want you there.'

His fingers moved up and down the back of David's hand, caressing, soothing. David was constantly amazed that these same fingers, which could tear at a guitar with such violence, could be so gentle when they touched him.

'Don't you see what a big strain it would be on me,' Barry continued, 'knowing that my biggest critic and my greatest fan was out there in the audience. I'd never be able to do me best.'

'You're askin' me to miss your big moment,' David complained, 'the one we've both worked so hard for.'

The one he had submitted to Archie's foul embraces for.

'This is just the start,' Barry promised. 'There'll be bigger things than this, an' you can see 'em. Keep away for this one tour, then I'll get so confident it'll never bother me again when you're there.'

'You'll be away seven weeks,' David said.

Seven weeks, forty-nine long nights without the comfort of holding Barry in his arms.

'Don't be daft,' Barry said. 'I'm not playing every night, am I? Sometimes, we get two or three days clear.'

His fingers made delicate music, plucking at David's veins, sending messages to his heart.

'When that happens, you can come and see me. We'll have a nice relaxin' holiday, just the two of us, alone together. Maybe we'll go up to the Lakes. You'd like that, wouldn't you? We could find a place where there's nobody else, and swim all day – in the nude.'

He stopped stroking his hand and stood up.

'Let's go upstairs and have a lie-down,' he suggested softly.

So David gave way to Barry, telling himself that it was reasonable, that the first major tour was important and it was natural as Barry's lover his being there would make Barry nervous.

But he had never seen any lack of confidence in the young man before.

Chapter Fifteen

The very idea of it – its boldness, its improbability – left Paul momentarily stunned. How long had Ben Moore been planning this? How could he even have thought of it?

He looked around the pleasant green wood basking in the sleepy heat of a warm August afternoon. Looked at his wife and saw that she was watching him seriously and intently, waiting for him to speak. Glanced at baby Paul, crawling gleefully through the grass. And finally returned his gaze to Ben Moore, who still had that wicked grin on his leathery face.

Paul squeezed the potted meat butty in his hand. Yes, it was real, he could see the brown paste oozing out from between the layers of white bread. It was real, they were real, Ben had actually said what he'd thought he'd heard.

The afternoon had started ordinarily enough. Maggie had decided that it was too nice a day to have tea at home and had made a picnic. The fresh air would do Paul good, she said; he'd been working too hard. So they walked to the woods, past the sites of innumerable Secret Camps, and chose this spot under the spreading oak tree.

It wasn't until Maggie had dished out the sandwiches and mugs of tea that Moore made his suggestion.

'Sam Holland's not standin' at the next election,' he began.

Paul was not surprised. Holland had contested the seat for Labour three times – a thankless task. There was a pause. Ben seemed to be expecting Paul to say something. He took a thoughtful sip of his tea.

'Thinking of contesting the seat, Ben?'

'What? A clapped out old bugger like me? No chance, lad. I was thinking of you.'

Paul almost choked.

'For Christ's sake, Ben,' he said, 'I'm not old enough to vote yet. I may not even be old enough by the time they call the next election.'

'When will you be twenty-one?' Moore asked, unperturbed.

'March 1970. That's nearly two years away, Ben.'

'Then there's no problem, Harold'll not call an election till he has to.'

The idea seemed totally outrageous to Paul.

'I'm a kid,' he said. 'I'm still at college.'

Moore's eyes followed a dragonfly as it drifted by them, then returned to Paul.

'You've been married for a year,' he said. 'An' you've got a child an' a home of your own. Who the bloody hell do you think's got more stake in the town than you have?'

If Paul had had time to think about it, he would have felt flattered. As it was, his first reaction was blind panic.

'How would the Constituency Association feel about it?' he asked.

Moore smiled.

'They'll be right enthusiastic about it,' he said, '. . . if I ask them to be.'

True, Paul thought. They would rubber stamp anything he put forward.

'But would the voters actually elect anyone so young?' he asked, still trying to find a way out of it.

'Don't be dense, lad,' the old man said. 'You're not goin' to win! I never thought that. Neither would anybody else on a Labour ticket. The Tories are going to get in next time, no question about it. But when '74 or '75 rolls around, you just might be in with a chance. You'll be older, and you'll already have made your mistakes in an election that didn't count.'

Paul glanced across at Maggie. She merely smiled to show that whatever he did she would support him.

'Give me time to think about it, Ben,' Paul said.

'Time to think!' Moore sounded both offended and surprised. 'What the bloody hell is there to think about?'

'You don't understand, Ben,' Maggie said softly, showing that she *did* understand – both her husband and Moore. 'Paul would never take a big step like that without talkin' to Jimmy an' David first.'

It was two weeks later that Jimmy came home. Though his summer job was finished, he still had a lot of work to do for the Conservative Association before term started. Despite that, he had managed to steal a weekend with his mates.

They walked along the tow path, stopping now and then to

watch the swimming insects make small circles in the water, or to skim stones across to the other bank.

'This canal, the woods – everywhere we used to play – they're all like a giant time machine,' Paul said. 'Put us all in it at the same time, and it's as if the years had never happened.'

'Eee, by gum,' Jimmy replied. 'I can remember this canal when it were thick, absolutely thick, wi' salt barges. Pulled by 'orses an' all. None o' them new-fangled motors.'

Paul laughed – but that was not what he had meant at all.

As they drew level with The Pack Horse, Jimmy said, 'Shall we pop in there for a pint?'

Paul tried to measure his reactions to the suggestion – he had not set foot in the pub since the night they had played the game of Odd Man Out. His heart was beating normally, his hands were not shaking, he did not feel sick.

'Why not?' he asked.

They sat in the corner, under the leaded windows, drinking pints of best bitter.

'So how's university?' Paul asked, expecting Jimmy to gloss over it as he usually did.

'I've met a girl,' Jimmy said. 'Her name's Claire. I think I'm in love with her.'

Paul was amazed that cool, smooth Jimmy could look and sound so much like a love-sick youth – and he was surprised to find that he felt no resentment that Jimmy was still free to choose while he was loaded down with responsibilities.

'Tell us more,' he said.

'Not now.' Jimmy picked up a beer mat in his slim fingers and shredded the edge of it with his thumb nail. 'I'm hoping I can persuade her to come up here, then you'll meet her.' He turned to David. 'I hear the group's doing well.'

'Doin' *very* well,' David said. 'I hired an agency when they kicked off in Brighton, so I could get clippin's from the local newspapers. I don't need 'em any more. If I want to read about Urban Decay, I've only got to open *The Daily Mirror*.'

'And the record?'

'Number Six. They reckon it'll be Number One next week.'

There was none of the animation and excitement in his voice that Paul would have expected. He did not understand why, but he suspected it would be a mistake to push it further. And Jimmy was acting strangely as well – being in love had naturally unsettled him, but it seemed to have depressed him, too. He had been wrong about the time machine, Paul thought. They had all changed since they were kids. It was as if their childhood had been nothing more than a film set, convincing but flat – and thus easily understandable. Now, though the buildings looked the same, there was more, much more, behind them – a labyrinth of complexity and confusion.

'What have you been doing?' Jimmy asked.

Paul told him about Ben and the offer. It seemed to depress Jimmy more, or rather, it seemed to sadden him. He looked like a man who has lost something – or is about to.

They sat in silence for what felt like an eternity, then Jimmy said, 'Are you sure you really want it, Paul?'

'In the end – definitely. I'm just not sure whether I'm ready yet.'

The worried look was replaced by one that Paul knew well, one that had at least remained unchanged since the simple, one-dimensional days of childhood. It was the expression Paul had first seen on Jimmy's face the day the Secret Camp had been wrecked – the face of the planner, the tactician.

'If you want it,' Jimmy said, 'you've got to start going for it now. And you'll need a strategy.'

How like Jimmy that was, working on the second move while he himself was still puzzling over the first.

'You've got to get yourself known,' Jimmy said, 'well before your candidature is announced. Get Ben Moore to appoint you his political secretary.'

'His what?' Paul was incredulous. 'Have you any idea what a town councillor's life is like? Ben doesn't get a salary, he has to fight like the devil even to claim essential expenses. He doesn't get any secretarial help, nobody does his research for him. There isn't any such post as *political secretary* in local government, and there are bloody good reasons for it.'

'You wouldn't expect to be paid, would you?'

'Of course not!'

'Then it's all to your advantage,' Jimmy said. 'It'll make you stand out more. You won't have an official status, so you can't speak in the Council Chamber. But there's nothing to stop you attending ward meetings as Moore's representative. And you can visit all his constituents.'

Paul marvelled at Jimmy's flow. Five minutes earlier, he had not known about any of it, and here he was, improvising a whole campaign.

'Go and listen to their complaints. A widow's got a cracked drainpipe the Council won't repair. She tells you about it, you get Moore to put pressure on the maintenance department, the council fixes it. And who gets the credit? You do! It's economical too. You do one good deed, the old bag gossips about it, and you've got ten more people on your side.'

'Anything else?' Paul asked, deadpan.

Jimmy didn't notice. His mind was racing.

'Yes. Borrow David's van and drive the old biddies down to the library and the post office on pension day.' He clicked his fingers. 'No, scrap that. Organize volunteers to do it, but let people know you're behind it.'

'Why?'

'Because everybody *likes* people who help them directly, but it's the leader, the man in the background, they *respect*.'

It seemed so cynical. Don't do what is really necessary, do what will create maximum advantage for yourself. Yet he could see that Jimmy was right. If he ever was to get elected – if he ever was to be in a position to do real good – then this was the way to go about it.

It was dark when they left the pub. They walked back along the tow path, each wrapped up in his own thoughts. The only sounds were their feet on the cobbles and the water lapping against the bank. They reached David's home, and the other two waited until the door clicked behind him until they set off again. There would be people waiting for them – a wife and child for Paul, an ambitious bewildered mother and a silent almost-invisible father for Jimmy – but David had entered an empty house.

'Try and get David involved in all this political business,' Jimmy said, as they strolled down the street. 'He needs to throw himself into something new.'

It was typical of Jimmy, Paul thought. Tell one friend how to be successful. Then try to get another friend involved because he would be useful – and it might just do him some good as well. Jimmy was the perpetual balancer, the manipulator, the true believer in the reconcilability of all things.

'He's very worried about the group,' he agreed.

'The group!' Jimmy said. 'He doesn't give a toss about the group. It's Barry who's upsetting him.'

Why should Barry upset him? Of course, he was probably missing the young vocalist's company but . . . Suddenly, he understood.

'You don't mean that they're . . .'

Jimmy's surprise was even greater than Paul's.

'You didn't know?' he said. 'I only come up here occasionally, and I spotted it immediately.' A large stone lay on the pavement.

He kicked it, and watched as it disappeared into the darkness. 'Listen, Paul,' he continued, 'if you're ever going to get on in politics, you're going to have to develop better antennae for people's weaknesses than that!'

Urban Decay were Number One in the charts the day they opened in Manchester. They were making front page news and the hysteria that greeted their appearance was being compared to Beatlemania. When the tour moved to Newcastle, they were top of the bill, and The Zoots, the group that Barry had idolised only weeks before, were relegated to second place. It had all worked out exactly as Goldsmith had promised.

Still, David was troubled. Barry hadn't called him to say when they could have their two- or three-day holiday together. He hadn't called at all! He would drive up to Newcastle and catch the act, he decided. Barry wouldn't mind. After so much acclaim, he'd have all the confidence in the world. And if he hadn't written or called to suggest that David should travel up to share his triumph, it was only because things had happened so fast and he had been overwhelmed by them.

It was a fine afternoon when David set off, but by the time he reached Manchester the rain was pelting down. The road over the Pennines was awash and the sky was a heavy, charcoal grey. He forced himself to go slowly round the twists and turns of the Snake Pass. He didn't want an accident. He didn't want Barry to be told that he was in hospital just before he was due to go on stage. The poor boy would probably drop everything and rush down to see him. Even if they forced him to go on and do the set, he would give a poor performance because he was so worried.

He made better time on the A1, despite the continuing downpour. Then, fifty miles outside Newcastle, in the middle of nowhere, the engine coughed and died. David pushed the car to the side of the road, lifted the bonnet and tried to find out what was wrong. But he was much better at dismantling cars than he was at fixing them, and after half an hour he gave up.

It was two miles to the nearest garage and it poured down on him all the way. He was wearing a new suit, one that he knew Barry would like. By the time he saw the Esso sign the cloth was sodden, clinging tightly to his body and itching. He had brought no change of clothing with him.

He rubbed the moisture off his watch and saw that it was six o'clock. The show started at seven-thirty, but Urban Decay would not be on until at least nine. If the garage could repair the car quickly, he would still have plenty of time.

The forecourt attendant was wearing heavy yellow oilskins and the same rain that had drenched David simply bounced off him.

'I need my car lookin' at immediately,' David shouted over the noise of the wind.

'Can't do it, son,' the man shouted back.

David pulled out his wallet.

'I don't mind payin' extra.'

'It's not a question of that. There's only me 'ere, and I've got to look after the pumps. I can fix it, but you'll 'ave to wait till I close up.'

'What time will that be?'

'Eight o'clock.'

Eight o'clock. Get the repair done by half-past. Count on at least an hour to drive to Newcastle, another thirty minutes to find the theatre and a place to park . . .

'Where's the *next* garage?'

'Nothin' for the next fifteen miles.'

'I'll wait,' David said miserably. 'Can I sit in the office?'

'Er . . . well . . . you could if it was left up to me, but it's against Company policy. The cash register's in there, you see.'

David spent two hours sheltering under the awning of the garage forecourt, listening to the rain pounding down, watching the purple petrol swirling in the puddles. He was cold, wet, bored, hungry and miserable. He thought of hitch-hiking, but that was out – no one would pick up a large man in a sopping-wet suit. It was too late to make the concert now, he would have to content himself with seeing Barry backstage after the show was over.

The repair was not completed until nine fifteen and he got lost twice in the complexities of the Newcastle traffic system, so it wasn't until after eleven that he reached the theatre. Although the concert was over, there were still a number of girl fans, huddled under raincoats, hanging around near the stage door.

'I just thought I'd die when Barry sang that one about the car,' David heard a thin blonde girl say to her friend. 'I mean, he was just so far out.'

David felt very proud.

The stage door was locked, and when David rapped on it, an elderly voice on the other side shouted, 'Bugger off! I've told you, they're not comin' out.'

David knocked again, really hammering it this time. The door opened a few inches and an old man peered out.

'I'm warnin' yer,' he said, 'I'll call the police.'

He saw the tall young man in the wet suit and began to close the door again.

David slipped his foot in the gap.

'I'm Urban Decay's manager,' he said.

The old man heaved and pushed, then realised he was wasting his time.

'Look,' he wheezed, 'we don't want no trouble an . . .'

'Are Urban Decay still here?' David demanded.

'Yes, they are,' the caretaker replied, leaning on the door as much for support as to keep David out, 'but you can't see 'em. Not without permission.'

A number of fans were crowding around David saying that they wanted to see Urban Decay too. It wasn't making his task any easier. He thought about pushing his way past the caretaker. Even though he might end up spending a night in the nick, he would at least see Barry first.

'I'm their manager,' he repeated.

'They're one of Mr Goldsmith's groups,' the old man countered. 'Why don't you go home and sleep it off, son? Best all round.'

'Ring through to their dressing room. Tell them it's David. They'll vouch for me.'

The pensioner looked embarrassed.

'I can't just go disturbing *artistes* after a performance. It's more than my job's worth.'

Was there anything he could do to convince the old fool?

'OK, wait!' he said.

He reached into the inside pocket of his jacket and pulled out a piece of paper, damp at the edges. It was a copy of the contract he had signed with Zeb Goldsmith. He always carried it around with him.

'Read this.'

The caretaker reached out cautiously and took the contract from David.

'I'll have to go inside,' he said. 'I haven't got me glasses on.'

David withdrew his foot and the door closed. It was at least five minutes before the old man returned, glasses perched precariously on his nose, the contract in his hand.

'And how do I know you're this Harrison of "Harrison Enterprises"?' he asked.

David gave him his driving licence. The old man held it at an angle and squinted.

'Well, I suppose it's all right then,' he said, grudgingly. 'But if I let you in, you'll have to help me stop this lot followin' you.'

David squeezed through the door and then turned to close it against the pressing girls.

'Tell Barry I luv 'im,' one of them shouted.

'Tell him I'm Julie from Brighton and I've seen all his concerts,' another screamed.

The old man went into his cubicle and consulted a list. He pointed down a long badly-lit cream corridor.

'Fifth door on the right,' he said.

'In a minute,' David thought, 'I'll be with Barry.'

The frustrations of the day – the breakdown, the rain, the bloody-minded door keeper – would all have been worth it. They wouldn't be able to act naturally at first, not with the rest of the group there, but later they could, when they were alone together. Then they would make up for all the sad, solitary nights. He took his comb out of his pocket and ran it through his hair. He had wanted to look nice and instead he was a complete mess. It didn't matter. Barry would be so pleased to see him that he'd hardly notice.

The sound of loud rock music blared out of the dressing room. David recognised it. Urban Decay's first album, due to be released the following week. He knocked but there was no answer. Of course they couldn't hear him with all that noise going on.

There was a tiny voice in the back of his head telling him to go away and come back the next day, but that would have been stupid after such a long drive. He opened the door.

The group were all sprawled out on armchairs. The floor was strewn with beer cans, and the air was thick with the smell of pot. They had only been on the road for a few weeks, and already they looked like hardened veterans.

Part of this was his fault. He should never have let Barry persuade him not to come on the tour. If they carried on like this, they'd destroy themselves within a year. He would have to get a firm grip on them once they got back home.

At least Barry wasn't there. He was too sensible – he knew that he needed to preserve his strength for the performance.

It must have been the gush of cold air as he opened the door that alerted them to his presence. They all looked at him through bleary eyes.

'Well, look who it is,' the drummer said. ''S David, our wonderful manager. You look wet, David.'

The others giggled. He was not going to get any sense out of them that night, but he would certainly give them a talking to in the morning – or get Barry to do it, because it was Barry they were really letting down.

'Where's Barry?' he asked.

They giggled again.

'Barry doesn' share a dressin' room with ush now. Haven' you heard? He's a fuckin' star. Got his own fuckin' dressin' room – an' everythin' that goesh with it.'

The other two seemed to find this hilarious. They laughed and laughed until tears came to their eyes, and they banged the arms of their chairs with their hands. David waited patiently until they had quietened down.

'So where is he?'

'In the star's dressin' room, nex' door. He's probably waitin' for you.'

And they seemed to find this funniest of all.

He entered Barry's room without knocking. It was the woman he noticed first. A blonde in her late twenties, she was heavily made-up, but this could not disguise the fact that her face bore the signs of fast living. Her body was still in good shape, though, high pointy breasts and firm buttocks; David could see it all clearly, since she was completely naked.

For a split second he thought she was just kneeling on the floor and bouncing her body up and down. Until he saw who was lying underneath.

Both heads turned when the door opened. The blonde registered initial surprise but quickly assumed a look of indifference. Barry was stunned for a moment, his face was frozen like a still photograph. Then he smiled, a lop-sided, boyish, rueful grin.

'Guess what, David?' he said. 'It turns out I'm not queer after all.'

After the big betrayal, everything else was an anti-climax – even Barry's visit to David's house shortly after the tour ended. For once, his confidence seemed to have deserted him. He knocked, even though he had a key, and stood awkwardly in the doorway when David answered.

'I've come for my things,' he said. 'I think it's best.'

'Yes,' David said sadly. 'I think it probably is.'

It was less than a year since David had discovered the group, less than six months since Barry had seemed almost pathetically grateful. And less than three months since they had happily, lovingly, shared the bed upstairs. Now it was all over. David helped Barry collect his gear and together they loaded it in the back of Barry's flashy new sports car.

'Is there somewhere we can talk?' Barry asked, as he locked the boot. 'I've got somethin' to tell you.'

Where else but in the kitchen – Barry on one side of the table, David on the other – the scene of so many previous discussions. It was there that Barry had told David he loved him, there that he had screamed that David had too much respect for Paul and Jimmy to want to stick his prick up their arses.

'You've been very good to us, David,' Barry said, 'and we'll always be grateful, honest we will.'

There was none of the old harshness in his voice, yet David would have preferred the biting edge, the demands that showed he was still needed. This new, soothing, coaxing tone was more suitable for addressing an injured child or a ga-ga old lady.

And if Barry must be grateful for something, why did it have to be for what he had done for the group? Why couldn't it be for the love and tenderness they had shared?

'The thing is,' Barry continued in a rush, 'we're in the big league now. We've outgrown you. You'd be out of your depth tryin' to manage us, so Zeb Goldsmith is going to do it instead.'

'We've got a contract,' David said, but only half-heartedly. He knew the outcome was inevitable – he was only going through the motions.

'It wasn't a proper one,' Barry said. 'We wrote it ourselves.'

'In the days when we loved and trusted each other,' David thought. 'In the days when we didn't think we really needed a contract at all.'

He said nothing.

'Anyway,' Barry continued, 'Zeb's lawyer's had a look at it, and he says it's full of holes. It would never stand up in court. But Zeb wants you to have compensation.' He paused, and smiled magnanimously, as if he were bestowing a gift on his former lover. 'Fifty thousand pounds, David!'

If Goldsmith was offering that much without a fight, what was the group he had built up from nothing really worth? But even if he was losing a fortune, he didn't care – money had never been a consideration.

'I don't want any compensation,' he said dully. 'I just want it all finished. Tell Goldsmith's lawyer to send me a release, and I'll sign it.'

Barry stared down at the table. He seemed embarrassed and uneasy.

'Take the money,' Barry urged. 'Do this one last thing for me.'

David had hurt his father, and because he'd had no chance to make it up to him, the guilt was always there. If he didn't accept the money, he would be giving Barry a cross to carry, too. It would not be as heavy as his own. He saw, for the first time, that even when Barry had loved him, it had been a selfish love. But just because the young guitarist had rejected him did not mean that he had stopped loving in return.

He had done a great deal already; neglected his business, submitted to the humiliation of Archie's embraces – suffered so much. This seemed a small thing in comparison.

'All right,' he said. 'If it will make you feel better.'

Barry smiled at him gratefully.

'Would you like to go upstairs,' he said, almost shyly, 'one last time?'

David yearned for it, the last chance to express his love for Barry. But Barry was only offering out of pity – and David didn't want to be pitied.

'It wouldn't be worth it to either of us,' he said. 'I think you'd better go.'

He saw Barry to his car and they shook hands like casual acquaintances. David went upstairs to bed, the one they had shared – and wept. He didn't get up again for three days.

Chapter Sixteen

In the house's more prosperous days, the attic had been servants' quarters. It was reached by a flight of narrow wooden stairs. It contained a battered sink in the corner across from the door, an army surplus bed at the far end of the room next to the rail for clothes, and a rickety dining table in the centre. A bookcase, constructed of bricks and planks, ran most of the length of the long wall. Opposite it, the roof sloped down to touch the floor, drastically reducing the available space for any tenants other than mice and cockroaches. The cheap linoleum underfoot had worn away in places, revealing bare, unvarnished wood. The whole room was cold and uncomfortable, and yet it became the centre of Jimmy's universe, the focus of his hopes and dreams.

The primitive conditions didn't bother Claire. The sloping roof was north-facing and had a skylight. Light was all that mattered, precious light, by which she could paint.

Throughout the autumn and winter of 1968, Jimmy visited the studio as often as he could and sat at the table, watching Claire work at her canvases. Some of her paintings were surrealistic, like the works of Salvador Dali. Others were impressionist – corn fields and hazy summer scenes. There was a third group which showed an almost Rousseauesque naivety. Whatever the style, they were all infused with an energy and intensity that was uniquely Claire's.

Sometimes it was so cold in the flat that Jimmy shivered, despite his overcoat, but the girl seemed as impervious to the temperature as she was to everything else when involved in the act of creation. She could become so absorbed in her painting that she would miss lectures for a week or go for days hardly eating anything.

They had no social life together. Claire didn't seem to have any friends, nor to need them. Occasionally they would go out, usually to the local theatre or else the West End. Although it was expensive, Claire never offered to pay her share. It wasn't because she hadn't got the money. Nor would she have refused to pay if he'd asked. It was just that she never gave a second's thought to his financial position or to what a drain on it these trips must be.

He knew that he was not unique in receiving this lack of consideration. Claire, who was devoted to emotion in the abstract, was little affected by its manifestation in the real world. Words and images moved her – people didn't.

He had given up his comfortable life with Rosemary for her. He had put a brake on his driving ambition. She had made no concessions in return. Sometimes it angered him almost beyond the point of endurance, but there was little he could do. He suspected that if he quarrelled with her, he would lose her – she would simply cast him aside.

He yearned to make love to her, yet dared not risk making a sexual advance. There were plenty of other girls who were willing. But he did not want other girls, he wanted Claire, and he felt his body would burst if he could not have her.

Finally, one day when the snows had at last melted and the first buds of spring were thrusting outwards, Jimmy found that he could stand it no longer. As he sat watching Claire at work with her brushes, he decided that he had to take the gamble, to play for all or nothing.

'Do you paint from live models?' he asked.

'No.' Claire didn't even look up from her work as she spoke. 'Don't know any.'

'I'll pose for you, if you like.'

Claire gave the matter some thought.

'Yes,' she said. 'Yes, I think I can use you.'

It was as simple as that – no thanks, just acceptance. He was adequate raw material, like a log or a vase of flowers. He wondered why he loved her, and only knew that he did. Perhaps it was her unavailability. Perhaps when he had bedded her, he would be able to exorcise her and find a much more suitable partner.

She took the canvas off the easel and replaced it with a virgin one.

'Take your clothes off,' she said.

He felt ridiculous, like a male stripper at a hen party. He removed his pullover, shirt, trousers, socks and finally underpants, and placed them on the chair. When he looked towards Claire, he saw that she was busy mixing up a new set of paints.

'Stand over there,' she ordered.

He did as he was told. For some minutes she stayed by her easel, just examining him. Then she walked over to him. She took hold of his arm and moved it. She got down on her knees, her hair brushing against his penis, and pulled his ankle a little to the left. Finally, she cupped his testicles in the palm of her hand.

He would not have believed it possible that he could feel nothing – no stirrings, no sexual excitement – but it was true. He felt nothing because he knew that she didn't either. She moved his testicles to the side, released them, and seemed annoyed when they swung back.

'Maybe it would help if you moved your leg a little,' she said, her face less than a foot away from his organ. 'Yes. Perfect. Hold that.'

She began by making a charcoal sketch, and as her arm moved, Jimmy watched her breasts against the coarse material of her smock. After half an hour, she put down the charcoal and reached for her palette.

'Can I see it before you put any paint on?' Jimmy asked.

The request seemed to annoy her.

'Oh, all right,' she said. 'Don't move, I'll bring it to you.'

She lifted the canvas off the easel and walked towards Jimmy. With the light behind her, he could see her legs and hips clearly outlined. He was sure she was completely naked beneath the smock.

'You said you wanted to look at it. Look!'

It was a conventional study, almost like an art school exercise. The figure was the one he observed in the mirror every morning. The elegance, the muscles, had been captured perfectly. The face was what troubled him. It was handsome and it was his – but the expression on it was terrifying. Was that uncertainty, that complete lack of confidence, really there? Did he always look like that in the studio? Was that what this woman had done to him? He tried to hate her, but he couldn't.

Claire returned to her easel and began to apply the paint. Her strokes were firm at first, then more hesitant, and finally she threw her brush on the floor in exasperation.

'It's all wrong,' she said.

'I thought it was very realistic.'

Too realistic, if that was reality.

'It's all surface, all camouflage,' Claire shouted, pacing the room. 'As bad as those buildings on campus.' She sobbed with frustration and disappointment. 'It's a soap opera view of life. I just can't get deep enough. Can't reach what matters.'

He wanted to comfort her.

'Don't move,' she said, fiercely. 'I haven't finished. I haven't given up – yet.'

She picked up her brush from the floor and started work again, her brow furrowed in deep concentration.

It was her tears, the moment of vulnerability, that gave him the courage to speak.

'Claire,' he said, 'have you ever slept with a man?'

'No.'

She was not proud of it, nor was she ashamed. She was simply stating a fact.

'Has a man ever kissed you? Fondled your breasts? *Anything*?'

She cocked her head slightly to one side to get a different angle on him, then made two delicate strokes on the canvas.

'No.'

'Don't you think you're missing out on something? Don't you see that there's a whole area of human experience you're denying yourself?'

She laid down her palette and looked him in the face.

'I've never had cancer,' she said. 'That doesn't mean I can't imagine the pain. I've never killed anyone, but I think I know how it would feel if I did. It's from *within us* that true feeling comes. Everything else is just decoration.'

'Claire,' Jimmy said desperately, 'how do you *know*?'

She frowned – then realization hit her.

'*You* want to sleep with *me*,' she said, as if it were a strange and novel idea.

She returned to her painting, leaving Jimmy posing stiffly, his skin goose-pimpled, his mind in turmoil.

Over the months, the studio had become as familiar to him as his own home. He knew its smell – a blend of must, turpentine and curry from the flat below. He could close his eyes and point to the damp patch on the wall, the stack of discarded canvases, the mouse hole in the skirting board. He wondered if this was to be the last time he would ever see it. Perhaps Claire, once she had finished the painting, would tell him not to bother coming back. He was vaguely aware of her voice, cutting through his thoughts. Was this it?

'I'm sorry, Claire. What did you say?'

'I said, yes. All right. If that's what you want.'

With a single movement she lifted her smock over her head. Jimmy gasped. He had often imagined her naked, but had never thought she would be as beautiful as this. Her long slim legs were superbly proportioned – even her knees seemed to be there less to provide a joint than to add balance and form to her shape. Her pubic hair was a perfect triangle, as if it had been sculpted rather than grown. Her belly curved delicately, her waist was tiny, her breasts, with dark, dark brown nipples, were firm and thrusting.

He dropped his pose and walked awkwardly over to her. He wrapped his arms around her body and felt her breasts pressing against him. He kissed her. Her breath was hot and sweet and her tongue darted in and out of his mouth, making his whole body tremble. She kissed like a woman with a lifetime's experience of making love, yet she had said she had never done it before. And he believed her – she wouldn't bother to lie.

'Well,' Claire said when they broke off the embrace, 'are we going to do it standing up or do you want to use the bed?'

'The bed.'

She walked over to it and lay down, spreading her legs. He knelt beside her and began to rub her clitoris.

'No need for that,' she said impatiently. 'I'm ready.'

'Are you sure?'

'Yes. Let's do it.'

Despite the fact that she was a virgin, he had little trouble entering her. She lay still at first, then her body began to move in time with his. Soon, it seemed as if her hands were everywhere – stroking, scratching, pinching. She was taking control. He was frightened that he would come before she did, then she cried out – a deep, sensual scream – and he knew he could relax.

No sooner had he withdrawn than she was on him, her mouth engulfing his penis, almost swallowing it whole. Her lips rubbed the shaft, her tongue teased the head – he felt himself hardening again.

She straddled him and as her vagina tightened around his organ he realized that it had never been as good as this before – not for him, not for anybody. She began to rotate her pelvis, slowly at first and then with increasing ferocity. He held her breasts in his hands and felt the current of sexual electricity surge through him.

'Again!' she said, when it was over.

'Claire, I can't. Not straight away.'

'Again!' she insisted.

And looking at her beautiful body, feeling the intensity of her energy, he knew that though it would have been impossible with any other woman, he could achieve it with her.

They lay side by side. Jimmy felt completely spent, totally drained. He wanted to hold Claire in his arms and tell her that she was wonderful. He reached over to pull her towards him. As his hand touched her, she stiffened.

'Don't!' she said.

She was lying on her back, staring at the ceiling, as if there were some message written there that only she could see. Slowly, a broad smile formed on her lips, and she jumped out of bed and rushed to her easel.

'Claire?'

'Not now!'

Her brush strokes had been slow and hesitant before, now she painted as if driven by a demon. She was often oblivious to everything else when she was working, but Jimmy had never seen her as intent as this. He hoped it was because they'd *made love* and through that she'd discovered that she actually *loved* him. That she wanted to finish the picture as a tribute to that love.

He fantasised about the completed work. The look of uncertainty would be gone. Though the portrait would still be of him, it would be more than just his appearance, because Claire would have built into it what she felt about him.

It had taken nearly a year to come to this, but it had been worth it. He looked at Claire's naked body and found, incredibly, that he already desired her again. He would wait, and the waiting would make it all the sweeter. He drifted off into sleep and dreamed happily of his new life.

When he awoke, Claire was still at work. He swung his legs off the bed and padded across the room, so that he could look at the picture over her shoulder. What he saw horrified him.

The changes had been subtle, a brush stroke here, more shading there, but the overall effect was devastating. The figure had ceased to be him, ceased to be a man at all – became instead a primeval being, single-mindedly devoted to satisfying the great thrusting urge of sex. The picture totally absorbed him, consumed his whole essence, and spat out as worthless anything that was not animal.

He gazed into Claire's eyes and saw fiery passion there – but it was not passion for him.

'It's the best thing I've ever done,' she said.

And still he could not throw her off. The encounter had made his obsession with her greater than ever. They slept together regularly, and it got better every time. She came to know his body perfectly, so that she could play on his synapses until he felt he would almost die with pleasure. After each session she would leave him in bed, amongst the rumpled, soiled sheets, and throw herself into her painting.

She was beautiful. She was the most exciting lover he had ever had. But she was selfish, too – totally absorbed in the world of her art. Was it this single-mindedness, a driving energy even greater than his own, that captivated him? He did not know. He only knew that he had to have her, that he could not bear to lose her.

He was plagued by dreams in the night, vivid technicolour nightmares of Claire with men. Claire and a succession of lovers, some of them his friends, others nothing more than vague shapes. Coupling, rutting, making the beast with two backs – as prime as goats, as hot as monkeys.

He woke up drenched in sweat, filled with a desire to rush to Claire's flat to make sure that the dreams weren't true. But what if they were? What would he do if he found her with another man? If she were still faithful, how long would it be before she tired of him and went in search of fresh gratification?

He did not neglect his normal political activities. He delivered urbane speeches to the Young Farmers and local Conservative Associations. He produced brilliant apologias for the Chamber of Commerce magazine in which the narrow self-interest of the local businessmen was magically transformed into a pursuit of the general good. Yet it was Claire who occupied his mind, his emotions, his very soul. And even that small part of himself that he did not offer her, she took – sucking the life from him just as she sucked the sperm from his throbbing penis.

As the Easter Vacation approached, so his fear increased. He had released a force in Claire that demanded satisfaction. Would that force lie dormant while she spent a month with her parents in Hampshire? He didn't think so. If she were to work at her painting, her passion must be fed. Men he did not know, country types in riding boots and hacking jackets, would be found to fill the need. The thought – the image of it – was too much to bear. He had to prevent it, and there was only *one* way he could do that.

He had his own key now, but he hesitated on the threshold, listening for the sound of creaking bed-springs and loud ecstatic moans. He heard nothing and, steeling himself, he opened the door. She was alone, painting, catching what little light there was on that grey day.

'What's that?' she asked, pointing.

He held it up for her to see.

'A Fortnum and Mason's hamper!'

Claire clapped her hands. She did not ask him why he had brought it, it was enough that it was there. Nor did she thank him; she accepted it as she accepted everything – as if it were a natural right.

Though she could go for days almost without food, she always had a hearty appetite when it was there. They sat cross-legged on the floor as she wolfed pâté and turkey, savouries and sweets, washing it all down with red wine. If she noticed that Jimmy was hardly touching the food, she didn't mention it.

They opened the brandy and drank straight from the bottle. Jimmy needed it. Even with the fiery liquid inside him, he would find it hard enough to speak. On the way to her flat, he had rehearsed a carefully balanced, beautifully phrased speech, but once in Claire's presence he could no longer remember any of it, and in the end he simply blurted out, 'Will you marry me, Claire?'

'Marry you?' she asked. 'When?'

Immediately. At Christmas. When they graduated. It didn't matter as long as she would agree, as long as he would have the right to be with her all the time.

'Whenever you want,' he said. 'Will you?'

She frowned, as she had done when considering whether to sleep with him, and when she spoke again, it was in the same tone: not cold, not calculating, just matter-of-fact.

'All right,' she said. 'If that's what you want. But I won't make you happy, you know.'

He knew it was true, but life without her would be intolerable.

He went to Hampshire with her for Easter. Her parents were solid country gentry: her father a stocky ruddy-faced Major, her mother smaller, thinner, but with the same healthy glow. Jimmy could see little resemblance between them and their pale, artistic daughter.

He had expected trouble. They were bound to see him as a working class upstart, a fortune hunter. But everything went remarkably smoothly. Major Peel, who thought himself a good judge of men, decided that Jimmy had no need to marry into money – if he didn't have it now, he would soon. And Mrs Peel, like so many women, fell victim to Jimmy's charm. Besides, she was so relieved that her strange child had a boyfriend at last that it wouldn't have mattered if he'd been a dustman.

The holiday period was packed with parties and balls. Jimmy divided his time between cultivating new contacts in the Hampshire set and jealously watching the way Claire behaved with other men. He need have had no worries on the second score, she was perfectly content with the way her life was arranged. For the moment.

He had promised his mother he would spend a few days with her, but somehow he never managed to get home. Though he eventually settled back in Norton, in a sense he never went home again.

Chapter Seventeen

Tonight it was surburban streets, tomorrow it could be country lanes. It didn't matter to David. He wasn't going anywhere, he was just driving. Often he had no idea where he was or how far he had gone. He would find himself in Preston or Stoke-on-Trent without any knowledge of the route he had taken or of what he had seen along it.

It had been a year since Barry had driven off up the street and out of his life. He saw photographs of his ex-lover in the newspapers from time to time, and occasionally switched on the television to find Urban Decay lurking there, waiting for him – like an emotional booby-trap. There had been no more affairs. He knew of clubs in Manchester and Liverpool where he could have picked up a casual lover, but though his body ached for relief, he was not prepared to submit to promiscuous embraces.

To fill the gap that Barry left, he'd thrown himself into other activities. He was working hard for Paul, running a shuttle service to the library, busing volunteer decorators all over town. He expanded his scrap business too, buying another yard. Still, he was left with too much time on his hands, time when others were in their beds and he could not sleep. So he drove and drove, along impersonal arterial roads, through anonymous council estates, whatever the hour, whatever the weather.

It was chance that took him to Stockport, and chance that steered the van in the direction of The Diamond Theatre Club. But it was not chance that made him stop outside it – it was a refusal to run away from the past.

The car park, large enough to accommodate hundreds of cars and a score of coaches, was empty. As David walked across it, rain fell thinly on his broad shoulders. The building was in darkness, even though it was only a little after eleven, and just as he remembered it: square, solid, unimaginative. It was a club, but could just as easily have been a warehouse.

His eyes travelled up the red-brick wall until they came to rest on the sign that spelled out the club's name. Green bulbs made up the background, *Diamond Theatre Club* was in blue, and the diamond itself, hovering over the middle of the name, was red. David began to count the bulbs, then gave up. There must have been a thousand of them at least.

The night he had gone there with his father, the sign had been illuminated and had held a magical quality – up there, as if above the entrance to an Aladdin's cave. Now, denied the miracle of electricity, it looked commonplace, a shoddy illusion exposed for what it really was.

The front of the place was designed like a Wild West saloon with swing doors and walls of solid-looking knotty planks.

'Be a man!' it seemed to challenge. 'Leave your drab pathetic life behind you and get a little excitement – a little danger.'

Even before he tapped the wall with his knuckles, David knew it would be nothing more than veneered plywood.

He was just about to leave when he noticed a piece of paper, made sodden by the rain, hanging from the door by a single drawing pin.

'These premises for sale or rent,' he read.

He took a notebook out of his pocket and wrote down the telephone number.

David was supposed to meet them in the car park at three o'clock on Wednesday afternoon, but traffic was light and he got there early. The main door was open, so he went straight in. He walked past the entrance desk and toilets, and turned left into the concert room.

It was still furnished, though it was clear from the dust that it had not been used for some time. Even the subdued lighting could not disguise the fact that the place badly needed re-decoration. Some structural work looked necessary too.

David picked his way between the tables. The last time he had done this, the room had been packed, and he had been going the other way, running after his angry, humiliated father.

The men he had come to see were sitting near the stage. One was tall and goofy, with unruly hair. The other was shorter and smoother. They looked like a comedy double act. They followed his progress with interest, and when he reached the table the small, smooth one glanced at the suitcase he was carrying and said, 'There's no work for you here, son.'

'Mr Spooner? Mr Clancy?' David asked.

'I'm Peter Spooner,' the small one said, 'he's Tony Clancy. Who are you?'

'David Harrison. We spoke on the phone.'

'Listen, lad,' Clancy said, his voice verging on anger. 'We're very busy men, so if you've had us trail all the way down here for a joke we don't find it very funny!'

'No joke,' David said, sitting down uninvited. 'You're in the business of sellin' clubs, and I'm in the business of buyin' 'em.'

He was serious, but he didn't know *why*. He had no idea how to manage a club, and this particular one held painful memories for him. He'd had no idea about how to manage a group either, before he had met Barry. And the fact that his memories *were* so painful seemed to be what had drawn him there – like a powerful magnet.

'You want to keep it goin' as a club?' Clancy asked, surprised.

'Yes.'

'Listen, son,' Spooner said. 'We've been in this business for over twenty years. We know what we're talking about. Clubs are dead, killed off by the telly. *We* couldn't make a go of this place any more – and if we couldn't, nobody could.'

'We're not thinkin' of sellin' it as a club at all,' Clancy said, the comic delivering the punch line his straight man had set up. 'It'll end up as a supermarket or summat.'

'In that case,' David said, 'you don't want payin' for the good will, do you?'

'Do you know how much a buildin' like this would cost you?' Spooner asked.

'I know what you're askin', but I'm not goin' to pay it.'

'I think we're wastin' us time,' Clancy said, rising to his feet.

David stayed where he was.

'I said I think we're wastin' us time.'

'You may be wastin' my time, Mr Clancy,' David said, 'but I'm not wastin' yours. I've got over fifty thousand pounds in the bank, and I'm willin' to give you some of it.'

Clancy sat down again.

'I've been checkin',' David continued. 'This place has been on the market for nearly a year, and nobody's so much as nibbled. An' for all that time you've been shellin' out for rates and maintenance. You're goin' to have to get shot of it soon, and to do that, you're goin' to have to drop your price.'

'I want to get rid of this place, God knows I do,' Spooner said. 'But I wouldn't like to see you take on more than you can handle. Fifty thousand quid is a lot of money, but it's not enough, even if we do take less than we're asking. There's the refurbishin' for a start. Then you'll have to find the cash to get your stocks in, pay your staff, book your acts. All that before the money starts to roll in – if it ever does.'

'I know that,' David said, 'but I can raise the rest. I'll mortgage my scrap yards, if I have to.'

'Are you old enough to own the club?' Clancy asked, sceptically. David shook his head.

'No, not until next year. Till then it will be in my mother's name, like the rest of my businesses.'

For all his goofy appearance, Clancy was the tough one, David decided. He was the sort of man who would rather have nothing than take less than he was asking. If they discussed the price later, Clancy would refuse to budge. Best to deal with it now. He was glad he had brought the suitcase.

'If you're prepared to drop your price by, say, thirty-five per cent,' he said, 'we could reach a gentlemen's agreement right now.'

'Thirty-five per cent!' Clancy scoffed.

'And as a sign of good will I'd be prepared to give you this,' David continued.

He swung the suitcase on to the table, flicked the catches, and opened it. Then, slowly, he turned it round, so that they could see what was inside.

'Sweet Jesus,' Clancy said.

The club owners gazed, wide-eyed, mouths open. Spooner's hand crept forward, wanting to make sure that it was real. But it was not his to touch, and with reluctance he let his arm flop down by his side.

'How much is in it?' Clancy asked, making an effort to keep his voice steady.

'Twenty thousand pounds.'

Clancy looked at the money again.

'We could take maybe a fifteen per cent drop in price.'

'Thirty.'

'Twenty?'

'Twenty-five.'

Clancy looked across at his partner, who nodded, then he held out his hand.

'You're on, Mr Harrison.'

If he had offered them a cheque or a bank draft, Clancy would have turned it down. Purchasing the club had been just like buying an old banger at the scrap yard. The seller could not resist the sight of all those lovely crisp blue notes. The magic power of ready money!

*

That summer saw all the pageantry of Prince Charles' Investiture as Prince of Wales and the drama of the first two men to walk on the moon. The Beatles opened the Apple Boutique and Blind Faith gave a free concert in Hyde Park. None of it caught Paul's imagination. He was impatient for the autumn and the annual party conferences. Because the coming year might just be *the* year when Harold Wilson went to the country and he would have his chance to stand as a Labour candidate.

Though he had enjoyed his teaching practices, his heart was not really in education. He had a secret hope that despite the sitting MP's majority of over eight thousand, he might win, that he would never have to get a job in a school.

As eagerly as he had anticipated it, when the Tory Conference finally came around, Paul found he had to force himself to watch. Ever since David had had to leave school, Paul had identified Socialism with good and Conservatism with evil. Not that he thought the Tories were actively evil in themselves – at least not many of them – but by their stupidity, complacency and narrow-mindedness, they were certainly evil by default. Seeing all those smug, self-satisfied faces, both on the platform and on the floor, incensed him. They were all so *sure* that they were right. Whereas he *knew* they were wrong.

It was on the Thursday that the unthinkable happened.

When the Chairman announced that the next speaker would be the President of the Seahaven University Conservative Association, Paul wasn't even watching the television. Instead, he was keeping his eye on young Paul who was lying on the rug and trying to cram a very large building brick into his very small mouth.

'I've got a mate at Seahaven,' Paul said to Ben Moore, who was sitting opposite him. 'He's in his final year.'

'Oh aye,' Moore said. 'Well if he's a mate, let's hope he doesn't go mixin' with this rubbish.'

He was pointing to the screen. The camera was right at the back of the hall and Paul could see a slim figure progressing down the aisle towards the podium at the front.

'He walks a bit like Jimmy,' Paul thought.

It would be fun to take the piss out of Jimmy over it, next time they met.

'You move just like a Tory,' he'd say. 'Got ideas above your station, have you, you arrogant bugger?'

The speaker reached the podium and leant his head forward slightly so as to be closer to the microphone.

'Mr Chairman, Ladies and Gentlemen,' a clear, confident voice rang out. 'We have heard a great deal in both the press and at this conference about challenges and opportunities in Britain today, but none of it seems to have really met the issue head-on.'

Paul's blood ran cold. It couldn't be true!

'Sounds like a Cheshire man to me,' Ben Moore said.

The camera zoomed in and Jimmy's face dominated the screen. Jimmy couldn't be the President of the Seahaven University Conservative Association. He was an impostor, a fifth columnist. He had left the real president tied up in the toilet. Any minute now he would begin his attack, ridiculing the delegates for believing that an intelligent working class boy, educated for the last five years under a Labour government, could ever subscribe to their Tory drivel.

But even Jimmy wouldn't have the brass nerve to pull a stunt like that!

Jimmy knew he looked calm and confident, but he had rarely felt so nervous – except with Claire. To get this slot, he'd had to call in a lot of favours, and he must use it well. It had taken Disraeli a long time to recover from the fiasco of his maiden speech and Jimmy couldn't afford years out in the cold. He was in too much of a hurry.

'I am from a working class background,' he said, 'yet I am studying at one of this country's fine universities. I have a friend who left school at fifteen and who is now well on the way to becoming a millionaire. What lesson can we learn from this? That if you want to be rich, you shouldn't go to university?'

He paused here for the anticipated laughter. If he didn't get it, he thought, he would probably drop his speech and flee the hall.

He needn't have worried. Humour had been thin on the ground at the conference. Besides it was the right kind of joke, because it was plain to all of them that in a moment he would say something to the greater glory of the Conservative and Unionist Party. The laughter died down, and Jimmy continued.

'No! That is not what it proves. It shows that in Britain today there are many different routes to success, many different opportunities.

'Yet this is Labour Britain. Am I saying that my friend and I are products of a Labour miracle? Again, no! Things do not happen overnight. The benefits that we are reaping are the benefits of thirteen years of Conservative rule, thirteen years of expansion, of increasing prosperity, of ever-widening opportunity. Benefits which in five years, the Labour Party has done so much to dismantle.'

It was going well, Jimmy could see that. He shifted gear, changing his tone from the moral outrage of the last few sentences to one of compassion.

'If Labour is re-elected, I will weep for the next generation. Because under Labour it will be denied the chances I have had. And I will weep for this country, because it is Britain that will be the loser if these young people's talents are left untapped – if their initiative is thwarted.'

Only a few lines left. He injected fierceness and confidence back into his voice.

'It is not too late to prevent the rot, to turn the tide. But we must act soon. Only a Conservative government can save us now, can put the "great" back into Great Britain. Only Edward Heath can lead this country as it deserves to be led, with decisiveness and imagination. We must win the next election, and we *will* win it.'

The applause was thunderous, and as he walked back to his seat, the delegates rose to their feet. They were clapping his words, but more than that, they were clapping him. He was a symbol of the opportunities that existed for the working class if only they were sensible enough to take them – he was a young man intelligent enough not to want to bite the hand that fed him.

Jimmy waited until the audience's attention was diverted onto someone else, and then slipped quietly out of the hall. He had made his impact; any new gesture of congratulations could only be an anti-climax, detracting from the standing ovation. He didn't leave unnoticed. A man in a tweed suit with a large walrus moustache was waiting in the doorway, legs akimbo, hand on hips.

'You from Cheshire, Mr Bradley?' he asked.

'Norton.'

'Aye, I thought you were,' the man said. 'Me too.' He held out his hand for Jimmy to shake. It was strong and callused. 'Name's Blackthorne. Stan Blackthorne. I run a little business up there.'

'A little business' was not the way Jimmy would have described Blackthorne Engineering. It was one of the biggest employers in Norton. And Stan Blackthorne didn't strike him as the sort of man to be overly modest. So, he was playing games, testing Jimmy out.

'I've heard of it,' he said.

'Aye,' Blackthorne said, 'but you wouldn't have done thirty years ago, because it didn't exist. I built it up from nothin'.'

He looked Jimmy up and down.

'I'm tryin' to decide whether you're a really bright lad – or if it's all show,' he said.

Different background, different age, but he sounded just like Hawsley the first time he had invited Jimmy to his room for sherry.

'Why don't you ask me?' Jimmy said.

'Are you bright?'

'As a button.'

Behind them there was the sound of applause.

'It didn't show in your speech,' Blackthorne said.

Jimmy flicked a thumb at the clapping delegates.

'They seemed to like it.'

'That lot,' Blackthorne snorted in disgust. 'Pampered, virtually to a man. There's a difference between soundin' smart and bein' smart, and when you start out with nowt, like I did, you soon learn to tell 'em apart. Now that speech of yours sounded smart, but you said sod all. It was just platitudes.'

'I know,' Jimmy agreed. 'But they were the *right* platitudes.'

'You're a cynical young bugger, aren't you?' Blackthorne asked.

Jimmy grinned at him.

'You wouldn't be here talking to me if I wasn't!'

Blackthorne smiled back.

'You're right,' he said. 'I wouldn't. What are you studying, lad?'

'Accountancy,' Jimmy said. 'I finish next summer.'

Blackthorne put his hand into his heavy waistcoat pocket and extracted a card.

'My private number,' he said. 'Give me a call round about March. I just might be able to come up with somethin' that might interest you.'

'A traitor to his class,' Ben Moore said in disgust, when Jimmy's speech had finished. 'And you say he used to be your mate?'

'No,' Paul said firmly. 'He *is* my mate.'

He had asked himself how Jimmy could do this to him, betray him in such a way. And then he realized that he didn't feel betrayed at all. Jimmy had spoken against everything Paul believed in, but he hadn't spoken against *him*, and try as he might, he could feel no resentment towards his old friend.

But he was worried. Their paths had separated, but they had to cross again. Could even Jimmy, the master tightrope walker, continue to balance friendship and ambition? If they ever became irreconcilable which one would Jimmy choose? And which would he choose himself?

Chapter Eighteen

The neon lights flashed and flickered, their garish colours cutting through the night, reflecting off the still-wet pavements of the Reeperbahn. Music blared from speakers fixed to the walls under the signs and David found himself caught in a cross-fire of conflicting rhythms and melodies. The air smelt of dampness, of bratwurst, of the odour of anticipation that lonely men exude when they are chasing a dream.

The area was full of men, sometimes alone, more often in groups, Many of them wore white uniforms and caps that proclaimed HMS Something-or-other. Others were in mufti, but rode the pavements as if they were rolling decks.

'Fake,' David thought. 'Unreal! All of it!'

It had been different down at the docks. That had been real, all right. There, the air had smelt of oil, of sweat and of the tangy salt that blew in off the sea. There had been no pictures of half-naked women twisted into almost-impossible positions – only massive, ugly ships and stark, skeletal cranes looming up on the sky-line. The sounds had been groaning and straining, not of men caught in the grip of brief sexual ecstasy, but of heavy machines loading and unloading relentlessly.

His father would have been comfortable in either environment; he felt ill at ease in both.

He had had many offers on his walk around the dockland. Some came from powerful, broad men, almost as big as he was. Some from thin, delicate waifs – cabin boys who, from the time they first put to sea, had been the love slaves of older, stronger crewmen. He turned them all down and headed instead for a dockside bar. He wanted to meet sailors, but they had to be a special kind.

There were so many clubs to choose from. David walked slowly along the street, inspecting the pictures and ignoring the exaggerated claims of the touts. Der Berlinerkeller seemed to offer what he was looking for. The women in the photographs looked exotic yet available, without any of the apathetic sleaziness that marked the strippers he had seen in some of the rougher clubs back home. One of the girls in the glass display case, he noticed, bore a close resemblance to the woman he had last seen astride Barry.

'Is it a good show?' he asked the doorman.

'Very goot. Ze best, ze dirtiest, in Hamburg.'

'I'll be back soon,' David said. 'Keep me a place.'

He held out his hand. The tout stared at it for a while, then reluctantly shook it.

As David walked away, he looked at his watch. Fifteen minutes should be enough to get the thing set up. He went and bought himself a currywurst.

The entrance fee was high but, as the man on the desk explained, it included membership subscription. He was left to make his own way along the narrow corridor and down the steep stairs. At the bottom he was met by another man, this one carrying a pencil torch. Together, they negotiated the twisting hazardous trail between the tightly packed tables until they reached an empty one. Suddenly the beam of the attendant's torch seemed locked on his hand. David placed some DMs in it, and the man went away.

The light in front of him was tiny, and it was only just possible to see the edge of the table. Around him, a score more flickering beacons floated on a sea of darkness. Heavy, sweet muzak seeped out of the speaker system, and on the stage a man and a woman, naked and bright pink under the spots, were softly stroking each other's bodies.

A weaving, wavering light made its way through the blackness and stopped at David's table. The torch-bearer's shape was vague. Only the fluffed-out hair told him that it was probably female. The girl lifted her beam so that it shone on David's face.

'English,' she said with certainty. 'Hello, Englishman. Ve sit and talk, you buy me drink.'

'No, thank you,' David said, wondering, 'What is it about us Brits that always makes us so formal and polite?'

The girl leant across the table, so that he could feel her breath on his face, smell her body, with its sickly mixture of perfume and sweat. Before he realised what was happening, her hand was on his chest, then moving swiftly downwards until it came to rest on his crotch.

'Come on,' she cooed into his ear. 'And later we haf a goot time.'

The touch made his skin crawl and he removed the hand. Gently, because the girl was only doing her job.

'Please go away,' he said.

She shrugged her shoulders and left.

The man and woman on stage had moved on to a low, rotating couch. The man was lying on his back, the woman kneeling, her rear end hovering over his face, her head slowly descending towards his penis.

Another flickering light, a new person, this time a waiter.

'Drink, sir? Champagne?'

David took out a thick roll of DMs and held them so the waiter got a good view. He peeled off some and handed them across the table.

'I want to see the manager,' he said.

The waiter pocketed the money.

'Zer iss no need,' he said. 'Vatever you vant, I can provide. A girl? A boy? A girl und a boy? You vant to fuck or only vatch? Is no problem.'

David gave him more money.

'The manager,' he said firmly.

The office was furnished in impeccable taste. The carpet was thick and luxurious. The soft armchairs blended with the expensive wall paper. Antique prints hung on the walls. The only thing that did not seem to fit was the man sitting behind the rosewood desk.

David remembered an action comic he had read as a boy. The head of the Gestapo, against whom the gallant British commandos were battling, had been totally bald, with a deep scar across his left cheek. He wore a black eye patch and had a Jolly Roger on his jersey. It had all been over-done, of course, David realised that at the time. Yet this man came close to that Gestapo model. There was no eye patch, but the scar was dramatic enough, and even though he was wearing a smooth dinner jacket, there was something piratical about his manner.

'I am Heinz Schüte,' he said. 'And you are. . . ?'

'David Harrison.'

'English. I spent several years in England. I learned the language well, did I not?'

'Very well,' David admitted.

Schüte ran his hands over his bald skull.

'Yes, I learned it from the prison guards. What were you doing in 1939, Mr Harrison?'

'I wasn't born.'

Schüte chuckled at his own joke.

'Of course you weren't. In 1939 I was what I suppose you would call a thug. I carried a razor. I offered protection. Zen – then – I was arrested by the police. They gave me a choice – prison or the army. I chose the army and soon became captured by the British.' He shrugged his shoulders. 'It was not so difficult. In the PoW camp I ran the rackets and learned my captors' language. After the war, I returned to Hamburg.'

He reached into his pocket, pulled out an expensive silver cigarette case, and offered it to David. When the young man shook his head, he took a cigarette himself and lit it with a solid onyx desk lighter.

'You should have seen this city after the war, Mr Harrison; so much devastation. But for a man who was smart, for a man who knew how to speak to the conquering heroes, it was a place of unlimited opportunities.'

'The black market.'

'The black market,' Schüte agreed. 'Food, cigarettes, girls, petrol, sometimes even drugs. I made a lot of money. And then, when people were becoming rich again, and they could afford to indulge their taste for luxury and depravity, I opened this club and several more like it.'

He inhaled deeply on his cigarette, then let the blue smoke ooze out of his wide nostrils.

'I am a rich man now. I have a big house, a Mercedes car and all my children were educated at very expensive private schools – but I still carry my razor.'

David listened patiently, knowing that Schüte was merely establishing his credentials, building himself up as a hard man. It wasn't necessary, David was already convinced. Still, it was a pity he didn't have an eye patch.

'So, Mr Harrison,' Schüte continued, 'I am only talking to you now because I am always interested to meet anyone who wants to see me so badly that he will pay my waiter such a large bribe. What do you want?'

David slid a piece of paper across the desk. Schüte scanned it.

'So you are in the process of buying a club. What is that to me?'

'I'll need acts,' David said. 'You could get them for me.'

Schüte lit another cigarette.

'Why should I?'

'Because it will make you a lot of money.'

'Are you sure?'

'Yes,' David said. 'The time's right. The government's relaxin' the obscenity laws. You're not gettin' pubic hair in men's magazines yet, but they're hintin' at it, and you'll soon be seein' full frontal nudity. Then it'll be the turn of the clubs.'

Schüte nodded.

'An' at the same time, the punters in the clubs are wantin' more for their money.'

'The poonters?'

Schüte frowned, obviously annoyed that he was not familiar with the word.

'The customers. They want class acts and more variety – the sort of show you're puttin' on here. It's not available in Britain. We've never been allowed shows like yours. We haven't got the experience. But once the punters see what you've got to offer, they won't be able to get enough. So you provide the acts, an' I'll guarantee the bookin's.'

Schüte smiled and stubbed out his cigarette.

'Let us go back into the club, Mr Harrison,' he said.

They stood by the bar. The man and woman had left the stage and been replaced by a girl with a Shetland pony. The pony was standing completely still, a blank, uninterested expression on its face. The girl was writhing, rubbing her body against its shaggy coat.

'We will have a drink,' Schüte said. 'I recommend the beer. The other things I sell are poison.'

The barman pulled them two beers.

'It is a good idea you have,' Schüte said. 'But now you have told it to me, why do I need you?'

'You'll have to have a partner in Britain,' David said.

'True, but I do not think you are the right partner.' He gestured into the darkness. 'Look at my clients.'

The only customers David could see through the darkness were four hard-looking merchant seamen at the table nearest the bar.

'They are not nice men,' Schüte continued amiably. 'They are almost like animals. Also, I have other problems. There are gangsters who would like to take over my business. There are policemen who want bribes or else a free hour with one of the girls. You are a big, strong man, Mr Harrison, but I do not think you are tough enough for this business.'

David said nothing.

'I will prove it to you,' Schüte said lightly, 'and in a quite not too expensive way. You showed my waiter that you had a lot of money. That was a mistake. I would not have made such a mistake, even in my early days. Now I know that you have the money – and I have the power to take it off you.'

Schüte moved away from the bar, so that he was facing David.

His place was taken by a large man with a shaved head and a broken nose. His dinner jacket strained against the bulging muscles it was covering. A second big man was standing on the other side of him.

'Put the money on the bar,' Schüte said smoothly, 'and then get out.'

'An' if I won't?'

Schüte laughed.

'Don't be stupid. Then my men will take you outside. You will struggle, but it will be useless. My customers – my . . . er . . . punters? – will say nothing. They are used to seeing drunks thrown out. Once these men have you in the alley, they *will* take the money off you. Then, because you have caused them trouble, they will hurt you. Perhaps they will even slash your face a little. They also carry razors.' His voice hardened. 'Hand over the money, Mr Harrison.'

David looked around the club. The girl on the stage was on her knees near the back end of the pony. The animal was becoming agitated. The little lights on the tables glittered in the darkness. The muzak seemed impossibly loud and syrupy.

'No!' he said.

'Very well.'

Schüte nodded. David felt his arms gripped, vice-like, but before the bouncers had time to move, the four merchant seamen were on their feet and blocking the exit.

'Havin' trouble, Mr Harrison?' one of them asked.

'I don't know,' David said, looking across at Schüte. 'Am I?'

The German's face had turned red. A vein throbbed on his bald skull.

'I have other men,' he rasped.

'And do you know that I don't?'

Schüte hesitated.

'We could start a fight that'd close this club,' David said. 'Couldn't we, lads?'

The seamen grinned as if they relished the prospect.

'But we don't want to do that,' David continued. 'Call your blokes off, and we'll leave quietly.'

Schüte nodded and the bouncers released their grips on David's arms, and stepped clear.

As David turned to go, Schüte placed a restraining hand on his shoulder. The seamen began to move in, but David shook his head. The German had got over being out-manoeuvred, and was grinning widely.

'Shall we go back into my office, Mr Harrison?' he said. 'I think I was wrong about you.'

It had to be done eventually, but it was still with reluctance that Jimmy invited Claire to go home with him for Christmas. He no longer hid the fact that he was working class, indeed he had made great play of it at the Party Conference. But there was a big difference between an abstract concept and the actual reality of his parents' small terraced house.

If Jimmy was worried, his mother was almost hysterical. The girl was posh, she would look down her nose at them – it was only natural! Mrs Bradley spent the weeks before their arrival in a frenzy of activity. Touching up the paint all over the house, re-decorating Jimmy's old bedroom – where Claire would sleep – scrubbing and polishing everything. And when it was all finished, she looked around in despair. It was the best house in the village, but it would never be good enough for Jimmy's young lady. She'd be used to one of them big mansions, like you saw on the films.

She need not have worried about the house. Claire's own comfort had never bothered her, and she found the village itself fascinating.

'I didn't know places like this existed,' she told her future mother-in-law as they walked down the street. 'Just look at those roofs. Thick rough slate, hacked out of the earth. Aren't they so wonderfully bleak and stark? And the light is different here. It's so grey. So hostile. I don't know – so *primitive*. It all makes the south look over-civilised, effete, don't you think?'

'Well, as long as you like it, luv,' Mrs Bradley replied, mystified.

She checked herself. You didn't call girls like Claire 'luv'. That was common.

'And who's that old man walking up the street? The one with the demented eyes and that evil hooked nose?'

'You want to keep away from him, lu . . . Claire. He's been inside, he has. In prison like.'

'Really! What for?'

'Well, he took this girl under the canal bridge and asked her to show him her knick . . . And asked her to show him somethin'. An' when she wouldn't, he just picked her up and threw her in.'

'And did she drown?' Claire asked.

'No,' Mrs Bradley admitted reluctantly. 'But she could have done. Anyway they locked him up, and they should never have let him out again if you want my opinion.'

'Marvellous,' Claire said. 'Simply delicious. No veneer. Everything stripped right back to the bone.'

'She isn't always easy to understand, Claire,' Mrs Bradley thought, 'but that's only to be expected, comin' from her background.'

'You want to get that chimney swept, Frank,' someone called to the landlord, who was collecting empty glasses.

'He's comin' tomorrer,' the landlord replied, as he always did when anyone complained.

Paul had been resentful of this get-together at first. He'd wanted to meet Claire, of course he had. But not under these circumstances. Jimmy should have brought her round to his house, then taken her to David's. It was all wrong that she should be with the three of them. Maggie never had been, nor had Barry during his brief period of residence. It was almost sacrilegious.

The moment he met Claire, all these thoughts melted away. She was beautiful. She was artistic, but completely different to the arty-crafty girls he had met at college. She was nothing like Maggie.

They talked about poetry, their conversation leaping from the Metaphysicals to the Georgians, then back into the Middle Ages. Paul was vaguely aware of his two friends – Jimmy gazing adoringly at his fiancée, David just looking bemused – but most of the time he was totally absorbed by Claire. If he had gone to university, he might have met someone just like her.

'What are your favourite lines of Eliot's?' Claire asked, after she had summed up the meaning of the *The Waste Land* to her own satisfaction.

Paul smiled.

'Almost impossible to say. There's so much good stuff. What about you?'

'That's easy,' Clare said.

> *'I should have been a pair of ragged claws,*
> *Scuttling across the floors of silent seas.'*

For a brief instant, the whole pub seemed to go silent. The dominoes had ceased to click, the fire was no longer spitting. Then Paul was aware of a shape behind, casting a shadow over the table. He looked round, and saw his father.

'Now then, Jimmy,' Wright said. 'Home on yer holidays? How long is it this time?'

'A month, Mr Wright,' Jimmy said. 'But we won't be here all the time.'

Wright shook his head in disbelief. 'A month,' he said. 'You don't know the meanin' of work, you lot. You should try graftin' for a livin', like what me and young David do. That's how you learn about life – not from books.'

Jimmy smiled, good-naturedly. He had heard the same words from half the men in the village, and by and large they were usually delivered as Wright said them now, without rancour.

'Anyway,' Wright continued, 'where's yer manners? Introduce me to yer young woman.'

Jimmy rose to his feet.

'Sorry. Clare Peel – Mr Wright, Paul's father. Mr Wright – Clare.'

Paul watched as his father's large callused paw, stained with a lifetime's oil, engulfed Clare's small artistic hand.

'How do you do?' Clare said.

'Very well, lass,' Wright said. 'I'm very pleased to meet yer.'

Paul found his eyes were glued to the interlocking hands. His father's thumb, thick and clumsy, its nails black and chipped, pressed down on delicate blue veins – a snake coiling around its prey, a cat toying with a mouse. The contact was broken and Claire's hand was free once more, yet Paul fancied it was stained, besmirched, polluted.

'Will you have another pint, Mr Wright?' Jimmy asked.

'No thanks, I've got to be goin'.' He turned to Claire. 'I'll be seeing you again, lass.'

Claire returned to the theme of modern poetry, sketching out her views on the way Ezra Pound had influenced Eliot, but her thoughts no longer flowed as they had done earlier.

'I'm tired,' she said after ten minutes. 'I think I'll go to bed.'

Jimmy stood up, helped her on with her coat and then reached for his own.

'No,' Claire said, 'you stay. I'm sure you three have heaps to talk about.'

As he watched her leave, Paul felt slightly ashamed. First he had resented her being here, and then he had given her all his attention, totally neglecting David and Jimmy.

'You were very impressive on television, Jimmy,' he said, by way of compensation. He had not meant to add any more, but he couldn't restrain himself. 'How could you do it? And how could

206

you have kept it all secret for so long? We didn't even know you were President.'

Jimmy put down his beer and looked Paul straight in the eye.

'I didn't tell you because we would have argued about it,' he said, 'just as we're about to do now. And our time together is too short, and too precious, to waste on a fight.'

Our time together is too short, and too precious, to waste on a fight.

Was he talking bullshit? Paul asked himself. Was he using emotional blackmail to head off a confrontation? He gazed back into Jimmy's clear blue eyes and found only sincerity there as, deep down, he had known he would. Jimmy was capable of distorting the truth – he was capable of telling complete bloody lies – but only to the outside world. However difficult it was, the Gang had always been honest with each other.

'Drop it,' he told himself. 'What Jimmy does in Seahaven has nothing to do with *us*. Don't take the risk!'

'Did you really believe that drivel you spouted?' he asked.

'Yes,' Jimmy said. 'Perhaps not as simplistically as I stated it, but fundamentally, yes.'

'But the Tories are so bloody self-seeking.'

'I agree,' Jimmy said, disarmingly. He took a long swallow of his pint. 'That's what makes then pragmatic. They don't approach a problem weighed down by dogma, they see it for what it is. So Conservatism works.'

'For the privileged few!'

'No. The wealth is shared out unevenly, but at least there is wealth to share out. Give your lot another few years, and this country will be ruined.'

They both turned to David, as they had always done in times of disagreement. He was uncomfortable under their scrutiny and for a moment it seemed as if he would shrug his shoulders – just as he had done when they argued about the Secret Camp Gang – and say he didn't mind. Instead, he addressed himself to Paul.

'You can't make everybody equal,' he said. 'There'll always be blokes like me who make more than most.'

Paul was about to protest, but David hadn't finished.

'An' I'm not the only one to benefit. There's five fellers working on the scrap who wouldn't have jobs at all, but for me. Then there's the club. It'll need waiters, door-keepers, maintenance men. They won't earn as much as me, but then I'm the bugger who's takin' all the risk.'

'Is it risky?' Paul asked, suddenly concerned for his friend.

'Course it bloody is,' David said. 'By the time I've finished, I'll

207

have used up all the cash I got from Goldsmith, the yards will be mortgaged and I'll be up to me neck in debt with the bank. An' that's before the place even opens.'

It had never really occurred to Paul before that David took chances. It just seemed as if everything he touched turned to gold. He looked at his old mate, so strong and solid, his pint mug made tiny by his huge hand. When David spoke of the club, did he tremble or was he only imagining it?

'It's a big gamble,' David continued, 'but I'm willin' to take it – an' that's why O'Malley's workin' for me, rather than the other way round.'

It sounded so logical and reasonable, but it wasn't. What if David hadn't been David, but some other kid without his drive? Some other kid forced to leave school, to exchange the possibility of becoming an engineer for an unskilled job in a scrapyard, a lifetime of misery and frustration? David had saved himself, but there were other people who couldn't, and they were the ones Paul wanted to help.

David seemed to read his thoughts.

'I'd do anythin' for you two, you know that,' he said. 'You have to be loyal to your gang, Paul, but a country's just too big a gang for anybody to manage.'

The talk got easier, drifting into the old days. The dominoes clicked, the fire hissed. The room itself was a part of their past, and they were warmed by its cosy familiarity.

At eleven o'clock, when last orders were called, Jimmy was feeling a little drunk. It was a rare sensation for him. Boozing was a dangerous activity, one that might loosen his tongue and let the real Jimmy break through the image – like a chicken poking its way from the shell. Only with David and Paul could he relax, only with them did he feel safe.

As he walked back to his parents' house, he was feeling happy and optimistic. He was the Chairman of the Conservative Association. He had made a big impact at the Tory Conference. Stan Blackthorne would almost definitely offer him a job – a good job – in the Spring. He had Claire . . .

There were problems, too, he realised. Claire could be difficult at times, and he worried when he was away from her. And then there was Paul. Why had he discovered politics? Why couldn't he be a writer like he'd always wanted to be? The world was big enough for both of them, there was no need to fight each other for the same bit of space.

'Getting morbid,' he told himself.

It might never come to a conflict with Paul, and even if it did, it could be years away yet. He would handle it when it arose. He could handle anything – there was no obstacle he couldn't overcome.

His mother was sitting in the kitchen polishing the brass ornaments from the mantelpiece.

'Where's Claire?' she asked.

'Claire,' he slurred the word slightly. 'She came back hours ago.'

'She did not. I've been sittin' here all night an' I've seen neither hide n' hair of her.'

He was instantly sober, as if he had been doused by a bucket of icy water. Claire missing! People went missing in Manchester and London, not Buckworth.

'I – I'm going to look for her,' he stuttered, opening the back door.

Most of the houses were in darkness. Jimmy ran down the street shouting Claire's name. Not caring if he woke anyone up, not caring if they thought him insane. He had to find her.

He stood at the crown of the hump-backed bridge and looked at his old school in the pale moonlight. He could see no movement. He knelt on the hard cobbles of the canal tow-path and plunged his hand in the freezing water, breaking up the paper-thin layer of ice. He followed the old railway line past abandoned salt mines, almost to the wood. He heard only his own gasping breaths and the sound of his feet on the cracked, frozen earth. All else was still – silent.

His mother was so distracted she had let the fire go out, but she still sat there in front of the ashes, polishing with maniacal fury.

'You haven't found her,' she said.

Jimmy shook his head.

'Oh my God! She could be anywhere!' Rub, rub, rub, at the brass iron-holder, until it seemed she would wear the metal away. 'She could be absolutely anywhere. Whatever will we do? Whatever will we tell her poor parents?'

Jimmy put his hand on his mother's shoulder.

'Go up to bed, Mum,' he said gently.

'But what about Claire? Who's goin' to . . .'

'I'll wait up for her.'

'I won't sleep,' Mrs Bradley said, as Jimmy eased her out of the chair and shepherded her to the foot of the stairs. 'I won't sleep a wink, not knowin' where that poor girl is.'

'Don't you worry yourself,' Jimmy soothed. 'It'll be all right.'

His mother's heavy footsteps reached the top of the stairs, and a little while later he heard the bed creak. He settled down in the armchair to continue the vigil alone. Closing his eyes, he saw Claire's bloated body float down the canal. Opening them again, he saw her lying under a bush, her face puffed and purple, a strangler's scarf wrapped tightly around her neck.

It was half-past one when he heard the latch being lifted and saw Claire walk in.

'Hello,' she said, as if nothing out of the ordinary had happened.

'Where've you been?' he demanded, his voice a mixture of anger and relief.

'For a walk,' Claire said.

'You said you were going to bed. You've been missing for more than four hours!'

Claire took off her coat and hung it behind the door.

'I decided I wasn't tired. And it was a long walk!'

'Why didn't you tell me?' he pleaded. 'I would have gone with you. You must have known I'd be worried.'

His anger had simply bounced off her, but this new tone made her furious.

'Don't you try to control me with your petty emotional games!' she said.

'Claire, I've got a right to . . .'

'You don't have any rights. You don't own me – I'm a free person.' Her voice dropped low. 'Do you want to know *why* I went for a walk?'

It was a threat, and it frightened him, though he could not have explained why. He just knew that it was suddenly very important not to find out why Claire had gone for a walk, and that if he pressed her any more, she would tell him. He sat there, still and terrified, while Claire made her way upstairs.

On previous nights, Claire had obeyed the strictures of working class respectability, and retired chastely to her own room. But later, when the Bradleys were asleep, she had always gone to Jimmy, her body hot and demanding. She did not visit him that night, and he lay in a lonely bed, tossing and turning, hugging his pillow. He didn't fall asleep until dawn.

He woke depressed. The room was cold and frost had formed an icy, intricate pattern on the outside of the window. He did not want to get up. If Claire was so angry with him that she would even forgo the slaking of her sexual thirst, would he be brave enough to face her? He steeled himself, threw off the blankets, and planted his feet firmly on the chilly floor.

His mother was in the kitchen, black-leading the fireplace.

'Have you seen Clare?' he asked.

Mrs Bradley sniffed, but did not look up.

'I heard her come in last night. Must have been half-past one.'

And she must have heard them arguing too.

Jimmy wanted to grab his mother and shake her until she answered his question, but instead he said, 'Yes, it was about that. She went for a walk.'

'Well, she got up early enough,' his mother said.

Had she packed her bags and left? Was that it – all over?

'Where is she now?' he asked, keeping his voice as level as he could.

'She's in the yard – drawin'.'

She was sitting on top of an upturned dolly-tub, her sketch pad balanced on her knees. She was well wrapped up, a scarf around her neck, a woolly hat on her head, but she wore no gloves and her exposed hand moved over the paper, drawing a line here, shading an area there.

'Aren't you cold?' Jimmy asked timidly.

She glanced up from her work.

'A little,' she said, 'but I need the light. I wanted to get this down on paper before I lost it.'

There was none of the previous evening's anger in her voice, not even a hint of annoyance. It was as if the row had never happened.

He looked over her shoulder to see what she was drawing. The sketch was in its early stages, but it was clearly a tree, with a man standing looking at it. He thought it an odd choice of subject.

Claire made innumerable sketches, but did not begin the painting until they were back in Seahaven. Then, she locked herself in her studio and it was a week before Jimmy was invited round to see the finished result.

'What do you think?' she asked, although she wasn't really seeking his opinion. She never sought anyone's opinion.

'It's very powerful,' he said.

It horrified him! It was a man and a tree, as it had been in the drawings, but paint and texture had brought about a great change in it.

The tree was no longer a sapling, yet it still looked young and vulnerable. Its fresh, green leaves gave it an almost virginal quality. The roots grew either to the left or the right, creating the impression of spreadeagled human legs. It seemed to tremble with fear – or perhaps, anticipation.

The man's body was more wood-like than the tree's; it was hard and unyielding and his muscles were bunched and knotted. He was naked, and his huge penis, its blue veins standing out, thrust forward as he approached the tree. The face – as in all Claire's faces since they first made love – had an inhuman quality about it. It was a face stripped of all experience, all emotion, save lust. The eyes were fiery and piercing, seeming to burn their way into the tree. The lip curled in animal anticipation of the sensations to come. It was not a human face – but it was clearly recognisable as Paul's father.

PART FOUR

Snakes and Ladders

Chapter Nineteen

Ben Moore had based his strategy on an autumn election, because that was when everyone said it would be. But the Socialists had done well in the May local elections and were leading the Conservatives in the opinion polls for the first time that year. Besides, the warm weather was coming, and that always had an effect on the Labour turnout. So on the 14th of May, the Prime Minister told his colleagues that he would be going to the country in the middle of June.

As soon as the news came through, Sam Holland, the Labour candidate, announced that he would not be contesting Norton. There was pandemonium in Transport House, followed by a personal call to Holland by one of the party bigwigs.

It was very late to renounce his candidacy. Yes, Holland said, he realised that, and he was sorry. Couldn't he just fight one more election? No, his doctor had told him that his health would not stand it.

There were more frantic calls, this time to the constituency association. They had the Approved List of Candidates, didn't they? Then they'd better get on with the job of choosing a replacement for Holland right away.

The constituency association committee held the interviews the following Monday morning. There were four candidates from the Approved List, and one local man, Paul Wright. The home-town lad got it.

The news came through to Transport House at one o'clock. By one-thirty, while most of the party bureaucrats concerned were still running around like headless chickens, Frank Sutton had cleared authorisation and was sitting in a taxi on the way to Euston.

He was not an attractive man. His face was long and thin, all angles, as if it had been chipped out of stone by someone who had lost interest half-way through. His eyes were pale, hard and angry and his greying hair was cropped almost like a prisoner's. Some of his colleagues wondered openly whether he had got the job of trouble shooter — or hatchet man, if they were feeling less charitable – because of his appearance. But it wasn't a case of type-casting. He loved his work, and his looks were just a bonus.

The Norton constituency association had been a thorn in the side of the Party machine for years, and Sutton had been waiting for a chance to pay them back. Now they'd served themselves up on a plate. Maybe that old shit Ben Moore had forgotten what happened in the Liverpool Royal Exchange constituency, but he hadn't. By evening, this Paul Wright – whoever he was – would no longer be the Party's candidate for the seat. And with a little bit of luck, Ben Moore would have gone too.

Paul had found the morning's interview tiring. All the other candidates seemed more competent, more self-assured – older – and it had almost come as a surprise to him, despite Ben's assurance, when the committee selected him.

Now it was early afternoon. The surprise had worn off and should have been replaced by elation – he had taken the first step towards success. Instead, there was this nagging, undefined worry, eating away at his brain, weighing down on his soul. He waited until young Paul was having his afternoon nap then sat down in the front room to try and isolate the cause of his depression.

What was the worst thing that could happen? He could lose the election. The Conservative candidate, Major Yatton, had had a parliamentary career only distinguished by its lack of distinction, but he had held the seat since 1945, and his majority had never dropped far below eight thousand. So, Yatton was likely to win again. That would be a blow, but not a crushing one. He could get a teaching job until the next election, and then fight Norton again. Or perhaps the Party would give him a safer seat next time.

He realised that his main worry was not Yatton, but the Party. If they allowed him to fight this election, he would have a chance of showing them what he could do. But would they let him? Despite what Ben said, Paul could not see them accepting him, untested, untried, over the candidates from the Approved List. They would kick him out – and then he'd be a marked man. They would never seriously consider him again.

He wished he hadn't listened to Ben, wished that he had waited a few years until he was more acceptable. The ladder of success had seemed so easy to climb. Only now could he see that there were rungs missing.

His gloomy thoughts were interrupted by a tapping on the

window, and he looked up to see a face smiling in at him. He jumped to his feet and opened the door.

'Jimmy!' he said, delightedly. 'It's the middle of term. What the bloody hell are you doing here?'

'I thought you might like a pint.' Jimmy glanced at his watch. 'There's still time if we hurry.'

The back room of The George was empty, as it usually was at lunchtime. They sat at the domino table, frothing glasses in front of them, grinning at each other.

'So what *are* you doing here?' Paul asked.

'I assume I'm talking to the prospective Labour Party candidate for Norton.'

'I was picked this morning,' Paul said, 'but I'm not sure if the P . . .'

'Then that's why I'm here. To help you.'

'What about your finals?'

Jimmy chuckled.

'They're not until the end of June. And I'm at Seahaven, not Oxford, remember. The exams should be a piece of piss. Besides, I figured Labour might try to make a dash for safety instead of waiting till the Autumn, and I've already done most of my revision.'

'You mean you – a Conservative – are willing to canvass for me?' Paul asked, adding mentally, 'if I'm ever allowed to stand.'

Jimmy shook his head.

'I'd be wasted canvassing. I'm much more valuable organising the campaign than I'd ever be tramping door-to-door. Besides, I'm not quite prepared to cut my political throat yet.'

'So you haven't undergone some sort of roadside conversion? You *are* still a Tory.'

'Of course I'm still a Tory.'

'Then why are you helping me?'

'Because you're my mate, and that's more important right now.'

Paul nodded gratefully, accepting it at face value as Jimmy had known he would. And it was true – but it wasn't that simple. Nothing Jimmy did ever was. He wanted to help Paul while he still could, before it would damage his own interests to do so. He wanted to build up merit, at least in his own mind, so that he wouldn't feel guilty when, in a few years' time . . .

But that was all long-term. There was something much more pressing. He had talked to Stan Blackthorne again and now had a pretty good idea of what the job at the engineering works would involve. There would be trouble – lots of it – and if Paul was around, he would be a formidable opponent. Far better to have him in London, too concerned about national issues to devote much time to a parochial little problem at Blackthorne's.

After Sutton had paid off the taxi from Norton station, he stood for a second outside Ben Moore's house.

'Not much to show for a lifetime's work,' he thought. 'The bloody fool!'

He rapped hard and waited impatiently until Moore opened the door.

He was shocked by how much the other man had aged since the last time they had been at loggerheads. His eyes were watery, his neck looked as if it belonged on a scraggy chicken. His hands were covered with liver-spots and his clothes hung loosely on him. He had been a hell raiser, now he was just an old man. This was going to be a doddle.

'It's not often we see you up here these days, Mr Sutton,' Moore said.

'You've tried to pull a fast one,' Sutton answered, 'and we're not fucking having it.'

'Aye, it's nice to see you an' all,' Moore said mildly. 'Are you comin' in?'

They went into the front room. Sutton sat down, opened his case, and pulled out a sheaf of papers.

'Would you like a drink, Mr Sutton?' Ben asked.

'This isn't a social visit,' the other man snapped, 'and I've no time for pissing about with the niceties. I've got to be back in London tonight. There's an election on and I've got more important things to do than bugger about in no-hope constituencies.'

Moore reached for the whisky bottle and poured out a measure. His hand shook.

'You won't mind if I have one meself?' he said. 'I think it's very good of you to spare us any time at all.'

'You didn't give me much fucking choice, did you?' Sutton said angrily, running his hand, fingers outstretched, through his cropped hair. 'What the fuck did you think you were pulling this morning?'

'Me?' Ben asked innocently, 'or the constituency association?'

'It's the same thing,' the other man snorted, 'and don't try to tell me different.'

'All right,' Moore conceded. 'I won't. So what's the problem?'

'You have an Approved List of Candidates. *Approved.* That means Transport House has vetted these people and found them suitable. But you couldn't select one of them, could you? You had to choose this fucker Wright.'

'He was the best man for the job. I believe we are entitled, by Party rules, to use our own discretion.'

'Only if you apply it sensibly. For Christ's sake, Wright's only twenty-one!'

'Bernadette Devlin was only a few months older than Paul Wright when she was elected.'

'And now she's in fucking jail.'

Ben laughed, a noisy rattle that barely left his throat.

'Oh, I don't think you need have any worries on that score,' he said. 'Paul's not the sort o' lad to go around throwin' bricks at anybody.'

Sutton looked at his watch. There was a train back to Manchester in less than an hour. If he could wrap things up speedily, he could be on it. And it would be over a lot quicker if he gave the old fart a chance to save a bit of face.

'What about a compromise?' he suggested. 'You withdraw Wright now and put someone more experienced in, and we'll promise to consider your lad for another constituency at the next election.'

He made a mental note to see to it personally that Wright was never considered for anywhere – ever again.

'Get rid of a candidate who knows the town and its problems, so that you can fill his place with a blue-eyed boy from Transport House?' Moore said. 'No chance!'

Fine, if that was the way the geriatric shit wanted to play it.

'Remember what happened in Liverpool Exchange in the fifties?' Sutton asked.

'Aye,' Ben said. 'I think so. The constituency association wasn't happy with its MP, Bessie Braddock. Thought she was payin' too much attention to what you lot wanted, an' not enough to the folk who'd elected her. So they refused to re-adopt her, and selected a bloke called Murphy instead.'

'Go on,' Sutton said.

'Party machine didn't like it. They tried to make the association toe the line – just like you're tryin' to make me do now.'

'And when they wouldn't?'

'They expelled the whole association an' set up a new one full o' good little boys an' girls who'd do what London wanted.'

Sutton flicked through his papers and found the one he wanted.

'The new association selected Mrs Braddock,' he said. 'Murphy stood as Independent Labour.' He glanced down at his statistics. 'In the 1955 election, he polled less than three thousand votes. She got over nineteen thousand.'

'Is there a moral behind this, or what?' Moore asked.

'Do you want us to expel the constituency association? Do you want us to expel you personally from the Party, after a lifetime's membership?'

Moore's mildness disappeared. His eyes blazed and his chest puffed out. He seemed suddenly bigger, Sutton thought with alarm.

'You don't belong to the Labour Movement because of a bit o' paper,' Moore said, banging his heart with the palm of his hand. 'You belong to it because o' this. But that's somethin' a bureaucrat like you will never understand.'

He began coughing uncontrollably.

'You had me worried for a minute,' Sutton thought. 'You looked like you were really fighting back.'

But it had only been the last stand of an old campaigner. And seeing him now, it was debatable whether they would be able to revoke his life membership before the Great Party Machine in the Sky revoked his membership of life.

'You can't expel us,' Moore said, between coughs. 'It was different in Liverpool. You had plenty o' time then to set up a new organisation. You haven't got that here. There's only three weeks to the election.'

Sutton shuffled his papers again and came up with a sheet of tightly written notes. He waved them at the older man.

'I've been doing the calculations on the train,' he said. 'We only need a few people from the constituency as rubber stamps. The rest of the organisation we can draft in from outside.'

That was it. The final, crushing fact. He sat back complacently and waited for the old man's surrender. But Moore didn't look defeated. Instead, he had a dreamy expression on his face. Maybe the old man had gone ga-ga already.

'Split in Labour ranks on eve of election,' Moore said, in an airy, far-away voice.

'What?'

'Sorry, I was just thinkin' aloud. I wonder what would happen if you expelled us and we fought back. Political parties are a bit like families.'

'Like families?'

'Aye, an' I don't just mean that they've got some right proper

220

sods in 'em. It's all right for them to have fights – everybody expects it – but there's a time an' a place for everythin'. You don't row at weddin's. An' you don't row just before General Elections. As soon as you've gone I'm off down to the phone box to call *The Express* an' *The Telegraph*.' He chuckled, and it brought his coughing on again. 'I've never bought 'em in me life,' he gasped, 'but I wouldn't miss 'em tomorrer for anythin'.'

'You old cunt!' Sutton thought.

'Should cost a few seats,' Moore continued. 'An' somebody's head'll have to roll at party headquarters. By, I wouldn't like to be in his shoes.'

Moore was sick, all right, Sutton decided, but not half as sick, not half as defeated, as he'd pretended to be. He'd been playing a game all along, thoroughly enjoying himself.

'All right,' Sutton growled.

'Am I to take that to mean that you've examined our choice of candidate and find him satisfactory?' Ben asked innocently.

'You really are an awkward old bastard, aren't you?' Sutton asked.

'So they tell me,' Ben said. 'I'll show you out, shall I?'

Ben watched Sutton's angry back retreating down the street. He had enjoyed himself, but he had been worried as well. He had never been quite sure, until the very end, that Sutton wouldn't call his bluff. And the coughing had been no act, nor were the heart palpitations he was experiencing as he stood in the doorway.

Sutton had never liked him, but now he was a sworn enemy. That meant that he was Paul's enemy too. If his young friend was ever to have any future in Labour politics, he would have to make a name for himself in this election, a name big enough to over-ride whatever damage Sutton could do in Transport House. He put his hand on the door-post for support.

'I've done me best, Paul lad,' he gasped. 'From now on, it's up to you.'

Chapter Twenty

The pointed gravestone was covered in green lichen. Despite the heat of the afternoon, it was still cool to the touch. Paul removed his hand and turned towards the old church. When it was first built, it must have been the most impressive building for miles. From its elevated position, it still looked down on most of the town.

'Why are we here?' he asked.

'Because,' Jimmy said, 'it gives us a clear view of at least half the constituency.'

They could have sat at home with a map, but Jimmy had always had a flair for the dramatic.

'We've got to target you,' Jimmy said. 'That way, we get maximum impact.' He pointed to the west. 'We ignore the executive estates, they'll never vote for you whatever you do.' His finger swung to the south, over the railway tracks. 'And we don't waste time on the solid Labour wards; *they'd* vote for you if you were a monkey.'

It made Paul feel uneasy.

'I don't want to ignore my supporters.'

'Who said we'll ignore them? Come Election Day, David will have his vans and volunteers round there, making sure we get them to the polling station. But we don't waste any of *your* time on them. It may be gratifying to preach to people who eat up your every word, but it won't win you any extra votes.'

That made sense, but it still seemed wrong. They walked slowly along the path, towards the far end of the graveyard.

'I've been talking to your agent,' Jimmy continued, 'and we've worked out a provisional list of speaking engagements. Now – your image.'

'What image?' Paul asked. 'I'm a person, not a box of soap powder.'

Jimmy laughed.

'I know you are, and a complicated bugger at that. But we can't hope to represent the many sides of Paul Wright to the electors, so we're going to have to refine it down. I think we should make a lot of play of you as the family man – you and Maggie, you and young Paul, the three of you together.'

That seemed honest. He *was* a family man. He loved his child and he was very fond of his wife. Besides, it would take the voters' minds off how young he was.

'And we've got to play up your youth,' Jimmy said.

'Isn't that dangerous?'

'It's a gamble, but it's one we've got to take. We have to make a clear distinction between you and Yatton – the crusty old landowner set in his ways and the dynamic young teacher.'

'I'm not a teacher yet.'

'We haven't got time for subtleties,' Jimmy said impatiently. 'You'll be qualified soon. You've already been in the classroom on teaching practice. We don't want to confuse the electors.'

'Confuse them?' Paul thought. 'With the truth?'

'Besides,' Jimmy said, 'there's another angle on this youth thing. If you don't mention how young you are, you can be sure that your opponents will. So rather than treat it as a weakness, we'll make it a strength. And there may be a spin-off. The tabloids are still looking for new angles on this election. What better one than the youngest candidate?'

'I don't care about national fame,' Paul said. 'At least,' he added honestly, 'not at the moment.'

'You should. People like to vote for nationally known figures. That's part of the reason why Heath and Wilson get such large majorities.'

They reached the boundary wall, and wheeled round.

'What do you think of England's chances in the World Cup?' Jimmy asked.

'The World Cup? Not a clue. I'm not interested in football.'

'Neither am I,' Jimmy said, 'but then *I'm* not running for office.'

He reached into his pocket and pulled out five sheets of foolscap paper, covered with his small, neat handwriting. He laid them on a flat tombstone and smoothed them out.

'I did some research while I was in Seahaven,' he said. 'These are the details of the teams that are still in the competition. Basic strategies, goal averages, weaknesses and strengths of individual players. Learn them.'

'Learn them!'

'Don't ever underrate patriotism, Paul,' Jimmy said. 'If England does well, it will reflect on the government. Don't you think your glorious leader has taken that into his calculations?'

Was all this really necessary, Paul asked himself. Couldn't he just stand on his own merits? He looked down at the river, the Drill Hall, Blackthorne's Engineering. He had long ago lost his religion, but he remembered that Satan had taken Christ up to a high point and offered him the kingdoms below if only he would fall down and worship him. He was getting above himself, he thought. He was no Messiah and Jimmy wasn't the Devil.

'Anyway,' Jimmy continued, 'you may not be interested in football, but your voters are. And they like to think you're one of them. If you want the support of the common man, you've got to have the common touch. Now, we need an efficient research unit . . .'

David stood in the centre of The Diamond Theatre Club and looked around him. It had changed a great deal from the time he and his father had visited it. It might have been a little seedy then, but now it looked as if a bomb had hit it.

It wasn't the sub-contractor's fault. The structural weakness in the room had been invisible until they had gutted the building. They'd been lucky that the whole place had not fallen down around their ears. But fixing it had taken much more time and money than David had anticipated.

He had thrown all his energy into the project since the defect was discovered. Sometimes he would act the gaffer, the man who was paying for it all, urging the workers on. At other times, he would strip off his coat and work side by side with the labourers, clearing rubble. Rarely was he absent.

The club had been scheduled to open in April. The acts had been booked through Schüte, the staff had been engaged. And still, in the middle of May, there was no sign that the work was near completion.

'You've had some bad luck, Mr Harrison,' O'Malley shouted over the hammering and banging.

True, but would that satisfy the bank manager on the first of August, when the first massive payment on the loan fell due?

David watched the workmen on the scaffolding, chipping away at the ceiling. A huge chunk of rotting plaster detached itself and crashed to the ground, throwing up a cloud of thick white dust.

'I'm goin' to take a few weeks off,' David said. 'Put somebody else in charge of the yards and take over here yourself.'

O'Malley rubbed his stubbly chin with the palm of his hand.

'Oi tink you're makin' a mistake,' he said. 'You've got good workers on this job, you always had an eye for men, but dey won't be *quoite* as good if you're not here.'

'That's why I want you to take charge.'

O'Malley grinned and shook his head.

'Remember when you gave me de start?' he said. 'You were little more than a child. But you had *sometin*. An' as you've got older, it's got stronger. Oi can run de yards for you, I can supervise dese men, but Oi'll never get de results you would, and roight now you need de best result you can get. Don't walk away from de job when it really needs you.'

More plaster hit the floor, and David watched the dust swirl. Every day this went on, it was costing him more than he could afford. He was spending money like water, and getting nothing back in return.

'Stay wid it, Mr Harrison,' O'Malley urged.

'I can't,' David said. 'There's something else I have to do.'

Only yesterday, it had been David's front parlour. Now, it was unquestionably Jimmy's office, dominated by an old kitchen table heaped high with plain paper and graph paper, pens of all colours, lists of local rate payers and Labour Party literature. A battered duplicating machine stood silently in the corner. Jimmy was busily writing.

'What are you doing?' Paul asked.

'I'm drafting a local opinion poll,' Jimmy said, hardly looking up. 'David's canvassers can take it round with them.'

The tone was light, casual, but Paul knew his friend of old. Jimmy was planning something devious.

'Won't that slow the canvassers down?' he asked, probingly.

'It'll be worth it,' Jimmy said, picking a ruler and drawing a straight line across the paper.

'Why? What sort of questions are you asking?'

'Nothing outrageous. What they think of the main issues, what qualities they look for in candidates. Things like that.'

'How will that help us?' Paul asked suspiciously.

'Even if we just threw them into the bin, they would do us some good,' Jimmy explained. 'Voters like people who seek their opinions. Makes them feel important. And they'll remember it was the Labour candidate who was interested.'

Jimmy was stalling. Paul was sure of it.

'But you're not going to throw them away, are you?' Paul asked.

'No, I'll analyse them.'

'And then?'

'And then,' Jimmy said, realizing that Paul was on to him, and abandoning his plan for a more subtle approach, 'and then I'll use the information to write your speeches.'

Paul was incensed.

'No you bloody well won't!' he said. But he found himself wondering *why* Jimmy wanted to do it. 'Is there something wrong with my speeches?' he asked.

'No,' Jimmy replied. 'They're very good. Clear, well thought out, logically argued. They'd be a smash at the Oxford Union. But they won't go down too well with the Old Age Pensioners' Association. The only thing that interests them about the EEC Common Agricultural Policy is what it will do to Fluffy the cat's dinner.'

Paul could see the point, he was sometimes aware of talking over his audience's head – but he still didn't like it.

'This isn't America, you know,' he said.

'Just try it once,' Jimmy pleaded. 'Then, if you think it didn't work, I'll drop the idea.'

So Paul *did* try, three days later, at the Junior Chamber of Commerce. They were a potentially hostile audience, but he went away feeling that he had been given a basically good reception. On the way home, he analysed the speech Jimmy had written. There was nothing in it that he didn't fervently believe in, and yet he knew that he would not have said any of it in quite that way. He knew, too, that if he had said it his way, he would have ruffled a lot more feathers.

He gave Jimmy the go-ahead to write the rest of his speeches. It left him more time to canvass, to address meetings, to talk to people in the street. And anyway, Jimmy seemed to have been right about everything else so far. Paul had already featured on the front page of three national newspapers, and the result of the first poll showed that local people were flattered by the national attention focused on their election.

It was only a week into the campaign and Paul did not know how he would survive until the end. His voice was nearly gone, he had shaken so many hands he thought his fingers would drop off, his feet and legs ached from so much walking and standing, and lack of sleep had reddened his eyes. It was a relief to finally go home and submit to the cosy warmth of Maggie's ministrations. Or at least it would have been, if he hadn't promised Jimmy he would ask her the question.

As soon as he entered the house he flung himself into his favourite armchair, kicked off his shoes and put his feet up on the coffee table. Maggie brought him a glass of malt whisky – one of the many things Ben Moore had taught him to appreciate – and sat on the rug, her back resting against the arm of his chair. Paul looked down on his wife's blonde head. How could he ask? It wasn't fair.

Maggie raised her hand over her shoulder, and Paul took it.

'What is it, Paul?' she asked after a second. 'You're more than just tired. Somethin's wrong.'

'Mrs Bloody Major Yatton,' he admitted. 'She's doing even more campaigning than her husband.'

'Is it costin' you votes?'

'Jimmy thinks so.'

'An' does he want me to do somethin' about it?' Maggie asked heavily.

There was no easy way to say it. 'Yes,' Paul told her. 'He wants you to campaign as well.'

Maggie was silent for a while, then she said, 'What would I have to do?'

'Just talk at a few meetings. Women's Institutes, places like that. It would all be very easy. Jimmy would give you a full briefing before you ever went.'

He felt her hand tighten with tension.

'Do I have to?' she whispered.

'It would help me a lot,' he said. 'And there's really nothing to be frightened of. You should never have an audience of over thirty or forty.'

'No, you don't understand,' she said. 'It's not *that* that worries me. I don't mind goin' on the platform. It's the part *before*. The bein' alone with Jimmy.'

The park! It always came back to the park!

'Jimmy's changed,' he said softly, 'we've all changed.'

Maggie twisted round to face him, and he could see that she was crying.

'Jimmy's not changed,' she said. 'He's just got worse. He's spent his whole life pretendin' – so that he'll impress people, so that he can get on. An' now he's forgotten what he's really like himself. He treats life – people – like it was just all part of a game, an' that scares me.' She put her head in his lap, and her last words were so muffled that he didn't hear them. 'You treat life serious, as if it mattered. That's why I love you – that's why I'll do what you want.'

It was as much of an ordeal as she had anticipated. For three hours they were closeted together in David's front room, while Jimmy explained, slowly and clearly, what Labour's policy was on all the major issues. Maggie couldn't complain about his behaviour, there was no attempt to charm her as there had been in the past. Rather, she suspected, he didn't see her as Maggie at all, only a part of his master-plan to get Paul elected, as mechanical and impersonal as the duplicating machine.

Yet even his physical presence was enough to disturb her. When his slim hand passed over hers to reach for a page of statistics, a wave of revulsion swept through her. As he bent forward to make a point, and his breath fell lightly on her cheek, she thought she would vomit. She was oblivious to most of his words, his careful explanations. It took most of her will not to run from the room screaming.

It was hopeless, thought Jimmy when Maggie had gone. She seemed incapable of grasping most of the facts he gave her, unable to absorb all but the simplest details. Even the few things he did manage to drum into her head, she could only repeat woodenly. If Mrs Yatton's numerous appearances hadn't been so damaging, he would never have considered using her at all. As it was, he gloomily arranged for her to speak at a local Women's Institute about her life as a parliamentary candidate's wife. He prayed she wouldn't be too much of a disaster.

At the end of the second week, Jimmy announced that his polls showed that Yatton's majority was down to five thousand and still dropping. The news seemed to push Paul over the pain threshold – give him a second wind. It did a lot for the morale of the volunteers. Walking around the campaign headquarters, slapping shoulders, giving encouragement, Paul was aware of the excitement, the camaraderie, and of the overwhelming feeling that with just a little more effort, they could win.

Only one face looked out of place – Ben Moore's. He was sitting in the corner, his expression mournful, his old gabardine mac belted tightly around him despite the warmth of the day.

'What's the matter, Ben?' Paul said.

'I'm just under the weather, lad,' he said.

But he refused to look Paul in the eye as he spoke.

'Oh, come on, Ben,' Paul said. 'We're mates. I deserve a better answer than that.'

'Aye,' said Moore. 'I reckon you do. I don't like the way this campaign is being run.'

'What do you mean?' Paul asked, puzzled. 'The gap's narrower than it's ever been, and it's getting smaller by the day.'

'I've been to some of your meetings, lad,' Ben said. 'I hardly recognized yer. What ever happened to yer socialism? Where's the great sweepin' reform you used to talk about? All you do now is appeal to their grubby self-interest. You've no heart any more. You sound like a Tory.'

He would not have taken it from anyone else, but he owed Moore a great deal.

'We want to win this election, Ben,' Paul said. 'Isn't that important?'

'I didn't fight Sutton so you could get to be just like him,' Moore said quietly.

'What? Who's Sutton?'

'Forget it, lad,' Moore said.

'No I won't. Tell me what you mean.'

The old man took off his cap, and scratched the top of his head.

'Don't sell yer soul for a parliamentary seat, Paul,' he said. 'It's not worth it.'

This was too much, even from Ben.

'You're jealous,' Paul said, 'because you've tried for years to get a Labour man elected, and you've failed. You're all twisted up inside because it looks like I'm going to make it – and without your help!'

The old man looked at him sadly.

'Aye, lad,' he said. 'Think that if you want to.'

He rose stiffly to his feet and shuffled out of the room. He had never shuffled in the old days. Paul wanted to go after him and apologise, to say that most of his inspiration came from Ben and Ben's experiences in life. But he couldn't bring himself to do it. He felt that he had behaved dishonourably, and he simply hadn't the courage to face the old man.

'I'll see him later,' he told himself, and turned his mind back to the task in hand.

The meeting was held in a draughty church hall. Jimmy stood at the back and watched Maggie twitching uncomfortably through Madam Chairman's introduction. Embarrassed, he turned away and examined the notice board on the wall beside him. Last week's speaker had lectured on cake making and next week's would tell them how to grow a herb garden. He looked at the audience, a motley collection of middle-aged and old women. Maggie was in good company, he thought, this lot looked like they had the IQs of retarded hens. But however stupid, they were all entitled to vote.

Maggie began falteringly, hesitantly, but as her talk progressed, she gained confidence. She described her life with Paul, and how much of his time had been devoted to politics even before he became a candidate. She gave a thumb-nail sketch of him in a bad temper, standing with his back to the fire, arms crossed, and had her audience in stitches, because they had husbands too, and knew that all men could be little boys at times. But it was in the question and answer session that she really came into her own.

'Are you lookin' forward to livin' in London, luv?' one old biddy asked her.

Maggie smiled.

'My husband has not been elected yet. But no, I'm not. I'm a Norton girl, born an' bred. London seems so big an' unfriendly. But if Paul does win, I expect I'll make the best of it. You have to go where your man goes.'

Jimmy noticed several heads nodding agreement.

Later, in his office, Jimmy examined the polls the volunteers had taken before and after the meeting and found to his amazement that several women who'd said they were voting Conservative when they went in had changed their minds after listening to Maggie speak. They couldn't have undergone a political conversion, Maggie hadn't talked about the issues at all. They'd changed their minds because they liked her, because she was a nice lass, and if she said her husband was all right, then he must be. And it didn't matter a toss *why* they voted, as long as the stupid old bags put their crosses in the right place on the ballot paper.

'Christ!' Jimmy said to himself, 'Maggie's a bloody asset.'

He picked up the phone and organized more speaking engagements.

It was on Maggie's fourth outing that they had the trouble. Jimmy cursed himself for not having spotted it earlier, although even if he had, there was no way he could have headed it off.

It was a ward meeting. A few of the audience were young mothers with children, but most were pensioners, glad of anything to kill an hour or two. As Maggie talked, the old women knitted furiously and the old men rolled cigarettes or fiddled with their pipes. The place echoed with hacking coughs and wheezing.

Maggie spoke with the confidence of a veteran now, and her listeners lapped it up – it was just like having their favourite granddaughter round to tea.

'But it's specially hard on my husband that he doesn't see much of our son,' Maggie was saying. 'When Paul comes home at night, the baby's in bed, and when he leaves in the mornin' he's still not got up. Still, he plays with the baby every chance he gets, and he loves to feed him. You should see the look on young Paul's face when he hears the door and knows his daddy's comin' home . . .'

Jimmy looked around the hall and noted with satisfaction that a few of the old ladies in the audience were sniffling.

'Get 'em to weep,' he thought, 'and you can get 'em to vote.'

It was then that he saw the man come in, walk quietly to the back and sit down. He was wearing a smart suit, and couldn't have been more than forty. He should certainly have had better things to do at that time of day. Maybe he was a reporter.

Maggie finished her set talk, and it was question time. Most of them were predictable and she fielded them well. Then the man in the suit stood up. He wasn't a reporter, Jimmy realised with horror – he was a ringer.

'That's all very interesting, Mrs Wright,' the man said, 'and I'm sure we'd all like to thank you for the touching picture you've given us of your home life.'

Maggie smiled her thanks.

'You stupid bitch!' Jimmy screamed mentally. 'Can't you see what he's going to do? Can't you spot the danger signs?'

'I was just wondering,' the man went on, still mildly, 'why you're here, instead of your husband.'

Maggie looked puzzled. She had never had to deal with this kind of question before.

'He does speak at a lot of . . .' she began but the man was no longer looking at her, he had turned to address the audience.

'What has Labour done for the pensioners?' he demanded. 'Oh, I know she'll say that pensions have gone up, but so has everything else. Everyone knows that money doesn't buy what it used to. If I didn't help my mum out, I don't know how she'd manage.'

A number of old people nodded, both to show that they agreed and as a sign of approval of this young man who knew where his duty lay.

He was there to win over the audience, but that was not his prime function. He wanted to wreck Maggie's nerve so that there would be no more vote-winning appearances. And it was working. Maggie's uncertainty was turning to distress.

'You bastard!' Jimmy thought, although he knew it was a good tactic and one he would have used himself.

'What's the old age pension these days?' the man asked. 'Seven pounds a week?'

'I wish it was, luv,' an old woman called out. 'It's a fiver.'

The man feigned amazement.

'Five pounds a week! And do you know what Mrs Wright's husband will be earning if we send him to London?' He spelled it out slowly. 'Three thousand two hundred and fifty pounds a year. That's nearly sixty-three pounds a week.'

Which was exactly what Major Yatton would be earning too, Jimmy thought. But the man was not trying to appeal to their logic, he was working on their emotions and their sense of grievance.

He turned to Maggie again.

'What is Labour's policy on pensions, Mrs Wright? What exactly is it planning to do for these poor old folk who even have to struggle to save up for a bag of coal?'

'I don't know,' Maggie stumbled.

Her jaw was quivering, she would be crying in a minute. And she'd get little sympathy from the audience. She was the wife of a man who could soon be earning sixty-three pounds a week. Jimmy wanted to drag her off the platform before she could do any more damage, but he forced himself to stay where he was.

'She doesn't know,' the man said to the pensioners. 'Does your husband know, Mrs Wright?'

Maggie nodded her head and Jimmy could see the tears starting to form in her eyes.

'Then I ask you again, why isn't your husband here? Is it because he's hiding behind your skirts,' he pointed his finger accusingly, 'avoiding awkward questions? Does he always run away from his responsibilities like this?'

Jimmy had been watching the exchange like a tennis umpire and now, moving his head from Maggie to the man and back again, he saw that the attacker had made a mistake – and that he realised it too. Maggie's jaw squared and though there were still tears, her eyes blazed with anger.

'My husband has *never* run away from his responsibilities in his life,' she said in a voice that would have sliced through brick.

The man started to speak again, but Maggie ignored him.

'I may not know much about politics, but I do know Paul. He's good, and he's hardworkin' and he's honest. And if he's elected, he'll do his best for everybody.'

The man in the suit stood still, his arms drooping by his sides. The pensioners sat in stunned silence, overwhelmed by the depth of Maggie's passion. Then a few people in the front row began to clap and the sound spread like a wave until the whole audience was applauding.

Jimmy whistled softly to himself.

'Jesus,' he thought, 'if she had a few more brains, I could get her elected Pope!'

Jimmy was on the phone when Paul went to see him. He motioned with his hand that he wouldn't be long, and Paul should wait.

'I don't *know* if there's anything,' Jimmy was saying into the receiver. 'I just want you to look.'

Paul examined the chart Jimmy had tacked to the wall – bold figures written in reverse order, crossed off as each day passed, until only five remained.

'You may want my help some day, Hawsley,' Jimmy said, and Paul noticed that an edge had entered his friend's voice.

Five days and it would all be over – one way or the other.

'Well let me put it like this,' Jimmy said, and his tone was definitely threatening, 'there are people who might be interested to know that certain funds, allocated for quite a different purpose, were actually used to top up your cellar.'

Who was Hawsley, Paul wondered. Perhaps it was personal business. He tried hard not to listen, and failed.

'Oh, *I* know you used it for entertaining,' Jimmy sounded more conciliatory now, 'but as I said, it is open to misinterpretation. So you'll do it for me, will you, old chap? Thanks ever so much.'

Jimmy replaced the receiver on its cradle.

'What was that all about?' Paul asked. 'Something I should know?'

'No,' Jimmy said carefully. 'Not yet, anyway.'

Headlights shone through the window, forming large white blotches on the far wall.

'David,' Jimmy said.

They had hardly seen him since the campaign started. He was out till all hours, organizing the volunteers, driving around. He was as much a prisoner of his van as Jimmy was of the office. When he entered the house, he had a large sheaf of papers under his arm.

'Latest opinion polls,' he said. 'How we doin'?'

'Yatton's majority's down to two thousand,' Jimmy answered.

'But there's a lot of sitting MPs would be happy with a margin that wide. We've got to squeeze more votes from somewhere.'

But they had squeezed hard already. That was how they had managed to turn four thousand voters around. They sat down and discussed possibilities they might have overlooked, areas where they could put on just a little more pressure. They had been talking for over an hour when the phone rang.

'Yes?' Jimmy said. 'Yes, okay. Wait a minute, I'll write it down.' He reached for a pencil and pad, and made tight neat notes. 'Thank you. I owe you for this.'

Paul knew the look on Jimmy's face as he put down the phone, that strange mixture of triumph and malevolence. It was the look he had seen the day that Jimmy had planned his revenge on the wreckers of the Secret Camp.

'Paul,' Jimmy said, 'how do you feel about discrediting Yatton?'

'What do you think I've been trying to do?' Paul asked warily. 'These last few weeks I've attacked everything he stands for.'

'I'm not talking about discrediting his policies,' Jimmy said. 'I'm talking about discrediting him personally. I've found a skeleton in his cupboard. Will you use it?'

A financial scandal? That was all it could be. Paul felt a great surge of relief. If Yatton was a crook, he could use that, play it for all it was worth – and still hold his head up high.

'It's nothing to do with money,' Jimmy said, reading his mind. 'It's sexual.'

'Sexual? That pompous old duffer having it off with another woman? I don't believe it.'

Yet even as he spoke, Paul could feel the hairs rising on the back of his neck, his heart beating a little faster. He shuddered – Jimmy was about to try and suck him into something very unpleasant. He tried to make a joke of the whole thing.

'Now if he was having it off with a fox hound,' he said, 'or a gun dog – that I could believe.'

Jimmy didn't laugh. Neither did David.

'Not a woman,' Jimmy said. 'Nor a fox hound. Boys!' He picked up his pad from the table. 'In 1956 your Major Yatton was arrested for accosting a young man outside the public conveniences on Paddington Station.'

'But he's married,' Paul said. 'He's got grown-up children.'

Jimmy kept silent.

'Was he convicted?'

'Well, of course he wasn't convicted,' Jimmy said, impatient with Paul's naivety. 'He wouldn't even have been arrested if

234

they'd known he was an MP, but he panicked and refused to say who he was until they got him down to the police station.'

'And you're sure it's true?'

'I got it from someone with connections in Central Office. It's true.'

'Yatton's a bloody awful MP,' Paul admitted. 'But what you've just told me has nothing to do with the way he performs his duties. I won't use it.'

'You've got to,' Jimmy said, through clenched teeth. 'Do you think I've run the risk of leaving Claire alone for a month just to see you lose?'

'The risk of leaving . . .'

'Forget that!' Jimmy said, as angry with himself as he was with Paul. 'Focus on your own problems. You're two thousand behind. *You've got to use it.*'

Paul looked to David for support – David who, like Major Yatton, felt the desire for young men.

'If you believe in yourself,' David said, 'if you believe in everythin' you've been fightin' for – use it.'

Paul shook his head.

'I can't,' he said. 'It's not honourable.'

Five days became four, four melted into three, Day Three evaporated – leaving two. And suddenly it was only an hour to the public debate in the Town Hall between the two main candidates.

'Are you nervous?' Jimmy asked, as he stacked away the documents, the facts and figures from the last-minute briefing session.

Paul grinned.

'Not at all,' he said. 'I know the issues inside out. I'll run rings round old Yatton.'

'It's very important, this debate.'

'I know.'

'The press will be there. The *Norton Chronicle* is bringing out a special edition tomorrow.'

'I know all that,' Paul said, getting irritated.

'We're still about seven hundred behind.'

'For Christ's sake, Jimmy!' Paul said. 'What are you trying to do, *make* me nervous?'

'Use it!' Jimmy said.

There was no need to ask what.

'No,' Paul said firmly. 'I won't do it.'

They might have carried on arguing until they left for the

meeting, covering the same barren ground again and again, had not the phone rung. Jimmy answered it.

'Yes?' he said. 'Yes . . . I see . . . right . . . I'll tell him.'

He looked grim.

'It's Ben Moore,' he said.

'Does he want to speak to me?' Paul asked.

He had not seen Ben since the argument at party headquarters. He simply hadn't been able to find the time. He would visit him as soon as the campaign was over and apologise for what he'd said. He desperately wanted them to be friends again.

'It isn't him,' Jimmy said. 'It's about him. He's had a stroke.'

'Where is he?' Paul demanded. 'In the hospital?'

Jimmy shook his head.

'At home.'

Paul was already in the hallway.

'David!' he called up the stairs. 'David! I need a lift – right now!'

Jimmy was just behind him, his hand on Paul's shoulder.

'Paul,' he said urgently, 'I know you're upset, but the debate starts in less than an hour.'

'Bugger the debate!'

'You have to be there.'

'Tell them I've got urgent personal business,' Paul said. 'Tell them I'll get there as soon as I can.'

Jimmy waited until David's van, carrying Paul on his errand of mercy, had disappeared into the distance. Then he picked up the phone and dialled.

'Hello,' he said, when his call was answered. 'Conservative Club? Can you put me through to Major Yatton's campaign manager please? No, he doesn't know me, but I've got some information that I think he'll find very useful.'

Chapter Twenty-One

Paul's knock was answered by the district nurse, a middle-aged lady whose bulk seemed somehow reassuring.

'Are you Paul Wright?' she asked.

He nodded.

'Yes, of course you are. You're the Labour candidate, aren't you? Well, thank heavens you've come. Mr Moore wouldn't rest until you'd arrived.'

'Will he be all right?' Paul asked.

She shrugged her heavy shoulders.

'Who knows?' She saw the obvious distress in his eyes. 'To tell you the truth, luv, he could last for another five years – or he could have gone in the time it's taken me to answer the door.'

He could be dead already! Ben had been his inspiration and in return he had insulted the old man and accused him of jealousy. He'd never found the time to apologise – and now it might be too late. He climbed the wooden stairs slowly, heavily, as if each succeeding step was draining more and more of his strength. When he knocked on the bedroom door, there was no answer.

'Go straight in, luv,' the nurse called from the bottom of the stairs.

Paul pushed the door, and it squeaked open. The room was papered in a soft, feminine, pattern. It had probably not been re-decorated since Ben lost his wife. A fire burned in the grate even though it was the middle of June, and the air had a hot, sticky-sweetness about it. The old man himself was lying in bed, his head propped up by two pillows.

'Dear God,' Paul thought.

The skin on Moore's neck hung in loose flaps, like that of a bloodhound, but on his cheek-bones it seemed to have tightened, as if it were pressing in, in, to crush his skull. His face was the colour of *papier mâché* and his glassy eyes were fixed on an unremarkable section of the ceiling.

Paul found it hard to believe that this was the man he had seen standing in the Council Chamber, blazing away at his opponents, cutting through their detailed objections and quibbles with a cry that came straight from the heart.

Was he still breathing?

'Is that you, Paul?' the old man asked in a weak, rasping voice.

'It's me,' Paul said, moving across the room so that Ben could see him.

'You're goin' to win, lad,' the sick man croaked. 'You're goin' to take Norton off 'em.' He coughed. 'It's a pity I'll not be around to see it.'

'You'll be fine, Ben,' Paul said. 'Get some rest and you'll be up on your feet in a couple of days.'

The old man shook his head. It scarcely made a dent in the pillow.

'This is it,' he said. 'You know, I wish I could believe in God. I wish I could believe that when they're puttin' the pennies on me eyes, I'll already be somewhere else, playin' dominoes with my missus in some big Labour Social Club in the sky.' He swallowed, but the air got stuck half-way down and his throat rattled, like the machine guns he had become so used to during the Siege of Madrid.

'But it's too late to teach old dogs new tricks,' he said. 'When yer gone, yer gone. The only belief I've got left is me Socialism. I've got to know it'll go on after me, Paul, that it'll win in the end. If it doesn't . . .' his eyes rolled and he seemed to have lost his train of thought '. . . if it doesn't, then what the bloody hell have I been here for?'

Paul felt the tears pricking his eyes.

'It'll go on, Ben,' he said. 'Ben, I'm sorry for what I said to you. You were right. You can't sell your soul for a parliamentary seat.'

Moore shook his head again, even more weakly this time.

'*I* was wrong, lad,' he said. 'It was nowt more than sour grapes. That's the trouble with old buggers like me – we could never learn to play the capitalists at their own game.' His voice had dropped so low that Paul had to put his ear close to Ben's mouth to hear him. 'It doesn't matter how you win, lad, just as long as you do some good once you're in.'

He tried to lift his arm to look at his watch, but the strain was so great that it fell back before it was more than six inches off the bedspread.

'What time is it?' he asked. 'You've got a debate at the Town Hall. You mustn't be late.'

Paul glanced at his watch. He should already be there.

'There's plenty of time, Ben,' Paul said. 'Don't worry about it.'

'There's no time,' Moore said. 'Not for me.'

He made a superhuman effort and raised himself off the pillows just far enough to wrap his arms around Paul.

The younger man returned the embrace. He could feel the shallow, irregular breathing in Moore's chest, and hear the air gurgling in his throat.

'Don't worry about me,' Ben said, in little more than a whisper. 'I don't need you here. I can go peaceful as long as I know that you're at the Town Hall, givin' that Tory bastard some stick.' The hands which had once been so powerful clung feebly to Paul. 'An' remember what I said,' Moore wheezed. 'It doesn't matter how you win – just as long as you get elected.'

There was a rattle in the old man's throat and Paul felt the arms behind him go slack. He gently lowered his dead comrade back onto the bed.

The Council Chamber, with its oak panelled walls and portraits of nineteenth-century mayors looking sternly and humourlessly down, was the biggest room available. But it was still crowded.

Major Yatton sat on the platform, his natural ruddy glow heightened by his increasing annoyance. He did not like socialists at all. He considered it an affront they should ever contest the seat. The fact that he should be running against a boy, losing ground to a boy, bothered him even more. And what a boy – a Moscow Red and a moral degenerate. He wanted to lay into his opponent – with words since riding crops weren't permitted – and the infernal young lout had the nerve to keep him waiting.

The audience were restless too. The seats were uncomfortable, the room was hot, and they had been left twiddling their thumbs for the past half hour.

Yatton's temper snapped.

'Mr Chairman,' he said, 'if my opponent cannot be bothered to turn up, I don't see why we should all . . .'

The large double doors at the back of the hall swung open, and Paul walked in. His face was ashen, he seemed to be unsteady on his feet, and he looked as if he had been crying. He made a great mental effort, walked to the platform and addressed the Chairman.

'I'm sorry I'm late,' he said, 'but I was unavoidably detained.'

There was a murmur of disapproval from the audience. What could be more important than this meeting? Didn't the young bugger want to get elected?

Jimmy silently cursed Paul from the back of the hall. He could

239

have told the Chairman, privately, why the candidate was going to be late and left it to him to tell the audience. But he hadn't, because he knew it would be more effective to wait until Paul arrived, looking as he did now and have him announce that he had been visiting the dying Ben Moore, Norton's greatest socialist. He would have had them weeping in the aisles.

He stopped cursing his friend and cursed himself. He should have anticipated this. Paul was too bloody lily-white to use his private life – or anybody's – to win votes. Well, they would see how he fared later on, when his principles were really put to the test.

Paul took his seat, at the opposite end of the table from Yatton. The chairman, sitting in the middle, addressed the audience.

'Each candidate will make a statement,' he said, 'and then we will be open to questions from the floor. We are rather late starting, so could I please ask you to keep your questions short.'

Paul started shakily, but it didn't matter. Yatton had not had an original thought in his life, and even in his emotional state, it was easy for Paul to score off him. And as the debate progressed, the facts and figures started to take over, crowding out the image of Ben Moore, lying dead, already starting to stiffen. He began to make his points more clearly and to expose the inaccuracies and inconsistencies in Yatton's statements in a cool detached manner.

Yatton himself was far from cool.

'The young upstart's making a monkey out of me,' he thought angrily, 'and I'm not going to stand for it.'

He hadn't been sure he was going to use his secret weapon, but the little swine had given him no choice. It was just a question of waiting for the right opportunity.

It came near the time allocated for the debate to finish, when his opponent was answering a question on foreign policy.

'. . . and whilst the Labour Government has been unable to solve the Rhodesia Crisis,' the Labour candidate said, 'it has at least avoided the kind of debacle that the Conservatives led us into over Suez, in which the morality of Sir Anthony Eden's policy was definitely open to . . .'

Yatton was suddenly on his feet.

'Morality!' he sneered. 'You talk about morality.'

The audience shifted expectantly in their seats. Paul glanced at the chairman. He was one of the town aldermen, a fussy little solicitor, and though he knew that Yatton was out of order, he had no idea how to deal with it.

'Bugger it,' Paul thought, 'I'll handle it myself.'

'Yes,' he said, 'the belief that might is not always right.'

240

'It's your own morality I'm talking about,' Yatton said in a voice oiled by half a lifetime of whiskies and soda, 'not your party's.'

So it was a personal attack. Well, what else had the old fool got left? Paul still felt completely in control, calm and confident.

'My personal record is always open for inspection,' he said.

'Your personal record.' Yatton's lip curled in contempt.

He swept his eyes across the audience then he turned back to glare at Paul over the top of the chairman's head.

'Isn't it true,' he said, 'that your wife was pregnant when you married her?'

'You bastard,' Paul thought. 'You ineffectual, vicious old bastard.'

But he still did not panic. This was, after all, 1970. Many of the young electors had 'had' to get married too.

'Major Yatton, I really must protest,' the chairman spluttered, finally galvanised into action.

'It's all right,' Paul said. 'I'll answer the question.' He looked not at his opponent, but at the audience. 'Yes,' he said firmly. 'My wife was pregnant when we got married.'

'And isn't it true,' he heard Yatton say over his shoulder, 'that your wife was not even sure that it was your child?'

This was not even a personal attack on him – it was an attack on Maggie, and a monstrously unfair one. She had not sought the walk in the park, she had not offered herself to them. She had been a virgin, and Yatton was making her sound like a whore! Paul's face turned white, not with the paleness of sorrow as it had earlier, but with a deep, all encompassing rage. His body seemed to shake and grow, like an emergent volcano, and when he turned to face Yatton, the Major shrank back, even though they had the table and the worried Chairman between them.

'Don't you mention my wife,' Paul said. 'Don't you dare soil her name with your filthy lips. And if we're talking about morality . . .'

Time warped and became like a movie run in slow motion. He looked at Yatton and saw that the other man realized that he knew about the sad, sordid yearnings that had driven him to hang around outside public toilets.

Paul watched as beads of sweat formed on the Major's forehead and above his military moustache, then made their tortuous, erratic way downwards, leaving a sticky trail behind them. He saw Yatton's eyes widening in horror and his mouth crank open in despair.

But if the picture had slowed down, the soundtrack had become louder and more insistent, attacking all the corners of his brain.

'Use it,' Jimmy urged. 'Use it!'

'If you believe in yourself,' David's voice echoed around his head, 'if you believe in what you're fighting for – use it.'

'It doesn't matter how you win, lad,' the dead Ben Moore croaked, 'just as long as you can do some good once you get in.'

The Chamber was completely silent, the audience was holding its collective breath and waiting for Paul to speak, waiting for him to finish off his sentence.

Yatton looked at him expectantly, pleading, a dog that knows it is going to be whipped and yet hopes against reason that its master will change his mind.

'If I speak now,' Paul thought, 'I'll walk this election. And I'll destroy Yatton. He'll never be able to live with the shame. He'll shoot himself.'

'Mr Wright?' he heard the chairman say, and life returned to its normal pace.

'This debate has degenerated to the level of personal abuse,' Paul said. 'If you will excuse me, Mr Chairman, I have no desire to continue to share a platform with a man who can behave in such a dishonourable and ungentlemanly way.'

He rose to his feet and walked down the aisle between the chairs. When he was half way to the door, some of the people behind him were already standing up and applauding. By the time he turned the handle, it was the majority.

It took David and Jimmy a while to fight their way through the departing crowd and when they got outside there was no sign of Paul. They drove around for half an hour looking for him, then gave up.

'He probably wants some time by himself,' David said as they entered The Rifleman's Arms, a seedy town pub, chosen because it was near to where they had parked the van – and they needed a drink quickly.

There were a few sad-looking customers in the bar, so they took their pints to the back room. It was in darkness and they heard the landlady sniff disapprovingly as they turned the light on. The ale was good, but the room was depressing, one of those places that seems cold and unwelcoming even in the middle of summer.

They had hardly spoken since the end of the debate, but now Jimmy said, 'It'll lose us some votes. There are still a few strait-laced sods around. But,' he continued, trying to sound cheerful, 'it'll gain some too. Paul stood by Maggie – sense of responsibility. He probably knocked her up in the first place – shows spirit. And there are *some* people in this town who just don't like mudslinging, whether it's true or not. On the whole, I think we came out ahead.'

His attempt at good humour failed. He slammed his fist down on the table.

'If only Paul had mentioned the fucking station lavatories, we'd have had the bastard. It would have cost him thousands of votes.'

David sipped moodily.

'I don't understand how he got to find out about it,' he said. 'There's only four of us know how Maggie got pregnant and none of us would have . . .'

He put down his pint and examined the idea that had just entered his mind with the same methodical precision he used to size up a load of copper.

'You told him,' he accused. 'It came from you.'

'It was for Paul's own good,' Jimmy said. 'I was trying to force him to use the only weapon we had left – and it almost worked.'

'And so you humiliated him – and Maggie – in front of all those people?' David said.

Jimmy looked uncomfortable, but unrepentant.

'It's a question of what matters most,' he said. 'Paul wants to get into Parliament very badly. It's the most important thing in the world to him. For that, he's got to be ruthless. And if he won't do it off his own bat, he's got to be forced into it.'

David tried to put himself in Paul's shoes. What would make him feel like Paul must have felt? He had a vision of Barry, beautiful Barry, standing up in the Council Chamber, hands on his hips, and laughing as he said, 'I'm all right now, but when I was younger I used to let David Harrison stick his prick up my arse!'

Would he have undergone the shame in return for The Diamond Theatre Club being a success? Never! Not even if the alternative was a lifetime of poverty. He asked himself if there was anything for which he would have paid that price. Yes, there was. If he could have changed the past – made his dad choose another theatre club, stopped the lorry breaking down – he would gladly have suffered the shame.

And standing in Paul's shoes, he saw things clearly, perhaps even more clearly than Paul saw them himself. There was one thing, possibly two, that would have been a fair reward for what he had gone through – but it had nothing to do with a seat in Parliament and £3,250 a year.

He didn't try to explain what he had been thinking. He knew Jimmy would never understand.

*

The light was on in David's front room, and through the window he could see Paul hunched over the big kitchen table. He opened the door and Paul looked up and smiled wanly at him. The candidate's eyes were blood red and his skin looked like wax.

'I'm trying to write Ben Moore's obituary for the *Chronicle*,' he said. 'I can't seem to get it right. How do you put a lifetime of struggle into a few lines?'

'Maybe a whisky would help,' David suggested.

'Yes,' Paul said sadly. 'Ben always liked his malt.'

When David returned from the kitchen, two generous tumblers in his hands, he found Paul staring blankly at the wall.

'How could he have found out?' Paul asked.

'What?'

Though David knew exactly what Paul meant, he was doing his best to play down its importance.

'Yatton. About Maggie.'

David placed the glass by Paul's elbow.

'Take a sip of this,' he said. 'Can't have been that difficult. Everybody in the village knew Maggie was in the club – an' some of 'em'll be Tory voters.'

He knew he was not answering the question. He still hoped he could avoid it.

Paul took a gulp of the whisky.

'Not that,' he said. 'The other thing . . . the park!'

There was no way round it. David delivered the short speech he had carefully prepared on the way home in the van.

'I think you're readin' too much into it,' he said. 'Folk like Yatton are narrow-minded and bigoted. They think any girl who gets pregnant must have been sleepin' around.'

Paul looked at him gratefully.

'You're probably right,' he said.

Paul *wanted* to believe him, David thought. Besides, he was still in a state of shock from the emotional gymnastics he had been through that night. David only hoped that in the cold light of morning, Paul would still believe. Because if he did not, he would work out the obvious – and David was frightened of what would happen then.

Harold Wilson was later to blame his defeat on the weather. It was so hot, he claimed, that a great number of Labour voters simply could not be bothered to turn out. That was not the case in Norton. David had assembled an unprecedented fleet of vehicles and had toured the pickup circuit at a furious rate, taking people to the polls and back home.

Paul kept busy, too, touring the polling stations. It was hard for him to assess what damage the debate in the Town Hall had done. Yatton had pulled a shabby trick, resorted to gutter politics, and the special edition of the *Norton Chronicle* was largely on Paul's side. But it still mentioned the fact that the candidate's wife had been pregnant when they tied the knot. He received many pledges of support offered despite, or perhaps because of, what Yatton had said. But that proved nothing either. Those who had turned against him would not bother to approach him at all.

And then it was all over. After more than three weeks of speech-making, canvassing, pushing volunteers on to greater and greater efforts, the polls closed, the boxes were taken to the Town Hall. There was nothing more they could do.

The pubs around the centre had an extension and at midnight, when the first results came up, David and Jimmy were sitting in the bar of The Wheatsheaf, watching them on the TV. The pundits said there were signs of a swing to the Conservatives and that if the trend was repeated country-wide, then Edward Heath would have an overall majority, probably a comfortable one.

'Doesn't prove a thing,' Jimmy said to David. 'Norton's different. We've turned it around.'

Oh – why hadn't Paul exposed the old pervert?

It was hot and sticky in the counting room. Paul, in his shirt sleeves, watched the tellers flick through the white slips of paper and stack them in appropriate piles. It seemed about even to him, but he couldn't be sure. At the other end of the room Major Yatton, still wearing his tweed jacket and regimental tie despite the heat, was also watching the counting with keen interest. There were TV cameras there too, inactive now but ready at a second's notice to capture the moment of victory on the face of the youngest candidate in the election – or to record his disappointment.

At one o'clock, the counting was completed. The Mayor, acting as returning officer, asked the two candidates to approach him. Yatton looked at Paul with a mixture of arrogance and contempt. It was hard to imagine him as he had been only two nights earlier, a quivering wreck, begging with his eyes for silence.

'He knows he's safe now,' Paul thought. 'If I'd ever intended bringing it up, I'd have done it then. And he despises me for not using it, because *he* would have. What a bloody fool I am!'

245

But he knew that if he had to go through it again, he would behave in exactly the same way.

The Mayor spoke to Paul first.

'Major Yatton has a majority of seventy-seven and . . .'

'Well, that's over,' Yatton said. 'Now you can crawl back to your dump.'

The two men squared up to each other like prize fighters – the stocky middle-aged landowner and the smaller, thinner trainee teacher. Yet it seemed to the Mayor that despite the difference in size and weight, the younger man was the more powerful of the two. He saw the hatred burning in both men's eyes and coughed nervously.

'Either candidate is entitled to demand a re-count,' he said. 'Mr Wright?'

'Oh, yes,' Paul said, never taking his eyes of Yatton, 'I'd like a re-count all right.'

It took two hours, and at the end of it, Paul emerged with a majority of thirty-five. Yatton demanded a second re-count.

Another re-count! That wouldn't be completed until at least five o'clock. The pubs were all closed, and anyway they had had enough ale for one night, so David and Jimmy wandered around the town.

The Drill Hall loomed up in front of them, solid, square, almost menacing in the darkness. It seemed so many years, David thought to himself, since they had perched on the ledge outside and watched the older kids dancing. It had been a golden place, a symbol of the freedom that would be theirs when they had grown up. Well, they were grown-ups now; tomorrow Paul could be an MP, soon Jimmy would be a manager, he himself owned an – as yet unopened – club. They had all the privileges of adults. So why didn't he feel free?

'What do you *want* out of life, Jimmy?' he asked.

Jimmy found the question disturbing.

'I want Claire not to have changed her mind about marrying me,' he thought. 'I've been away from her for nearly a month. God knows what could have happened in that time. I want her not to have found someone else who can satisfy her needs better than I can.'

Aloud, he said, 'To be in control, to sway events.'

'Why?'

In a way, he found this second question more unsettling than the first. He had never asked why, it was enough to know that there was a force in him, pushing him on to greater and greater efforts, more and more victories. He tried to rationalize it.

'Because somebody has to,' he said, 'and I would rather it was me than some other fucker.' But he was still not happy with his answer.

'No need to ask what you want,' he said, changing the subject. 'You want to be a millionaire.'

'I'm going to be that, all right,' David said, 'and before I'm thirty. I'm good at making money. But it's what I do, not what I want to do.'

He talked so casually about money. Jimmy remembered how he and Paul had been amazed at the off-hand way in which he had announced that Zeb Goldsmith had given him fifty thousand pounds.

'So what do you *want* to do?' he asked.

'Me dad wasn't a particularly good man,' David said heavily, 'but he was me dad. An' just before he died, I made him very unhappy. I'd like to make up for it somehow. I'd like to know that I'd done one thing that had made somebody's life really better.'

'If you get Paul elected . . .'

'You don't understand,' David said, harshly for him. 'I'm not talkin' about the trappin's. If that's all it took, I'd have succeeded already – with Barry. What I want is . . . to bring somebody deep inner peace.'

As they continued to walk, Jimmy turned his head and gazed at David's profile, only vaguely visible under the inadequate street lighting. It was strange, he thought, how the three of them were such friends, would always be such friends, and yet sometimes they didn't seem to understand each other at all.

By five-fifteen, the cameras were already panning round the excited crowd in the main lobby of the Town Hall, but it was not until five thirty-two that the Mayor, flanked by the candidates, appeared on the balcony at the top of the circular staircase.

It was almost a Douglas Fairbanks set, Jimmy thought, gazing up at the heavy, ornate pillars. And there was the dashing hero, Paul Wright, looking small and frail. It was impossible at that distance to tell whether his face bore the signs of triumph or dejection.

The Mayor unrolled his sheet of paper.

'I, Harold James Openshaw, being the Returning Officer for the Borough of Norton, do declare that this is the true record of the votes cast in this election.'

Jimmy heard a disturbance behind him and turned to see three skinheads, arms tattooed, bottles of Newcastle Brown in their hands, pushing their way through the crowd. They forced themselves into the centre of the room and shook their clenched fists at the figures on the balcony.

'What are you gonna do about the darkies?' one of them demanded, making an expansive gesture with his arm and spilling a trail of brown ale over the people standing closest to him.

'Yeah!' a second shouted. 'Wogs out! Get rid of the niggers! Britain for the British!'

The police moved in quickly, roughly escorting the trouble-makers out of the building. The Mayor waited until everything had completely calmed down again. He knew the cameras were on him and that this was his big moment.

'. . . the record of votes cast in this election,' he continued. 'Green, William Peter – two thousand, four hundred and seventy-two.'

The Liberal. He had had no hope, even at the start, and they had spent three weeks squeezing his supporters, encouraging defections into the Labour camp. It seemed to have worked – his share of the vote had gone down.

'Wright, Paul – fourteen thousand, seven hundred and eighty-two.'

A cheer went up from the Labour supporters.

'We must have won,' Jimmy thought, 'even if it's been a very high turnout, we must have won.'

'Yatton, Cedric Henry.' The Mayor coughed, extracting the full dramatic impact from the occasion. 'Fourteen thousand, seven hundred and ninety-three.'

The rest of his words were drowned by the cheers from the Conservative side.

Eleven votes, Jimmy thought bitterly. Eleven lousy votes! And how many people who had voted Conservative would have switched sides rather than support a child molester? They wouldn't even have had to vote for Paul. If only twenty-three of them had given their support to the Liberal, or stayed away altogether!

Yatton's speech, like the man, was commonplace and mundane. Jimmy could detect no triumph in his voice. He had won, but only just. In a year when the swing was towards the Tories and his opponent was barely twenty-one. Next time he would lose – and he evidently knew it.

It was Paul's turn to speak. He sounded exhausted but was

making an effort for the sake of the Party workers to seem optimistic and cheerful. It was a victory, he said, they had gained over five thousand new voters for Labour. Next time, they would break the Conservative stranglehold on Norton.

His volunteers cheered him again, trying to return his enthusiasm with their own. Then slowly the crowd began to drift away.

He had meant it; it was a victory, not just for Labour but also for him. He would get the Party's nomination next time, even without the political wanglings of Ben Moore, and by then he would be older, more mature, better able to deal effectively with life as an MP. Still, it hurt. Four or five years was a long time to wait!

'I'll show the bastard next time,' he confided to Jimmy and David later. 'I'll really show him!'

He forgot, for the moment, just what fun Fate had messing around with his life.

Chapter Twenty-Two

Sunlight streamed through the window onto the four or five paper clips that were lying on the desk. Smythe picked one up, straightened it out and then tried to bend it back into its original shape. He was half-way there when it snapped.

'I've been ringing the club for a fortnight,' he complained. 'You're never there.'

It was more of a whine than a complaint, David thought.

The bank manager was a nervous little man, with pointed features and darting eyes. But he was also greedy and ambitious, and in the hope of a quick fat return he had lent David more than had perhaps been prudent.

'I've been busy doin' other things,' David said, 'but I'm back at the club full-time now.'

'And what state is it in?'

'We'll be ready to open next week.'

Smythe unwound another paper clip and started to bend it round the broken one.

'You should have been open months ago,' he said, a hint of hysteria in his tone. 'That was the understanding when I gave you the money.'

'There've been snags,' David replied.

Even so, it would have been ready weeks earlier if he, not O'Malley, had been supervising the operation.

'The loan's on ninety-day call,' Smythe said.

He dropped the paper clip sculpture and started to chew his thumb nail.

'I know all about that,' David said coldly. 'But you told me when I borrowed it that was just a formality. You said I could have it for a year at least.'

Smythe spread his hands, palms upwards, in a gesture of reasonableness.

'Well now, Mr Harrison, I didn't say quite that. I said you could *probably* have it for a year. But circumstances have changed, haven't they? And I'm . . . er . . . afraid I'm going to have to have the money back.'

David slammed his hand on the desk. The bank manager visibly jumped.

'I haven't got the money,' David said. 'It's all in bricks and mortar.'

Smythe stared down at David's strong fingers, as if assessing whether or not he was within their reach.

'In that case, Mr Harrison, you'll have to sell the club and if you don't, we'll . . . er . . . well, we'll just have to file for your bankruptcy.'

He would never get what the club was worth. As soon as it was known that he was bankrupt, it would become a buyers' market. Besides, no one in the business thought the club could be run at a profit.

'What if I can manage to pay the interest charge on time *an'* ten per cent off the loan?'

'You'll never do it,' Smythe protested, 'not by the end of August. You'd have to have full houses every night.'

'What if I did?'

Smythe was hesitating between the paper clips and his thumb when his eyes lit on the rubber band. He picked it up and twanged it between his fingers.

'If you could do that,' he said cautiously, 'then I'd agree to extend the loan for, say, another six months.'

It was the best deal he was going to get, so he took it. But he could tell from Smythe's tone that the bank manager didn't believe it was possible to raise the money in time. He wasn't sure of it himself.

Schüte's German dancers arrived two days later. David met them at the airport. There were four women and one man in the troupe. David was very satisfied with them. The women all had good figures and come-hither eyes, and were a million miles from some of the slags who toured the northern strip-tease circuit. The man was blond and muscular, but quite ordinary looking. That was good too. The more ordinary he was, the easier it would be for the punters to imagine themselves taking his place.

David booked them into their hotel and then took them straight on to the club. When they got there, the arc lamps had already been set up, and Harry Woolidge was waiting to get to work.

'This gentleman is a photographer from the *Stockport Advertiser*,' David told the strippers. 'He'll be takin' photos of you as you rehearse.'

The Germans looked dubiously at the man in the trenchcoat. David was not sure whether it was because the coat itself was so grubby or because its owner had chosen to wear it on a hot day at the end of June.

Woolidge caught their expression too.

'Part of the uniform,' he explained. 'I never go anywhere without it.'

'Zis is not in our contract,' said the male dancer, obviously the spokesman for the group and a firm believer in having everything spelled out in Teutonic black and white. David dug into his pocket, extracting a wad of notes, and saw it have the customary effect.

Woolidge licked his lips.

'Mind if I have a drink before we start?' he asked.

David gestured towards the bar. He had been buying Woolidge drinks for months. The rest of the local journalists too. At least this time it was wholesale.

Woolidge ducked under the counter, picked up a glass, and held it under the Scotch optic until it had dispensed a treble.

'So,' he said to David, 'What kind of pictures do you want?'

'Just this side of obscene.'

'And how many copies?'

'Two hundred.'

Woolidge whistled softly.

'What the fuck do you want that many for?'

'I'm goin' to send a set to the secretary of every social club in the north-west,' David said.

Woolidge drained his glass and looked longingly at the optic.

'Have another,' David offered.

'It's none of my business,' the photographer said over his shoulder as the amber fluid gurgled into his glass, 'but you could get into trouble, you know, sending unsolicited dirty pictures through the post.'

Of course he knew, but it was a necessary gamble. He had to hope that the photographs, combined with cheap group rates and free coaches for parties of more than thirty, would do the trick. He needed to raise a lot of money – fast.

It was packed on the first night, but that was hardly surprising. Admission was half-price, drinks were half-price; David wouldn't even cover his costs. He looked around at the bar staff rushing to and fro, the four-piece group who provided the music, and the *artistes* on the stage. All of them employees, all of them expecting to be paid at the end of the week. He turned towards the audience, sitting goggle-eyed through acts the like of which they had never seen before. They would tell their friends about it; but would enough of their friends come?

He walked over to the bar where the Stockport and Manchester press were enjoying their freebies.

'Wonderful stuff this, David,' one of them said, pointing to the girl on stage, 'but we can't tell it like it is – our editors wouldn't stand for it. We all work for family newspapers.'

'Don't then,' David said, signalling for another round of drinks. 'In fact, I'd rather you didn't. I'd take it as a big favour if you suggested in your pieces that it was far too lewd to describe at all.'

The reporters looked puzzled, but before they could ask him anything else, David felt a tap on his shoulder and looked round to find one of his waiters standing there.

'A man wants to see you,' he said into David's ear.

'Is it important?'

'I think you'd better come.'

David told the reporters to order more drinks when they felt like it and followed the waiter to the other end of the bar where the man was waiting for him. He was a burly bloke in a pale suit. His face had the battered look of an ex-rugby player about it, and his eyes were sharp and observant.

'You the boss?' he asked.

David said he was.

'Bit young to be running this kind of thing, aren't you?' the man asked, and without waiting for an answer he took a leather note-case out of his pocket and flicked it open so that David could see his warrant card.

'Hoskins, Inspector, CID. Don't worry, son, it's my night off. I wouldn't even be here if a feller hadn't given me a free ticket. I'm not looking for trouble, and I certainly wouldn't like my missus to know where I've been spending my free time.'

'Would you like a drink, Inspector?' David asked. 'On the house, of course.'

'No chance, son. What I'm giving you is in the nature of a friendly warning. I've seen a lot of these shows, part of my job, and I can tell you now that as it stands, it won't last a week. The Watch Committee will have it closed. So if I was you, lad, I'd tone it down a bit.'

'Thanks for your advice,' David said. 'I'll certainly give it some thought.'

*

They played to a less-than-capacity crowd on Tuesday. On Wednesday, it was only half full.

'It's only to be expected, Mr Harrison,' said the old barman who had seen clubs come and go. 'Folk don't get paid till tomorrer. Right now all they've got in their pockets is the price of a couple of pints – if they're lucky.'

David leant on the bar and sipped thoughtfully at his own pint. Yes, that was the way it had always gone. Thursday, Friday and Saturday were the big nights in the pubs and clubs. Trade started to fall off on Sunday and was reduced to a trickle the day before the men queued up to collect their cellophane packets. He supposed that he was doing well to get even this many people on a Wednesday night.

'Most clubs only have a stag night once a week,' the barman continued helpfully. 'You can get away with it every night in London, but there's not really the demand for it here. Why don't you try summat else? Bingo. A few straight turns – singers an' the like. Pull the women punters in an' all.'

He was probably already looking through the *Manchester Evening News* for another job, David thought. And he was right, in a way. If David diversified, he could make a steady living. But not enough to pay off Smythe in time. He had to go for all or nothing.

He glanced around at empty tables and chairs. At the moment, it looked like nothing.

The black van turned off the road and pulled onto the car park, but instead of looking for a space it drove straight for the entrance. The doorman knew what it was, even before the back doors flew open. He stood aside and let twenty or more blue-helmeted policemen rush past him. He only gave a cursory glance at the piece of paper the sergeant at the back showed him. This had been bound to happen sooner or later, and he had no wish to get involved.

The moment the first uniformed policeman appeared in the doorway, a number of men sitting at the tables rose to their feet – plain clothes officers, they had spent a very pleasant evening posing as punters.

It was the drummer who noticed the blue uniforms first. He stopped pounding out his bump and grind tattoo, leaving the rest of the group to carry on without a beat. The organist looked puzzled, followed the direction of the drummer's gaze, and stopped playing too, his frozen fingers stretching out the last note until he got a hold of himself and removed them from the keyboard. The guitarists, whose minds were miles away, wishing they were playing with a really good group like Urban Decay, were the last to come to their senses, but they finally broke off mid-chord, abandoning the girl on stage to writhe with her artificial snake totally unaccompanied.

Inspector Hoskins had positioned himself so that he could get onto the stage quickly. He picked up the microphone that the comic used when he was telling his smutty jokes.

'You have been witnessing lewd and obscene acts,' he said. 'No charges will be pressed against you, but I must request you to remain in your seats until my officers have completed their investigations.'

The snake-girl didn't understand the words, but she could recognise the *politzei* when she saw them. She picked up her scattered clothes and retreated to the dressing room.

Hoskins put a hand to his forehead to shield his eyes.

'Kill the spot,' he ordered. 'Put on the house lights.'

He became aware of David, concerned and pale, standing next to him. He cupped his hand over the microphone.

'Well, I did warn you, son,' he said. 'You've only got yourself to blame.'

Realization of what was happening sank slowly into the drink-sodden, sexually-stimulated minds of the audience. A low growl of annoyance swelled until it became an angry roar of complaint. Several men stood up, shouting and waving their arms at the stage. The policemen on the perimeter started to move, then hesitated, awaiting instructions from Hoskins.

'Please remain in your seats,' the Inspector repeated.

A pale ale bottle flew through the air, missing a standing constable by a good four feet and smashing against the wall. Another followed.

Hoskins peered into the audience, trying to locate the throwers, but the tables were too tightly packed. He wondered, fleetingly, why the customers had been seated like this. It was more normal to spread them out, to make the place look fuller than it was. A third bottle hit the wall. There were cries of 'Fuck off!' and 'Leave us alone, you bastards!'

'This shouldn't be happening,' Hoskins thought.

He had raided scores of clubs, much rougher places than this, and at worst the customers had been sullen.

'Sit down!' he ordered, realising as he spoke that his voice sounded less confident this time. 'Anybody causing trouble *will* be arrested.'

By way of a response, a fourth bottle arced through the air and landed on the stage. It shattered, and small pieces of glass flew around Hoskins' feet and legs.

He caught the eye of the sergeant, standing at the side of the room. The uniformed man pointed into the middle of the mass of angry men. He had spotted one of the bottle throwers. Hoskins nodded, and the sergeant began to edge his way through the audience. He had not gone three yards when he was tripped and fell heavily forwards, disappearing between two tables.

The audience whistled and shouted and one wag called out, 'Fallen over yer Size Tens, have yer, P. C. Plod?'

Other policemen began to move in on the crowd.

'Stay where you are!' Hoskins ordered.

He had twenty-six officers under his command, against something like five hundred men. He dared not risk a full-scale confrontation, not unless the sergeant was in real danger.

The fallen policeman rose to his feet, dusting off the arms of his serge jacket. He stood hesitantly for a moment, then turned and walked slowly and carefully back the way he had come. A group at one table put their hands to their mouths and blew a bugle retreat. No one tripped the sergeant this time.

They'd start throwing chairs next, Hoskins thought. He wondered if his men could hold off the mob until reinforcements arrived. And how would it look down at the station, him running to the superintendent for help?

'Give me the microphone, please,' he heard David say.

Hoskins hesitated, as his sergeant had done earlier.

'Give me the microphone,' David insisted. 'Otherwise you'll have a riot on your hands.'

Reluctantly, the Inspector passed it over. He had no idea what David was going to say, but he couldn't think of anything else to do.

There was a buzz of anticipation when the punters saw that the tall young man – who didn't look like a policeman at all – was about to address them.

'I'm David Harrison,' David said, slowly and clearly. 'This is my club. I'm as sorry as you that your evenin's been spoiled, an' I'd like to make it up to you. On the way out, you'll be given your money back and free tickets for a show next week. And,' he paused for dramatic effect, 'that ticket will include free drinks *all night*.'

Cheers and whistles greeted the announcement.

'If you'll just sit quiet in your seats until the police give you permission to leave, I'm sure there'll be no trouble, no arrests. Isn't that right, Inspector?'

Hoskins would dearly have loved to have nicked the bottle throwers, but he saw the sense behind the young man's comment. No serious damage had been done and it was better to let a few of them get away with it than be remembered as the man who couldn't control the crowd at The Diamond Theatre Club. He nodded.

The mood of the audience was changing.

'Well done, lad!' someone called out.

'That's the stuff to give 'em,' a second one shouted.

'You can bribe me like that any day of the week,' a third said, and everyone laughed.

The men sank down into their chairs – there were no more bottles.

David handed the mike back to Hoskins, who covered it with his hand again.

'Thanks, son,' he said shakily. 'I owe you for that. But I'm going to have to run you in anyway.'

'That's all right, Inspector,' David said. 'I know you're only doin' your duty.'

The punters sat quietly, joking and finishing their beer, while the uniformed policemen moved quickly among them, taking down details and checking names against driving licences. As they dealt with each table, the customers were allowed to go. Among the first to be released were two reporters from the *News of the World*, who made their excuses and left.

Smythe's paper clip sculpture had expanded, and now resembled a star.

'You're ruined,' he moaned. 'The police have closed the club.'

'It's only until after I appear before the magistrates on Monday,' David said calmly.

Smythe reached for another clip and nervously added it to one arm of his creation. It spoiled the symmetry, but he didn't seem to notice.

'You don't think the magistrates are going to let you open again, do you?' he demanded. 'Ruined, completely ruined. I'm calling in the loan. I don't have any choice.'

'You gave me three months,' David said. 'I've used up less than a week so far.'

'But you can't possibly pay us back now,' Smythe protested.

'The longer this goes on, the more you will lose. You could go to jail, you know that.'

'Of course I know that,' David snapped, losing his temper for the first time.

'You've still got all your running costs and you'll have no income. Sell now!'

'No,' David said firmly.

The office was cool, but Smythe's hands were glistening with sweat.

'I'll get a court order,' he threatened.

'I'll fight it,' David said. 'An' by the time we've got through that, the three months will be up anyway.'

So there was nothing for Smythe to do but admit defeat, and worry.

On Sunday, the *News of the World* gave it full play. '*Naughty goings-on at the club of Britain's youngest porn king!*' screamed the banner headline which took up more space than the story below it. There was even a photograph of David standing next to the stripper, the snake draped over her arm.

'Miss Brandt's antics with her python defy description,' the paper claimed, and spent another two paragraphs attempting to describe them anyway.

Paul suggested the names of two Norton solicitors he knew, but David turned them down.

'They're both good men,' Paul said.

'That's as maybe,' David replied, 'but I'm gettin' one from Stockport – one that'll know the local beaks.'

Paul met David's choice of solicitor in one of the conference rooms before the hearing. He was middle-aged and had a smooth, round head, soft, melting eyes and cuddly body. He looked, Paul thought, like a bald teddy bear in a suit. One of the Norton men would have been much better.

'Don't you think it would be better if Mr Wright . . . er. . . ?' the solicitor said, waving a hairless paw.

'I'd like him to hear what you have to say, Mr Thompson,' David said. 'If I end up in clink, Paul will be runnin' my business interests for me.'

'Captaining the sinking ship,' Paul said to himself. 'Supervising the fall of an empire.'

'Fine,' Thompson said, getting down to business. 'We've not drawn a bad pack on the Bench this morning. There's Rogers, head teacher, liberal – Samuels, big wheel in the Chamber of Commerce – and Mrs Jenkins.'

David smiled.

'What's she famous for?'

Thompson grinned back.

'Good works. Widows and orphans.'

'And what are David's chances of avoiding a term in prison?' Paul asked.

He had already given up any idea of the club re-opening. The *News of the World* story had put paid to that.

'Goodish, I would say,' Thompson replied. He turned to David. 'Try to look sincere,' he said, and winked heavily. 'Repentant too, if you can manage it.'

Paul assessed the three magistrates: the trendily dressed middle-aged headmaster who was chairman; the no-nonsense 'flog 'em till they bleed' businessman; the lady in the elaborate hat who looked as if she would never allow a homeless pussy cat to wander off alone into the cold dark night, but might not extend the same kindness towards Britain's youngest porn king.

His gaze moved on to take in the spectators. The *News of the World* story had ensured that the wood-panelled courtroom was unusually crowded for a Monday morning, both with the public and the press. And there, right in the front row, was David's mother, brothers and sisters. His mother was softly crying to herself. Paul wondered what would happen to the family if David were sent to prison. Even if he managed to avoid a jail sentence, they would still be broke – David would still have to start again from nothing.

As corroborating statements from other officers had already been submitted, and accepted by the defence, the prosecution produced only one witness – Inspector Hoskins. He stood in the box, calm and confident, and described the show he had seen presented in the club. Yes, he said, in his opinion it had been lewd and obscene within the terms of the Act.

Thompson got up to question him – the Fluffy Toy versus Superman.

'Isn't it true, Inspector,' he said, 'that there was a near riot at the club?'

For the first time since he had begun giving evidence, Hoskins looked uncomfortable.

'There was a certain amount of disturbance, yes.'

'But only as much as normally accompanies a raid on a club?'

'No,' Hoskins admitted reluctantly. 'More than that.'

'Would you describe it for us?'

'There was a certain amount of noise.'

'Some of the audience were shouting at you?'

'Er . . . yes.'

'Would you mind telling the Court what it was they shouted?'
Hoskins was beginning to redden.

'I'm not sure that the Court would wish to hear . . .'

'In other words, they were obscenities.'

'Yes.'

'Directed against the police?'

'Yes.'

He wasn't a teddy bear, Paul thought, he was a mongoose, stalking his victim.

'And what else happened?'

'A bottle was thrown.'

'One bottle?'

'No, several.'

'But you had the situation under control?'

'Yes,' Hoskins said firmly. 'Yes, I did.'

The mongoose struck.

'Then why did you hand the microphone over to my client?'

'I . . . er . . . because . . .'

Hoskins' hand went up to his collar and loosened his tie.

'What did my client say, Inspector?'

'He . . . er . . . offered the customers free tickets and free drinks if they would quieten down.'

'I see. At considerable expense to himself. And did that work?' the solicitor demanded. 'Did they quieten down?'

'Yes,' Hoskins admitted defeated. 'Yes, they did.'

'Your client was still in charge of an establishment in which there was disorderly behaviour,' the Chamber of Commerce Magistrate snapped.

'With respect, Your Worship,' Thompson said smoothly, 'he wasn't. The police were in charge. And there was no trouble before they barged in.'

'My client is a young man,' Thompson said, pointing to David.

The club owner was looking unusually respectable with his conservative grey suit and pale tie. His hair was neatly smoothed down and he bore more resemblance to a solictor's clerk than to a man on trial.

'I do not offer his youth as a defence should the Court find he has done wrong,' Thompson continued. 'But I must ask you to consider the circumstances. When he was only fifteen years old, his father died tragically and, although little more than a child, he was forced to give up a promising academic career to look after his mother, brothers and sisters.'

The solicitor did not point out the family. He did not have to, Mrs Harrison sniffled and all eyes were on her.

Paul saw the good-works lady on the Bench give a sad-sentimental smile.

'He did not make himself a burden on the State,' Thompson said, 'as so many young people nowadays do. He stripped off his jacket and got down to work. And everything he has, he's earned by the sweat of his brow.'

The businessman magistrate nodded his head sagely.

'He's ticking them off his list one by one,' Paul thought. He wondered what plum the solicitor would have for the Chairman.

'Times are changing,' Thompson continued. 'The barriers of illiberality, of prudery and censorship, which have for so long threatened the very nature of truth itself, are gradually being pushed back. But sometimes the pioneers are over-zealous, especially if they are as young and inexperienced as my client.'

Aimed at the chairman, of course; a *Guardian* reader if Paul had ever seen one.

'I would remind you that on the evidence of Inspector Hoskins we learned than it was this young man who prevented a civil disturbance which would have been a black mark on the image of this community.' Thompson paused. 'If you should send my client to jail, or even close the club that he has worked so hard to build up, his family will not starve, but they will be thrown on the mercies of the State – and it will be seen as a victory for the narrow-minded salaciousness of the *News of the World*.'

'Brilliant!' Paul thought. 'Three in one.'

The magistrates conferred with each other and the Clerk of the Court. Then the chairman addressed himself to David.

'You are undoubtedly guilty of a criminal act,' he said sternly. 'The show you presented is both a breach of the law and an affront to decency. However,' his voice softened a little, 'there has been a great deal of publicity in the gutter press about this case, and my colleagues and I are conscious that this may have made it appear more sensational than it actually is. In addition, we have taken into account all that your solicitor has said on your behalf. You are a talented young man, Mr Harrison, who has worked hard for what he has achieved, but you have still broken the law.'

'How did David ever think he could get away with it?' Paul asked himself.

'However,' the Chairman continued, 'we will not send you to prison, nor will we close your premises. You will be fined one thousand pounds. But I solemnly warn you that if you come before us again, you *will* go to prison and your club will be closed. Do you understand that?'

David nodded his head like a penitent schoolboy.

'Yes, sir,' he said.

'Very well,' said the magistrate. 'Next case.'

Local shoplifters were of no interest to the press. They left their seats and flooded out into the lobby.

While David was giving his details to the clerk, Paul looked around for another exit. There wasn't one. The only way out was through the big double doors into the lobby where the journalists were waiting to ambush them. Paul took his friend by the arm.

'Leave all the talking to me,' he instructed. 'Don't say a word yourself.'

David was silent, but when they reached the door, he stopped, took off his tie and jacket, and ruffled his hair. As he slung his jacket nonchalantly over his shoulder, Paul thought how little of the respectable, repentant young man was left. Now, David had the rakish air of a playboy.

The reporters crowded round, all shouting their questions at once, while the flash bulbs popped.

'Mr Harrison, Mr Harrison, have you any statement to make?'

'Will the club be re-opening soon?'

'Will there still be strip acts?'

'No comment,' said Paul, 'Mr Harrison has no comment to make.'

'Aren't you "Paul Wright, the youngest Labour candidate"?' one of the sharper reporters asked. 'Don't you think you'll be damaging your image consorting with a porn king?'

Paul turned his back on the man. They were jackals, all of them. David had had a narrow escape – why couldn't they leave him alone? He tried to push David through the pack of reporters, but the other man stood firm.

'I do have a statement to make,' David said loudly.

Instantly the reporters stopped shouting and waited in anticipation, their pencils poised over their notebooks.

'The laws of this country are out of date,' David said in a firm, almost evangelical voice. 'All the acts at my club appear perfectly openly in Germany. Furthermore, to close my club – even for a week – is to deny the Englishman's basic right to go where he wishes and see what he wants. I will fight to preserve that right at whatever cost to myself.'

Paul looked on in amazement. This was not the David he knew – the tone, the words, the eloquence, were simply not his.

'Does this mean you'll be re-opening the club and putting on the same acts in defiance of the magistrates?' someone shouted.

David smiled. '*I* didn't say that. You must draw your own conclusions. I have nothing more to add.'

They were not satisfied, but David had had his say. He elbowed his way effortlessly through them to his van. Paul climbed in the other side. The newsmen were still taking photographs and shouting questions as they drove away.

'You've done it now,' Paul said. 'I can just see the headlines: "Young vice king unrepentant", "The show *will* go on", "Porn – an Englishman's basic right"!'

David glanced into his rear-view mirror and saw that the journalists were no more than specks in the distance.

'Didn't you like my speech?' he said. 'I worked very hard on it.'

'You wanted all this to happen!' Paul said. 'You planned it.'

'As nearly as I could,' David chuckled. 'I couldn't be certain they'd raid on Wednesday night, but after I made sure Inspector Hoskins had a free ticket for Monday it was a pretty good bet. Anyway, that's what I told the *News of the World* an' the reporters would've come back on Thursday if they'd had to. They knew the police would turn up eventually – they couldn't let that kind of filth go on for long.'

'But damn it, David,' Paul said exasperatedly, 'they might've closed the club! You could have gone to jail!'

'There was always a danger of that,' David said. 'But I figured that preventin' a riot would be in my favour.'

'You didn't know the audience would turn nasty.'

'I knew some of 'em would,' David replied. 'I had four or five lads from the scrap yards planted down there to make sure that they did. Promised to pay their fines if they got done.'

Paul still did not understand.

'You've been fined a thousand pounds,' he said.

'And how much free publicity do you think I got? I'll be playin' to packed houses every night.'

Paul began to wonder if all the worry had not unhinged his friend's mind.

'But if you put on the same show, they'll raid you again,' he protested. 'And you heard what the magistrate said. Next time, they'll lock you up.'

'I'm not going to put on the same show,' David said. 'I'm just going to say that I am. I won't fool the Watch Committee, they'll know they haven't enough to pull me in on. But it'll fool the punters, *because punters are born to be fooled.* They've been told that it's the dirtiest show in England, and they'll believe it. It wouldn't matter if the girls kept all their clothes on. It was in the papers – so it must be true.'

David had manipulated the police and distorted justice to serve his own ends. His solicitor had played on the emotions of three basically well-meaning magistrates. It was all wrong.

Paul was prepared to stand by his friend whatever he had done – he just wished he didn't feel a sneaking admiration for David's coup.

Chapter Twenty-Three

The house was absolutely huge. Goodness only knew how many rooms there were. Claire's mum must have to employ a full-time cleaner. And then there was this place they were having the drinks in – the library – absolutely full of books, from floor to ceiling. They couldn't have read them all themselves. Was it like the library in Norton? Did Mr Peel get paid for keepin' the books there? An' if he did, were they forever bein' bothered by people trampling over their lovely carpet to borrow them?

In spite of it all, Claire's parents were very nice, no side to them, although Mr Peel had looked funny that mornin' when she'd asked if it wasn't a waste of such a lovely room only to use it for breakfast.

Jimmy watched his mother moving around the room – inspecting the carpets, picking up the china to see if anything was printed on the bottom. He smiled. It was like letting an alcoholic loose in a distillery.

He was not embarrassed by his parents' presence. His father was not really there at all, just as he was never really anywhere. He blended into the background, making no more impact than the umbrella stand. As for his mother – whatever outrageous comments she made, they could never equal the imbecilic outpourings of the county-set prats. He wondered how Claire could tolerate these people. But, of course, she didn't. If something didn't interest her, she simply shut it out of her mind.

He looked at his watch. Twelve-thirty. The wedding was at two. What had happened to David and Paul? He needed them badly. He was afraid that, despite all the preparations, all the guests, Claire would suddenly call it off. Yet he had another fear – that she would do no such thing, and the wedding would go ahead as planned. Where the fuck were David and Paul?

To distract himself a little, he cast his mind back to the interview he'd had with Stan Blackthorne the previous April. They'd had a lunch in the Conservative Club – haute cuisine by Norton standards. Blackthorne had kept the conversation general during the meal, and did not get down to business until they were relaxing in the leather armchairs of the Members' Lounge, coffees and brandies on the low table in front of them.

'The job I have in mind,' Blackthorne said, 'is a new one. Call it my Special Assistant, call it what you like, I'm not bothered. It'll pay two and a half thousand a year.'

It was a fabulous sum by any standards. Jimmy knew that no other employer would offer him anything approaching that amount.

'I'm not sure I want it, Mr Blackthorne,' he said, carefully.

The older man did not seem put out.

'Oh, don't you, lad? Why?'

'Because I've done some research,' Jimmy said, 'and you're in the wrong business. Most of your work force is employed in making components for the British car industry.'

'And?'

'You're doing all right at the moment, but British cars are getting a decreasing percentage of the market each year. It can only get worse. When we go into the Common Market – and we will – the Europeans will no longer be at a disadvantage. And the Japs are coming up with some neat little numbers that'll be a real challenge. I don't want to get involved in a declining industry.'

Blackthorne took a cigar from his case, snipped the end and warmed it with a match.

'Three thousand,' he said.

'No,' Jimmy replied.

Blackthorne grinned, and Jimmy caught a glimpse of a younger man, the cocky engineer of thirty years earlier, convinced he could build an empire out of nothing.

'You've just passed the test,' Blackthorne said. 'As things stood, you'd have been stupid to take the job even at five thousand a year.' He lit his cigar and puffed out some smoke. 'An' a thickie is the last feller I want workin' for me at the moment.'

'So you're going to diversify?' Jimmy asked.

'Correct.'

'What into?'

'I don't know, lad,' Blackthorne said. 'That's what I want you to find out.'

Under-estimating his own ability had never been one of Jimmy's weaknesses, but even he was astounded by the suggestion.

'I've not got my degree yet,' he said. 'I've never worked in industry. There's teams of industrial consultants you could call on

266

who would do a much better job than me. They've got the specialists, they've got the expertise. They could be in and out of the place in three months.'

'I don't want somebody who could be in and out in three months,' Blackthorne said. 'It's not how I built up my business, and it's not how I run it now. I want a smart lad who's committed to the firm, and I think you'll fit the bill.'

He flicked the end of his cigar over the ash-tray.

'No,' he said. 'That's not true. I want me – as I was thirty years ago.' He sighed. 'But I can't have that, can I? And you're the next best thing.'

It was a wonderful job, a marvellous job. Jimmy couldn't resist it, and the smile on Blackthorne's face showed that he knew it too.

'But before you jump in with both feet, lad,' the older man said, 'you might like to consider this. I'll give you complete freedom of movement, whatever budget you ask for, and any outside help you need. The first six months you'll be learnin' the job, and I'll be paying you for nowt. I don't mind that. But if you haven't come up with some very good ideas by the end of the year, you'll be out on your arse.'

It might have given a lesser man pause for thought, but it hadn't worried Jimmy. He lacked experience, but he was smart. He would deliver on time. He just wished he was as confident about this wedding. Where the fucking-pissing-shitting hell were David and Paul?

'There's plenty of time,' David said, glancing at the dashboard clock as he eased his new TR6 round the bend of the country lane. 'Can't be more than another three miles, an' it's still only quarter to one.'

David had changed since the court case, Paul thought. It wasn't just that his clothes were trendier or that he had had his hair cut in Mario's, a fashionable and outrageously expensive salon in Manchester. It wasn't even the designer sun-glasses he was wearing. He had a different aura, and the changes, though subtle, were definitely there. Take his body. It was as massive as ever, but his broad shoulders no longer brought to mind the brute physical force of the scrapyard, rather they seemed to belong to a gentleman-sportsman – a polo player or a yachtsman. He seemed to be courting publicity too. He appeared regularly in the local papers and occasionally in the nationals.

'There's one thing I still don't understand,' Paul said, realizing as he spoke how much he sounded like the gormless assistant at the end of a classic detective novel. 'When the reporters saw your new show and realised you'd toned it down, why didn't they expose you as a fraud?'

David grinned and slipped into a higher gear to take advantage of a straight stretch of road.

'I'm sure they thought about it,' he said. 'It would have been a good story. But the continuin' saga of David-Harrison-Britain's-Youngest-Porn-King is a better one. That's why I bought this car. Part of the image.'

'Do you really care about image?' Paul asked.

'No,' David said, 'but the people I deal with do. I've only done business in London once, and because of the way I looked, I got screwed.'

It was Goldsmith he was thinking of, but the words automatically conjured up a picture of Archie and he shuddered. *'One day you'll be a lonely old queen,'* Archie had said.

'Anyway,' he continued, 'the next time I don't want to be treated like a hick. I want to have somethin' goin' for me before I arrive.'

The next time. He had only just got the club on its feet, and he was already planning another step up the ladder.

'Maybe that's what's wrong with me,' Paul thought. 'I can only handle one thing at a time.'

'I think we're there,' David said.

Paul snapped out of his musings and looked up at the Peel family farm. *The Peel family farm.* It was a Jacobean manor house with a heavy stone roof and mullioned windows. The Bradleys' humble terraced cottage wouldn't have filled a corner of it. Yet it had still not been considered big enough to house one family of landed gentry. Extra wings had been added – nineteenth century by the look of them. The man standing by the five-barred gate swung it open to let them pass.

'He almost touched his forelock,' Paul thought in disgust.

They drove up to the forecourt and parked near the Jaguars, Volvos and Range Rovers of the other guests. Paul looked across at the stables and the ornamental gardens with their sloping terraces and fountains.

'What! No bloody peacocks?' he demanded.

David was casting his eye around too, probably costing the place and working out whether it was economically viable to turn it into a country club.

'You've got a long way to go before you're in their class,' Paul joked.

'Maybe,' David said, seriously. 'They've had four hundred years' start on me – but I'll catch up with 'em eventually.'

Jimmy appeared in the doorway almost immediately, an elegant young man in an immaculate morning suit, standing under the stone-carved family crest of the girl he was about to marry. Now that Paul and David had arrived, the hired waiter could stop acting as look-out and go back to the job for which he'd been employed.

Jimmy started to walk the fifteen or twenty yards that separated them, but the walk soon became a trot and then a sprint. He hugged them and slapped them on their backs as if they had been apart for years instead of two short months.

'You're looking great, Jimmy,' Paul said encouragingly.

'Thanks, pal.'

Jimmy's expression was soft, vulnerable, overcome with emotion.

'How many times has he let it show on his face like this?' Paul asked himself. 'How many times has he let the mask slip?'

He flicked through the mental history of their lives together. It did not take long – he knew all the pages off by heart. Never, not even in the days of the Secret Camp, had Jimmy so abandoned his protective covering.

'I'm glad you could come,' Jimmy said. 'No! Fuck it! What I mean is, I'd never get through it without you. I need you both so much today.'

Then his muscles snapped back into place, and he was the crisp, efficient host again.

'We're having cocktails in the library,' he said. 'Not the bride, of course, I'm not allowed to see her until we're in the church. Follow me and I'll introduce you to some people.'

The small parish church looked almost unbelievably like the snow-covered ones which graced Christmas cards. It was full to capacity and not just with people who had been invited to the reception.

'The local peasantry,' Paul thought, 'paying respects to the squire's daughter.'

It was so different from his own wedding; the number of people, the obvious affluence – and the fact that the bride and groom had *chosen* to get married.

The organ struck up the tune and Paul turned and watched Claire walk down the aisle. She looked beautiful, so serene and calm as she glided towards the altar. Yet she wasn't a combination of pride, radiance and nerves, as most brides are. It was almost as if she was untouched by the whole thing.

Jimmy, standing next to him, was thinking about Paul's wedding too. He remembered his speech. He remembered taking Maggie's drunk little cousin behind the club for a quick knee-trembler. It had all been so simple then. It could be again. He had only to turn now, and walk down the aisle, passing Claire as he headed for the door. But then Claire was by his side, and the service began.

There was a buffet rather than a sit-down meal. It was strange, Paul mused, how opposite ends seemed to meet. The only people in Buckworth who held wedding receptions in their front rooms were the ones who couldn't afford a proper 'do'. Yet here were these people, rich beyond the wildest dreams of the folk back home, doing exactly that. Except that this front room was more like a banqueting hall, and the spread included smoked salmon and caviar instead of boiled ham and tinned sardines.

Paul had seen his friend married, and had no interest in the rest of the affair. But he was best man and he felt he should fulfil his duty by circulating amongst the chinless wonders. After all, it was the first and last time he would have the job – they would never attend David's wedding.

He tried his best, but it didn't work. These people bored or offended him as he did them.

'Ted Heath may be a bit of a tradesman,' one young man in the Grenadier Guards said to him, 'but at least he's got his priorities right. No more soakin' the gentry and pamperin' the Great Unwashed. And about bloody time, don't you think?'

'Not really,' Paul said. 'I stood as a Labour candidate at the last election.'

'What! Oh really! Frightfully interestin',' the man said, looking at him as if he'd confessed he was a mass murderer with an acute case of leprosy. 'Do excuse me.'

He hurried away to a less polluted part of the room.

'I say,' Paul heard an arrogant voice just behind him chortle, 'you're not *the* Harrison chappie, are you? Britain's-youngest-porn-king?'

'That's me,' David came back. 'Why d'you ask? Are you famous an' all?'

Paul grinned. Good old David!

But really, he'd had enough. It wasn't just the noise they made

270

or the inane things they said, he was starting to feel hot and giddy from all the drink he had knocked back.

He wandered down to the front hall. The big oak door was open and a pleasant breeze was blowing in. Paul looked for a chair to sit on, but they were all covered with guests' coats and bags. He climbed half way up the main staircase and sat down.

With his elbows resting on his knees and his head in his hands, he thought about the future. It was all very well for David, with Harrison Enterprises getting more prosperous every day. And for Jimmy, with a good job in Blackthorne Engineering and a beautiful wife who had money in her own right.

But what about him? He was the cleverest of the three, they all accepted that, and he was the only one in a hole. He didn't feel resentment against his two mates, only against life, which seemed to have given him so much and yet so little.

There was the sound of footsteps below him. Paul turned his head, but he was sitting in the centre of the broad stair, and without moving he couldn't see over the banister rail.

The footsteps stopped and he heard a door creak on its hinges, followed by the sound of water hitting water. So there was a bog under the stairs and the dirty bastard who was using it hadn't even bothered to shut the door. The man below grunted and pulled the chain. The cistern gurgled and then flushed.

More footsteps. Someone else was coming up the hall.

'How are you, Charles?' said a voice that was a mixture of Hampshire and public school, overlaid with an alcoholic slur. 'Haven't seen you for ages.'

'Busy, Rodders, old chap,' the other replied. 'Breakin' in a new horse. Wonderful mount.'

'They sound like a third rate variety act,' Paul thought from his unintended hiding place. 'Rodders and Charles, comedians to the gentry.'

One of the men chuckled throatily. Paul guessed it was Rodders.

'Speaking of wonderful mounts,' he said, 'that Bradley chap's a lucky man!'

'Certainly is,' Charles chimed in. 'Used to think old Claire was a bit odd. Well, still do, all this paintin' and poetry and stuff, but thought she was sexless as well. Just goes to show how wrong one can be.'

'Can't stand chattin' to you all day,' Rodders said. 'Came out for a piss. Need one badly. 'Scuse me, old man.'

As Charles walked away and Rodders emptied his bladder, Paul sat and marvelled at the levelling effect of alcohol. These two upper class twits had had all the advantages of a privileged education, yet once in their cups they talked about women in much the same way as the most illiterate lout in Buckworth would.

There were new footsteps, two sets of them, and by the clicking sound one of the people appeared to be a woman.

'I say, this really is very sportin' of you, old girl,' the man said.

This was getting ridiculous. Paul had no desire to be accused of eavesdropping on any of these petty conversations. He stood up.

'It'll have to be quick,' the girl said.

Paul recognised her voice and instantly knew that he didn't want to be near any of this. But if he went down, he would run into them. He looked desperately up the stairs, and realised he would never make it in time. When he turned again, they had rounded the corner and were on the first step.

Claire was in her blue going-away dress. The young man was still in his morning suit, one of his hands held tightly in Claire's, the other squeezing her left breast.

When he saw Paul, the man's expression changed from lust to horror. He released his hold on Claire's breast, and his arm fell to his side. The hand on the end of it continued to flap pathetically, as if embarrassed at being caught in such a position. He became aware of his other hand, the one interlocked with Claire's. He tried to pull it away, but Claire kept a firm grip.

The three froze – looking at each other – for no more than two seconds, but in that brief space of time, Paul had learned more than he ever wanted to know.

Claire began climbing the stairs again, pulling the young man reluctantly along with her. When they reached Paul he had to stand to one side to let them pass.

'Hello, Paul,' Claire said, as if they were meeting casually on the street.

'Hello, Claire,' he answered numbly.

It was a long staircase and the young man couldn't hold his thoughts in until he reached the top.

'That's his friend,' he said in a whisper that nevertheless carried back perfectly to Paul. 'Won't he tell him?'

Claire made no effort to keep her voice down.

'Do you really think Jimmy doesn't already know?' she asked scornfully.

They reached the top of the stairs and disappeared down the corridor. Paul was racked with indecision. Should he tell Jimmy? What if he *did* really know? And if he didn't know, what good would it do anyone for the groom to burst in on his adulterous bride? Anyway, perhaps he might prefer not to know. Perhaps he would never forgive his friend for telling him.

He thudded heavily back down the stairs to the reception. Jimmy was talking to a group of young women. A canapé plate was perfectly balanced in one hand. With the other he managed both to hold a glass of champagne and make gestures to illustrate the story he was telling. The girls laughed admiringly, almost adoringly. Jimmy was so poised, so much in control – while upstairs his new wife was humping away with a callow youth she'd probably grown up with. Paul knew then that he couldn't tell him. Not until he had consulted David first.

He didn't get a chance until after the couple had left for Italy under a shower of rice and good wishes and he and David were once more in the TR6 heading home. Then he told it all, including Claire's last words.

'But of course he knows,' David replied, changing gear to overtake a lorry. 'It was obvious to me that first night in The George when she started sendin' out messages to your . . . to every man in the place. Of course Jimmy knows. He's not a fool.'

'Then why has he married her?' Paul demanded angrily, though it was not David he was angry with.

'Because he loves her,' David said.

He reached into his pocket, pulled out a cigarette, and lit it from the dashboard lighter.

'Listen,' he continued, 'when you're in love with somebody, you'll forgive 'em anythin'. Why do you think me an' Barry split up? Not because he was unfaithful to me with a girl. I could have stood that. I could have stood any number of girls, as long as he kept comin' back to me when he'd got tired of 'em.'

'Then *why* did you split up?' Paul asked.

'Because he didn't want me any more. It was as simple as that. And that's the only thing that would have stopped Jimmy marryin' Claire.'

'Well I don't understand it,' Paul said. 'I don't see how you can love someone who isn't loyal to you.'

David shook his head.

'That's because you've never been in love yourself,' he said.

'I'm not ever likely to be,' Paul said sadly. 'I *am* loyal, you see, and that makes it impossible.'

But he under-estimated the power of love. He was to fall into its grasp twice, and it would turn his life completely upside down.

Chapter Twenty-Four

In late August, Edgar Adams, a teacher at Stanley Street Secondary Modern School, found that he coveted his neighbour's wife so much that life without her would be unbearable, and the pair ran away to Bournemouth. To Paul, desperate for work, it seemed at the time like a huge stroke of luck. Later, in his more depressed periods, he was to see it as one more step in the wrong direction, one more misleading card the gods had dealt him as they manipulated the huge joke that was his life.

The school was a solid, red-brick Victorian structure, with long thin windows like those in a church and crenellations topping the walls. It reminded Paul more of a prison than a castle. The playground, inadequate even by Victorian standards, had been further reduced by shabby, pre-fabricated classrooms rapidly constructed to deal with the post-war baby boom. There was an air of apathy and neglect about the whole place.

It depressed Paul, but did not surprise him. He had sat in on a great many Education Committee meetings, and had heard Robert Macintosh, the chairman, arguing for the diversion of funds away from the secondary moderns and into the grammar schools.

As he walked across the run-down playground, he could see the lowland Scottish exile in his mind's eye – bulbous nose, flabby cheeks, five o'clock shadow. He could hear the man's voice, the soft rolling of his 'r's as he made his points.

'As a businessman, I say it's no good thr-rowing good money after bad. We're investing in the future here, and we've got to make quite sur-re that we invest in children who are going to be of value.'

'Yes,' Paul thought, as he opened the main door, noticing as he did that the paint was peeling off, 'if there's one Tory in this town I despise above all others, it's that narrow-minded, self-seeking, pseudo-puritan Scottish bastard.'

It crossed his mind that Macintosh's opinion of *him* was even less complimentary, and he smiled.

There were two other candidates sitting on the uncomfortably low mock-leather settee outside the headmaster's office – a thin young man with dandruff and a middle-aged woman in a severe suit.

The office door opened and a pretty, brisk young girl emerged.

'How did it go?' the thin man asked.

His voice expressed sympathy and solidarity with someone in the same position as himself, but also contained the suggestion of a hope that she might have cocked it up.

'Pretty well, I think,' the girl said, with a slight Midlands accent. She sat down next to the woman in the severe suit.

With the instinct that even trainee teachers learn to develop very quickly, Paul knew the girl would get the job and that the rest of them were just there to legitimise her selection.

The door opened again and the headmaster, Martin Charlton BA, stood framed against the light that was pouring in from his office window.

'Mr Wright?' he asked.

They shook hands and Paul followed him into the office. Sitting behind the desk, a cup of tea in his hand, was the Chairman of the Education Committee.

He might as well write it off as a bad job, Paul thought, and use the rest of the afternoon for something useful. He was on the point of telling Charlton just that when he changed his mind – he would not give that bastard Macintosh the satisfaction.

Macintosh stood up and extended his arm. The corners of his mouth drooped in a thrifty, sadistic smile.

'He's enjoying this,' Paul thought, as they shook hands. 'Well, so will I!'

Charlton put Paul through the standard set of questions about his educational background, his teaching philosophy and what contribution he hoped to make to the school. As Paul delivered his concise, well-considered answers, it was clear that the headmaster was not really listening.

'And why should he?' Paul asked himself. 'He's only going through the motions.'

Paul was both wrong and right. Charlton was not listening, but not because Paul had no chance. He hadn't listened to what the other candidates said either. Instead, his attention had been focused on the way Macintosh responded to them.

Charlton had reached his present position by correctly guessing which way the wind was blowing and bending with it – a tendency made easier by his own complete lack of convictions of any sort. He had a lean and hungry look, but the gleam in his eye came not from burning ambition but from a constant fear that he couldn't even hold on to what he'd got. He was a fake and he knew it. But worse, the Chairman of the Education Committee knew it too.

Inviting Macintosh to take part in these interviews was only one part of a long campaign of ingratiation. He couldn't hope the other man would ever respect him, but by carefully flattering his ego he might, at least, induce in the chairman a feeling of benevolent superiority. He didn't mind being Macintosh's spaniel – as long as the Scot let him keep his kennel.

The headmaster looked at his watch and saw that the interview had been going on for twenty-five minutes. That was long enough. No one could accuse him of being unfair, of not giving Wright a chance to express his views. He glanced across at Macintosh. The face told him nothing, but then it rarely did. The Scot was as thrifty with his expressions as he was with the ratepayers' money.

'And now perhaps Mr Macintosh would like to ask you some questions,' Charlton said lamely.

The Scot leaned forward, his hands clasped in front of him and fixed Paul with a gimlet eye.

'Yes, indeed,' he said. 'I'm surprised at you applying for a job in Norton, Mr Wright. I would have thought that a socialist – even one who has taken advantage of a grammar school education – wouldn't have wanted to work in a borough that had refused to go comprehensive.' His mouth twitched in a minimalist sneer. 'Or do ideals go out of the window when your own job is concerned?

'No, Mr Macintosh,' Paul said. 'Ideals – at least mine – do not go out of the window. I would prefer to teach in a comprehensive school, but, as you say, there are none in this unenlightened borough.'

'Then why . . . ?' Macintosh began.

'Because my wife doesn't want to move away from her family while our child is so young.'

The sneer on the chairman's lips was widening.

'Ah yes,' he said. '*Your* child.'

So he had either been at the debate with Yatton, or had heard about it.

'Besides,' Paul continued, his voice rising, 'I'm a good teacher, and schools like this need good teachers. It's the only thing they've got going for them.'

'What exactly do you mean by that?' Macintosh demanded.

'Well, they certainly haven't got any money. Have you looked around this building – I mean, really looked? It's a disaster area, because most of the resources have been siphoned off, taken away from the kids who need them and are entitled to them, just so the middle class can have a privileged education.'

Macintosh's mouth moved into what those who knew him well would have identified as a scowl. It was people like Wright who were causing all the problems, he thought.

'Schools like this are the bastions of society,' he growled. 'They're fighting a rear-guard action in a country that has lost its sense of discipline and morality.'

'I completely disagree with you,' Paul said coldly. 'But then we both knew that before I ever came to this interview.'

There were no further questions and Paul went through the ritual of going outside and sitting with the other interviewees, waiting to be told that he had not got the job.

It was time to make a decision.

'So which one do you think, Robert?' Charlton asked nervously.

Macintosh ran his fingers over his sandpaper chin. He knew exactly why he had been invited to the interviews, and if anything it only made him despise Charlton more. He really was a pathetic case, certainly not the sort of man this school of young savages needed. He would have dearly loved to get rid of the headmaster long ago, had it not been for the danger of union action. So . . . he couldn't give Charlton the push, but he just might be able to force him into a position where he would jump.

'You're the headmaster, Martin,' he said. 'What do you think?'

'That isn't the question,' Charlton thought to himself.

Wright was obviously out, so that left the other man, the middle-aged woman and the girl. Macintosh had seemed interested in the girl, but most of his attention had been focused on her legs. Still, it was necessary to take the risk and plump for one of them.

'I . . . er . . . thought the little girl from Birmingham was quite impressive,' he said.

Macintosh's mind was ticking over. He was surprised at how forthright Wright had been. If he was that bolshie at interview, he would be insufferable if he was appointed.

'You hadn't thought of giving the job to Wright?' he asked.

Charlton picked up danger signals. Was Macintosh pushing Wright? And if he was, what earthly reason could he have?

'I thought about him,' he said, playing for time. 'But . . .'

He left the last word hanging in the air, hoping that Macintosh would come in.

The chairman made him sweat.

'Well, it's up to you, Martin,' he said finally. 'I never like to interfere with internal decisions.'

'Since when?' Charlton thought.

'But,' Macintosh continued, 'you must always bear in mind that if you *don't* give it to Wright you could be accused of political bias. And you never know, come the next local elections you may find yourself dealing with a Labour Education Committee. As I say, it's *your* decision . . .'

It was a day for leaving things unsaid.

'So what *do* you think, Robert?' Charlton asked desperately.

Macintosh looked at his watch.

'Good Lord!' he said. 'Is that the time? I've got another meeting. I must dash.'

He rose to his feet, picked up his briefcase and headed for the door.

'I'd really like your opinion,' Charlton called after him.

Macintosh turned the handle and glanced over his shoulder.

'My opinion?' he asked, as though surprised to be consulted. 'Oh, on purely educational grounds I recommend that you appoint the girl from Birmingham. But I bow to your superior knowledge of what will be best for the school as a whole.'

He opened the door and was gone. Charlton looked down at his hands and found that they were shaking. The Chairman had dropped him right in the shit. If he didn't choose Wright, and there was a political outcry, Macintosh would claim it had been the headmaster's decision. If he did choose Wright, and there was trouble, Macintosh would say he had recommended someone else. The bastard!

Macintosh, getting into his car to drive away to a non-existent meeting, smirked to himself. He was sure that Charlton would appoint the bolshie, and equally sure that once in the school, Wright would cause trouble. Then Charlton would have to deal with it – or be pushed into dealing with it – and would just keep on digging himself into a deeper and deeper hole. Or perhaps 'grave' might be a better word.

Paul decided to give it up. He had seen Macintosh walk through the outer office. He knew that Charlton was now alone, letting a respectable time elapse to create the impression that he was still thinking. Soon, he would call in the candidate of his choice – the young woman with the Brummie accent. It was all a farce, and he didn't want to play in it any more. He was steeling himself to get up and go home when Charlton opened the door and said, 'Could you step in here for a moment, Mr Wright?'

Paul sat in the interview seat facing the desk, but Charlton, instead of returning to his own place, paced the room.

'I'm very impressed by your background, Mr Wright,' he said. 'Your . . . er . . . educational background, that is.'

He realised that what he had said was open to interpretation – probably the correct one.

'Not that I have any objection to your political views,' he added quickly, 'at least, as long as they don't affect the school. Would you describe yourself as an . . . er . . . political activist?'

Paul gave a thin, humourless smile.

'Anyone who is not a political activist has no right to stand for Parliament,' he said.

'Quite,' Charlton replied. This was all very difficult. 'If you were appointed to this school, I would expect you to leave your political views at the door, as it were.'

For the first time, Paul realised that there was a chance he might get the job. After three years of struggling and making do, there was the possibility of a decent wage coming into the house. Maggie could have new clothes – and God knew, she deserved them. All he had to do was promise to be a good boy. But he had not signed away his soul for a parliamentary seat. How could he do it now?

'If appointed,' he said, 'my teaching would be completely apolitical. But at the same time, I would reserve the right to express my views in the staff room – just as any other teacher would.'

'Get out!' Charlton wanted to scream. 'Get out! I don't want you in my school!'

But Macintosh's warning still weighed heavily on him.

'Could you wait outside for a few minutes?' he asked.

Paul went back into the outer office. The other candidates looked up at him expectantly, but Paul smiled and shook his head.

'He hasn't made up his mind yet.'

Inside, Charlton was sweating.

'You bastard, Macintosh,' he said aloud, slapping his forehead with the palm of his hand.

Why, oh why, had he asked the Chairman to come to the interviews? It had been a huge mistake, and now he was trapped. Wright spelt trouble – reeked of it. He didn't want him – but he dared not contemplate the consequences of turning him down. In the end, he settled on a gut-wrenching compromise. He would offer Wright the job, but watch him like a hawk. Any signs of political rabble-rousing, and he'd be out of the school.

Lucy Green, fourteen and a half, jet black hair, pretty as a picture, just happened to be passing her school gates as the man was leaving. She stopped dead in her tracks. She always did when she saw anyone looking at her. She knew that unseen eyes must always follow her wherever she went, and that heads would nod with compassion and tongues click in sympathy, but it was somehow different when she could see the watcher herself.

The man gave her a vague, friendly smile, their shoulders almost brushed, and then he was off down the street. She turned awkwardly round and watched his retreating back. She guessed from what he was wearing – smart but inexpensive suit – that he had been to the school for an interview, and from the spring in his step that he had got it.

He would be replacing Mr Adams. He didn't look old enough really. He didn't look big enough, either. Mr Adams was a massive feller, able to get away with clouting even the toughest lads in the Fifth Form, even if he wasn't supposed to. But although the new teacher was small and thin, she thought he looked very nice – sensitive.

He gave her a funny sensation in her tummy. When she got home, she'd write a poem about him. That would help her understand how she felt. It always did. She'd read the new poem through once or twice, then put it with all the others in the small tin box under her bed, praying that no one was ever curious enough to find out what she kept there.

She dreaded discovery. She knew exactly how they would react, her mother and sisters laughing at her, her big, brawny father shouting and thumping about, telling her that girls had no business writing poetry.

She wished there was someone, just one person, who she could show them to, these precious things that she created with love and then buried in secret. She sighed and checked up and down the street to see if there was anyone around. It was deserted, and she started walking again, dragging her shorter left leg clumsily behind her.

Maggie was painting the skirting board in the front room when

Paul got home, but she jumped to her feet as soon as she heard the kitchen door click, and rushed to meet him.

'Well?' she asked.

'Well what?'

She poked him in the ribs.

'The job! You got it, didn't you? I can tell.'

'You've got a blob of paint on your nose,' Paul said.

Maggie put her hands on her hips in mock exasperation. Then a worried look crossed her face.

'You did get it . . . didn't you?' she asked timidly.

Paul smiled broadly.

'Of course I got it!'

She threw her arms around his neck and kissed him, wetly, all over his cheeks.

'You're so wonderful,' she said. 'So clever.'

She was ecstatic. She would have done anything for Paul, even move down to London and try to be an MP's wife, but she was much happier to stay in the village, her home, the place she knew.

'Well, aren't you going to put the kettle on and make the conquering hero a cup of tea?' Paul demanded finally.

She kissed him once more and broke off the embrace.

'I might think about it,' she said.

As she busied herself with the tea-tray, she thought about the difference that Paul's wage would make. It wasn't a fabulous sum, but combined with what she earned at the post office they would have enough. They could buy little luxuries – but more, much more important, they would at last be free of the weight that had been on her for the last two and a half years.

She turned to her husband, who was lounging with his elbows on the table, a smile still on his face.

'Paul,' she said, 'would you write to Jimmy and David *today*, and tell them that we won't need their money any more?'

For a second, Paul was puzzled. Maggie handled the household accounts, and he had almost forgotten about the weekly allowance his two friends paid towards the upkeep of young Paul.

'We needed it at first,' Maggie said, 'but we don't now. It's not right havin' other men payin' to support your son.'

Had she forgotten how the deal came about, Paul wondered? They had all contributed precisely because they didn't know whose baby it was – because they were all responsible. Had Maggie wiped all that had happened completely out of her memory?

'We can manage now,' Maggie said urgently.

But it wasn't the money that was bothering Paul. The gang still came together, but their lives were growing apart. It wasn't just that David was rich and that Jimmy had married someone who was virtually aristocracy. Their experiences, their world-views, were pulling them all in different directions. Paul suddenly felt a sense of loss.

His friends were still very important to him. He loved the baby more than anything else in the world, but after that came his feelings for David and Jimmy, with Maggie ranking a very poor fourth.

'Paul! I said we could manage.'

She had cut through his musings as last. He looked up and saw that she was nearly in tears.

'Sorry, love,' he said, pulling her to him and stroking her silky blonde hair, 'I was miles away. Yes, I'll write to them.'

He knew that he had hurt her, that she thought his mind was on his new job when she wanted to talk about something that mattered so very much to her. But better that she should be hurt by this than that she should know what he had really been thinking about.

Chapter Twenty-Five

The honeymoon in Venice was the happiest three weeks Jimmy had ever spent. Though she had never visited it before, Claire knew the city as if it were her home. She led him from art gallery to church to piazza. She showed him buildings and explained how their creators had struggled to reconcile the magnificence of their concepts with the mundane laws of civil engineering. She spoke as if she had actually been there, looking over the builder's shoulder, her own brow pursed in concentration.

They stood by the Bridge of Sighs which stretched from the Doge's Palace to the State Prison, and across which countless men had taken their final walk.

'What a place to die,' Claire said wistfully.

She pointed out frescos and mosaics, and made them seem fresh and exciting. She took an old bedraggled whore of a city, its cracks badly plastered over, its crumbling limbs propped up, and turned it into a beautiful young girl. She made Venice live for him.

There were days when they would stay in one place, St Mark's Square or a canal bank, and Claire would sketch while Jimmy looked lovingly on. Her drawings were of buildings, as clear and accurate as the pictures the pavement artists sold to tourists. Yet there was more to them. Claire infused each line with the yearnings – the driving force – of the builder, and every sketch became an emotional biography, a synaptic system laid bare.

Sometimes, her work pleased her, and she'd tear it carefully from the pad and place it in her folder. Other sketches exasperated her, and she clawed them out, screwed them up, and watched them float away on the murky, swirling water. Occasionally, Jimmy went to a nearby café and brought her back a beer or a sandwich, and she would consume them one-handed, while her pencil moved up and down the white pad.

They took a moonlit gondola ride and lay in the curtained *felze*. They watched the lights of Venice drift past them, listened to the water slurp against the sides of the sleek craft, smelt the sea, the

283

pasta, the spices of the East. And as they slowly passed under the Rialto Bridge, Jimmy felt Claire's hand groping at his crutch.

'I want to do it *now*,' she whispered urgently.

'We can't,' Jimmy protested.

Claire glanced through the curtains at the gondolier, a black shape standing on the *poppa*, ploughing his single oar through the dark water.

'He can't see us,' Claire said, 'and do you think he'd care if he could? Do you think we're the first?'

Her slim fingers pulled at his zip and then his penis was in her hand. He could feel her nails running down his shaft, digging tiny trenches in the flesh – hardening him.

She was on him in a second, her panties pulled hastily to one side, her vagina wet and hot and gripping him. As the boat cut through the night they twisted and moaned until the final release exploded over them.

Claire looked through the curtains again. The gondolier was where he had always been – an impassive, solid, almost malevolent silhouette, perched like a raven on the end of the boat. He swung his oar, she could see his powerful shoulders take the strain and could imagine the tight hard muscles in his arms and legs flexing as the air rushed into his barrel-chest.

'Jimmy,' she said, 'do you think we could . . .'

'Could what?'

'It doesn't matter,' she said. 'You wouldn't enjoy it.'

David had not been wrong when he said that Jimmy knew of his wife's promiscuity, but he had not been exactly right either. Jimmy had seen the open, carnal look with which Claire favoured men she guessed would be good in bed. And part of him knew what happened when she suddenly disappeared for an afternoon – or even an hour. But another part of him said that nothing was proven. Maybe, like Othello, the Moor of Venice, he felt it was 'better to be much abus'd/ Than but to know't a little.' Certainly, when they were making love, he did not find other men's kisses on her lips.

Even at the times when he was convinced of her unfaithfulness, he tried to tell himself that it was unimportant to him because it was unimportant to Claire. She was just using these men, and however many of them she slept with, he was the only one who mattered to her. But that was not true either. It was her art that mattered – all else was just the food on which the monster fed.

As they strolled through the shady piazzas or drank coffee under the benign late-afternoon sun, he wondered if the answer might not be to stay in Venice for ever. Claire's work would absorb most of her time, and he would be happy with what was left over. Yet he knew it was not possible. Even if Claire's rich parents were prepared to subsidize him, he had to make his own way in the world. If he did not, he would rapidly dry up, become a husk of a man. Then he would have even less chance of holding on to her.

There was no rest for David that August. The club was making money, and he intended to see that it stayed that way. He was there when it opened and did not leave until well after closing time. He watched the barmen to make sure they provided rapid service and didn't fiddle, he checked the stock, he dealt with customer complaints. There was simply no time for a holiday. Besides, what was the point of lying on a sun-drenched beach alone?

It was only a minor annoyance when his MC gave a week's notice. A good barman was like gold, to be cherished and cosseted, but the compère at a stag night only needed to be able to say 'fuck' and 'cunt' to pass himself off as a comedian. David put an advertisement in the *Manchester Evening News*, sat back and waited.

The afternoon edition had only been out for an hour when there was a knock on his office door and one of the barmen came in. He was trying to keep a straight face, but David could see that something had really tickled him.

'Yes, Terry?' David said.

'Got a bloke outside, Mr Harrison. Says he's seen your ad and wants to apply for Walt's job.'

His face cracked and he chortled.

'Funny, is he?' David asked.

Terry made an effort to regain his composure, but it was no good.

'Oh aye, he's funny all right. Dead comical. Wait until you see him.'

'Show him in then,' David said. 'And Terry . . .'

'Yes, Mr Harrison?'

'I've no objection to you having a good laugh. But do it on your own time – not mine.'

'Right, Mr Harrison. Sorry about that, Mr Harrison,' the barman said, spoiling the effect of his contrition by giggling as he went through the door.

David could see why he had been so amused. He returned with a tall but slight man of about twenty-five who had a long sensitive nose and bright blue eyes. His fluffy blond hair grew thickly, yet seemed as fine as gossamer. He was wearing a pale shirt, a broad floral tie – and a bright pink suit! David found himself glancing down at the man's wrist and was relieved to see that he was not carrying a matching handbag.

'I'm Phil Watkins,' the man said with a lisp, and held out his hand in such a way that it was not clear whether he expected it to be shaken or kissed.

Terry was almost beside himself, clutching at the desk for support.

'You can go,' David said.

The barman's laughter echoed after him as he crossed the concert room.

David wondered, momentarily, if it had leaked out that he was homosexual and this was an elaborate practical joke. But since Barry there had been no one. Not for two long, lonely years. Besides, none of his staff would dare pull a stunt like this.

He found he was getting angry with the man. Watkins was wasting his time – he was not the sort of comedian who would go down well in the club, and he must know it. And David did not like prancing, mincing queers. They took homosexual love, which to him was the sweetest, most beautiful thing he had ever experienced, and made it nothing more than a gross, disgusting parody of itself.

'I don't think there's much point in this, Mr Watkins,' he said briskly. 'You're not what I'm looking for.'

If Watkins had protested feebly, or even become abusive, that would have been the end of it. But instead, the comedian placed his hands firmly on the desk, and looked into David's eyes.

'Mr Harrison,' he said, and though the lisp was still there, there was firmness and conviction in his voice, 'I won't lie to you, I need a job badly or I wouldn't be here now. But I'm good – very, very good, and I can work with any audience. Just give me a chance, one chance. Let me perform tonight – free.'

David kept his staff in order well enough, but he knew that he could not afford to relax his grip for a minute. Even though he owned the club, he was still the youngest man working there. Just the fact that Watkins was coming to see him had been enough to make Terry the barman abandon his normal show of respect. How would he react if David allowed Watkins to go on stage?

'Sorry, Mr Watkins,' David said. 'It just wouldn't work.'

The blue eyes were deep, incredibly deep, deep like the pool they had played by as children. David tried to turn away, and found that he couldn't.

'Please, Mr Harrison,' Watkins said. 'Hasn't anybody ever gambled on you?'

Yes. Old Fred Rathbone, dead now. On the day of his father's funeral, when he had begged for work, begged to be given the chance to prove himself.

'All right, you can go on,' he said gruffly, 'but I'll have my regular comic standin' by. The second you start to die, you're off. No arguments, no excuses.'

Watkins smiled, an even, confident grin.

'I'll not die,' he said. 'Just you see.'

David stood at the bar. It was a rough crowd that night. Phil would be murdered. He would give him two minutes, and then if he hadn't had the sense to come off the stage himself, David would pull him off.

'Hear you've got yourself a new comedian, Mr Harrison,' one of the waiters guffawed as he passed.

It had been a mistake, and you couldn't afford them in business, not when you were only twenty-one and still had a long way to go. His staff worked well because they thought he was some sort of superman who never slipped up. Well, he had slipped now, and it would take a while to climb back. He could minimize the damage by not allowing Phil to go on at all, but he had given his promise. It would all be over soon. Phil would be booed off and leave – probably in tears – never to return.

The house lights went down and a group of miners occupying a table near the stage began to chant, 'Bring on the strip – pers!'

A single spotlight fell on the microphone. Phil emerged from behind the curtains and pranced onto the stage. He had changed into a lilac suit and this time he *had* brought his handbag.

For a moment, the audience sat in stunned silence. They had been expecting a big, virile lad who would talk about the size of his prick, not a simpering queer.

'Hello,' Phil said lispingly, hand on hip. 'I'm your compère for the night.'

So it wasn't a joke. The nancy boy wasn't going to disappear and be replaced by the real comedian.

'Get off, you big puff!' one of the miners shouted.

'You want to watch yourself being rude to me,' Phil said, pointing at him. 'Until last week I was a rough, tough soldier.'

287

He made a gesture with his hand, and several of the audience laughed.

'Yes, I was stationed at Aldershot Barracks. And you'll never guess what my job was,' he challenged the heckler.

'You were the camp comedian,' the man said sarcastically.

'Got it in one, sweetie,' Phil said, 'the *very* camp comedian.'

The heckler realised he had been turned into a dupe and scowled, but most of the audience laughed delightedly.

Phil hadn't finished with him yet.

'Anyway,' he said, 'how did you know? Were you there? You weren't the one in the showers with the teeny-weeny rubber duck, were you?'

The miner's cronies punched him in the ribs, and he laughed too, making the best of a bad job.

'Anyway, as I was just about to say,' Phil continued, 'it's terrible back-stage, I mean really terrible. You can't move for girls with no clothes on. All those horrible naked bodies in the way when you're trying to put on your make-up. Well, you know what it's like yourself, don't you?' he said to the miner who had become his reluctant stooge. 'And that's another thing – they use your cosmetics as if they were their own. I swear to you, I had to buy three mascaras last week. And those big nasty bosoms! I said to my friend Cecil, I said, I ought to get danger money on this job, I can't tell you how many times I've nearly had me eye poked out.'

He had the audience completely on his side. They laughed, slapped each other on the back, banged their hands on their knees.

'And these girls, they keep making – you know – advances at me. It's me body they're after.'

He turned sideways so that the punters could see his thin delicate frame.

'Some of the things that go on behind that curtain. I can't tell you – I'd just die. Oh, all right then, I will. Well, last night . . .'

When he finished his turn the audience, forgetting that he was mere padding and that the strippers they had come to see were on next, clamoured for more.

Terry the barman looked at David with a respect that bordered on worship.

'I would never have believed it,' he said. 'I don't know what it is you've got, Mr Harrison – but you've done it again.'

He had done it again. He had the golden touch and everything he laid his hands on was a success. When word got around, Phil would be almost as big a draw as the girls. Yet David couldn't help

288

wishing that he had bombed out, so that he wouldn't have to keep looking at those deep blue eyes every night.

Jimmy's parents walked silently and respectfully around the detached house that he had bought on the outskirts of Norton. It had cost a fortune, but when you were Special Assistant to Stan Blackthorne there was no problem getting a large mortgage.

Never in her wildest dreams had Mrs Bradley imagined that Jimmy would *ever* own a house like this. And he had it already – and him only just left college! Well, he'd certainly done a lot better for himself than that mate of his, Paul. That was what came of bein' responsible an' not givin' in to your urges.

She was a bit disturbed by the specially converted loft with its large dormer window. She supposed it was all right for Claire to paint. After all, you couldn't expect somebody posh like her to do her own cleanin' and bakin', and she had to have somethin' to occupy her. But some of her pictures were not quite – well – nice. Still, they probably all did that sort of thing in Claire's circle.

When the tour was finished, and Jimmy's mother had expressed her admiration for the bathroom and the fitted kitchen, his father said, 'Do you fancy a pint, lad?'

Jimmy was astonished. He remembered David going out for his first pint with his father, the day he turned fifteen and was judged to be a man. And Paul with Mr Wright – the night he told him that Maggie was pregnant. But what could have brought about the suggestion from *his* father? The house? The job at Blackthorne's?

'You wouldn't mind, would you, mum?' he asked.

His mother sniffed her assent.

'But just mind you choose somewhere respectable,' she cautioned. 'You've got a position to keep up now.'

All the local pubs were respectable – it was that kind of area. They chose the nearest, which was full of men in expensive casual-wear talking about the pound and the advantages of having four-wheel drive. If Bradley felt out of place in his grey-flannel trousers – the marks of bicycle clips permanently imprinted on them – he didn't show it. He hardly seemed to notice his surroundings at all. Something else was on his mind.

They took their drinks and sat down at a small circular table. Jimmy sensed that his father wanted to speak but couldn't find the right words.

'So you like the house, dad?' he said, just to fill in the silence.

'It's very nice,' his father replied.

Bradley gazed down at his pint, like a gypsy looking for answers in her crystal ball.

'Jimmy,' he said finally.

'Yes, dad?'

'I've never tried to tell you what to do, given you advice, like. You never seemed to need it, always knew what you wanted. An' I've never really said much about what you've achieved. But I've always been proud of you, you know, son.'

No, Jimmy didn't know. He had hardly ever stopped to consider what his father thought of him. He was touched by the older man's attitude – and ashamed of his own.

'Thanks, dad,' he said.

But Bradley was still getting to his point.

'You've got a pretty wife,' he said, 'an' a big house an' a good job. Are you happy?'

The question knocked Jimmy completely off-balance. He laughed, a sophisticated, cynical noise such as he might make at a cocktail party.

'Define happiness,' he said.

His father looked puzzled and perhaps a little hurt, as if he thought Jimmy was playing games with him, showing him up in his ignorance.

'Oh you smart-arsed, educated, cultivated bastard,' Jimmy cursed himself. 'You intelligent, insufferable little shit.'

Aloud he said, 'What I mean is that it's very difficult to say what happiness is. Are you happy?'

'Of course I'm bloody not,' the older man replied. His face became creased with sadness. 'The only thing I've ever hoped was that you would be.'

Chapter Twenty-Six

Through the window, he could see children skipping, running, talking animatedly in groups. But in the room itself an atmosphere of gloom hung in the air and mingled with the smoke of last-minute cigarettes.

'There must be nowhere in the world more depressing than a school staff room at ten to nine on the first day of term,' Paul thought.

'The thing to do,' said the tall man with the heavy horn-rimmed spectacles, 'is to jump on 'em at the start. After that you can ease off a bit if you like – not that I'd recommend it with the load of tearaways we've got here.'

He stood clear of Paul and took a practice swing with the golf club he held in his hands.

'Speak softly and carry a Number Seven iron,' he said.

'Do you ever use that on the kids?' Paul asked.

The golfer shook his head.

'No – not much anyway. We don't believe in corporal punishment in this school.' He raised his hand in a clenched fist salute. 'Capital punishment – that's what we want.'

It was the jokes that got them through, Paul thought, gave them just enough strength to go on year after year, teaching kids in whom they had no faith, in a building that was crumbling and decaying around them.

A bell rang in the corridor.

'Better get moving,' the other man said, 'or we'll have Uriah in here telling us off.'

'Uriah?'

'Our esteemed leader, Martin Charlton BA. And that's another thing. Don't expect any backing from that bugger. You get into any trouble and he'll throw you to the wolves.'

Paul looked at the rows of teenagers gazing back at him. Thirty-four faces – some of them attractive, some of them spotty, some thin and angular, others pouchy with puppy-fat. Sixty-eight eyes, watching him, assessing whether he was easy game or whether they would have to tread carefully. If they decided he was weak, they'd eat him alive.

He didn't like it, but he didn't blame them. To these kids, education was not a joy, a liberation of the spirit. It was simply a tedious grind imposed on them by authoritarian adults, something that had to be endured until they gained their freedom at the end of the year. Except that with no qualifications, they would probably be exchanging one kind of boredom for another – and from that there was no escape.

'What's your first name, sir?' asked a ginger girl with her hair in bunches.

It had started, a tentative probing to see how he would react.

'Jump on 'em,' the old hand in the staff room had said.

'My first name's Paul,' he said.

'Ooo, Paul,' a boy called out from the back of the class.

'Yes,' Paul said. 'That's my name and you can use it – but not in that tone of voice.'

'You mean we call you Paul, sir?' the ginger-haired girl asked. 'To your face, like?'

'It doesn't matter what we call each other,' Paul said. 'It's how we treat each other that's important.' He swept his hand around the room, with its flaking paint and cracked window panes. 'We're stuck in this place together, six hours a week, for the next year. Now you can make my life hell,' some of the girls giggled, and he waited until they had finished, 'and I can make yours pretty unpleasant. But what's the point of that? Isn't it better that we get on with some work we can all enjoy?'

'Work's borin',' a bullet-headed boy at the back of the room complained.

'It doesn't have to be. What was the last book you studied in English?'

'*A Treasury of . . .* somethin',' one of the girls said.

'*A Treasury of Verse,*' Paul supplied. 'I won't make you plough your way through that again. We'll look at modern poems. And we'll read things *you* suggest as well.'

'Can we read comics?' a fat, curly-haired boy asked.

'Yes,' Paul said. 'But not all the time. And we must remember that there are good comics and bad comics.'

Several kids groaned. They had no doubt in their minds that the ones they liked to read would be classified as bad.

'We can read any comics you want,' Paul said, 'as long as you can explain to me *why* you like them.'

'What's the point anyway?' Bullet-head asked. 'It's not goin' to get us good jobs, is it?'

There was a standard answer, the one about *every* qualification helping, the one that said even a good report card could impress an employer, the one that offered an illusory reward in the future in return for compliance now. Bullet-head sat back in his seat and waited for Paul to spout it.

'No, it isn't going to get you good jobs,' Paul said. 'We'll do some grammar and spelling, and that might help the girls who go on to shorthand and typing. But for most of you, what we do in this room won't help you in your work – not at all.'

He had their attention and interest – at least for the moment.

'But do you really want to spend the next fifty or sixty years just working, watching the telly and going to the pub?' he asked. 'There are other things in life, and I can show you some of them. Will you give me a chance?'

Heads nodded, not all, but some. It was going to be an uphill battle, but he would get there.

Paul was half-way through a Roger McGough poem when the bell rang. Some of the boys started to move, then thought better of it. When he reached the end of the poem, he said, 'We'll talk about it next time. OK, you can go now.'

The kids jumped to their feet and headed for the door. Some of the more forward ones said, 'See you tomorrer, Paul.'

He put his books in his briefcase, and when he looked up he saw that the classroom was empty apart from one girl who was still sitting at her desk. He had a vague idea he had seen her somewhere before. She was a pretty little thing with jet black hair and green eyes. She still wasn't fully grown, but her school jumper hugged firm, well-rounded breasts. In some ways, she reminded him of Claire – her mouth, her nose, suggested the same sort of sensitivity. But whereas Claire was both confident and detached, this girl was vulnerable.

'Hadn't you better run along now . . . er . . .' he asked.

'Lucy, sir. Lucy Green.'

Her voice was nice too, artless and unaffected, yet soft.

'Yes. Hadn't you better run along now, Lucy?'

She seemed reluctant to move, but it was against the rules to leave children in the classroom alone, and he had no intention of coming into conflict with Charlton over such a minor, unimportant matter.

'Well, Lucy?'

Her jaw quivered. Her eyes were glassy, as if she was trying not to cry.

'Look, Lucy, I really have to go and . . .'

She placed her hands on her desk, levered herself into a standing position and then swivelled herself clear.

He couldn't work out what was wrong at first. Her body, which had looked so beautifully symmetrical when she was sitting down, twisted and distorted as she walked. Oh God, and he had been telling her to *run* along.

She was looking at him, pleading for something, yet he didn't know what the right response was. Dragging her foot behind her, she had almost reached his desk.

'Does it bother you a lot?' he asked.

'The leg never really hurts, sir,' she said, 'but sometimes I get aches in other places. I suppose it's because I've got to twist my body when I walk.'

'I didn't mean that,' Paul said. 'I wasn't talking about physical pain.'

Lucy smiled. Sadly. Beautifully.

'I know,' she said.

Paul sat on the edge of his desk, so that their eyes were level.

'I've got two friends,' he said. 'One of them is handsome and very graceful. The other is big and strong. When I was growing up, I wanted to be like one of them. It didn't matter which – just as long as I wasn't me. I don't want that any longer.'

'Sometimes I'd love to run about like everybody else,' Lucy said.

'Yes,' Paul replied. 'I'm sure you would. And sometimes other girls in the class must cry themselves to sleep because they're not as pretty as you are. We are what we are, Lucy, and it's what goes on inside us that really matters.' He should have let it rest there, but he knew that she wanted him to ask her, and he did. 'What goes on inside you, Lucy?'

'I write poetry,' she said, in a rush.

As simple as that. No, 'I've written some poems.' 'I write poetry,' as if it were the very core of her being.

'You mustn't tell anybody.'

'You know I won't.'

'They'd all laugh at me, you see. But sometimes I see things.' She waved her hands helplessly. Her breasts moved. 'I don't know, a sunset, birds, even water drippin' into the rain barrel, an' I've got to write about 'em. Do you know what I mean?'

He had been like that once, when he was in the grammar school.

294

But then he had married, become interested in politics, studied for his external degree – and all his works, all the products of his imagination, had ceased.

'Yes,' he said softly. 'I know what you mean.'

She nibbled her lower lip.

'Could I show 'em to you, sir? Would you tell me what you think of 'em?'

'Of course,' he said, gently.

Her face lit up in an ecstatic smile. She began to move towards him – then suddenly stopped.

'Thank you, sir,' she mumbled.

She turned and limped out of the room.

If she hadn't stopped herself in time, he thought, she would have hugged him. He almost wished she had.

Phil Watkins – The Camp Comic – went from strength to strength. David watched him on stage, marvelling at the way he handled his audience, varied his routine, swept down and exploited unforeseen opportunities for humour. He was an artist in the most complimentary sense of the word. And David couldn't stand being near him.

He tried to treat the comedian like any other member of his staff at first, but it didn't work. There was something about Phil's doe-like eyes that seemed to bring out the worst in him. The most innocuous remark would come out gruff and off-hand, Phil's eyes would well up with tears, and he would walk away. But he was soon back, clutching the bar like a limpet a few feet away from David.

Finally, one early evening just before the first punters arrived, David felt he had been pushed beyond the limit of endurance.

'For fuck's sake, Phil,' he shouted, though he made it a rule never to swear at his staff, 'what are you doin' here now? I pay you to be on that stage between eight-thirty an' eleven – an' that's the only time I want to see you in this club.'

He might lose a good comedian, but he didn't care. He wanted nothing to do with the camp queer. He had loved Barry and he had been deeply hurt. There would be no more affairs – he was strong enough to resist.

The warning seemed to have an effect. Phil started to turn up only when he was due on stage and left as soon as he had introduced the last act. It should have made David more comfortable, but all he felt was guilt.

He always locked up himself, walking round the outside of the building to check the windows after he had double-locked the main door. It was his club and it was his responsibility. Besides, unlike his bar staff, he was in no hurry to get home – he had nothing to go home to.

It was more than a week after the scene with Phil that he noticed the shadowy figure standing at the far end of the car park while he was doing his routine check. There could only be one reason why anyone was there. He had taken most of the money out of the till, but there was the float – and a fortune in booze. He thought of calling the police, then dismissed the idea. He would handle it himself.

He heard footsteps, coming down the street, close to the watcher. The rest of the gang? Two youths passed under the street light – skinheads, hands in their pockets, bovver boots noisily assaulting the pavement. They weren't planning any robbery.

The skinheads noticed the figure in the corner of the car park.

'What you doin' here?' the taller of the two demanded loudly. 'Havin' a wank?'

The shorter, broader one laughed nastily.

Phil's voice, high pitched with terror, carried clearly across to where David was standing

'I'm not doing anything,' he said, 'I'm just standing here.'

'You sound like a puff,' the short skinhead said. 'Are you? We 'ate puffs.'

Before Phil had time to reply, the boy punched him in the stomach. Air whooshed from his mouth and he sank to his knees. A kick to his chest sent him toppling over backwards.

'We're goin' to stomp you, you fuckin' queer,' the tall one said, planting his toe-cap in the base of Phil's spine.

'Leave me alone,' Phil screamed. 'Please! I haven't done any – thing!'

He wrapped his hands around his head and tried to curl up into a ball, but it was useless. In the few seconds it took David to run across the car park, the hooligans had managed to land several more kicks.

The skinheads turned as the sound of pounding feet got closer and saw the big running man. He was obviously looking for trouble, but that didn't bother them. The puff had been too easy – this would be much more fun.

The tall skinhead waited calmly until the running man was in range, then launched out with his foot and caught David a heavy blow on the shin. It should have stopped him in his tracks, the skinhead knew that, but he might as well have tried to stop a runaway lorry. David swung his huge fist and struck his attacker's nose. He could feel the bone crack. The boy gave a muffled cry as he fell backwards.

The smaller skinhead threw a punch at David's head, and connected just above the ear. It felt like he had hit a brick wall. David swung round and delivered three rapid, powerful body blows. As the boy began to fall forwards, David kneed him in the face, grabbed him with both hands and lifted him high above his head. He was in a blinding, towering rage – he wanted to destroy, to pulverize. He swung his arms and flung the shorter skinhead onto his friend, who was only just, groggily, rising.

The two boys were not afraid of a good scrap, not worried about getting hurt. They had fought pitched battles in Manchester and Blackpool and carried the scars as badges of honour. But this man was crazy – he would kill them both. They pulled themselves painfully to their feet and staggered off down the road as fast as their injuries would allow them. They were very lucky – if David hadn't been more concerned about Phil at that moment, he would have finished off the job.

Phil had managed to pull himself out of the foetal position and was on his hands and knees.

'Does it hurt much?' David asked.

'A few bruises, but I'll get over that. I should be used to it by now. It's been goin' on ever since I was a kid.' He coughed. 'That's why I became a comic. On stage, they only take the piss, and I can fight back. Out here, they want to kick the shit out of me, and there's nothing I can do about it.'

He laughed bitterly, and winced at the pain it caused him.

David put his huge hands under Phil's armpits and lifted him gently to his feet.

'Why does it have to happen?' Phil asked. 'I don't want to harm them. Why can't they leave me alone?'

'I don't know,' David said heavily. 'I just don't know.'

He half-helped, half-carried Phil back into the club. He sat him in a chair and eased off his jacket and shirt. There were already bruises and swelling, but as far as David could tell, running his fingers up and down Phil's slim chest, there were no ribs broken.

'What were you doing in the car park anyway?' David demanded.

Phil looked up at him, his deep eyes both frightened and earnest. It would be easier to lie, the eyes said, it would be better for everyone – but he couldn't bring himself to do it.

'I was watching you, Mr Harrison,' he said. 'You don't want me close to you in the club, so it's the only chance I have. I'm there every night when you lock up.'

'Why?' David asked.

Phil's lip quivered.

'Because I love you.'

And then, of course, it happened.

Blackthorne's was still making substantial profits, but it couldn't last. The orders from the British motor manufacturers were bound to fall off, and the company would go into decline. Jimmy had been given one short year to come up with a suggestion that would stop the process.

But he wasn't fooled into thinking that that was really why Stan Blackthorne had taken him on. Changing the company's focus would be revolutionary, and in revolutions it is often the instigators who lose their heads first. Stan Blackthorne had no intention of losing his, but he would be quite prepared to sacrifice Jimmy's if anything went wrong. So it was not the new product that was most important, it was how to accomplish the change-over. And to determine that, Jimmy needed to understand what made the factory tick – its political dynamic.

He started his first week in the company by meeting the section managers. At best they were wary, at worst hostile. Jimmy was neither surprised nor disconcerted. He was young, he had been brought in from the outside, it was only human to resent him. He assured them that he was not there to tread on their toes, that as a new boy he had a great deal to learn from them. Most seemed reassured by his earnest declaration – which suggested to him that they should never have been given their jobs in the first place.

He met the Shop Steward's Committee on Wednesday, three men in light overalls representing three generations of workers.

'I'm Jimmy Bradley,' he said, holding out his hand to the oldest one, a grizzled man with a mane of white hair.

'Sid Higgins, Senior Shop Steward.'

His handshake was firm and held the promise of tough negotiations. Higgins had been a shop steward for over thirty years and a Labour Councillor for twenty. He was tough, he was smart – but he was old. He only had another twelve months to go before he retired.

'This is Ray Monk,' Higgins said.

The heir apparent for Higgins' job. Jimmy shook hands with the middle-aged, sandy-haired Monk. His grip did not have the force of the older man's.

'An' this is Eddie Copeland.'

Mid-twenties, sharp featured, sharp-eyed, only recently elected.

'A new boy,' Jimmy said, 'just like me. Won't you sit down, gentlemen?'

They sat in the chairs around his desk and he returned to his executive swivel-seat. He picked up the phone.

'Shall I order us up some tea?'

'That would be very ni . . .' Monk began.

'We have our tea in three-quarters of an hour,' Higgins interrupted. 'We get it off the trolley. We pay for it an' all, Mr Bradley.'

'Forget this Mr Bradley business,' Jimmy said. 'Call me Jimmy.'

'You're a boss, Mr Bradley,' Higgins said. 'I think we'd better keep it formal, don't you?'

'As you like,' Jimmy said easily. 'So, there is no set agenda for this meeting. I just wanted to find out what was on your minds. Would you like to kick off, Mr Higgins?'

Monk twitched uncomfortably. His face flushed, and kept on flushing until it had turned a deeper colour than his pale red hair.

'He knows what Higgins is going to say,' Jimmy thought, 'and he doesn't like it. He's not much for confrontation, that one – he'd rather believe that everything in the garden is rosy.'

Young Copeland seemed to be taking no interest at all. Instead, his eyes were roving around Jimmy's plush new office, resting on a detail here or there, assessing it, moving on.

'I've seen management in other firms bring in men from the outside,' Higgins said, smoothing back his mane of white hair in an unconscious gesture, 'and whatever fancy title they give 'em, they're hatchet men, out to screw the workers. They don't know about our problems, and they don't care.'

'Mr Higgins,' Jimmy said earnestly, 'I'm not some fancy public school boy who's never lived in this area. I was brought up in a terraced house. My dad doesn't ride around in a Rolls Royce – he's got an old Raleigh bike with squeaky pedals. And when I was at university I worked as a market porter, humping heavy crates on freezing cold winter mornings. So please don't tell me I don't know about workers and workers' problems.'

Monk looked as if he were about to applaud. Copeland was staring at him through speculative, calculating eyes. Only Higgins seemed totally unaffected.

'So if you're not a hatchet man, why are you here?' he asked.

'I'll tell you why,' Jimmy said. 'There's nearly a million unemployed in this country now, and the figure's going up all the time. It's my job to see that nothing goes wrong with Blackthorne Engineering.'

He explained the decline in orders. He produced charts and pages of figures and waited patiently while they examined them.

'We need another string to our bow,' he said when they had finished, 'and that's what I'm looking for.'

'It'll mean changes,' Higgins said.

'Structural changes, yes.'

'You mean people'll lose their jobs?'

Jimmy shook his head.

'No, no. If whatever I eventually suggest does happen, and there's no guarantee it will – I'm just a new boy – we'll employ the principle of natural wastage. Some people will retire, others may not like the new set-up and will choose to leave. They either won't be replaced, or if they are it will be by someone doing an entirely different kind of job.'

'You might not be able to find the right kind of skills in the town,' Higgins argued. 'You might have to bring folk in from outside.'

'A few,' Jimmy admitted, 'but only to train local people.'

Higgins tried one last shot.

'You're a Conservative, aren't you?' he asked.

'Yes I am,' Jimmy replied. 'But above that I'm a Norton man, born and bred. And I'll consider I've failed in my job if we don't actually increase the number of people employed here.'

When they had gone, Jimmy assessed their reaction. Higgins didn't fully trust him, he would never fully trust any boss, but perhaps he was now less wary about Jimmy than he was about some of the others. Monk was completely convinced – and relieved; he would be in charge within a year, and he didn't want a battle on his hands straightaway. Young Copeland had not believed a word Jimmy had said.

The Ring o' Bells was not the sort of pub that Jimmy patronised, at least not these days. Its settles, running around the sides of the room, were covered with old, cracked leather; it had lino, not carpets; and the tables were formica-topped. He took another swig of his pint and looked at his watch. He would give it another half an hour and then call it a day.

The main door swung open and Eddie Copeland walked in. He

was wearing a smart jacket and trousers and could have been mistaken for a minor executive out slumming it.

Jimmy was not surprised to see him, it was the closest pub to Copeland's house. Copeland was not surprised to see Jimmy, either – though he pretended to be.

'Why, Mr Bradley,' he said. 'I never expected to see you here. I wouldn't have thought this was your kind of pub.'

'I asked you to call me Jimmy,' Jimmy said, 'and I'll drink anywhere as long as the ale's good. Can I get you a pint? Bitter?'

'Bitter'd do me fine,' Copeland said.

The two men leant against the corner of the bar, far away from the other customers.

'I thought we had a good meeting yesterday,' Jimmy said.

'Aye,' Copeland replied. 'I've been thinkin' over what you said – about natural wastage. It won't work, not in a place like Blackthorne's.'

'Why not?'

'There's a few old buggers like Sid, close to retirement,' Copeland said, 'but most of the workers are young married women with kids to bring up. The pay's good an' the job suits 'em. They'll be there for the next thirty years. So if you have to get rid of labour, it'll have to be through redundancy.'

'Have you mentioned this to the other shop stewards yet?' Jimmy asked.

Copeland grinned.

'No,' he said. 'I haven't had time to get round to it.'

'I wouldn't if I were you.' Jimmy's voice became more relaxed and casual. 'I'm sure we'll be able to find a way round the problem without redundancy. Anyway, I'd like to see what you think of another idea I've had – vertical mobility.'

'What's that?' Copeland asked.

'Promoting shop floor workers up to management level,' Jimmy said. 'It's been tried in other places, and it works well. Good for the company. Good for the employee too – after all, who wouldn't like to have his own office?'

'And there's a chance of that at Blackthorne's?' Copeland asked.

'Not at the moment,' Jimmy admitted. 'Not with the present set-up. But if we re-structured there would be plenty of scope. Of course, if we can't re-structure or if we find ourselves blocked in any way . . .' He looked at his watch. 'Good heavens, is that the time. I'd better be going.'

'Time for a quick half?' Copeland said.

'No, really Eddie, I have to go. My wife'll kill me. But I've really enjoyed talking to you. I always think that if management and workers can understand each other on a personal level, there's a lot more chance they'll get on at the institutional level. Don't you agree?'

'Oh aye,' Copeland said. 'There's no doubt about that, Mr Brad – Jimmy. You and me understand each other perfectly.'

PART FIVE

Piggy in the Middle

Chapter Twenty-Seven

A great many things happened between the summers of 1970 and 1971. Chile was the first country in the world to elect a Marxist President. General Charles de Gaulle, who had for so long blocked Britain's entry into the Common Market, died. Idi Amin staged a coup in Uganda. East Pakistan broke away from West Pakistan.

But these were only news stories, watched on the telly while you ate your tea and then forgotten about. They happened in places far away and had little effect on life in Norton. They were not as traumatic as the final, official break-up of The Beatles. They were not as complicated as decimal currency, which forced on everyone the need to calculate exactly how much 37½p was in real money. And they weren't as interesting as the newly fashionable hot pants, which clung tightly and erotically to the bums of attractive young women.

Yet even these things were ultimately less important than minor personal events. As the years went by, people would have only the vaguest idea of when exactly the Fab Four split or when they had first seen the small unimpressive coins which the government claimed were 2.4 old pennies. But they would remember exactly what happened to them between one summer holiday and another and it would be stored in their minds as 'The Year We Bought the Puppy', 'The Year We Moved to Sedgewick Road', 'The Year Mum Died'. For David, it was the year that Harrison Enterprises grew out of all recognition – and the year that *he* grew too, as a result of his developing relationship with Phil.

In his rare conceited moments, David would tell himself that his business had expanded because of his own innate ability. And that was true – but it wasn't the whole story. It sometimes seemed to him as if there was a force beyond him directing his money-making activities. He need not have bought The Diamond in the first place – though in a strange way he had felt compelled to – but once he owned it there was a logical path he followed almost blindly. He had to get customers, which meant successful stag nights, so he needed the Germans. And once he had the Germans, it was only to be expected that other club owners would start ringing him up.

'Mr Harrison?' a typical call went. 'Bill Lee, Showboat, Wigan. Listen, these strippers you've got on at the moment. Where are they goin' when they've finished at your place?'

'Back home.'

'An' . . . er, there's no chance they could do a few days up here instead, is there?'

The man sounded worried, and David was not surprised. He'd had three coach loads of punters from Wigan that week alone, men who would otherwise have been spending their money at The Showboat.

'Sorry,' David said, 'they've got bookin's in Germany next week.'

'An' what about the new lot you've got comin' over?'

'Same thing, limited contract only.'

'There's no chance is there,' Lee said, wheedling, cajoling, 'that you could get a few extra acts and let me have 'em?'

So that The Showboat could regain its lost customers at the expense of The Diamond?

'Sorry,' David said again, 'that's quite impossible.'

But when he started getting inquiries from as far away as Newcastle, from clubs that couldn't possibly damage his own business, he realized that it was not all that impossible. Schüte had plenty of acts and he was Schüte's only contact in England. All he had to do was make a long distance phone call.

Soon he was bringing acts into the country nearly every week, acts he never saw himself but which went directly to Birmingham or Leeds. And suddenly, Harrison Enterprises included a theatrical agency.

Then there were the buses. After the court case there was no longer any need to tempt customers to the club with the offer of free transportation, but David found there was a tidy profit to be made by running the buses and charging for them. There would be even richer pickings if he actually owned the transport. He acquired a couple of coaches.

It was an old punter in a cloth cap who came up with the best idea of all. David ran into him one night at the bar, watching the show with wide eyes and sucking on his dentures.

'Enjoyin' yourself, granddad?' David asked.

'I am that,' the old man replied. 'By, but we never had anythin' like this in my day.'

'Have another pint,' David said. 'On the house.'

'Thanks. Don't mind if I do.' He slid his empty glass across to the barman. 'Where did you say these lasses come from?'

'Germany.'

'They don't have shows like this in Germany,' the old man said, disbelievingly. 'They're a miserable load of buggers, your Germans.'

'They've got streets full of shows like this,' David said, laughing. 'Hundreds of clubs.'

'Have they, by God. Then why don't you organise a trip for us to see 'em? You'd have a sell-out.'

And for once a punter was right. David advertised the excursion in the club and it was over-subscribed almost immediately.

'Great trip, David,' one of the customers said on his return. 'You wouldn't believe the things they get away with over there.'

'Would you go again?'

'Oh aye. Definitely. But next time, lad, couldn't you make it coincide with United playin' in Germany?'

Why not? Sex and football – the perfect combination. It wasn't only the United fans who would be interested. There was Manchester City, and possibly even Liverpool and Everton. And whatever German city they played in, Schüte could be guaranteed to come up with top-class dirty entertainment.

He had the coaches, the drivers, the contacts. Weekly and fortnightly trips required very little more organisation than two-day excursions. As well as sex and football, Germany could offer the Black Forest and the Romantischestrasse. So Harrison Tours was born.

Phil could never be Barry, sweet virginal Barry, who had shared with David the voyage of discovery into the joys of love-making. In the early months, David closed his eyes in bed and tried to imagine that it *was* Barry who was doing all these wonderful things to him. And when it was over and he opened his eyes to see the slim comedian lying beside him, he swore that he would never let it happen again, that the pleasure could never compensate for the pain of the memories it revived. But the following night, Phil would look at him with those deep blue eyes and offer himself – and David could not resist.

It was in March, when winter had melted away and the first green buds of Spring began to thrust themselves forward, that David realized that he was no longer making love like a blind man. That he was no longer paying homage in his orgasms to the frail innocence that Barry once had, now gone for ever. And with that realization came another – Phil *could* never be Barry, but it was not Barry he loved any more. It was the camp comedian.

After the love came the fear! Phil, although he never worked anywhere but The Diamond, was establishing a reputation throughout the Manchester area. How long would it be before he was tempted away to a bigger, more prestigious club?

'I'm no innocent virgin,' Phil said in bed one night. 'There was a time when *anybody* who wanted me could have me. But I knew soon as I saw you that you were the man I wanted, the one I could be happy with – for ever.'

Barry had promised eternal fidelity too, sitting at the kitchen table in the little palace that David had built for them to share.

'You had faith in me,' Phil said. 'I'll never let you down.'

Hadn't Barry said the same thing, the same tone of gratitude in his voice? Ah, but when success came his way, it had all changed – and Phil was just as good in his own field as Barry had been.

David came to dread picking up the phone for fear that it would be some agent, some theatre owner, wishing to speak to 'The Camp Comedian'. Yet part of him knew that he was powerless to change events, and wished the whole thing could be over with as soon as possible.

Lucy's poems weren't great works of art, but reading them Paul found himself almost in tears. It was not so much the object she described – a summer swallow or snow clinging to the black skeleton of a tree – that affected him, it was what she showed him of herself. The beauty of the scene was merely a projection of the beauty and sensitivity that was within her.

He sensed anger too, anger at herself that she was not saying quite what she wished, because while her words were direct and honest, they were not exactly the right words. And though she understood this failing perfectly, she did not *have* the right words, had never been given a chance to acquire them.

He lent her books of poems – Herbert, Keats, Stephen Spender – and they would sit and discuss them in a dusty classroom after school, arguing over words, searching for expressions which would provide the simple distillation of a wider truth.

Contact with Lucy brought a change in him. For the first time in years, he began to write poems and short prose pieces. He showed them to her.

'They're wonderful,' she said. 'I could never, ever, write anythin' as good as this.'

'You'll be better,' he told her sincerely. 'Much better. I've got the tricks and the experience, but you've got the talent. I envy you.'

He noticed a change in her, too. At the start of the autumn term she kept herself isolated from her class-mates, conscious, as she'd always been, of the short leg that made her different from them, made her – in her own mind – inferior. But as the weeks went by and she gained confidence both from Paul's praise and her own growing mastery of the language, she seemed to become surer in social situations as well. She no longer clung to the shadows when she walked. She did not now enter the classroom first and leave it last, so that no one would observe her progress. She stood in the playground with the other girls, laughing at the boys who were showing off for their benefit.

If he had done nothing else, Paul thought, watching her chat easily to a handsome, strapping lad one break, he had helped Lucy to break out of her cocoon and see what a beautiful butterfly she really was. He was happy for her, really happy, but at the same time he felt a gaping void within himself, as if he had lost something very precious.

Even if Charlton had felt brave enough to face the political flak, he had no grounds for failing Paul on his probationary year. The young teacher threw his drive and enthusiasm into his work – producing syllabuses, re-organising resources, running excursions. It was true that some of the little savages called him by his first name, and far too many of them went to talk to him when he was on duty in the playground. Despite that, his discipline was among the best in the school, as Charlton had discovered when he lurked outside Paul's classroom and listened to the sounds of the lesson drifting through the door. And though discipline mattered above all else, he had no real objection if the little bastards were learning something as well.

Wright seemed to be keeping his politics out of school too. Charlton knew that he attended countless meetings in Norton and gave innumerable speeches, but there had been no red banners raised in the playground, no Wright-inspired sit-down strikes.

Only once was there a potential conflict, and even then Charlton could detect no political motivation behind it. It happened just before the Easter holidays. Wright asked for an appointment, and Charlton, not without misgivings, granted it.

'We need a Sixth Form,' Paul said the moment he entered Charlton's office.

The headmaster shifted uncomfortably in his seat.

'I don't see why,' he said. 'Any of our children who want to follow further education can go onto another school or to the tech.'

'And only three or four of them do,' Paul said. 'It's too big a change for them – all new kids, all new teachers. They've little enough confidence anyway. They're afraid to take the risk. Now if we had our own Sixth Form, we'd keep between twenty-five and forty. I know – I've been talking to them.'

Change meant danger – uncharted waters.

'We couldn't afford it. We haven't got the resources,' Charlton complained. 'We'd need all sorts of things – more space, a teacher in charge of the Sixth Form, extra money . . .'

'I've done the calculations,' Paul said. 'We can squeeze the space – just. I'd be willing to run it . . .'

'I can't pay you any more,' Charlton said. 'I can't reduce your teaching load.'

'I don't want any of that,' Paul continued, evenly. 'We can get some extra money from the capitation allowance – that should enable us to employ an additional teacher. And the rest of the classroom time could be filled by some teachers giving up their free periods.'

'Giving up their free periods!' Charlton thought. 'That lot!'

'They'd never agree to it,' he said aloud. 'I'd have the unions snapping at me the second I tried it.'

'They've already agreed,' Paul said.

'*All* of them?' Charlton asked, incredulous.

'Nothing like all of them,' Paul admitted, 'but enough. It can work, if only you'll let it. It'd be good for the staff, too. We'd go from being a Group Nine School to a Group Ten. And that means more money for responsibility allowances.'

'And the headmaster's salary would go up,' Charlton thought.

'You say you'd be prepared to run it for no extra pay?' he asked.

'Yes,' Paul replied firmly.

Charlton was not a man to take hasty decisions, or indeed any decisions at all, but this seemed too good an opportunity to miss. It would keep Wright out of trouble for one thing. If he ran the Sixth Form well, all credit would go to the headmaster. If he made a cock-up of it, there was an excuse to get rid of him. Even Macintosh, Chairman of the Education Committee, could not object to a scheme that promised to keep the little hooligans off the street for another couple of years.

Producing the plans took a great deal of time. As spring progressed into summer, Paul sat determinedly at his desk, ignoring the smell of flowers, shutting his ears to the call of the birds, forfeiting his chance to walk hand in hand with young Paul in the woods. He was doing it for all the kids in Stanley Street. He cared about them, every single one of them, but the inspiration that drove him on day after day was the slim, pretty girl with a limp.

'All girls need is this here domestic science,' her father, a solid, bone-headed brickie's labourer, had told him. 'Cookin' an' mendin' an' that.'

'But if she wanted to stay at school for another year or so, would you stop her?'

'No harm in it, I suppose. It's not as if she's goin' to get a job in a shop with that gammy leg of hers.'

Lucy was just beginning to develop her talent. If she left school and went straight into a world where books were regarded with suspicion and a woman's place was in the kitchen, it would wither and die – however much she might try to save it. Just as his own artistic aspirations had perished.

So on days when all the planning seemed too much, when he did not know how he was going to drag up the energy to carry on, he would think of the girl – and it would give him the push he needed.

The plans were accepted, the extra resources found, and the Sixth Form was inaugurated at the start of the Autumn Term. True to his word for once, Charlton had not given Paul any additional free periods, and running the new group was an exhausting business. But it was worth it. For the first time in their lives, the kids were in the school through choice, and because they had made that choice they were demanding and challenging in the classroom – exciting and stimulating to teach.

It had an effect on the staff, too. Several of the old guard, who had scoffed at the idea originally, approached Paul and said that they would be willing to give the odd lesson should he need them. They had emerged from years of sleep, from years of seeing the job only as a way of paying off the mortgage, and were starting to remember why they had decided to become teachers in the first place.

And Paul, who had never thought of the sixth form in terms of advancing his own career, began to see that it might. He was accorded new respect in the staff room. Two members of the Education Committee had visited the school and gone away impressed. Even the headmaster had smiled at him once or twice.

Yes, Paul thought, as he stacked books in the stock room at the end of the day, even though the scheme had been running for less than a month, it was clearly a success.

He heard the door open and turned to see Lucy standing in the opening. Her presence disturbed him. As her effect on him had grown steadily stronger, he had found it more and more difficult to be alone with her. She stepped inside the room and closed the door behind her. It clicked so loudly that he was sure the noise must have been heard throughout the school. She leant with her back against the door, cutting off his retreat.

'Yes, Lucy?' he said, his tone more brusque than he would have employed with any other pupil.

The girl seemed nervous, hesitant, as she had been the day she offered him her poems.

'It's my birthday, sir,' she said.

She had never been one of the kids who had called him by his first name, and he had been glad, because it had helped to keep some sort of distance between them when all other forces were pulling them closer together.

'I'm sixteen today.'

Paul felt helpless. If she had been any other girl in his class, he would have ruffled her hair good-naturedly. Yet because he knew her so well, because of the depth of their relationship, he could not bring himself to act naturally. Instead, he held out his hand stiffly to shake hers.

'Happy birthday.'

She ignored the gesture.

'I love you, sir,' she said.

In different circumstances, in another life, the words would have filled him with indescribable joy. Now they assailed him, battered his heart, sent tiny waves of nausea all over his body.

He looked into her eyes.

'You don't love me,' he said. 'You have a crush on me. It's perfectly normal at your age. When you find yourself a nice boyfriend, I think you'll find your feelings for me will disappear over-night.'

Her lips were trembling, she was scared to death, but she was determined to go on.

'Yes,' she said. 'I could have plenty of boyfriends, because you've taught me to take pride in myself. I don't want them. I want you.'

'You can't have me,' he said firmly.

'Tell me you don't love me,' she said, 'and I'll go away.'

His mouth refused to form the words that would make her leave.

'You're a child,' he said.

'I'm sixteen today. I'm old enough to . . .' she looked down at the floor and her face reddened '. . . to make love to anyone I want to.'

'I'm your teacher. It wouldn't be ethical.'

'Then I'll leave school.'

No, not that. She couldn't throw away her chance, the chance he had worked so hard to make possible. His grip on the book in his hand tightened, and his knuckles turned white.

She started to walk towards him, a frail figure between two mountains of dusty books. He could sense her adoration, could smell her sweet, young scent. He had to do something to shatter the atmosphere, destroy the electricity that was building up between them.

'Don't take her seriously!' he told himself. 'Treat it as a joke. Make her hate you.'

'You may be a big, grown-up person of sixteen,' he said, 'but that's still rather young to be the Other Woman.'

The barb hit home. She stopped in her tracks, two feet away from him, and tears came to her eyes.

'I don't think I am the Other Woman,' she said. 'I think your wife is.'

He knew it was true. Maggie was a loyal, wonderful wife. He respected her and admired her more than any woman he had ever met – but he could not love her. It was this small, dark-haired girl with the green eyes and the crippled leg who had captured his heart. His nails dug deep into the book cover.

'It's easy for you, isn't it?' he said. 'You're young. You haven't got any responsibilities. But what about me? I have a wife and child.'

'It's not easy for me,' Lucy gasped between sobs. 'D'you think I don't know I'm goin' to end up with a broken heart?'

His head was pounding. His fingers slackened and the book he was holding crashed noisily to the ground.

'I don't want to break up your family,' Lucy said. 'I just want a little bit of you for myself. Please . . . Paul.'

'Make her hate you, make her hate you,' his brain chanted to the rhythm of his beating heart.

'You don't want *me*,' he said. 'You want an *experience*, something you can stick into one of your adolescent verses.'

Her lips trembled, her eyes were full of sorrow.

'Well done, Paul,' he thought bitterly. 'You're a fine human being and I'm really proud of you.'

313

'You don't love me after all,' she said, blinking back tears.

'Of course I don't,' he replied harshly. 'Now fuck off and let me get on with my work. Go home and write a silly poem about unrequited love.'

'There won't be any more poems,' she said.

She turned and started walking back to the door. Her body was heaving with sobs, and her limp seemed more pronounced than ever before. Though the passageway was narrow, she managed to cling to the left-hand bookcase, as if she hoped it would swallow her up.

'I've destroyed her,' Paul thought. 'I've not just taken back what I've given her, I've stolen everything she ever had.'

'Lucy!' he said.

She stopped and turned awkwardly. Her face was bloated with her tears.

'Lucy, I didn't want to hurt you, love. It was the only defence I had. I . . .'

Four steps, and he was holding her in his arms, soothing, comforting. And then he was lost. He kissed her and felt her lips – burning him, engulfing his soul. He fondled her breasts and it was as if this, and only this, was what his hands had been created for. They sunk slowly to the floor and made sweet, wonderful love on the hard boards.

With Lucy, there were no memories of what had gone before, no David lying between them, no Jimmy watching Paul have his share. There were no shares at all this time. The girl was his, and his alone.

Jimmy's tremendous effort in his first year at Blackthorne's won the admiration of the entire staff. He did not hide in his office like most managers. He visited every department regularly and got practical experience in them all. He spent a week on each of the production lines – assembling components, checking their quality – just as if he was an ordinary worker. He travelled around with the reps. He even found time to visit other firms, some of them as far away as Slough.

There were improvements made in working conditions that year, and though the orders came down from Stan Blackthorne, everybody knew that Jimmy was behind them. It wasn't a coincidence that a few days after Jimmy had worked on the assembly lines – chatting to the working mothers during the tea breaks – Blackthorne should announce that in future he would be employing nursery nurses and that any worker who wished to could deposit her young children in the crèche. It wasn't just chance that the tea breaks were suddenly extended, without any union pressure at all, giving the mothers time to visit their children during the day.

Middle management liked him too, because he was not the pushy young man they had feared, but someone genuinely eager to learn, who sympathised with them over their own problems.

If the factory had been a democratic institution, he would have been elected the boss by an overwhelming majority. And Jimmy knew that none of this mattered a damn. He was employed by Stan Blackthorne, and his was the only opinion that counted.

When Jimmy made an appointment to see him about something important, Blackthorne checked back through his diary. He had given the young man a year to come up with something new, and it was a year to the day.

'Cheeky young sod,' he thought.

Still, he had to admire Jimmy's style.

Jimmy entered the office looking as impeccable as always; smooth blue suit, blond hair perfectly in place, shirt brilliantly white, shoes gleamingly black. And while any other manager would have been laden down with files, Jimmy was bare-handed.

Blackthorne lit a Cuban cigar. He hoped he had been right about this young man. If he hadn't, he would soon be giving up some of the finer things in life – and he had rather got to like them.

'You've cost me some money this year,' he said gruffly, because even if Jimmy had come up with an answer, there was no harm in keeping the bugger on his toes. 'What with your salary and expenses. And these nursery nurses! Have you seen what their wage bill comes to?'

'It'll be worth it,' Jimmy said confidently.

'It'd better be,' Blackthorne growled. He settled back in his seat. 'So, what have you got to tell me?'

'If the current trend for buying foreign cars continues,' Jimmy said, 'we should still make a profit next year even if we don't diversify. But the following year we'll just about break even – and after that we'll be running at a loss.'

'So what's the alternative?' Blackthorne asked. 'Rubber ducks?'

'Solid-state electronics.'

'What the bloody hell's that?'

'Miniaturisation, the micro-chip. They're doing a lot of work on it at Manchester University.'

It was all gibberish to Blackthorne. He realised that it was many years since he had been a working engineer.

'What good is pure research to us?' he asked.

'It's got practical applications. Twenty years ago, a computer as complex as the human brain would have needed to be the size of Greater London. They reckon in Manchester they'll soon be able to make one that's only as big as a portable typewriter. In ten years, everybody will have a personal computer.'

'We haven't got ten years,' Blackthorne said.

'There'll be other gadgets in the meantime which use the same technology,' Jimmy argued. 'Digital watches and pocket calculators.'

'I think I prefer the idea of makin' rubber ducks,' Blackthorne said. 'Digital watches an' pocket calculators. Who'll want 'em? We've never needed 'em before.'

'We never needed transistor radios before the technology was available. They created their own market.'

'Aye,' Blackthorne agreed reluctantly, 'but that was a mass market.'

'This will be too. Prices will be high initially, just as they were with ballpoint pens when they first came out, but they'll soon drop. And the people who are in on the ground floor will make a killing.'

Blackthorne scratched his nose thoughtfully.

'Sounds very good,' he said. 'Where's the catch?'

'The research department we have here isn't good enough. We need to bring in new blood, probably some of the whizz-kids from Manchester.'

'I suppose it'll cost,' Blackthorne said.

Jimmy smiled.

'Oh yes.'

'How much?'

Jimmy told him and Blackthorne choked on his cigar.

'Sweet Jesus!' he said when he'd stopped coughing. 'And suppose you tell me where I get the money for that.'

'All right. You're producing less than you were two years ago, but you're still employing the same number of workers.'

'More, if you count the bloody nursery women.'

'I told you they'll be worth it. Trust me.'

The casual confidence had gone from his voice, and his words were now clipped, precise. After thirty years of business negotiation, Blackthorne recognised the signs. The young man was beginning the hard sell.

'You're over-manned as it is. Or maybe over-womaned might be a better word for it. There's scope for technological improvements which would cut out a few more. You could speed up the belts a bit – I know, I've worked on them – and get higher productivity out of less people.'

'The union would never accept it,' Blackthorne argued. 'The bloody shop stewards stand next to the belt with a stop watch as it is.'

'They'll accept *anything* by the time we've finished with them. Then there's the question of management. It needs tightening up. Get rid of the dead wood, the softies, and hand it all over to the hard men. I'll give you a list.'

'An' what would all that mean in terms of reducing the workforce?' Blackthorne asked.

'We could get rid of about two hundred and fifty of them.'

Blackthorne whistled.

'That's nearly a third. It'd cause a strike.' He drew on his cigar. By, but he did like Cuban tobacco. 'Nasty things, strikes. They're like a family row, they create a lot of bitterness.'

'Does that bother you?' Jimmy asked.

'You cheeky young bugger!' Blackthorne said indignantly.

And then he saw that Jimmy was grinning at him. Well, he'd hired the lad because he didn't look like the sort who could easily be taken in. He grinned back.

'No,' he said, 'it doesn't bother me particularly. Not as long as I'm sure that I'll win.'

Chapter Twenty-Eight

That his two friends would eventually come into conflict, David was sure. The whole situation had a frightening inevitability about it. Paul had almost achieved the impossible feat of taking Norton away from the Conservatives. Next time, he would win. In the meantime, he was the town's leading left-winger, the champion of workers' rights. And Jimmy? Jimmy was the bright new symbol of capitalism. Stan Blackthorne had not given him so much freedom, paid him such a high salary, without expecting something big in return. That something could only be a hatchet job on the very people Paul was pledged to protect.

He rarely thought in images, but one came to him now. Jimmy and Paul were like express trains heading for one another. At first, each was convinced that he had the track to himself. Then, as the other came into view, they told themselves there was double-tracking ahead, or a siding that the other could pull in to. Finally, when it was clear that a collision was inevitable, each hoped to de-rail the other without causing damage and to continue his own journey with his friend or their relationship intact. And David himself, like a helpless signalman, could only stand and watch.

For Paul, the first signs of trouble came in the middle of October. He was attending a Labour Party Social, more from a sense of duty than for pleasure. As he stood by the buffet table, loading his plate with lettuce, chicken breast and potted shrimps, he thought about the spread that had been laid on for Jimmy's wedding. He had not tasted lobster since.

'Hello, Paul,' a thin voice said behind him.

He turned and saw it was Ray Monk. He disliked Monk. Not personally, he hadn't enough about him to really give offence, but because he held a union post that could have been filled by a better man, another fighter like Sid Higgins. Still, he supposed it wasn't really Monk's fault. He probably wouldn't have stood for election at all if Sid Higgins, wanting a nonentity as his Number Two, hadn't insisted.

'How you doing, Ray?' he asked. 'How are things at the works?'

Monk ran his hand through his hair in a futile attempt to push the wispy red locks back into place.

'Never better,' he said, grinning.

'And how are you getting on with Mr Bradley?' Paul asked innocently.

'What? Jimmy? He's a great lad. Likes us to call him Jimmy even though he's one of the bosses. No side, see?'

Paul felt his political antennae – which Jimmy had taught him to tune – tingle.

'So he's not a bad boss, then?'

'You don't really think of him as a boss at all. See, he's not like the rest of 'em, only out for the company.' He was speaking slowly, explaining with the care of a stupid man imitating the way he is habitually addressed. 'He's workin' class himself. Knows what it's like. Cares about the workers.' He chuckled. 'If he goes on like he has been, we won't need shop stewards.'

It worried Paul. He loved Jimmy like a brother. But he did not love him uncritically, and the description of J. Bradley, The Workers' Friend, did not match up with the man he knew.

Sid Higgins formally retired on the 29th of October. It was customary on such occasions to hold a short ceremony at which the retiring man was presented with a gold watch, thanked for his many years of service – and shown the door. That wouldn't do for Sid, Jimmy said. He had done stalwart work both on the production line and as a shop steward. He deserved a good send-off in the canteen, with booze flowing like water and a group for the dancing. And people shook their heads in admiration, and said wasn't that just like Jimmy.

When Paul arrived in the streamer-festooned canteen, the party was well under way. He had only just had time to order up a drink when the group stopped playing and Jimmy climbed onto the stage.

'Ladies and gentlemen,' Jimmy said, 'I'd like to thank you all for bein' here tonight to honour our Chief Shop Steward, Sid Higgins. I've not been workin' against Sid for long . . .' He put his hand over his mouth in mock-horror and everyone laughed. 'Sorry, I'll re-phrase that. I've not been workin' *with* Sid for long, but I've learned a lot, and I'm goin' to miss him, as I'm sure you all are.' He turned to the drummer. 'Can we have a roll, please, an' I don't mean a ham roll.'

The drummer gave him a tolerant smile, and obliged.

'Right then, Sid,' Jimmy said, 'come up here an' say your piece.'

Higgins's speech was short and commonplace. He talked about his years with Blackthorne's and the changes he had seen.

'I'll miss all me old mates,' he said, 'especially Ray and Eddie, whose assistance on the Shop Stewards' Committee I have found in-val-u-able.'

Paul glanced across at the two men. Monk wore a bland, complacent grin; Copeland looked alert and watchful, as he always did.

'Eddie's worth ten of Ray,' Paul thought. 'If it ever came to a fight in this place, he's the one I'd rely on.'

'An' I'm sure that Ray will fill the post of Chief Shop Steward conscientiously and faithfully,' Higgins concluded.

Paul went to get himself another drink.

The conscientious and faithful new Chief Shop Steward lurched into Paul a little while later, obviously the worse for booze.

'Shee what I mean about Jimmy, Paul,' Monk said. 'He'sh one of ush.'

One of us! What an idiot the man was. He simply couldn't see that Jimmy was playing a game – deliberately dropping his 'g's' during his speech, making jokes far less subtly than he normally would. Talking down to them!

Paul stood alone for a while, thinking about his own problems. Whichever way he looked at it, his life was a fucking mess. He understood now why David had been willing to have Barry on any terms, how Jimmy could marry Claire even knowing what he did about her.

Yet their choices, between having or not having one partner, had been so much easier than his.

He kept having a recurring nightmare in which he, Maggie and Lucy were in a car. He was driving, which was strange, because he didn't know how to. They were on a twisty road, high up a cliffside. They were going too fast, but whichever pedal he jammed his foot on, it made no difference. The speedometer needle climbed higher and higher. He wrenched desperately at the steering wheel, pulling the vehicle around the tight corners. The car rocked and swayed. He did not know how much longer he could keep control. Ahead of him, he could see the road dividing, the left fork carrying on, the right climbing further up the mountain. He had only seconds to decide which route to take. The choice terrified him. He looked up at the right fork. Too steep, they would never make it. He pulled the car to the left, the road suddenly disintegrated beneath them, and they were falling, falling, into the black sea below.

Then, somehow, they were out of the car and in the water. Maggie was spluttering and struggling, holding out her hand expectantly, waiting for him to rescue her. A gasping sound behind him. Lucy, her jet-black hair spread across the water, her green eyes only just above the surface. Lucy, holding out her hand to him, too. It was impossible to reach them both in time. Lucy was crippled, she couldn't swim without help. But Maggie didn't seem able to either. He had to . . .

He would wake up sweating, his heart beating furiously, his mouth dry. He wouldn't dare go back to sleep in case he had the dream again, and found himself treading water – hesitant, indecisive – while both the women in his life slipped down into the black sea for ever.

'Doing a bit of politicking?' a voice asked.

Paul smiled.

'No, Jimmy. I'm only here because Sid Higgins invited me. But,' he added honestly, 'if the chance comes up, I'll take it. These are my natural constituents.'

There were shouts of 'Give us a song, Sid!' from the other end of the room. Sid Higgins climbed onto the stage. He had a quiet word with the group, who nodded, then turned to face his audience.

'With a voice like mine, there's only one song I can sing,' he said. '*Wanderin*' *Star*.

The group played the intro, and after it Higgins came in with a throaty, creditable impersonation of Lee Marvin.

'Born under a Wanderin' Star. That's a laugh,' Paul said. 'Sid's never been further than Blackpool in his life.'

Jimmy grinned. Paul sensed that the other man was not sharing *his* amusement, but rather laughing at a private joke of his own.

Higgins droned on.

'D'you think Sid'll be able to keep away from this place?' Paul asked.

'Oh, I think so,' Jimmy said confidently.

Paul shook his head.

'I'm not so sure. When you've given your life to the union, it must be hard to relinquish the reins of power.'

Jimmy's smile was broadening. Paul probed a little further.

'Very hard to give it all up. Especially when you're leaving somebody like Ray Monk in charge. I wouldn't be surprised if you didn't see him dropping in two or three times a week.'

'Be a bit difficult, that. He's going to live with his married daughter in Darwin.'

'It's a fair way,' Paul admitted, 'but it can't be more than a couple of hours by train.'

'Not *Darwen*, Lancashire,' Jimmy chuckled, '*Darwin*, Australia.'

It was about a week after Sid boarded the Qantas flight for Australia that the rumours started. No one knew where they originated from, but most people believed some or all of them. Blackthorne's was in big trouble – there was going to be a temporary close-down, they'd all be out of work by Christmas. Ray Monk was besieged. Anxious members demanded answers and he didn't have any. So naturally, he went to see good old Jimmy.

He didn't knock. Jimmy had told him never to knock, the door was always open to him. He found the Special Assistant in his shirt sleeves poring over a mountain of coloured charts and spidery graphs. Jimmy glanced up and Monk could see his brow furrowed with worry lines. The look was gone in an instant, replaced by the usual optimistic smile. But it had been there all right, and Monk wondered how much it was costing the Special Assistant to seem so cheerful.

'Ray!' Jimmy said. 'Take a seat. What can I do for you?'

Monk lowered himself into one of the visitors' chairs.

'There's been rumours, Jimmy.'

Did he see alarm cross the younger man's face? It was difficult to say.

'What sort of rumours?' Jimmy asked evenly.

'About the place shuttin' down.'

'There's always rumours,' Jimmy said lightly. He frowned. 'No, you deserve better than that, Ray. Can you shut the door?'

Monk stood up and clicked the door closed.

'Lock it.'

Monk turned the catch and returned to his seat.

'I trust you, and I like to think you trust me,' Jimmy said, his voice almost a whisper.

'I do.'

'Can I tell you something in confidence?'

The shop steward nodded.

'We're in a hole. Oh, I know we're making a profit now, but if we don't modernise, get some new plant, we're dead.' He picked up a piece of paper covered with tight neat figures, and waved it. 'I'm trying to find the money somewhere, but it's uphill work.'

'Are we goin' bankrupt?' Monk asked, panic rising in his voice.

'No,' Jimmy said firmly. 'We *may* go bankrupt. I'm doing my damnedest to prevent it.'

Jimmy was silent for a while, and Monk could see that he was thinking, weighing something up.

'Will you do something for me, Ray?' he asked finally.

'If I can. What?'

'Let me ask you a question first,' Jimmy said. 'I know the workers won't learn about this from you, because you'll respect my confidence. But what would happen if they got it from somewhere else?'

'Well,' Monk answered, uncertainly, 'they'd be a bit upset, like.'

'And what do you think that would do to production figures?'

'I suppose they'd go down.'

Jimmy nodded his head wisely.

'I think I agree with you. And right now, that's the last thing we want. We can only dig ourselves out of this mess if we all pull together. So what I want you to do is reassure your members.'

'What d'you mean?'

'Tell them there's no truth in the rumours,' Jimmy said. He put up his hand to cut off Monk's interruption. 'I'm not asking you to do it for the company, Ray. I'm not asking you to do it for me. It's for those people down there,' he pointed through the window, 'the ones who need the wages, the ones whose jobs I'm trying to save. Will you do it?'

After Monk had left his office, head hung low, Jimmy analysed their conversation. He had wanted to give the shop steward the impression that he was worried, and he was sure he had succeeded. His concern had only been half an act. For perhaps the first time in his life, he was really questioning his ability to manipulate events. If his plans failed, he was out, the sacrificial lamb that Blackthorne would throw to the angry workers. He would never be given a management post again. He would be lucky to get a job in an accountancy firm, starting at the bottom.

The whole operation was a gamble, but gambling had never bothered him before. He remembered the way he had coolly sipped his pint during the game of Odd Man Out – that hadn't been an act. The stakes had not seemed so important in the old days. He hadn't met Claire then.

If the plan failed, if he ceased to be a perpetual winner, he would lose her. And it would always be the same. He would have to go on and on, from triumph to triumph, because without that he wouldn't be Jimmy, without that he couldn't hold Claire.

He sighed and picked up the pile of graphs he had drawn especially to confuse Monk.

Monk went back to the shop floor and told his members that everything was fine. He had to – it was quite true what he and Jimmy had agreed about the production figures. Besides, Jimmy had trusted him with a confidence, and the only way to safeguard it was to deny the rumours.

Few people believed him – Jimmy had never expected that they would.

'This comic of yours . . . what's-his-name . . . Phil Walton . . ?' the manager of The Silver Horseshoe said.

'Phil Watkins,' David replied, his hand squeezing the telephone receiver.

'Yeah, that's right, Watkins. I caught his spot last night. Very impressive, very impressive indeed. I was wondering if he could do a turn for us.'

It had finally happened, the thing he had feared for so long.

'Phil works every night. I can't spare him.'

'No problem,' said the other, cheerily. 'He's not on all the time, is he? It's – what? – a fifteen to twenty minute car journey between the clubs? There's no reason he couldn't work both places. And it would be a good chance for the lad. I mean, The Diamond is all very well, but . . . er . . .' he coughed to cover his embarrassment.

It was all very well for a start, David thought, but it was just a strip club. It didn't book acts that appeared on the telly, like The Horseshoe did.

What was the point in fighting it? He couldn't keep Phil caged up all the time. He had to open the door and give him the chance to fly away.

'I pay him by the week,' David said. 'He's not under exclusive contract or anythin'.'

There was no contract at all. He'd had Barry under exclusive contract and that had done no good when the final break came.

'So you don't mind, then?' the man from The Horseshoe asked.

'It's not up to me. I suggest you speak to him yourself.'

The other man sounded embarrassed again.

'I . . . er . . . have, actually,' he said. 'Last night. He said he wouldn't do anything unless it had your approval.'

'You won't do it unless I agree,' David said angrily, 'but you *want* to do it, don't you?'

'Well of course I do,' Phil said. He reached across the kitchen table and took David's hands in his. 'And now you're hurt, and I never wanted *that*.'

He began to stroke David's knuckles with his fingers – soft, feathery strokes.

'I love you, and I'll always love you – but I'm not in love with Harrison Enterprises. I've got all I can out of The Diamond. I need a new challenge.'

'You've been very good to us, David,' Barry said, 'but we've outgrown you. We're big league now, and you're out of your depth.'

'I'll be leaving the club behind,' Phil said, 'but that won't mean I'm leaving you as well. And can't you see what it would do to us if I didn't take the chance when it was offered?'

David could see it all too clearly. Phil in a few years, still a stag night comedian, a failure who could have been a success if only his jealous lover hadn't prevented it. Phil, no longer slim but merely scrawny, a bitter, twisted wreck of his former self. Phil sitting opposite him as he was now, hating him for what he had done, yet staying with him because there was nowhere else to go.

'You do it,' David said encouragingly. 'I know you'll be a smash.'

Phil leant across the table, put his arms around David's bull-like neck and kissed him tenderly.

'You're the sweetest, most loving, most understanding man in the world,' he said.

Chapter Twenty-Nine

The rumours of a shut-down at Blackthorne's got worse with each passing day. Stan Blackthorne had only to be a little late for the stories to spread like wild-fire – he had committed suicide, he had tried to commit suicide and was in hospital, he had had a nervous breakdown, he had taken what little money was left and fled the country.

The managers all walked around with perpetually long faces and nervous tics. Even Jimmy Bradley seemed to be cracking under the strain; he spent his days closeted in his office making, his secretary whispered, long desperate calculations.

A general air of gloom hung over the factory. Absenteeism was up, production was down. Blackthorne's was late with orders, and *that* had never happened before. Many of the workers started to look for new jobs, and found that there were none to be had. And when on the 9th of December a third of the workforce – including some management – got pink redundancy notices in their pay packets, the strongest emotion of many of those still in work was not anger that their friends had lost their jobs, but relief that they had hung on to theirs.

There probably wouldn't have been a strike at all if Monk, in a blind panic, hadn't phoned Paul.

Paul looked around the table, across the dirty tea cups and Woodbines smouldering in cheap plastic ash trays, at the men who would be his allies in the coming struggle. On the left were Ray Monk, looking more insignificant than ever, and Wally Harding, newly-elected to fill the space left by Sid Higgins and completely out of his depth.

'Thank God for the other two,' Paul thought.

Eddie Copeland, with his hard eyes and pointed features. He reminded Paul of a rat, but a rat could be dangerous in a corner. And Jack Becket, the Regional Organiser. Ruddy-red farmer's face and yardbrush moustache, a tough fighter, veteran of hundreds of conflicts like this.

'Now the first thing to establish,' Becket said, 'is: can you win the strike? Because if you can't, there's no point in staging one. You'll end up worse off. Ray?'

'I don't know,' Monk said. 'It's very difficult to say. If I could talk to Jimmy . . .'

'Who's Jimmy?' Becket asked.

'Jimmy Bradley. He's Blackthorne's Special Assistant.'

'It's a bit early to talk to the bosses,' Paul said coldly. 'First, we've got to get organised, so you can deal with them from a position of strength.' He turned to Copeland. 'We can win, can't we, Eddie?'

He was sure he would get support from that quarter. Copeland had only to show his leadership during the dispute, and come the next election, he could walk into Monk's job.

'There's a lot of women involved,' Copeland said. 'It's always difficult to get a solid commitment from women.'

Paul looked at his watch.

An hour till the general meeting. An hour to persuade these representatives of the workers that if you once let the capitalists walk over you, you were finished.

The management had given them permission to hold the meeting in the staff canteen. Public image, Paul supposed, showing they were being reasonable. The bastards!

The room wasn't anywhere near full, he thought gloomily, not like it had been for Sid Higgins' farewell party. A lot of people had not even bothered to turn up. Was it because they believed they had no power to change what had been done? Or were they thinking of the difference their fat redundancy payments would make to Christmas, and pushing to the backs of their minds the fact that after the holiday there would be no work, no wages. Would these people ever get their priorities right?

He tried to get the feel of the meeting. There were pockets of anger, buzzing like pylons discharging electricity, but they were almost swamped by the sea of sickly fear emanating from those who were too worried about their own jobs to rock the boat.

Ray Monk stood on a chair, lifted his megaphone, and said that it was the recommendation of the Shop Stewards' Committee that strike action should be taken. He did a rough head count and decided that there was a quorum present. He wasn't very impressive, but at least he was better than he had been an hour earlier.

'So, brothers and sisters,' he said, 'if we could have a show of hands . . .'

'Just a minute, Brother Ray,' Eddie Copeland said, and he didn't need a megaphone, 'I'd like to address the meetin'.'

This hadn't been planned at all. A leadership bid already, Paul wondered.

Mystified, Monk stood down and allowed Copeland to take his place.

'I've been givin' the matter some thought,' Copeland said, 'and I must respectfully disagree with Brother Ray. The company isn't getting rid of people because it wants to, it's doin' it because it has to. If it doesn't, Blackthorne's will go broke, and everybody will be out of work.'

There were some boos and cat-calls, but Copeland did not look the least put off.

'If we accept it,' he continued, 'there's a chance the company will do more than just pull through. And it's promised that the first new people it takes on will be them that's been sacked today.'

Both Paul and Monk looked at Copeland in amazement. He hadn't mentioned any of this at the Shop Stewards' Meeting. He said hardly anything, just voted with the others.

'It's all right for you, Eddie,' came one bitter voice from the audience. 'You've still got your job.'

There were cries of support from others who had suddenly found themselves unemployed.

Copeland reached into his overall pocket, extracted his pay packet and pulled a pink slip out of it.

'No, I haven't,' he said, waving the paper around.

He hadn't mentioned *that* at the preliminary meeting, either, Paul thought. He'd been keeping it back for just this moment. For the first time, Paul began to get an inkling of the management planning behind all this.

If they took a vote now, they would lose it. Paul looked up at Eddie Copeland.

'Since this seems to be an evening for impromptu speeches, do you mind if I have my say?' he asked.

Copeland smirked confidently down at him.

'Be my guest.'

Paul stood on the chair and looked out at the faces of all these people so impressed by Eddie Copeland, a man who had lost his job, and was still counselling moderation.

'You've got to fight this,' he said. 'OK, the management have promised, in the long term, to take on the sacked workers again. What guarantee is there of that?'

He paused and swept his eyes around the audience.

'None!' somebody shouted.

'That's right! None! They've promised to help them find other jobs in the short term. What guarantee is there of that?'

'None!' several people called out.

'None! There are nearly a million unemployed in Britain now and the majority of them are in the North. Can you be sure you'll ever find work again?'

He noticed heads slowly shaking, like trees in the wind.

'Can you be sure the management won't sack more people next month, or the month after?'

More head shaking, more doubt.

'Let them get away with this, and they'll think they can get away with anything. And next time there'll be fewer of you, so you'll have less muscle to fight back with. You have to strike *now*. Not tomorrow, not next week, not next year – *now*!'

The motion was passed by a small majority.

'We're in trouble, Paul,' Jack Becket confided in the pub later. 'The union'll give its official backin' to the strike, but that won't solve anythin' like all your problems. You had a majority tonight – just – but how many of the buggers that stayed at home will give you their support?'

'Less than half,' Paul guessed.

'Maybe a lot less. So what you've actually got is a minority in favour. You're goin' to have black-legs, you can be sure of that.'

'You've got the experience,' Paul said wearily. 'What would you do?'

'This strike will stand or fall by its picket lines,' Becket explained. 'Get a good solid picket and you'll not only stop them that are black-legs now, you'll discourage the ones that think about changin' their minds when the money starts to pinch.'

Was it all worth it, Paul asked himself. Socialism was about fighting for those who couldn't fight for themselves. But why should he make an effort for workers who could fight, but just couldn't be bothered? They weren't wicked, merely short-sighted. They couldn't see that solidarity was their only strength. They didn't understand that just because they were doing fine now, didn't mean they would continue to do so.

It wasn't only the people at Blackthorne's, he thought. Look at

David, down on his uppers a few years ago and now convinced, because he had made it, that the system worked.

It was freezing on Piccadilly Station, and David pulled his coat collar up around his ears.

'It's like starring in a bad movie,' Phil said. 'Pantomime Dame has heart attack just when Aladdin is showing her his lamp – dirty little bugger. "Where can we find a replacement at this time of year?" the impresario screams. "What about Phil Watkins, the Camp Comedian?" suggests the shy young assistant director. "I hear he's a big smash up North." "Get him!" says the man with the big cigar. "We'll give him a chance." And here I am, being whisked off to the bright lights of Chiswick without even time to pack me handbag properly.'

David laughed, and his breath turned into a white cloud in the cold air.

'Mind you,' Phil said, 'I haven't let it go to my head. I'm still the same sweet, unspoiled boy I always was.'

'Oh, you are,' David agreed. 'You haven't mentioned the Christmas Special for at least half an hour.'

'Ah, yes, the Christmas Special. Through the magic of television, we are able to bring into your very homes dancers, conjurors – and cheery Phil Watkins with songs around the Camp fire.'

He was taking off, David thought, and he deserved it. He had been a smash in The Horseshoe and an even bigger success when he appeared two weeks running on a regional chat show.

'I hope the bloody train comes soon,' Phil said. 'It's so cold there's icicles formin' on me false eyelashes.'

'I told you to dip 'em in anti-freeze,' David complained. 'But would you listen? You would not!'

They had been joking ever since they'd left the club, David functioning mainly as Phil's dupe, but occasionally scoring points of his own. It was an escape from reality, and David knew it – but reality looked so bleak.

A large electric engine advanced slowly along the track, pulling carriages behind it and blocking their view of the far platform.

'Do you think this is the train?' David asked.

Phil pretended to examine it.

'Well, it is *a* train,' he said, 'and it's on the right platform at the right time, so chances are it is *the* train.'

An unintelligible message was broadcast over the loudspeaker and the guard on the platform shouted, 'London train.'

David opened a carriage door and heaved the heavy suitcase

onto the train. He was about to step up himself when Phil said, 'I can manage it from here, love. Honestly.'

He climbed aboard, shut the door and pulled down the window.

'So,' David said, 'this is it.'

'It isn't anything,' Phil replied, suddenly angry. 'I'll only be gone for four weeks. And London isn't the moon, you know, you can be there in three hours. You will come, won't you?'

'Yes,' David said.

But he knew he wouldn't. He would not risk another scene like the one with Barry.

The guard blew his whistle.

'Give me one last kiss,' Phil whispered, stretching forward, but the train was already starting to move. 'I love you,' he called out as it slowly chugged away, leaving David behind.

'Did you hear that?' said a middle-aged women with a dog to the crusty gentleman next to her. 'Did you hear what he said?'

'Filthy, I call it,' the man said. 'You ought to be flogged,' he told David.

David ignored them and watched the train receding into the distance, until Phil's head became nothing more than a vague shape, his waving hand as small as a doll's. He felt hot tears running down his cheeks.

'He's crying,' the woman said in amazement.

'It's disgusting,' the man said. 'Absolutely disgusting.'

It wasn't disgusting, it was beautiful, but the man could save his righteous indignation, because it was probably all over. Once in London, Phil would be swallowed up by show business glamour. He would find himself a handsome, artistic, delicate lover and soon forget all about the big, clumsy brute whose bed he used to share when he was an unknown in the North.

David looked at his watch and saw that he was running late. There was something else he had to do, another duty of love to perform.

As Paul trudged up the road towards his home, he felt tired and demoralised. He was sick of greed, self-interest, stupidity. Let the black-legs go to work. Let the people who had been sacked just lie down and take it if they wanted to. He had his own life to live, and God knew, that was complicated enough.

He saw the man in the overcoat standing by a lamp-post fifty yards ahead. From his size, it could only be David. He wondered what Buckworth's richest man was doing there, in the cold.

'I was waitin' for you,' David said, as Paul drew level with him.

'Why didn't you go to the house? It's freezing out here.'

Because he hadn't wanted to be alone with Maggie and young Paul.

'We need to talk,' David said.

Paul looked at David's face, illuminated by the street light. His eyes were puffy, as if he had been crying.

'Phil?' he asked, sympathetically.

As tired as he was, if David needed him he would stay with him all night.

'I've just seen him off,' David said. 'It's not about that. Let's go for a walk.'

'Must be important,' Paul thought. 'David never was one for talking about serious matters while he was sitting still.'

Hands in their pockets, they set off down the street.

'I hear there's a strike at Blackthorne's,' David said.

'You're very well informed.'

'I have to be. That's how I keep a hold on my money. Don't get involved, Paul.'

'What makes you think I will?'

David sighed.

'Because I know you. You think the workers have had a rough deal and you'll stick up for them.'

'And haven't they had a rough deal?'

'Maybe they have and maybe they haven't. That's not the point. It's a lost cause. The strike's goin' to fail and it won't look good that you, the Labour candidate, have had anythin' to do with it.'

'It doesn't have to fail,' Paul said.

David shook his head.

'It does, it does. A strike just before Christmas? It's not happened by chance you know – it's planned. An' it's got Jimmy's trademark all over it.'

'And just because Jimmy's behind it, you think I'll lose?'

'Not because Jimmy's behind it, because of the *way* Jimmy's behind it. You're backin' folks' strength, he's backin' folks' weakness – so he'll win.'

David took his hand out of his pocket and laid it on his friend's shoulder.

'You're a very bright lad, Paul, an' you're very sincere – but you're not half the tactician Jimmy is.'

It stung. Minutes earlier he had been despairing about the workforce but now, in the face of David's certainty that Jimmy would win, Paul re-affirmed his belief in them. He had to have faith in the people, because if he didn't, there was nothing. And though he knew that David was trying to help, he still resented it.

'Thanks for your advice, David,' he said, 'but I have to do what I have to do.'

David shook his head sadly.

'You'll never bloody learn, will you?' he said.

Chapter Thirty

The sky was full of heavy grey clouds and there was a howling wind. It was a bitterly cold 13th of December, but walking briskly, Paul managed to generate a little body heat. He hadn't got long. School didn't break up until Friday and it was only by persuading colleagues to cover the two periods after playtime that he was able to get away at all.

Blackthorne's loomed up in front of him. British Industrial Design, circa 1940, red-brick, square and functional. It was perhaps not quite a traditional dark satanic mill, he thought. It conformed to the minimum standards of light and air, as laid down in the Factory Acts. But Blackthorne himself was as much a robber baron as any of the old cotton manufacturers.

The building was surrounded by a high wall, topped with broken bottles embedded in concrete. It looked like a prison, except that there were no guards and the heavy metal gates were not quite closed. A number of trucks were standing in the yard, waiting to carry Blackthorne products all over England. The chimney was belching out smoke as it did on any other working day.

There were fifty pickets, he estimated, wrapped up in duffle coats and scarves, huddling behind crudely painted placards which proclaimed the justice of their cause. Well under ten per cent of the total work force. And what a ragged, defeated group they looked already. Ray Monk was walking up and down dispensing coffee from a large thermos flask. The strikers took the plastic cups in their gloved hands and held them up to frozen lips.

'How many black-legs have we got?' Paul asked Monk.

'Ninety-seven,' the shop steward replied gloomily. 'There were a few more but we managed to persuade them to go home.'

There should have been hundreds of pickets. Angry, shouting people, shaming the scabs into turning back. But this was the best that Monk, the coffee dispenser, had been able to organise. Well, if weight of numbers had failed, perhaps reason would work. Paul looked at the big double gates that led to the factory.

'When's the tea break?' he asked.

Monk pulled back his glove and consulted his watch.

'About ten minutes,' he said. 'Why? You're surely not going to . . .'

Paul was no longer there. He marched to the gates and pushed the left one. It swung open, creaking loudly. When the gap was wide enough, Paul stepped through it and entered the factory grounds.

He skirted the lorries, stepped over the frozen puddles and headed for the main workmen's entrance. A couple of foremen were just emerging from one of the offices. One was about to speak when the other tapped him on the arm and shook his head. The two men turned away, pretending they hadn't noticed him. He tried the door. It wasn't locked and he entered the building.

A long wide corridor led to the central workshop, and as Paul strode purposefully down it, his footsteps echoed against the walls like the beat of a military drum. He looked neither to the left nor the right, but kept his eyes riveted on the tall slim figure standing at the end of the corridor by the workshop door. The man kept perfectly still. He wasn't going *anywhere* – he was waiting.

'Waiting for me,' Paul thought. 'How did he know I would come?'

Because Jimmy understood him, just as David did. He had known what Paul would do even before he knew it himself.

Jimmy looked completely at ease. There was even a smile playing on his lips. He was enjoying himself, as if this was no more than a game, one of the mock shoot-outs they had staged after Saturday matinée westerns.

Paul stopped two yards short of him. He realised that his hands were poised like a gun-fighter's, and felt slightly ridiculous.

'Hello, Paul,' Jimmy said. 'I hear you upset our plans a bit last night, undid all Eddie Copeland's good work with one fiery speech.'

Paul tried to analyse his tone. Jimmy was pleased about something, but not with himself – not at the moment, anyway.

He sounded like a doting father whose son had just won first prize!

'Jesus Christ! He's proud of me,' Paul thought. 'He's got a strike he didn't want because of what I did. And he's proud of me.'

It wasn't game! You couldn't treat life like that.

'I'm going to talk to the workers,' he said.

Jimmy narrowed his eyes, but the smile was still there.

'Do you have permission?'

335

'It's not a game! It's not a game!' a voice screamed loudly in Paul's head.

'It's their free time,' he said aggressively. 'They can do what they want with it.'

'It may be their free time,' Jimmy said, 'but you have no right to be here. Strictly speaking, you're trespassing.'

Paul wondered whether Jimmy would try to block his entrance. Surely they hadn't reached that point yet. Surely all the past years counted for something. Yet even as he thought this, he knew that *he* was prepared to fight if he had to.

'I'm going in,' he said firmly. 'If you want to call the police, that's up to you.'

'For goodness' sake, Paul, stop being so melodramatic. I'm not going to stop you, and I'm not going to call the police. Do you think I would have let you get this far if you could have done any good?'

Paul took a step and Jimmy held up his hand.

'Don't go in there, mate,' he said. 'They're going to lose this one. Cut your losses. Distance yourself from failure.'

Paul marched forward. Jimmy shrugged his shoulders, lowered his arm and stepped out of the way.

Jimmy was just like David, so sure that he would win and Paul would lose – so completely, arrogantly sure. Well, Paul would show him!

Some of them worked in other departments, but today all ninety-seven of them had chosen to take their tea together in the main workshop. Here at least was solidarity, even if it was only a solidarity of fear and guilt. They sat on boxes or perched at the edge of the conveyor belt – turban-headed women, blue-overalled men – sipping unhappily at their tea and not saying very much at all.

Paul closed the door loudly behind him. The black-legs turned towards the source of the noise. There was an embarrassing silence until one of the women, nervously fiddling with her curlers, said, 'Hello, Mr Wright.'

'What are you all doing here?' Paul asked, keeping his voice as level as he could. 'Don't you care what happens to anybody else? Don't you even care that you might be next?'

Some of the women looked down at their varnished nails, others developed a sudden interest in the ends of their cigarettes. One of the men tapped his foot on the floor, then realised it was the only noise in the vast room and came to a self-conscious halt.

'Well, do you care?'

'It's not that simple, Mr Wright,' a woman from headlight assembly said. 'There's no overtime at my Charlie's place any more, but we've still got the HP to pay.'

'We're talking about workers' rights, not HP payments.'

'Well,' the woman said determinedly, 'nobody in my family's ever had the bailiffs in, an' I'm not goin' to be the first. I couldn't hold me head up in the street.'

'What about you, Mrs Worrell?' Paul asked a woman he knew from past Labour Party Socials.

'I've promised our Tim a bike for Christmas. He's been so lookin' forward to it. I couldn't disappoint him now.'

He had told himself he would keep calm and present a reasoned, logical argument, but he found his temper rising. HP payments, bikes for Christmas! Would these people sell all their freedoms for a colour telly and fitted carpets?

'What about you?' he said, pointing to a woman near the tea urn.

'My husband says I'm to have nowt to do with strikes.'

'That's right,' one of the men called out. 'My missus would cut me ba . . . wouldn't like it neither.'

'Anyway,' said an older man with badly fitting dentures, 'it never does no good to get in bad with the bosses.'

Jimmy had been right, he would never move these people by idealism. Jack Becket had been right too. The strike would stand or fall by its picket line.

If Ray Monk couldn't get a decent picket together, then he would. He turned on his heel and left the black-legs in peace.

'Macintosh,' the voice said.

Charlton felt the telephone shake in his hand. What had he done to upset the Chairman now?

'Charlton,' he croaked.

'I've just been told by somebody down at Blackthorne's that young Wright was there this morning, stirring them up.'

It had finally happened. It had taken a year and a half, but Wright had started to cause trouble.

'Don't you keep a check on what your staff do in school time?' Macintosh demanded.

Charlton could almost see the Scot entering another black mark against his name in the big, leather-bound book of his mind.

'I . . . I . . .' he spluttered.

'The thing is, I do quite a lot of business with Stan Blackthorne.'

'He must have gone out on his free period,' Charlton said. 'They're allowed to do that.'

'Are they, by God? It's a wee bit different from when I was at school. Well in that case, until the strike's over, you'd better make sure he doesn't have any.'

Mrs Pilling received him with a sort of flustered, embarrassed deference, much the same way as she would have welcomed the vicar.

'You'd better come in to the livin' room, Mr Wright,' she said, patting her hair into place. 'Only you mustn't mind the state of the place. It's very difficult when you've little children, isn't it?'

A man, presumably Mr Pilling, was sitting on the sofa, watching television.

'Tom,' Mrs Pilling said, 'this is Mr Wright, the Labour candidate. He's come to see me about the strike.'

Pilling grunted a greeting.

'I'll just turn down the telly a bit then we can hear ourselves think,' his wife said. 'Would you like a cup of tea and a biscuit, Mr Wright?'

'No, thank you,' Paul said.

He had far too many other calls to make that night.

'Well, sit yourself down, anyway.'

She sat on the sofa next to her husband, he on the chair opposite.

'I am supportin' the strike you know, Mr Wright,' Mrs Pilling said. 'I didn't go into work today.'

'But you weren't on the picket line either, Mrs Pilling.'

The woman shrugged her shoulders helplessly.

'Well, I'm not what you might call an activist. Besides,' she continued, pointing to a small child crawling around on the yellow nylon hearth rug in front of the electric fire, 'it's too cold to have her standing outside for hours.'

'Who looks after her when you're at work?' Paul asked.

'The factory creech.'

'And before there was a crèche?'

'Well, me auntie used to, but since Jennifer's been goin' to the creech, she's got herself a bit of a part-time job.'

It was the same story everywhere. The women were in the union, but they did not see themselves as union-women. And most of the ones with children were finding, like Mrs Pilling, that it was difficult to get back to the pre-crèche days.

And Jimmy had planned it like that, Paul saw it all now. Set up a crèche, get them dependent on it, and then let the strikers see how

338

they manage without it. The strike had been in the making for much longer than he had imagined. What other cards did Jimmy have up his sleeve?

'Could you . . . er . . . just step into my office,' Charlton said after assembly.

Paul wondered what it was about. This was not like Charlton. Despite his approval of the Sixth Form scheme, he was still too wary of Paul to spend more time with him than he absolutely had to.

Charlton sat down behind his desk but did not offer Paul one of the visitor's chairs.

'It has come to my notice that you were not in school yesterday when you should have been teaching,' Charlton said.

'I had my class covered,' Paul protested.

'That is highly irregular. You are paid to teach the class yourself, not delegate it to someone else.'

'It's done all the time. And you know it.'

'Nevertheless, it is not what is supposed to be happening,' Charlton said, taking refuge in pomposity, 'and I must insist that in future you refrain from making such arrangements.'

The strike, Paul thought. That was what this was all about. Someone had been putting pressure on this worm who called himself a headmaster.

'In fact,' Charlton continued, 'I would appreciate it if you'd let me know whenever you wish to leave the premises during school hours. We are very close to Christmas and with all the activity going on, I may need you for a great deal of supervision.'

'Don't cause trouble,' Paul told himself. 'Don't give him any weapons to use against you.'

'You've been nobbled, haven't you?' he demanded. 'All this is to keep me away from Blackthorne's.'

Charlton's face reddened, but he kept silent.

'I won't stand for it,' Paul said. 'You're exceeding your authority.'

'If you look at your contract,' Charlton said, his voice definitely shaky, 'you will see that I am well within my rights. And I'm prepared to make an issue of this one.' He picked up some papers and pretended to look at them. 'That will be all, Mr Wright.'

Paul slammed the door behind him and stormed down the corridor. Without him at the factory for a couple of hours every day, Ray Monk would collapse and the strike would follow. But if he insisted on going, Charlton probably had grounds for sacking him. He couldn't do it to Maggie and young Paul. And he couldn't abandon Lucy. Shit! Shit! Shit!

Jimmy ran into Macintosh after lunch in the Members' Lounge of the Conservative Club. When he entered the room, the Scot was already ensconced in one of the leather armchairs.

'I've done you a good turn, young Jamie,' Macintosh said.

'Oh yes,' Jimmy said. 'What?'

He was suspicious. People like Macintosh didn't, as they said in Norton, 'do owt for nowt'. If he had really been of service, he would want something in return – probably soon.

'You know that bolshie trouble-maker Wright?'

Jimmy nodded.

'I've fixed him.'

'How?'

Macintosh was surprised by the alarm in Jimmy's voice.

'I've been on to his headmaster, made sure he's confined to barracks until the strike is over.'

The young man didn't look as pleased as Macintosh had expected. In fact, he looked positively shaken.

'I'll just call the waiter,' Jimmy said, recovering himself. 'Can I get you one?'

'I wouldn't say no to a wee dram.'

Jimmy pulled a chair across to Macintosh.

'Are you sure that's wise?' he asked in a confidential tone. 'Didn't you put Wright in the school in the first place so he'd cause trouble and you'd have an excuse to get rid of the headmaster?'

'Where'd you hear that?' Macintosh asked sharply.

'Nowhere. I just worked it out.'

It was the only possible reason for a neo-fascist like Macintosh agreeing to Paul working in a Norton school.

'Aye, well, you may be right,' the other man admitted, rubbing his five o'clock shadow with his hand.

'And isn't that just the sort of incident you could use to put the screws on?'

Macintosh thought for a while.

'It's too late now, I've already set it in motion.'

'You could unset it?'

'No, I'd look a fool.'

'I don't think so,' Jimmy said. 'It's a wise man who knows when he's made a mistake, and a brave one who'll admit it. Besides, I'd consider it a personal favour. I'd like to have Wright involved in the strike.'

340

'Why?'

The drinks arrived just in time, and while Jimmy fumbled for change, he had a few seconds to think out an answer.

'It's a bit like you and the headmaster,' he said, when the waiter had gone and he was sipping at his brandy. 'There are some people we can't get rid of at the moment, but with Wright stirring them up, we just might be able to find an excuse.'

Macintosh understood that easily enough.

'Still,' he said, 'I'm not sure . . .'

'I'd really appreciate it,' Jimmy urged. 'I'd owe you something big in return.'

Macintosh smiled magnanimously.

'All right, Jamie. Anything for you.'

Jimmy had been so busy acting on instinct that he had not really had time to think, and on the way back to the factory he tried to puzzle out why he had behaved as he had. He was convinced that he would win now, but he also knew that the strike would be over sooner without Paul. And making sure Paul stayed in school would be protecting him from himself – the Labour candidate would have had nothing to do with the final ignoble defeat of the strike. But Jimmy had tried to push Paul once before – over the debate at the Town Hall – and he now thought that it had been a mistake. Paul had to do things his own way, however bloody stupid that way was. And if he wanted to fight Blackthorne's it should be on fair terms – them against him – without any help from outsiders like Macintosh.

'Christ,' Jimmy said in disgust. 'I'm beginning to sound as lily-white as he is.'

Paul had little time to wonder about what had made Charlton change his mind. He managed to strengthen the picket line and the number of black-legs dropped a little, but it took a constant effort on his part. He spent hours outside the factory, encouraging the banner-holders, injecting them with his own belief that Blackthorne's could be beaten. He visited other strikers in the evening, and persuaded them to join the line. He organised a baby pool, so that some mothers could picket while others looked after the children. He was hardly ever at home when his son was awake, and even his few bitter-sweet moments with Lucy had to be sacrificed to the demands of the war he was waging with Blackthorne's.

On Friday, Stanley Street broke up for the Christmas holiday, and the pressure eased. Not only did that free Paul, but it also released the rest of the left-wing teachers in Norton. The picket line on the last Monday before Christmas was stronger than it had ever been.

'It won't matter to them that production is down now,' Paul told Monk as he stamped his feet to fight off the cold. 'Most of their customers will soon be closing down for the holidays. But come the New Year, they'll be screaming for their orders, and Blackthorne's won't be able to provide 'em.'

All they had to do was stand firm, endure the weather, do without their Christmas indulgences for once – and they would win.

It was midday when one of the strikers brought Paul the letter.

'Everybody's gettin' 'em,' he said.

Paul looked at the envelope. There was an address on it, but no stamp.

'They're not comin' through the post,' the striker said. 'They're bein' delivered by students on holiday.'

Paul took off his gloves – Christ, it was cold! – and extracted the single sheet from the envelope. It was a duplicated letter, but the name of the recipient had been hand written and it was personally signed by Jimmy on behalf of Blackthorne's. There was no prologue – it went straight into the bribe.

Because Christmas fell on a Saturday that year, it said, it had already been agreed that Monday the 27th and Tuesday the 28th were to be holidays. Blackthorne's did not consider it worth starting up the assembly lines for the rest of the week, so work would not begin until the 3rd of January. All workers who clocked in on the 24th would be entitled to the extra days' paid holiday, whether they had been on strike or not. In addition, there would, for the first time, be a Christmas bonus. To qualify for that, the same conditions applied.

'So suddenly they've got money to burn,' Paul said bitterly.

Of course Jimmy had had the letters hand delivered. Timing was important and he was leaving nothing to chance. Plant the idea now and let it grow. The closer it got to Christmas, the more the strikers would realise what they were missing.

Paul felt something burn his cheek and looked up to see that it was snowing. Not only was the calendar on Jimmy's side, the weather was too. Lucky bastard!

No, he told himself, being fair, he wasn't lucky. He had chosen his time carefully. If Christmas had fallen on a Tuesday or a Wednesday, Jimmy would have used an entirely different strategy.

There was almost a blizzard on Tuesday. Buses ran late, the snow ploughs rattled up and down the streets, there were temporary power failures. The decorations strung across the High Street rocked in the wind, the branches of the big Christmas tree outside the library drooped under the onslaught. Even young snowballers were occasionally driven indoors. The picket line was thinner, and though a lot of them arrived late, the number of scabs was up.

And so it went on for the rest of the week. A stream of strikers trickled back to work, picketers were more erratic in their attendance.

'I've got to do me shoppin' sometime, Mr Wright,' one of them told Paul. 'Me husband likes his comforts at Christmas. Though God knows how we'll pay for 'em this year.'

By Christmas Eve, there were two hundred people back at work. Then, at five o'clock, the workers poured out, the lights went off, and the battle was over for a few days.

Chapter Thirty-One

Paul, in a state of exhaustion, slept late, and by the time he arrived downstairs Maggie had already helped Young Paul unwrap all the presents that Father Christmas had brought him.

'He came down the chimley, Daddy,' Young Paul explained earnestly. 'He left his reindeer on the roof, and he came down the chimley.'

'And did you hear him?' Paul asked, smiling.

The boy pursed his brow.

'I think so . . . yes, yes, I did hear him, Daddy.'

Paul admired the toys that had come all the way from Fairyland and then he and the child played with the new fort, moving the cowboys and Indians around and making up stories about them. For the kids of the strikers at Blackthorne's, Paul thought, Father Christmas would not have been quite so generous.

At half-past twelve they put on their coats and set off up the road. Last year they had spent Christmas Day with Maggie's mum and dad, this year it was his parents' turn.

His mother was busy in the kitchen – arms flapping wildly, elbows seemingly pointing in all directions at once – preparing the dinner. His father sat at the table, a bottle of brown ale in front of him. His face was relaxed and for once the look of a hungry wolf forever searching out new victims, fresh fodder for his bed, was absent.

'Well, don't just sit there like a stuffed dummy, Jack,' Paul's mother said. 'Offer our Maggie an' our Paul a drink.'

Wright lumbered to his feet.

'What would you like, luv?' he asked. 'There's Cyprus sherry and I think there's a spot of port if you'd prefer it.'

His parents had changed little over the years, Paul thought, either in their appearance or their basic attitude to life. He wondered if his mother knew about his father's affairs. She probably didn't care. Maggie would care, if she found out about Lucy. It would hurt her deeply – and he would suffer with her – but she wouldn't take it lying down. She had always been a fighter.

He dreaded to think what she would do. But it was foolish to worry now. He was entitled to at least one day of peace.

His mother was a hysterical cook, but a good one. Every meal she made was a potential tragedy, doomed to failure, yet somehow she always managed to pluck it from the edge of disaster. The Christmas dinner was one of her best, the turkey succulent, the pudding rich, and Paul, who had hardly eaten at all while he was on the picket line, scoffed it down.

After the meal, tumblers of whisky in their hands, they retired to the front room. Streamers and balloons hung from the ceiling, a fire blazed in the grate for the first time since last Christmas. Paul and his father settled themselves down in armchairs. Maggie yawned and stretched out like a cat on the sofa. Paul's mother squatted on the hearth rug next to the child, her arms full of brightly wrapped boxes.

'Now let's see what Father Christmas has left for you at grandma's house,' she said.

Young Paul gazed, wide-eyed at the presents, but before he opened them he had a question he wanted answering.

'Why did he leave them here?' he demanded.

'Well, I expect he knew you were comin' here for your dinner.'

'If he'd left them at my house, I could have bringed them with me anyway,' young Paul complained, 'and then he would only have had to climb down one chimley. I think he must be a very silly man.'

The grandmother looked helpless.

'Yes, well, we'll tell him to do that next year, shall we?'

'But will he remember?' Young Paul asked stubbornly.

'Of course he will. Father Christmas remembers everything. Now let's open the presents, shall we?'

Paul grinned.

'Oh what a tangled web we weave . . .' he thought.

The feast had done its work. The Christmas pudding lay comfortably and solidly in his stomach. He knew that tomorrow the strike at Blackthorne's would seem desperately important again, but for the moment he was happy to let thoughts of it lie dormant.

He was about to make a casual remark to his father when he noticed that the older man's attention was riveted on Young Paul. He turned and looked at the child himself. He had his mother's golden hair, her eyes, too. And now that he was nearly four his face had lost its baby podginess and was setting into firm lines.

He was playing with a plastic train set, chugging it up and down

345

the carpet. His movements seemed controlled, calculated, as if he were planning every move in advance in order to extract the maximum pleasure from the experience. Paul remembered his own childhood, how, in his enthusiasm, he had almost attacked new toys, so that sometimes he would break them through misuse and on other occasions it was hours before he really understood how they were supposed to work.

Wright was still watching the child, but his look was not one of a doting grandfather. It was more like an engineer's as he sized up a job, or an art critic's assessing a painting. He finally seemed satisfied. His eyes shifted from the infant to the father. When Paul read what was in them all feeling of well-being left him. He felt sick to his stomach.

He stood up.

'It's stuffy in here,' he said to Maggie. 'I'm going for a walk.'

She swung her legs onto the floor.

'I'll come with you.'

'No!' he said, louder than he had intended. 'No, I've got some thinking to do – about Blackthorne's.'

As her husband slammed the door behind him, Maggie stretched out again. Paul was behaving strangely, but she supposed it was all the strain of the strike. He would be less nervous once he had had a good rest. The noise of her son and mother-in-law, playing in the background, soothed her. She closed her eyes.

She was almost dozing off when she suddenly started to feel uncomfortable. It was as if she were being lightly touched by many hands, or had thousands of tiny insects crawling all over her body. She opened her eyes and saw that her father-in-law was staring at her. She had never seen that expression on his face before. It seemed as if he was noticing her for the first time not as his son's wife, but as a woman in her own right. She shuddered and tugged her skirt down below her knees.

She was not fond of Wright; in some ways, she actually despised him. His son was worth ten of him; Paul was dependable, faithful and gentle, everything the father was not, and she loved him for it. Yet the older man had a strange power that both attracted and repelled her. She was frightened to be alone with him, but the fear was not of the man himself but of something deep within her, something unworthy and ignoble.

'I'd better get the washin' up done,' she said. 'No, you two stay where you are. It'll not take me long.'

*

'So he thinks like I do,' Paul said to himself as he sat on the wall, his head in his hands. 'Neither of us are sure, but we've looked at the baby and we both *think* we know.'

Damn his father! Damn life! Damn Blackthorne Engineering!

Blackthorne's. They thought they could do anything they wanted and always get away with it. Well, they couldn't. Their actions would catch up with them. He felt anger welling up inside him. How dare they treat their workers in this way, as if they were pawns on a capitalist chess board? They would *not* get away with it. If it took every ounce of strength he had, he would defeat them.

Less than forty pickets turned up on that first, cold, frosty morning of work.

'Where are they all?' Paul demanded angrily.

'They've got used to havin' a lie-in over the holidays,' Ray Monk said. 'It was as much as I could do to force meself to turn out on a bugger of a mornin' like this.'

That was part of Jimmy's plan too, Paul thought. The holiday had destroyed the rhythm of the strike, put a brake on its momentum.

'Anyway,' Monk said defensively, 'where are all your teachers today?'

Where indeed? At home, probably, doing last-minute preparation, grabbing their final chance for rest and relaxation before the long hard haul of the Spring Term.

They counted glumly as the black-legs filed into the factory. There were fifty more today.

'Suppose you can't blame 'em really,' Monk said. 'They're spent-up after Christmas.'

Yes, and now they had finally given in, they would be cursing Paul for persuading them to stay out so long, blaming him for the loss of holiday pay and the Christmas bonus. He would not get their votes again.

'It will only take one small concession,' Paul thought bitterly, as he stood behind the barrier, banging his hands together for warmth, 'and they'll all cave in.'

In the early afternoon the management requested a meeting with the shop stewards. Paul watched them walk into the factory for the first time in over three weeks, and then went back to his position by the gate. It was not a long vigil – within thirty minutes they were out again.

'They've made us an offer,' Monk said wearily. 'We're recommendin' to our members that they accept it.'

'Who is "they"? Blackthorne?'

'No. He wasn't available. We spoke to Jim . . . Mr Bradley,' Monk hastily amended, seeing the look on Paul's face.

'And what did he say?'

'He said that if they cut costs to the bone, and we're prepared to limit our pay demands this year to five per cent, they should be able to take some workers back.'

'How many?' Paul demanded.

Monk looked shame-faced.

'Thirty-five.'

Thirty-five! Out of two hundred and fifty. And apart from the reduction in the work force, the labour bill would be kept low because Jimmy had tied in next year's pay negotiations to the ending of the strike.

'I suppose Bradley insisted that Eddie Copeland be one of the ones that are taken back,' Paul said.

'No, he didn't. But Eddie will be. He's got seniority.'

'And what about the others? The two hundred and odd who won't have jobs?'

'None of them have got jobs now,' Monk argued. 'An' if we go on with the strike we'll lose anyway, an' even the thirty-five won't get back in.'

'You inadequate, ineffectual, spineless bastard!' Paul felt like shouting – but he didn't. What would be the point, Monk was right – they had lost.

But even that wasn't true.

'I have lost,' he told himself. 'It was my failure. I should have been able to persuade more people to stick it out, to stand up for what they believed in. And I couldn't do it!'

Maggie cosseted him and fussed over him, but it did no good. He didn't want sympathy, he didn't want reassurance. He was like an injured animal who needed to be left alone to lick his wounds. Maggie sensed this, and after tea, which Paul hardly touched, she dressed Young Paul up in his warm coat and took him round to her mother's.

Paul sat gazing blankly at the wall for perhaps an hour before he heard the knock on the door. When he opened it, he found a grave and serious David standing there.

'You've heard?' Paul said.

'Yes,' David replied. 'I've heard. Do you fancy a pint?'

'I might as well,' Paul said. 'I'll just get my coat.'

He turned to go back into the house, but David grabbed his arm.

'Just one thing. I've got Jimmy with me. He's waiting in the pub.'

'Forget it,' Paul said.

David kept his arm in a powerful grip.

'I think you should see him. I think you need to talk.'

'Do you enjoy being piggy-in-the-middle?' Paul sneered.

He knew he wasn't being fair, and felt ashamed.

'No,' David said. 'I don't like it, but I have to do it. Jimmy's beaten you, like I warned you he would. But that was business.'

'Business! We're talking about people's lives. We're . . .'

David's grip tightened.

'Business,' he repeated firmly. 'Remember the Secret Camp, Paul? Remember the rules?'

'What rules? We never made any rules,' Paul said.

But he knew what David meant.

'The rules that made us special to each other,' David continued. 'The rules about not lettin' each other down, never betrayin' the friendship. We never spoke 'em out loud, I can't even express 'em properly now. We never needed to say 'em. We felt 'em. Do you know what I'm talkin' about?'

Paul nodded his head.

'And can you say that Jimmy's broken one of them rules?'

Paul thought for a while, struggling with himself, trying to untangle his own feelings of failure and inadequacy from his membership of the Secret Camp Gang.

'It's chilly out here,' he said finally. 'Come inside while I get my coat.'

Jimmy was sitting in the back room of The George. When Paul entered, the other tables suddenly went silent. Everybody knew about the strike and the part the two young men had played in it. As Paul advanced towards his old mate, conversations started up again – loud meaningless conversations, conversations just to make noise to fill the empty air.

Paul looked down at Jimmy. He was as serious, as grave, as David had been. There was no look of triumph on his face.

'Hello, Jimmy,' Paul said.

'Hello, Paul.'

Paul glanced down at Jimmy's empty glass.

'You look like you've supped up. Same again?'

There was an audible sigh of relief from the surrounding tables.

It had to be discussed before it could be forgotten.

'You cost people jobs, Jimmy,' Paul said. 'It's easy for you, with a big house and a rich wife. But their wages matter to them. And you've manipulated the whole situation, as if it were a game.'

'I had to do it that way,' Jimmy said. 'We had to shed labour now, or we'd have gone bankrupt in a couple of years' time. And if we'd had a long successful strike, we'd just have gone broke sooner. So maybe I timed it right, and maybe I used some tricks, but I had no choice.' He took a swig of his beer. 'Don't forget, we've made concessions. We took back thirty-five workers today.'

A month earlier, Paul would have taken it at face value. But he had learned a lot during the strike about the way Jimmy worked, the way *things* worked.

'How many were you planning to take back when you worked the whole thing out?' he asked. 'How many more did you sack than you needed to?'

Jimmy smiled for the first time, an abashed, impish grin.

'Thirty-five.'

Paul should have been outraged, but he couldn't be. Not with Jimmy. Not at that moment.

He looked across the table at David and Jimmy, and realised how inexorably connected the lives of the three of them were. They were trees whose roots had criss-crossed and tangled; they were girders, welded together by struggle and experience. They could not have gone their separate ways even if they had wanted to.

Jimmy stood up, an empty glass in his hand.

'Is it my round?' he asked.

'Yes,' Paul said. 'But it's not your match – not by a long chalk.'

PART SIX

The End of the Secret Camp Gang

Chapter Thirty-Two

It was sometime in the years between the defeat of the Blackthorne strike and the fall of the Heath Government that the idea came to Paul that each member of the gang resembled an animal. Jimmy was a fox: wily, alert to all opportunities, taking chances but always leaving himself at least the *possibility* of escape. David was a crab, making little noise but scuttling rapidly sideways, using his pincers to claw more and more under the control of Harrison Enterprises.

And himself? He was a wasp, small, angry, with a sting in his tail – caught in one of the jam-jar traps of his childhood unable to climb out.

Well, he *would* climb out, Paul promised himself. He hadn't been able to go to Oxford, he hadn't been elected in '70, he could not be seen openly with the girl he loved – but he would keep on trying until he reached the top of the jar and re-gained a least a measure of choice. Of freedom.

Yet even Paul, for all his imagination and musings, did not see, during these quiet years, the seeds of destruction which would bring about the end of the Secret Camp Gang. How could he? The seeds were buried deep inside each one of them. Growing insidiously. Building up their strength. And while Paul might realise that he was cultivating a threat to his happiness, and David and Jimmy might reach the same realisation about their own seeds, none of them could anticipate the real danger. Not until the time was ripe and all the seedlings burst through together. Only then would the pattern be clear. Only then could the design of fate, like the corporation park's floral clock, be seen for what it really was.

Harrison Enterprises had moved the centre of its operations to London.

'It's where things are happenin',' David said. 'It's where you've got to be if you're in my kind of business.'

Neither Jimmy nor Paul were fooled. David didn't *have* to be anywhere – he could have made money in the middle of the Antarctic. But London was where Phil Watkins – the Camp Comedian – was happening. He had given up the Northern circuit entirely, and was concentrating his energy on the Smoke.

David started his southern operation cautiously, buying a small piece of a couple of clubs until he'd learned the ropes, then setting up rival establishments and driving his ex-partners out of business. He'd had, he said, 'a bit of trouble with the London gangs' but Schüte soon helped him sort that one out. Paul could imagine it – the Hamburg toughs travelling to England as ordinary tourists, cameras around their necks, cut-throat razors packed neatly in their suitcases.

David rarely came back to Buckworth now, but when he did, he always found time to visit The George. He spent an evening there with Paul in the spring of '73, six years since the Carnival, six years since it had been decided, on the toss of a coin, that Paul should marry Maggie.

The pub had changed very little. There was still the clicking of dominoes from the corner table.

– 'My drop? Double six, biggest in th' pack.'

Still the heated discussions on the merits of various racing pigeons.

– 'An' I tell you, that bugger's no good at all against a cross wind!'

It was almost like old times. Except that Jimmy wasn't there.

Jimmy was out of town on business. He'd been out of town a lot since he'd left Blackthorne's and set up his own independent consultancy.

He'd told his two mates all about his final interview with Stan Blackthorne, exaggerating the gestures a little, spinning out the story for everything it was worth, but essentially sticking to the truth. Blackthorne *had* been astonished when he said he was resigning.

'You've only been with the firm two years,' the old engineer said. 'Aren't you tryin' to run before you've learned how to walk?'

'I've served my purpose here,' Jimmy replied. 'And what I've done for this company . . . ("Cocky young bugger," Stan Blackthorne interjected) . . . what I've done for this company, I can do for others.'

'It'll take money,' Blackthorne warned.

'I'll get backers.'

'Aye,' Blackthorne admitted, 'I expect you will. I might even be willin' to invest a few bob in you myself.'

Thoughts of Jimmy reminded Paul of something.

'I hear Claire's father's gone broke,' he told David.

'Has he?'

'Yes. Apparently he's been a compulsive gambler for quite a while. Mortgaged the estate up to the hilt and eventually had to sell out.'

Paul remembered the house as he had seen it on the day Jimmy got married. Huge. Magnificent. Making David's little palace in the village seem no more than a hovel.

David wasn't saying anything. Not that that was unusual, but over the years Paul had become adept at spotting the difference between silence and evasion.

'You knew about it already,' he accused.

'Aye, I did.'

There was more he was holding back, and suddenly Paul knew what it was.

'Any idea who bought it off him?' he asked.

David grinned sheepishly.

'It wasn't *just* me,' he said. 'There's foreign money behind it.'

'Foreign?'

'Some Arab sheikhs. They had spare cash, and they were lookin' for somethin' to invest it in.'

'But what in God's name do they want a country estate for?' Paul asked.

'Bit of shootin'. You know the sort of thing, mowin' down pheasant with sub-machine guns.'

'And?'

'Bit of gamblin'. Somewhere it wouldn't be commented on.'

'And?'

'You do hang on once you get the bloody scent of somethin', don't you Paul?' David said. He shrugged his heavy shoulders. 'An' they like to have a few girls around the place.'

'Prostitution,' Paul said in disgust. 'You've become a pimp.'

David didn't take offence.

'I'm a businessman,' he said. 'I bring the goods to the buyer for a mutually profitable exchange. The girls don't need to do it. They all come from good homes – the Arabs insist on that – and they're far from starvin'.'

'So why *do* they do it?' Paul demanded.

'Because they want to make a lot of money quick, an' in hours of work an' effort involved, that's the easiest way to do it.' He took a long, slow draught of his pint. Northern beer tasted as good as ever. 'Enough of Harrison Enterprises, Brothel Division. How are you gettin' on?'

'I'm in a mess,' Paul thought to himself.

What right had he to criticise David's ethics when his own were so far from perfect? It had been a year and a half since Blackthorne's strike, a year and a half since the Christmas he had promised himself he would get his life in order. And it was still as bad as ever. Lucy wasn't in the school any longer, she was studying for her 'A' levels at the local tech. That, at least, was a relief, but it didn't solve his problems. There was simply no way out of his dilemma, not without hurting the girl he loved or the wife he didn't.

'Have you nodded off?' David asked.

'What? Sorry! Things are fine. Charlton may have to promote me whether he likes it or not. But that'll probably be irrelevant anyway. I've got the constituency tightly strapped down. Even if Heath doesn't make as big a balls-up as I expect him to, I should be home and dry come the next election.'

'That wasn't what I meant.'

'I know it wasn't,' Paul said. But he didn't want to talk about Maggie and Lucy, not right then. 'So tell me,' he continued, less condemnatory this time, 'are you turning the whole of Claire's ancestral home over to this glorified bordello?'

'No,' David replied. 'I'm keeping the West Wing for myself.'

The West Wing! How casually he said it, this man who had been brought up in the kind of terraced house Paul still lived in. The West Wing.

'For you and Phil,' Paul said.

'Yes, for me an' Phil.'

Just as his other little palace had been for him and Barry.

'How is Phil?' Paul asked. 'I see him on the box occasionally.'

Actually, he never seemed to be off it. He had his own weekly show and made guest appearances on nearly everyone else's. Paul heard his catch phrases on the bus, in the shops, even in the school playground repeated by hard cases who would normally keep well clear of anything which could be construed as even vaguely 'queer'.

'He's doin' very well,' David said. 'Makin' nearly as much money as I am.'

'That wasn't what I meant,' Paul answered, repeating David's phrase a few minutes earlier.

And like Paul, David said, 'I know.'

'I don't mean to press.'

'No, it's all right. I'd like to talk about it. I thought it'd all be over after the first panto season, 'specially when he was such a big hit. It happened with Barry, I didn't see why Phil should be any different. But he's been as lovin' as ever. No – even more lovin'. He takes me to all these fancy show business parties an' introduces me to his clever friends. I know what they're thinkin'. "Who's this big, uncultivated brute that pretty little Phil's brought with him?"'

'I'm sure they don't think that.'

'A couple of 'em even said it to his face at first. One bloke, a big TV producer who Phil really wanted to work for, said he'd never realised before that "butch" was short for "butcher". Everybody else laughed, but Phil didn't. He cut the feller dead, hasn't spoken to him since. So now people realise that if they want Phil as a friend, they've got to put up with me too.'

'Sounds great,' Paul said. 'So why the frown?'

'I keep worryin' about him suddenly findin' out that they're right. I am a big uncultivated brute, and I don't really belong in their world at all.'

Paul put his hand comfortingly on David's shoulder.

'Phil won't reject you,' he said. 'I'm sure of it.'

He felt a twinge of guilt. He had always been honest with David before, but he was not sure that he was being honest now.

Claire had changed since she met Jimmy. She was no longer the girl who could live in a garret, ignoring the physical needs of warmth and sleep. Not that she cared any less about her art – it was still the centre of her existence – but she had gradually got used to comfort, good food and drink and trips abroad whenever she felt like them. All these, Jimmy could provide. And only he, because her father was living in penury in some grotty little villa on the South Coast.

He'd known what she was like when he married her, and been prepared to pay the price, so he made no demands on her. But occasionally, he would drop oblique hints about something he would like her to do. He had not insisted that she stop having affairs, for example, but had indicated that she should at least be discreet about them. He had suggested that it would be valuable to him if she could be charming to his business associates when he brought them home. And though she was not prepared to change her life-style radically, she was at least willing to modify it – to compromise. A little. So, she played the hostess and kept her affairs secret, and the marriage looked to the outside like an eminently successful and suitable one.

She was content with it herself. In fact, she would probably never even have had affairs had it not been for her art. Jimmy was good in bed, probably the best lover she had ever had, it was just that sometimes, when she was working on a picture, she needed a different perspective, a fresh source of energy, and that inevitably meant a new man.

And then, shortly after David's visit, Jimmy *did* make a demand. It started as a suggestion but rapidly grew in force until it became an order: an order which, if she obeyed it, would turn her whole life upside down. He was angry when she refused, angrier than she had ever seen him. But she would not give way – she would leave him first.

It was on a warm and deceptively peaceful Friday in late May that it happened. Jimmy left his plush new office a little early and drove straight home. Claire was not there to welcome him, but that was not unusual. If she was working, he would not see her until the light faded.

His normal practice was to mix himself a drink which he would sip as he went through the documents he had brought home. On this day, because he had something to say which would not wait any longer, he chose instead to climb the stairs to Claire's studio.

She was painting furiously, and did not notice him at first. When she did, she smiled at him vaguely and returned to her canvas. He sat on a stool in the corner and watched her work. There was no variety in her style any more. She seemed obsessed by naked bodies. Sometimes they would be female, beautiful but full of the fear of violation; sometimes they were men, aggressive and unfeeling, driven only by their urge to ravage. Occasionally she would sketch a man and a woman together, coupling, making the beast with two backs, but these pictures did not have the power of the solitary figures. It was as if the fantasy could only be sustained at a distance, as if the act itself could never fulfil the promise.

The sun shone brightly through the attic skylight. Jimmy sat sweating in his tie and shirtsleeves. Claire, as so often when it was warm, was painting in the nude. He looked at her body, a blob of red paint on her firm left breast, a dab of white on her slightly curving belly. She was more beautiful now than when he had first met her, he thought, and he still loved her desperately, though he could not have said why.

She stopped, stepped back, and examined the painting.

'It's no good,' she said. 'It's shit.'

She turned and looked at him.

'Isn't it?' she screamed.

He looked at it seriously.

'There are others I prefer . . .' he began.

'Prefer!' Claire said. 'Prefer? It's not a car. It's not a meal. It's a painting. You don't *prefer* a painting. You react to it. You let it absorb you if it can. But this one can't. Because it's shit. They're all shit.'

She grabbed her palette knife and slashed through the canvas. She reached for the gin and tonic that she always kept close to the easel these days and took a long slug. She coughed, two or three times, and when she had finished, she started to cry.

'They're all shit,' she kept on saying, over and over again. 'All of them.'

He held her in his arms and stroked her hair gently. He had planned to be more subtle, more cautious in what he was going to say, but seeing her like this, vulnerable, needing him, he decided to speak now.

'Claire,' he said softly, 'I think it's time we started a family.'

She had not heard him. She was so wrapped up in her own misery that his words had not registered.

'I think it's time we started a family,' he said again, louder this time.

He felt her body stiffen. She pulled away from him.

'A family,' she said. 'You want children?'

'Don't you?' he asked.

'Of course I don't want fucking children. *These* are *my* children.' She swept her hand around the room, indicating her paintings. 'And they're all still-born.'

He was stunned. It had never entered his head that she did not have the normal maternal feelings.

'I seem to have picked a bad time. You're upset and . . .'

'You haven't picked a bad time, because there'll never be a good time. I don't want kids, getting in my way, making demands, interfering with my work. Not now, not ever!'

Jimmy's voice went suddenly cold.

'I give you everything you want,' he said. 'I let you do anything you want. But every man has the right to children, *and I won't be denied it.*'

It was strange, this desire to have kids. He'd always planned them eventually, always intended them to be a part of the well-ordered pattern of his life. But this urge to have them *now*, this roadside conversion, had taken him completely by surprise. It was as if he had suddenly felt the shades of his own mortality pressing down on him. He would *not* be denied!

Yet did he have any choice? He could divorce Claire even if she opposed it – God Almighty, he had grounds enough – but he was reluctant to.

He counted off the reasons on his slim fingers. One: despite it all, he still loved her. Two: the only people who knew she was betraying him were her lovers, but if it came to a messy divorce *everyone*, from his business associates to the readers of the *News of the World*, would have a field day with the sordid details. Three . . . three, Councillor Macintosh had been to see him that morning.

'Major Yatton won't be standing at the next election, Jimmy,' the dour Scot had told him.

'I didn't know that.'

'He doesn't know himself yet. But the man's become a liability. Norton's conservative with a small c. It's family men the voters want, not perverts who hang around public lavatories.'

'Yes, you're probably right.'

'I know I am. You're not involved in any scandal, are you, Jimmy? No skeletons in your cupboard?'

'Absolutely not.'

So there it was. As near as dammit, an offer of the nomination. As long as he could appear before the voters of Norton as a family man. He didn't need to have kids, not yet, but a divorce was definitely out of the question.

The offer had come as no surprise. He had been working for this, doing all the *right* things, manipulating the circumstances, so that he would be the obvious choice. Jimmy Bradley the Chairman of the Seahaven University Conservative Association, who had made a televised speech at the Party Conference. Jimmy Bradley the Special Assistant, who had broken a strike and turned the fortunes of Blackthorne's around. Jimmy Bradley the consultant, who knew so much about half the companies in Norton that he had their managing directors by the balls.

He'd come up through business, but business had never really interested him. It was politics with its scope for the dramatic, its possibilities of power – its risk of total crushing defeat – which had him in its grip. He'd been sure for a long time that a life in politics was what he wanted. And because he was only interested in a meteoric rise, he would have to start on home ground, in Norton.

And yet he had worked hard for Paul in the last election. Because Paul was his mate and you helped your mates whenever you could – without question. Because there would, inevitably, be a strike at Blackthorne's, and he had wanted Paul out of Norton when that happened. Because if Paul did win the seat, or even come close, the Party would lose confidence in Yatton and start looking around for a new man – a younger man– to replace him.

He could imagine how Paul would receive the news. He would be angry, just as he had been when he first heard about the redundancies at Blackthorne's. He would protest that Jimmy couldn't – shouldn't – stand, because his motives were all wrong, as he had protested about what Jimmy wanted to do to Maggie that night in the park.

It wouldn't make any difference. Jimmy had examined his conscience, the special conscience he reserved for David and Paul, and had found it clear. He would fight Paul fairly. Without any of the tricks he had wanted to employ on Paul's behalf in the last election. Using none of the tactics he would have adopted against any other Labour candidate. And he would still win. It would be a victory well within the rules of the Secret Camp, and whilst Paul would be unhappy, he would have no grounds for complaint.

He wished that Paul *could* have a seat too, but even he couldn't arrange that. So his friend would have to settle for a consolation prize. He could have given him a job at Bradley and Co., but he knew that Paul's pride would never let him accept that. Very well, then, the offer would have to come from David and Jimmy would find some way, in their business dealings, to compensate him.

Taking away an opportunity with one hand, presenting a second with the other. A balance. That was what life was all about. It was always possible to strike a balance. Except with Claire.

Paul would see reason, but Claire was so intense, so emotionally weighted, that it was impossible to conceive of pushing her, of tipping her towards equilibrium. He tried to examine the scales objectively: love, the fear of public humiliation and political ambition on one side, the yearning for children on the other. Both were heavy, and rather than give an inch themselves, they would prefer to break the scales.

There had to be a way to balance them. *There had to be.* But for once in his life, he couldn't see how to do it.

Chapter Thirty-Three

The threat of the miners hung over the Heath administration like a vulture hovering above its helpless victim. The NUM had closed the pits in '72 and brought the country to its knees. The great bird of prey returned in the autumn of '74, just as the government was about to introduce Phase Three of its pay policy, swooping ever lower, ready to strike. In every sense of the word.

In October, the NUM put in a pay demand of forty per cent and was offered thirteen. On the 10th of November, it imposed an overtime ban and the government declared a State of Emergency. By December there was such a shortage of fuel that Heath introduced further emergency regulations.

The three-day week. Factories operating at only sixty per cent capacity. Television shutting down at ten o'clock because the government believed that without its magic box the Great British Public would go straight to bed and stop wasting power.

When television was transmitting, it bombarded its viewers with ways to save fuel – improbable cooking instructions which involved producing meat and three veg using only one pan. Patrick Jenkin at the Department of Energy advised everyone to brush their teeth in the dark, then spoiled it all by leaving every light in *his* house on, much to the delight of a passing Fleet Street photographer.

Things couldn't go on like that. Something had to crack.

'There's going to be an election,' Paul told Lucy. 'There *has* to be.'

They were sitting in a quiet corner of a big, open-plan country pub some distance from Norton.

Paul had travelled there by bus, changing twice. The vehicle which took him on the last stage of the journey was ancient. It groaned and creaked as it slowly covered the distance between isolated, usually deserted, stops. The heating was almost useless and frost froze on the outside of the windows denying him even the diversion of the bleak winter landscape.

Lucy had arrived first, and she would leave first. They never travelled together. Their lives were dominated by the whim of the Crossville Bus Company's timetabling department.

Around them sat other couples, free from guilt, unhampered by subterfuge. Some were obviously out on a date – slightly nervous, slightly wary, tryng to impress. Others were married and sat in a comfortable intimacy almost bordering on the complacent. Oh, to be like them!

'It won't be easy, this election,' Lucy said. 'You'll be fighting Jimmy this time.'

It was odd to hear her speak about Jimmy as if she knew him well. They had never met. Maybe he talked about his two closest friends too much. But what else *could* he talk about? He couldn't discuss Maggie, nor could he mention the one person other than Lucy who he really loved – young Paul. And so he had told her about Jimmy and David and now she knew almost as much about them as he did.

'Yes,' he said. 'I'll be fighting Jimmy this time.'

He was ready for it. He'd learned a lot since the Blackthorne strike – about tactics, about exploiting his opponent's weaknesses.

Not that he would use Jimmy's major weakness – his wife – against him. It would be easy to start the rumours, get people laughing behind Jimmy's back, cut him down to size. But he would never do it – and Jimmy wouldn't use Lucy against him. He hoped!

He would win. He had almost carried the seat when there had been a swing to the right, and this time the pendulum must move to the left. Nothing could stop him. Not even Jimmy Bradley!

'And what if you do win?' Lucy asked, reading his thoughts.

'Then I'll be Paul Wright, MP for this borough.'

Trying to make light of it.

'What about *me*?' Lucy asked. 'You'll be going down to London. Maggie will be going with you. What about *me*?'

'I'll be up here a lot. I'm not going to be one of those MPs who deserts his constituency.'

'Coward!' he told himself angrily. 'How can you ever fight on the big issues if you're too scared even to face your own problems?'

'It's bad enough as it is,' Lucy said. 'All the lying, all the deception. Just once, I'd like to make love somewhere decent. Not in a committee room, not in the woods. In a real bed. Where we can take our time. Where everything isn't so sordid.'

'Keep your voice down,' Paul hissed, and was instantly filled with shame.

She was right, of course. She was entitled to better than this –

quick, surreptitious fumbles; cautious, whispered messages of love.

'Will you ever divorce Maggie?' Lucy asked, more quietly this time.

'I never promised that,' Paul said defensively.

Lucy smiled, a beautiful, sad smile that took his breath away. He wanted to reach across the table, to pull her into his arms. But he daren't with all these people around – because there was just a chance that one of them would recognise him from his picture in the paper.

'No,' Lucy admitted. 'You've never promised that. I suppose I should be grateful for what you've given me already. I've had moments of happiness I'd never have thought possible. I'm confident and outgoing and it's all because of you. And once, I *would* have thought that was enough. But I do so want to be your wife, Paul – so that I can be proud of you in public. Will you divorce her?'

'I can't now,' Paul said. 'Not with the election coming up.'

He saw disappointment in her eyes.

'That's a Jimmy answer,' she said. 'And you're not Jimmy. You wouldn't divorce Maggie even if you could, because you can't bring yourself to hurt her.'

He tried to speak, but she reached across and put her hand to his mouth to silence him. For once, he did not notice the display of public affection.

'I understand.' Tears were forming in those deep green eyes. 'I know you're too gentle to fight for you own happiness. But where *does* that leave me?'

Where indeed?

'Should we stop seeing each other?' he asked, and even saying the words brought a pain to his heart.

'It might be for the best,' Lucy replied. 'But I couldn't bear it.'

'Thank you, Lucy,' Paul thought. 'Thank you for saving one of the few things in my life which is precious to me. Damn you, Lucy! Why couldn't you have been strong enough for both of us!'

Councillor Macintosh stood at the bar, waiting for Elaine to finish powdering her nose. It was a good pub, this one, he decided in his dry, calculating way. Close enough to Norton for convenience, far enough away to ensure that news of this assignation didn't get back to his wife.

His eyes moved idly across the bar and what he saw made him almost choke on his double scotch.

Paul Wright, sitting as bold as brass in the far corner. Paul Wright, who had just happened to choose this pub on this night to take his wife out for a drink.

Wait a minute, Macintosh told himself. Wright's wife was a blonde – he remembered the bitch from those political meetings – and this woman had dark hair. Could it be – could it just be – that Wright was doing the same as he himself and having a bit on the side?

Macintosh edged himself behind a pillar, out of Wright's line of vision. If the other man had *already* spotted him, it didn't really matter – they had a mutual interest in keeping quiet. But suppose he hadn't!

Being a socialist in itself was enough to overdraw on Macintosh's good will, but Wright owed him other debts. He didn't show enough respect, he looked at the Councillor with contempt in his eyes.

And he hadn't done what he was supposed to in the Stanley Street Secondary Modern School. Macintosh had got him the job so he would bring about chaos and get rid of Charlton. Instead, the school's reputation was actually going up.

Oh yes, the left-winger had put himself very far in the red.

Left-winger. Far in the red. Macintosh chuckled drily at his own joke.

This could be a way of settling the account. Even if it were not enough to cost Wright the election, there was at least scope for personal revenge. Wright's wife would give him hell once she found out.

The woman with Wright had got up and was walking towards the toilet – towards where he was standing. Macintosh noticed that she was moving awkwardly and wondered why. She had a pronounced limp. A cripple! Wright was having it off with a cripple. Probably couldn't get a normal woman.

The cripple walked past him. He'd been thinking of her as a woman but now he'd seen her close up, he realised that she wasn't. She was little more than a girl – just out of school. Just out of school! In a sudden burst of inspiration it occurred to him that the school she was just out of might be the one in which Wright taught. Even if he hadn't been shagging her then, it would look as if he had been. And that was just as good.

And the beauty of it was that if she had been one of Wright's pupils, it should be easy to find out her name. Charlton couldn't have had many dark-haired cripples passing through his school recently.

Elaine was finally back from the lavatory. She sat down on the stool next to him, crossing her legs as far as her tight skirt permitted.

'Drink up,' Macintosh grunted. 'We're leaving.'

She giggled.

'You're in a hurry tonight.'

She leaned closer and perfume invaded his nostrils. It smelled expensive, and it was. He knew to the penny how much it had cost. He'd bought it for her as a reward for accompanying him on a business trip to Scarborough.

'Where are we going?' she whispered in his ear. 'Alderley Edge? Or Maggot Wood?'

Yes, she was working out rather expensive with her constant hints about presents, Macintosh thought. He did a quick calculation, pounds laid out over hours spent in the back of his Jag. Not a good ratio at all. If his car had cost him that much to run, he would have got rid of it long ago.

Besides, if he was going to make Wright's affair public knowledge, it might be wise to keep a low profile himself.

He contemplated one last fling. He might as well, he'd already paid for it. He pictured Elaine with her legs in the air, the big, firm bosom freed from that frilly blue blouse. No good. He couldn't get interested. The only thing which really excited him was the thought of returning to Norton and ringing up the headmaster.

Phil was not wearing one of the pink suits which had become his trademark. Instead, he was dressed in black trousers and a black crew-necked sweater. His own neck seemed unnaturally white against the darkness of the material, and not just thin but as scrawny as a chicken's. He looked like a man who had been burning the candle at both ends.

When had he had the chance? David thought. But that was a silly question. They saw each other as much as possible, but there were hours every day when Phil was working at the studio – or said he was. And how much time did you need for a secret affair? An hour? Half an hour? Just long enough to pull down your trousers and bend over!

'Well, take a seat,' David said, gruffly for him.

Phil stood in the centre of the thick carpet, shifting awkwardly from one foot to the other.

'I haven't got time,' he said. 'I just called in to tell you that I want to go back up north for a while.'

'But why?' David asked. 'London's the key. You always said it was.'

And London had been good to them both. David looked around his plush office. Good central location on Garrick Street, stylish decor created by one of Phil's little friends, original David Hockney on the wall. The cost of this one room alone would have been enough to buy up half of Buckworth.

Phil was silent.

'Why?' David asked again.

The Camp Comedian shrugged his thin shoulders. He usually contrived to make the gesture funny, but this time it merely looked pathetic.

'I just do,' he said. 'I need to get away.'

David played his trump card.

'I'm not sure that *I* can get away,' he said. 'I moved here because of you, you know, but now my business commitments make it very difficult to leave for long.'

The words sounded stilted, pompous, unlike anything he would normally say – especially to Phil.

'I'm sorry you can't come,' Phil replied. 'But I just have to get away.'

What new shows were opening in Manchester? Which of them was Phil's new friend – his new lover – starring in? David wanted to deal with this problem as he dealt with all others – head on – but for once his courage deserted him.

'Won't you miss me?' he asked.

'Of course I'll miss you.'

Phil was crying, but then, David thought, he'd always found it easy to cry.

'Look, David,' the Camp Comedian continued, 'I can't . . . I won't be questioned any more. I should never have come here. I should just have left you a note. I'll . . . I'll write to you.'

And he was gone. Across the expensive carpet, through the reception where David's highly-paid secretary was hard at work, and out of the door marked 'Harrison Enterprises (Theatrical Division)'.

Just like Barry. And just as with Barry, David had sat there and let it happen.

He tried to turn his mind to the new deal he was putting together with the Arabs, but it was impossible. Almost before he realised it, he was walking through the outer office.

'I'm taking the rest of the day off, Joan.'

His secretary looked surprised. Mr Harrison *never* left early.

'You're expecting calls from New York and Rome.'

'I know.'

'Where can I contact you?'

'You can't.'

'But what shall I tell them?'

'Tell them . . . tell them to ring me tomorrow.'

He drove back to Knightsbridge. To his flat – to their flat! Phil was not there. David checked through all the closets and drawers. Phil's show business suits still hung mournfully in their usual place, but his personal clothes, the ones he wore when he was not pretending, had all been removed. David searched around for an address or telephone number in Manchester.

There wasn't one.

So this was it!

He sat staring at the wall, his slow, careful mind going over their life together, trying to isolate the moment at which things had gone wrong. Darkness came – hours of darkness followed by the dawn. He did not notice. One day stretched into two. And then three. At some point he must have got up and made some food for himself – beans on toast, fried eggs, he could see the evidence in the pans – but he did not remember.

The phone rang any number of times, business associates desperate to get in touch with him. He didn't respond. What was the point of it? What was the point of anything? He could sell Harrison Enterprises and he would be a rich man. But money had never really mattered to him – he would have earned enough to keep him happy just from the scrapyards. It was the challenge which had appealed – the battle. And he had lost the will to fight any longer.

On the fourth day he made a token effort and drove to his office. He could tell, from the way his secretary stared at him, that he looked rough. He didn't care. He didn't care about anything.

He needed to be needed. Had done ever since that fateful night when his father had ploughed Fred Rathbone's van into the broken down lorry. Well, his family didn't need him – they were well provided for. Jimmy and Paul didn't need him – Jimmy had his consultancy and Paul would win Norton at the next election despite being up against the blond superboy.

And now, even Phil didn't need him.

He picked up one of the trade papers at random and flicked it open.

'Pop Star's Death!' the headline screamed.

His hands started to tremble and he knew what he was about to read even before he lowered his horrified gaze to the text.

He looked at the photograph first. The wide smile, the slightly pointed features. The eyes, which had once been filled with admiration whenever they looked at him.

He forced himself to take in the story below.

'Barry Crowther . . . lead singer and mainstay of Urban Decay . . . career in decline for the last two years . . . friends said he had been depressed recently . . . overdose of drugs in Los Angeles hotel room . . .'

He loved Phil, not Barry. Yet still he felt a tragic sense of loss – of waste. He had stood on the step of the little palace and let Barry drive away for ever. Maybe if he'd tried harder, the young guitarist would have stayed with him. It was unlikely, but there was just a chance. And if he'd stayed, if he'd had David's firm hand to guide him, he would never have ended up like this – dead at twenty-one.

He thought of Phil standing there, just across the desk from him. He could almost *see* Phil standing there. He'd looked tired and drawn. Well, they both knew why *that* was. Because he had been having an affair behind David's back – possibly more than one affair. Because the double life was exhausting. Because he was racked with guilt.

But that wasn't the point at all.

David had been concerned only with his own feelings, not with Phil's. He'd been looking not through the eyes of love, but through the eyes of jealousy. He would *not* let Phil end up like Barry. He wouldn't allow him to walk out of his life and go from one promiscuous affair to another, ending up the victim of drugs or the clap or the jealous rage of a new lover. If Phil wouldn't accept him as a partner, then perhaps he would let him be his protector, his guide. The Camp Comedian had given him more happiness than he'd ever been entitled to expect. He owed Phil a debt, and he was ready to pay it.

He flicked the intercom on his desk.

'Get me booked on the first flight to Manchester, please, Joan.'

Chapter Thirty-Four

Edward Heath should have 'gone to the country' in early February, while he was four per cent ahead in the public opinion polls and before the miners' dispute escalated into anything more than an overtime ban. If he had called an election, he would have won it easily. But he didn't. Instead he let the 17th of January deadline slide by, only to be confronted at the end of the month with a full-scale miners' strike endorsed by eighty-one per cent of the membership.

'We've poleaxed Ted Heath before,' one young pit-man said on television, 'an' we shall do it again.'

On February 7th, the day that Councillor Macintosh went to see Jimmy Bradley, the Prime Minister announced there would be an election after all, three weeks from that date.

'I'm surprised to see you still working at your business now the election's on,' Macintosh said, in the level, measured tone he habitually employed.

'I'm just tying up a few loose ends,' Jimmy replied cautiously.

He had thought this was just another client-consultant meeting, but it plainly wasn't. It was hard to read Macintosh's expression. The man moved his face with economy, as if he were saving his facial muscles from wear and tear. A small twitch, a slight frown, that was all you got, that was the only indication of what he was thinking.

And what did these minimalist movements show? Macintosh was not angry, despite his words. Nor was he exactly gloating, though there was an element of that. Malicious glee, Jimmy decided. Which was about as close as the dour lowlander ever came to expressing happiness.

'It's very important we win this time,' Macintosh continued. 'If Wright gets in, we'll have a good deal of difficulty prising the little bastard out again.'

Jimmy bristled at the reference to Paul, but he didn't let it show

– he never let it show. There were better ways of dealing with people like Macintosh.

'Why will it be so difficult to prise him out?' he asked innocently. 'Do you think Paul will turn out to be such a good constituency MP that the voters won't want to get rid of him?'

The gash in the middle of Macintosh's five o'clock shadow widened. From anyone else, it would have meant little, but Jimmy recognised it as the Scot's widest scowl of disapproval.

'You sound as if you're on his side,' Macintosh said.

'I'm on *my* side,' Jimmy replied.

But that had always included Paul and David.

Macintosh nodded, reassured. Unenlightened self-interest was something he understood.

'Wright's been putting a great deal of effort in the constituency over the last six years,' he said. 'There's a chance the bleeding-heart do-gooders will vote for him – unless we can come up with something to tarnish his shining armour a little.' He spread his hands, the glum magician revealing the rabbit in the hat. 'Did you know that he's been sleeping with a crippled school girl?'

'Yes.'

Macintosh was so deflated that for a moment he almost seemed human.

'And when are you planning to use it?' he asked. 'I'd leave it a while, until the week before the election. That way, the new candidate would have no time to establish himself before polling day.'

'The new candidate?'

'What's happened to your political acumen, Jimmy? You surely don't imagine the Labour Party will continue to support him after this becomes public knowledge?'

'I don't want it to become public knowledge.'

'You asked me to do something for Wright once before,' Macintosh reminded him. 'Remember? During the Blackthorne strike. You asked me to take the pressure off him with Charlton. And I did because I thought it was for you. But I won't be fooled again. We go public on Wright.'

'If you do that,' Jimmy said, 'then I'll resign my candidature.'

Macintosh put his large, hairy hands flat on the desk, and leaned across so that his face was only inches from Jimmy's.

'Don't threaten me,' he said in a voice which was almost a whisper. 'You're a good candidate, a very good candidate, but you're not completely indispensable. If it comes to a choice between having both you and Wright fight the election or having neither of you, then I'll choose the latter course.'

They were really afraid of Paul, Jimmy thought with pride. Little Paul had these bloated businessmen quaking in their expensive, well-cut waistcoats.

But that didn't solve the problem.

'I'll make a deal with you,' he said. 'You don't go public on Paul's affair and *I'll* get him to withdraw.'

'If I do go public,' Macintosh countered, 'Wright will have to resign anyway.'

This wasn't political, it was purely personal. Jimmy could feel Macintosh's cold dislike chilling the room.

'Oh, Paul,' he thought, 'why do you always land me in situations like this?'

'I'm asking you not to go public,' he said aloud.

'No more favours.'

Jimmy smiled at the grim, determined face opposite him.

'Speaking of favours,' he said. 'You remember that rush job we did on your books – getting them ready for the Revenue?'

'What about it?'

'We managed to plaster over a few cracks.'

'There's nothing illegal in my business dealings.'

'Illegal – no,' Jimmy said smoothly. 'Irregular – yes. I imagine the tax man would be very interested in knowing what I know.'

Macintosh was almost puce under his bristly black covering.

'If I go down, you go down with me,' he threatened.

'I think not,' Jimmy said. 'I haven't submitted reports to *anybody* yet.'

'I'll ruin you with the local business community.'

Yes, that was a risk, but, if pushed, it was a risk he was prepared to take.

'There's no need for either of us to go to extremes,' he said. 'Paul has to withdraw. I agree with you there. But after that, you keep quiet about what you know, and I'll keep quiet about what I know.'

'That's blackmail,' Macintosh growled.

'You could look at it like that,' Jimmy agreed. 'Do we have a deal?'

Macintosh nodded.

'But I won't forget this, Bradley.'

It was years since he had called Jimmy by his surname.

It was strange returning to Manchester after all these years. No,

David thought, it *wasn't* many years, it was just that a great deal had happened in them. He remembered tramping the streets, trying to get a booking for Urban Decay. And now he was doing it all over again, looking for Phil, his lost love.

He tried all the gay bars and pubs. He talked to club managers Phil might have approached for a booking. He drew a complete blank. His business was going to pieces in London and he didn't give a damn. He had to find Phil. Had to talk to him one last time.

He had been searching for a week when he got his first break. The club was called Joker's – flashing lights, all-pervading smell of pot, loud glitter-rock filling the room. The man was called Mark, an ex-public schoolboy who might have become a smooth City broker but instead was a mess. David looked at him across the table. Long blond hair encrusted with grease, thin intense face, frightened eyes which yearned for the next fix.

'I'm lookin' for Phil Watkins,' David said.

'Haven't seen him,' Mark replied, over-loudly. 'Now what about the other matter you wanted to discuss?'

'Other matter? What other matter?'

'For Christ's sake keep your voice down,' Mark urged him, looking anxiously around.

'*They* don't know anything,' David said, mystified.

'Of course they do,' Mark whispered. 'At least, the ones who remember him from the old days do. They're just not telling you.'

'What's he into that's so terrible? Is it drugs? S-M?'

Mark looked genuinely astonished.

'You really don't know?'

'No.'

'Then, Christ, I'm not going to tell you.'

David resisted the temptation to pick him up and shake him. That was not the way to deal with junkies – put the pressure on and they just retreated into their shells.

'You've seen him?' he asked.

'Yeah.'

'When?'

A vague shrug. Was this the sort of person Phil was getting mixed up with? Was his beautiful white arm already like a pin cushion?

'I should have seen the signs,' he told himself. 'I should have been *looking* for the signs.'

To the junkie, he said, 'Was it yesterday? The day before?'

'The day before,' Mark settled on.

'Where's he living?'

'Don't know.' A crafty expression came into his eyes. 'But I can find out for you.'

He paused, waiting for David to make an offer.

'I can pay you. How much?'

The eyes did a rapid calculation, not thinking of money as money at all, but only in terms of the number of fixes it would buy. He named a sum. It was laughable.

'All right,' David agreed.

'I'll need some of it now. For expenses. Say . . . half.'

Give him money and he would be high within the hour. Refuse, and he would never come up with the address. David palmed some notes into Mark's hand.

'How long will it take? When can we meet?'

Mark looked vague again. He travelled in his head, in his veins, not in time and space.

'I'll be around,' he said. 'You'll find me.'

It would do. It would have to do.

Paul and Jimmy walked slowly along the canal bank. The frosted cobble-stones glistened in the pale sunlight. Ice clung to the edges of the water, not strong enough – not yet – to extend its grip over the entire surface.

Jimmy was silent, thoughtful, almost as if he were not himself, and Paul realised that he had something very significant to tell him.

'They've found out about you and Lucy,' Jimmy said finally.

There was no need to ask who *they* were.

'Did *you* tell them?' Paul asked, and was instantly ashamed. 'I'm sorry, Jimmy. I didn't mean . . . What do they want me to do?'

'Withdraw, of course. But not yet. Not until it'll be too late to find a good replacement.'

'They didn't want you to tell me so soon, did they?' Paul asked.

Jimmy picked up a loose pebble and skimmed across the surface of the canal, just as they had all done when they were kids.

'No,' he said.

'So why did you?'

The taller man draped his arm over the shorter one's shoulders.

'To give you a chance to cover your back.'

Did Jimmy expect him to play along with their little game? He wouldn't withdraw! He would fight the election whatever they did.

No, he wouldn't. When it came out that he had fallen in love with one of his pupils, he'd lose the Party's support. The voters' too. He'd have to go. But he wouldn't do it their way, leaving the Party in the lurch at the last minute.

'I'll withdraw tomorrow,' he said.

'If you do, there'll be trouble.'

'For you?'

They stopped walking. They stood perfectly still, on a frozen tow path, looking into each other's eyes.

'Possibly for me,' Jimmy said, 'but I can handle it. I'm prepared. You're not.' He caught Paul's look of resentment, but still pressed on. 'You don't understand power, Paul, you never have. Part of the trick is knowing just how far you can push people – friends *and* enemies – and still keep them under control. You announce your withdrawal tomorrow and whatever I try to do, Macintosh is going to make you suffer.'

'I can't let the Party down,' Paul said, 'so I'm just going to have to take that risk.'

Jimmy sighed heavily.

'I knew you'd say that.'

Macintosh held the press handout between trembling fingers.

'Mr Wright, after long thought, has decided that he can more usefully serve the community in education than in Parliament. He is to be replaced by Alderman Thompson, whose experience in local government . . .'

Wright had been tipped off! By Jimmy Bradley! And Jimmy Bradley should have known better. The miners were getting more support than they deserved. Harold Wilson was looking good on television. The polls indicated that the gap between the two parties was narrowing. The Norton Conservatives needed all the help they could get, and discrediting the Labour candidate at the last minute would have given them just the push they needed. But now Wright wasn't the Labour candidate at all! He'd been replaced by a nice, safe, respectable alderman, a man who could never have swung the seat on his own, but who didn't need to – because Wright had done the work for him.

He considered his options. Fling mud at Wright and some of it might stick to the Norton Labour Party as a whole – the party which had selected a pervert as its candidate even if he had now withdrawn.

The Scot rubbed his bristly chin thoughtfully. How seriously did he take Jimmy Bradley's threat to shop him to the Inland Revenue? A threat was only effective while it was in the interest of the man making it to carry it out. And once Wright was exposed,

Bradley would have nothing to gain and a lot to lose. Jimmy was far too intelligent to prejudice his own political and business interests for the sake of a futile gesture. Macintosh picked up the phone and dialled the *Norton Chronicle*.

The editor was dubious at first.

'We don't really go in for sensationalism,' he said.

'You printed a special edition on the debate between Wright and Yatton in the last election.'

'That was different.'

'We've been friends for a long time,' Macintosh said levelly. 'I'd appreciate you doing this for me.'

He didn't need to mention the fact that he owned thirty per cent of the paper.

'I'll need solid proof,' the editor said.

'You just set up the story,' Macintosh replied. 'I'll get you all the proof you need.'

Paul had been expecting the call to Charlton's office ever since he had announced his withdrawal. It came as no surprise to find Macintosh there too.

'Councillor Macintosh has brought . . . er . . . certain accusations to me, Mr Wright,' the nervous headmaster said. 'Accusations concerning a relationship between you and a . . . er . . . certain young woman.'

'Lucy Green,' Paul said. He saw the headmaster's expression change from worry to astonishment. 'Did you expect me to deny it?'

Direct responses, commitment of any kind, always confused Charlton. He was at a loss.

But Macintosh wasn't.

'So you *do* admit it?' he asked.

'Yes,' Paul replied. 'Adultery is no longer a crime in this country. I don't even think it's grounds for dismissing me from my post, which is what this meeting's all about, isn't it?'

Charlton's mouth flapped open, but no words came out.

'Adultery isn't grounds,' Macintosh agreed. 'But what we are discussing here is a possible – a probable – case of gross moral turpitude.'

'You sanctimonious bastard!' Paul thought.

Gross moral turpitude. Depravity, baseness, had nothing to do wtih what he shared with Lucy.

'Go on,' he said.

'The question is, did this affair start whilst she was still a pupil

376

in this school, whilst you were still *in loco parentis*. In other words, Wright, did you abuse your position merely to slake your lust.'

He had chosen his words carefully. To anger. To provoke a confession. And yet it would also give him satisfaction if Paul lied, because then he could tell himself that for all his professed socialist principles, the young teacher was just like him.

Paul had no intention of lying. He would tell Macintosh that he was proud of his love for Lucy, that it wasn't sordid at all and he didn't give a fuck for the other man's salacious opinion.

The Scot had settled back in his chair and was waiting patiently for a response with something which could almost pass as a leer on his face.

Paul bit back the defiant statement which had formed in his brain. If he told the truth, it would mean Maggie finding out about Lucy, and though he could face her anger, he was not sure he could handle her sorrow. It would mean losing his job, too, and seeing his wife and child in semi-poverty again, making do and mending, spending their holidays at home instead of at some modest seaside hotel. They were entitled to better, and even if that meant sacrificing his precious principles, it had to be done.

'My relationship with Miss Green began after she ceased to be a pupil of this school,' he said formally.

'I don't believe you,' Macintosh said.

'I'm sure you don't – but can you prove I'm lying?' Paul asked. Even if he had let himself down, he would at least pull one small triumph out of this disaster.

There was no way Macintosh *could* prove it, not without Lucy's help. And Lucy would *never* betray him.

'You do realise,' the Councillor continued, unperturbed, 'that it will be in the papers.'

With a sickening jolt, Paul saw Macintosh's whole strategy. Why hadn't he been honest in the first place, and salvaged a little of his own dignity?

'Will it mention Lucy's name?' he asked dully, an actor reading his script with no interest because he already knows the surprise ending.

'That would depend,' Macintosh replied. 'If the affair started after she left school, she has to be regarded as a mature adult, responsible for her own actions, and her name would be printed. If, on the other hand, she was seduced while still a child, then her anonymity must be protected at all costs.'

'It started at school,' Paul admitted. He turned to Charlton. 'You'll have my resignation within the hour.'

'It's too late for that,' Macintosh said. 'Consider yourself dismissed. Subject to the headmaster's decision being ratified by the Board of Governors, of course. But I don't think there'll be any problem about that, do you?'

'No,' Paul agreed. 'I don't think there will.'

He had to tell Maggie before she heard it from anyone else. He found her in the kitchen, her sleeves rolled up, baking. White flour clung to the golden hairs on her arms.

She was a good wife, he thought, and a very pretty woman. *Why couldn't he love her?*

'Where's the boy?' he asked.

'Gone to town with my mum.'

Even the gods wanted him to get it over now.

'Why are you. . . ?' Maggie started to ask.

'Sit down, I've got something to tell you.'

She smiled, uncertainly.

'Something nice?'

But if it had been something nice, he would not have been home in the middle of the day.

He told it all. How he had first met Lucy. How he had wanted to help her. How his feelings had started to develop for the beautiful crippled girl. She listened in silence, her face betraying nothing. Only when he had finished did the tears start to flow from her eyes.

'Three years,' she said. 'It's been going on for three years.'

'Yes.'

'And you still carried on sleeping with *me* all through it. Why, in God's name? Is sex that important to you? After the way I've tried, have you no respect for me at all?'

He could have explained that he had nothing *but* respect for her, that he had forced himself to sleep with her because he recognised that she had needs too, and deserved to have them satisfied.

But that would have sounded too much like pity – and Maggie had never sought pity.

'Why?' she demanded again.

'Because I'm a shit.'

'That's not a good enough answer from you, Paul Wright,' she said. 'I know you too well. Do you love this girl?'

'Yes,' he admitted.

She wanted to ask him if he loved her too, but she didn't dare – because she knew he would give her an honest answer.

'Well, things can't go on as they are,' she said.

'I'll move out.'

'Don't be so bloody stupid, Paul,' Maggie said, suddenly angry. 'People like us can't afford that kind of luxury. You've no job so we'll be living on the dole. How the hell can we keep two places running?'

'It doesn't matter where I go. David'll find me space at the Diamond.'

'We're not accepting charity,' Maggie said, furious now. 'Besides, it wouldn't be good for our Paul. He's a right to have his father here. No, you won't move out, but I'm not having you sleeping in my bed. You'll have to manage on the sofa.' She lifted her pinafore up to her eyes. Baking powder stuck to her forehead. 'How could you, Paul?' she sobbed. 'How could you?'

She ran through the kitchen door and into the back yard. He made no attempt to stop her.

She was right, he thought. How could he? He had never felt so low in his life. He wished David was there. David, in his slow, taciturn way, would understand, even if he could offer no solution. Because there *was* no solution.

He'd tried to contact David when this whole thing had blown up; he hadn't been able to reach him. His London office didn't know where he was. Even O'Malley at the Diamond hadn't heard from him for weeks. Where the fuck *was* David?

David was still in Manchester, waiting for Mark the Junkie to turn up with Phil's address. And it had to be Mark, because nobody else would help him. Not *could* – would. Ever since Mark had planted the idea in his mind that Phil's old friends knew where he was, David had been watching them carefully, and now he was convinced that the junkie was right.

Individuals would flee at the sight of his square body in the doorway, groups would huddle together as if for mutual protection from this sad, angry giant. He was sometimes sure that as he entered a club, Phil was being discussed. But then the conversation would change to something else entirely, to a nice safe topic like police harassment or discrimination against gays at work.

They were shutting him out, shrouding Phil's whereabouts in a conspiracy of silence, and only Mark the Judas-junkie was prepared to break the pact. And where was Mark? High? Lying dead in some alley with his veins shot full of dope? David didn't know. He wished he'd never given him the money to get high on.

But he was sure of one thing – it was not fear that was making the gays shut him out. They knew all about him, knew he was one of them and not some menacing straight. So there had to be another reason – and that could only be because it was what Phil wanted them to do.

David wept that his lover – his ex-lover – could do such a thing to him. Had Phil learned so little about him during their time together that he felt it necessary to hide? Whatever he was into – a new boyfriend, or heroin – David would understand and try to help him. He only wanted to see Phil happy. When – if – he was sure that Phil *was* happy and safe, he would go back to London, taking his broken heart with him. But he had to know!

He was staying in cheap lodgings near Moss Side, a far cry from his luxury apartment in Knightsbridge, a far cry, even, from the little palace he had built for Barry. And a million miles from the mansion he had planned to share with Phil. He could have moved somewhere much better. He had cash – lots of it as always – in his hip pocket. But he did not move. The lodging, damp and dingy, suited the state of his soul.

He was drinking more than he used to, not just on his round of the clubs but even when he returned to his miserable room for another night's restless sleep.

London was only a phone call away, and he knew his office must be going frantic, yet he could not be bothered to give them a call.

He had told Jimmy, on the night of the last election, that he had a mission – to make one person's life better, to find one person whom he would not fail as he had failed his father. He thought he'd found that person in Phil. Poor, weak Phil, who had been a figure of fun from childhood, who had adopted his camp humour as a defence, a camouflage which was not really a camouflage at all. Phil, who had once searched for affection by sleeping with any man who wanted him. He'd thought he'd given the camp Comedian a better, happier life, but he must have been wrong – because now Phil was rejecting him.

David was coming apart at the seams – if Mark the Junkie didn't produce an address soon, it would be too late.

He didn't read the papers, he didn't watch television. He knew nothing about Paul's disgrace, which had merited an inside column in the quality press and glaring headlines in the tabloids. He didn't even know that Edward Heath had decided to call a snap election, nor that the election was being held very soon. He was blinkered, capable only of looking straight ahead – looking for Phil.

Chapter Thirty-Five

Four years earlier, Paul had stood on that balcony, conscious of the fact that the television cameras were on him, waiting expectantly for the result. He could have been standing there now, at the top of that Douglas Fairbanks staircase – next to Jimmy – but for his own foolishness.

He could not bring himself to regret it. All his life, he had done his duty – studying hard, marrying Maggie, going to teacher training college because he had a wife and child to support. Just this once, he had followed his instincts, and Lucy had made him happier than he had ever been.

And yet the guilt still consumed him. Every time he walked out of the door, he could sense Maggie's eyes following him, could hear the unasked questions on her lips. He didn't deserve her – and she didn't deserve him.

The Mayor, in full regalia, approached the microphone. So this was it. The moment which should have been his.

Paul wasn't sure what he wanted – *who* he wanted to win. Jimmy was his friend, closer than family. Alderman Thompson believed, as he did himself, in the rights of the weak and underprivileged.

The Mayor unrolled his sheet of paper.

'I, Stuart Charles King, being the Returning Officer for the Borough of Norton, do declare that this is the true record of the votes cast in this election. Abbot, William Robert, – 2,936.'

Slightly up on last time, Paul thought, but who had he taken the votes from?

'Bradley, James Peter – 13,843.'

Less than he'd got himself at the last election. Nearly a thousand less. The crowd realised it too. There was no wild cheering, just an expectant hush. So Jimmy had lost. Finally, after a life of nothing but victories, Jimmy had lost.

'Thompson, Albert Edward – 13,772.'

A low turn-out! Throughout the country the electors had been voting in unprecedented numbers. 79%, they'd said on the radio. And in Norton the poll had gone down! Why was Jimmy so lucky?

Why was Jimmy always so lucky? Why was fate, which seemed to place every obstacle in his own path, so willing to hack a way through the jungle of life for Jimmy?

The Conservative supporters, downhearted seconds earlier, went wild.

'It wouldn't have happened if I'd been running,' Paul's mind told him to the rhythm of their applause. 'It wouldn't have happened if I'd been running . . . it wouldn't have happened if . . .'

But now that it had finally come to it, he was glad that his old pal had won, glad he had some new triumph to celebrate. Because God alone knew how Jimmy was coping with his increasingly difficult home life.

There was to be a late-night victory celebration at the Drill Hall, and Paul was invited.

'A left-winger and a child molester,' he said. 'They'll all hate me.'

'Let them,' Jimmy replied. 'I don't give a fuck, so why should you? Ignore them. Don't listen if they talk a load of shit – and they will. You won't be representing your party, or any party. You'll be there as my mate.'

'It wouldn't do you any good with the constituency association.'

'Screw them! Now I've been elected, I don't need them any more. As long as I don't make any cock-ups in Parliament, they'll keep on nominating me for ever, even if they hate my guts. And I *won't* make any cock-ups.'

Same old Jimmy, Paul thought. Forever moving onwards and upwards. Planning three steps ahead, discarding old allies when they couldn't help him any longer, constantly looking out for new ones. And always confident that whatever he did next, he would be an outstanding success.

'Please come,' Jimmy said. 'I'd appreciate it.'

He would have liked David to be there too, but he seemed to have disappeared off the face of the earth.

'I can't come,' Paul said regretfully. 'I've got something else I have to do.'

'Tonight of all nights?'

Jimmy sounded terribly disappointed.

'It has to be tonight,' Paul said earnestly. 'I've just made up my mind and I might have changed it again by morning.'

So Jimmy was alone in his triumph. Not even Claire was there.

'Thanks for that at least, God,' he thought, toasting the ceiling with his champagne glass.

She had become progressively worse since the day she destroyed her painting. She was drinking more, she had lost all interest in her appearance. It had become harder to get her to put on a show for his business associates. She would spoil it by getting drunk, by flirting in a blatant way with one of the guests, by saying something so weird that they all·thought she was mad. In the end he had stopped even trying to persuade her to behave, and had given up entertaining at home.

Maybe she really was going insane. He remembered her last picture – and shuddered. She'd shown it to him proudly. Wanting – demanding – his approval. He'd felt only disgust.

The man was the usual figure, pulsating desire from the canvas. Only this time, he was almost three-dimensional, the product of layer upon layer of paint. Red paint. And yet it didn't really look like paint at all. And even at a distance, it didn't *smell* like paint. He glanced inquiringly at Claire.

'Bull's blood,' she said with relish. 'I got it from the abattoir.'

Jimmy lowered his eyes from the brutal, lascivious face, down the body of knotted muscles, to the space between the monster's legs. A huge erect penis jutted out aggressively, searching for something to violate, for soft tissue to ravage. But worse, far worse, were the testicles. Vast hanging balls totally out of proportion to the man. This was how she saw him. This was how she saw all men.

The balls were thicker, more real, than the rest of the body.

'Oh God!' Jimmy said.

He rushed across the room to have a closer look at the picture. There, fixed to the canvas, encrusted with dried blood, were a pair of real bull's testicles.

'It's not quite right,' Claire said, fixing him with demented eyes. 'It's not quite right, but I'm getting there. Soon, I'll be able to paint one perfect picture. And then nothing else will matter.'

He fled the studio, his stomach churning, bile rising in his throat. He . . .

'You'll show them what's what once you're in the House, won't you, Jimmy?' a voice said, snapping him back into the present.

Stan Blackthorne – glass of champagne in one hand, chicken leg in the other.

'I'll show them, all right,' Jimmy agreed.

'Just remember,' the industrialist added, lowering his voice, 'never take what these prats . . .' he swung his chicken leg in an arc, indicating almost everyone else in the room '. . . what these prats say seriously. It's the folk who are really making the brass who know what's really goin' on. The days of the landownin' chinless wonder have passed.'

'Country manor to poor house in one generation,' Jimmy said, thinking of his father-in-law. 'I'll remember, Stan.'

Blackthorne slapped him heavily on the shoulder.

'I'm sure you will, lad,' he said, and was gone.

What could he do about Claire? Jimmy asked himself. He couldn't take her with him to London, that was a certainty. She wouldn't go, anyway. She had her studio, her light, her bull's blood – she wouldn't be shifted.

He still loved her, but life with her had changed from being very difficult to becoming almost impossible.

This was the ideal time to start a career in politics. The final results weren't in, but the election looked like being a damn close run thing. Edward Heath had won one, lost one, and drawn one. That was simply not good enough. He would be ousted – and soon. And the new leader would be one who had – as he had told Hawsley while still at Seahaven – 'a low, shop-keeping mind'. The new leader would be no gentleman. He would control the Party with the same ruthlessness and indifference as a grocer controls his stock. He would last ten years, maybe longer, by making sure that there was no effective opposition from within the party. Which meant that the fortunes of those already eminent would go into decline, leaving spaces for younger men to fill. And if the new leader lasted long enough, then perhaps by the time he left his place could be taken by a pragmatic young politician, one who at an early age had shown himself adept at both business and manipulation.

Claire would simply have to go. Despite her lack of care over her appearance, she could still attract any man she wanted, because the sexual vibrancy she tried to capture on the canvas lived in *her*. She was still having affairs, he was sure of that, though he did not know – or want to know – the details. And that would not stop, however high he climbed in the Tory hierarchy. She would have to go – but not yet. Not until he was so firmly entrenched in the party that a divorce would not count against him. Balance again – not getting rid of her until he felt secure, but shedding her in time to have an established wife, and an established family, by the time it came to make a challenge for the leadership.

Balance. That was what it took.

Jimmy felt another slap on his shoulder and turned round to find himself facing Macintosh. The councillor had drunk too much, and for once the mask had slipped, revealing beneath the stiff puritanism a mindless Rangers supporter on a Saturday night.

'We showed them,' he slurred. 'Didn't we, Jimmy?' He held out his hand for Jimmy to shake. 'No hard feelings! All right? We both made promises we broke. You told Wright I had the goods on him, and I leaked it to the papers. So no hard feelings.'

Jimmy looked down at the proffered hand, but his own arm remained firmly by his side.

'I needed you until today, Macintosh,' he said. 'I don't need you any longer. The first thing I'm going to do when I get home is post the letter to the Inland Revenue. It's quite long – and very detailed. You can expect a visit from your local tax inspector in the near future.'

Macintosh's mouth dropped open in astonishment. For several seconds, his whole face froze as he tried to find the right words.

'You young bastard,' he said finally – and loudly. 'It's confidential material. You can't do that to me.'

'And on the subject of confidentiality and indiscretion,' Jimmy continued calmly, 'there's a bottle blonde called Elaine whom your wife will be finding out about soon.'

He wheeled around and walked away. To anyone watching the scene – and a number of eyes had been attracted by Macintosh's outburst – it could not have been anything other than a snub, a calculated insult.

Now why had he done that? Jimmy wondered. Taking revenge on Macintosh would not get Paul into Parliament. It wouldn't even get him his job back. All he was doing was storing up trouble for himself.

'Whatever happened to your famous sense of balance, Jimmy?' he asked himself aloud.

It was called The Pink Saxophone and it was no different from any of the other gay clubs David had visited, except that in choosing its name the owner had at least shown he had a sense of humour.

David was sitting with a bunch of ageing leather boys for whom, long ago, Phil had been a sort of mascot. Someone they used when they felt like a change. They were behaving like all the others David had spoken to – willing to talk for ever as long as the talk didn't involve David's lost lover.

'I 'ope that Edward 'eath don't get in,' one of them said, adjusting his metal-peaked cap. 'The Tories 'ave always bin a lot tougher on us than the other lot.'

'You've got it all wrong,' another of the gang said. ' 'eath's gay 'imself.'

' 'Ow do you know?'

'Stands out a mile, dunnit? Takes one to know one. Anyway, 'e's not married, is he?'

'There's millions of blokes not married. It dun't mean . . .'

'A general election?' David interrupted. 'Is there going to be a general election?'

The group looked at him in surprise.

'Where've you bin?' Peaked Cap asked. 'On the moon? Course there's a general election. Today.' He glanced at his watch. 'Well, yesterday now.'

Today. His two best mates had been fighting it out for weeks, and he hadn't been there to help, to be what Paul called the 'piggy-in-the-middle'. How could he have been so wrapped up in his own affairs that he hadn't noticed? He had to get back to Norton right away.

'I'll see you fellers,' he said.

He stood up and was heading for the door when he saw Mark the Junkie slumped at a corner table.

'You got the address?' David asked.

'Keep your voice down, for Christ's sake,' the junkie urged. 'If anybody finds out that you got it from me . . .'

'Why?' David demanded. 'What's he done? Why are they all bein' secretive?'

'You'll find out for yourself,' Mark said. 'Look, I'm not doing this for the money, you understand.'

But David could see that his fingers itched, that his eyes gleamed in anticipation of the fixes the cash would buy him.

'I'm not doing it for the money,' the junkie insisted again. 'I just think that you've got a right to know.'

David reached into his hip pocket and carefully pulled out a wad of fivers. He passed them under the table and felt Mark's hand claw them from him. A second later, the junkie's thin fingers were pressing a small piece of paper into his hand.

'And remember,' Mark pleaded, 'you didn't get it from me.'

Paul stood on the river bank, Blackthorne's – the scene of his biggest defeat – at his back. There was a slight breeze, and when it blew in the right direction it carried with it the sound of the victory celebrations at the Drill Hall.

He heard her coming in the distance. He knew it was her – and not just because it was unlikely to be anyone else at that time of night. It was her walk which was unmistakable, one foot solidly forward, the second dragged behind.

He should have run towards her, arms outstretched, like they did in all the Hollywood films. But Lucy could never float, not like all those fit, perfect, stars of the screen. And his mobility, his *ability* to reach her would only remind her of her limitations.

Besides, the longer she took to reach him, the longer he could put off what he had to say.

She was there at last, beautiful in the pale moonlight, her black hair spilling over her shoulders, her eyes deep and dark and wonderful.

'What's so urgent, darling?' she asked.

'Does anyone know it's you? Do they know you're the "teenager seduced by Wright while she was still a schoolgirl"?'

'No,' she said. 'We've always been very discreet.'

Yes, they had been, hiding their love, pretending indifference in public. Even though they longed to touch one another, to merge their bodies in a long embrace.

But they hadn't been discreet enough. Somehow Macintosh had found out, and now Maggie knew, too.

'It's got to end,' he said.

She didn't understand at first.

'End? What's got to end?'

'Us.'

'Us?'

Echoing his words again.

'It's the best thing for both of us,' he said.

It wasn't, but it was the best thing for her. Because he would never leave Maggie, and Lucy had the right to a full life with a loving husband and children of her own. He had only one child – there could never be any more.

'You're deserting me for *her*?' Lucy said.

'Yes,' he admitted.

'But I'm the one you love. I'm your real wife.'

There was more to marriage than love. Much more. Lucy had his love, but the bonds which tied him to Maggie were stronger than heart strings.

'You can't do it!' Lucy said. She was shouting, almost screaming. He had never heard such a crude, ugly tone in her voice. 'I
won't let you do it!'

The tears came now, cascading down her face like raindrops
spilling off the granite visages of the statues in the corporation
park. He stepped closer and took her in his arms. He couldn't help
himself. For ten minutes they stood locked together, while Paul
prayed to a God he no longer believed in to give him strength to be
resolute.

It was Lucy who broke from the embrace and stood clear of him.
Her eyes were swollen, her face was puffy from the tears she had
shed.

'You *can* leave me,' she said, a catch in her voice. 'You *have* to
leave me.'

He was grateful for the change in mood, though he did not
understand it.

'I've been fooling myself,' she continued. 'I know the Paul
Wright I love, and he's not capable of abandoning his wife. And if
he was, he wouldn't be my Paul any more.'

She twisted her head so that they could kiss. One last kiss and
then no more.

'I'll always love you, Paul,' she said. 'Even when there's
someone else, there'll always be a place in my heart for you.'

It sounded corny, like a line from the Hollywood films he had
been imagining earlier, but he knew that she meant it.

She turned, without saying another word, and hobbled away.

Paul looked down at the river, shimmering in the moonlight.
How easy it would be to walk down the bank and keep on walking,
letting the water lap around him, gently close on him, until
everything became black. No more worry, no more heartaches.

But what would Maggie and young Paul do then?

He shook his fist up at the sky, at the supreme malevolent being
who just might be there, grinning down at him.

'Why couldn't I be like my father?' he demanded. 'He does
whatever he wants. He doesn't know the meaning of guilt and
responsibility. Why couldn't I be like him?'

But he wasn't, and he knew it was time to go home.

The celebrations were over and Jimmy returned alone to his
expensive suburban house. There were no lights on, but that
didn't mean that Claire was in bed – or that, if she was, she was
alone.

'She has to go,' the cold, calculating Jimmy told the Jimmy who couldn't imagine life without her. 'She has to go.'

He unlocked the door and entered the hallway. He looked up the stairs and hesitated. He had never yet caught Claire in bed with another man, and he didn't want to do so now. Not on his night of triumph.

He walked into his study, opened the cabinet and poured himself a stiff scotch. A glittering future was opening up for him. He'd been brought up in a grotty terraced house, educated in a decaying primary school where they huddled around a smoky coal fire in winter. He had come from nothing! He was very rich for such a young man, and in a few years he would be an influential politician. He wished he could feel elated.

His eyes fell on the letter lying on his desk.

'Inland Revenue Department, Liver Building, Liverpool X.'

He didn't have to post it. He could see Macintosh in the morning and explain that he had only been making a joke in doubtful taste. The Scot would resent him for a while, but there would be no permanent damage done.

It wasn't wise to cross the Chairman of the Education Committee, the man who would probably be the next Mayor of Norton. Tearing up the letter was the best course. Posting it was a very Paul thing to do.

He sighed, picked up the letter and slipped it into his pocket. He stepped out of the front door and turned in the direction of the post box. The night air felt cold against his face.

He thought he heard a noise from upstairs. He could not be sure, but he thought it sounded like a cry of ecstasy.

Though it was four o'clock in the morning, Maggie was still waiting up.

'Why do women *always* wait up?' Paul thought.

Even when they knew it would inevitably lead to a row.

'It's over,' he said.

'Is it?'

Maggie's eyes were hollow, drained of the sparkle which had once filled them.

'I told her tonight I'm never going to see her again.'

'That doesn't make it over.'

No, it didn't, did it? It didn't matter whether he was seeing her or not. As long as he loved her, it would never be over.

'You'd better move back upstairs,' Maggie said flatly.

Oh, what had he done to her?

'I don't have to,' Paul said. 'I can . . .'

'I married you for practical reasons,' Maggie said. 'Because I was pregnant. And then, for a while, I thought we had something better than that. Well, we haven't, have we? So it's time to be practical again. If we can't have love, we still both need sex, and we might as well get it from each other because we *are* good together in bed. Besides, what will our Paul think when he gets old enough to notice that his mum and dad don't sleep together any more?'

He wanted to hold her, to comfort her as he had comforted Lucy only hours earlier. But he knew he did not have the right.

'I'll make a brew before we go to bed,' Maggie said.

'Listen . . .'

'Hush, Paul!' Maggie said fiercely. 'Don't say anything you don't mean, anything you'll regret in the morning. You can't always have the best in this life. We had our chance and we threw it away. Maybe it was your fault, maybe it was mine. If I'd been a better wife . . .'

'No, you were . . .'

'. . . if I'd been a better wife, perhaps none of this would have happened. But it did happen, and we're stuck with it. Stuck with second best. People like us usually are.'

She turned her back on him and started to fill the kettle.

David sat behind the wheel of a rented car looking at a respectable converted house in safe, staid Rusholme. He had waited so long – weeks – he could force himself to be patient a little while longer. No bull-headed, frontal attack. He would find out exactly what Phil was into before he approached him.

It was half-past nine before Phil emerged through the front door. God, he looked rough. He had always been thin, but now he looked positively wasted. Was *that* what heroin did to you?

David had been worried about Phil spotting him, but he needn't have been. Phil had the same single-minded intensity that he'd seen in Mark the Junkie. He had no eyes for anything that was going on around him. He walked down the road almost like a zombie and at the corner he turned left on automatic pilot. David started up the car and followed him.

They moved slowly through the suburbs of Manchester, the watcher and his tail, and then Phil suddenly stopped in front of a red-brick institutional building. He gazed up at one of the windows, and for a moment David thought he would turn round and walk away. Then he squared his shoulders as much as he could and executed a parody of a march through the main gate.

And David stayed in the car, sick to his stomach. So this was what it was all about. This was why Phil had asked everyone to tell him nothing.

It was four hours before Phil came out again. He looked, if anything, worse than when he had entered, but that was only to be expected.

David cruised until he was level with the other man, then stopped and opened the car door. Phil jumped like a startled rabbit.

'There's no point in runnin',' David said. 'I know it all now. So get in!'

Phil meekly obeyed.

David said nothing as he drove, just looked straight ahead, and though he could sense that Phil was fidgeting in the passenger seat, almost dying to speak, his lover was silent too. They reached Platt Fields and David parked the car on a double yellow line.

'We'll walk,' he said. 'I find it easier to think when I'm doin' somethin'.'

It was a sunny day. Mothers were out strolling with babies in trollies, grandfathers sat on park benches reading newspapers and arguing with each other over old memories.

David led Phil to an open stretch of grass.

'Why?' he asked.

'I didn't want to cause you pain.'

'You had no right to take that decision,' David said angrily. 'No right at all. I was entitled to know.'

Phil's head dropped onto his shrunken chest.

'I realise that now,' he mumbled.

'How long has it been going on?' David demanded. 'And how long is there left?'

'I found out just before I left London.' The other man looked up, and David could see a trace of the old Phil in his eyes. 'And how long has the Phil Watkins (The Camp Comedian) One Man Show got left to run?' he asked in his stage voice. 'A year. A year and a half at the most.'

'Does it hurt?' David asked gently, all anger gone.

'Not as much as the agony of being without you.'

'Come back to London,' David urged. 'I'll get you treatment. The best that money can buy.'

'It won't help,' Phil said. 'If the Christie Institute can't help, nobody can. The cancer's gone too far. I'm half eaten away inside.'

'I . . .'

'I'll come back with you anyway. I want to come back with you. I want you to be there when I die.'

And for the first time since he had watched Phil walk out of his office, David felt a faint glimmer of happiness.

Chapter Thirty-Six

A month had passed since the General Election. Jimmy was down in London, a new boy in a new Parliament. David was back down south too, re-winding the strands of his diverse business empire back around his thick finger.

Only Paul was left in Buckworth. He was still unemployed. He had looked for work, but no one would hire him. Paul Wright, the youngest Labour candidate in history. Paul Wright, the seducer of schoolgirls who had been drummed out of teaching. *Sic transit gloria mundi.*

He got some sympathy from men who knew how easy it was to fall, from women who could tell he was not a mindless child molester. And there were people who just shrugged their shoulders and said life was like that and he was no better and no worse than all them that hadn't been caught.

He even received unsolicited – and unwanted – support from his father.

'You've got to grab it while it's there, lad,' the older Wright had said. 'Because if you don't, some other bugger will.'

But there was the other side of the coin, too. Villagers who had known him all his life suddenly looked the other way when they saw him; anonymous voices hurled abuse after him as he walked down the street.

None of it mattered. He would have borne it all gladly if only he had been able to regain Maggie's respect. But that seemed impossible, because he just couldn't reach her any more. She never complained about the hardship now that they were living on the dole. Never mentioned Lucy. She treated him with polite formality, as if he were a lodger she didn't much like but whose rent money she needed.

And when they made love, which they still did occasionally, it was like a casual encounter on a summer beach, grabbed simply because it was there.

She had stopped explaining her movements. She would just leave the house when she felt like it, and return without comment.

Sometimes it was obvious what she'd been doing – going to the shops, visiting her mum. But other times, after dark, he had no idea where she went. He would nod when she asked him if he would stay in and keep an eye on young Paul, but he never asked her where she was going – he felt he had lost that privilege.

She was out the night David called, parking his flash sports car outside the front, knocking with his huge fist on the back door.

Paul showed him into the kitchen.

'I was sorry to hear about Phil,' he said. 'How is he?'

'Some days are better than others. That's not why I'm here. Fancy a pint?'

Paul shook his head. Entering The George was something of an ordeal these days.

'All right,' David said. 'I'll come straight to the point. Have you found work yet?'

'Not much chance of that,' Paul said bitterly, though his bitterness was directed at himself, not the outside world.

'I've got a job for you.'

'Did Jimmy put you up to this?'

'He suggested it,' David admitted, 'but only because he thinks quicker than me.'

'I don't want charity.'

'There's no question of charity between us, but if my mind was movin' that way, it'd have been money I was offerin', not a job. I really *can* use you, Paul.'

'What as?' Paul asked 'I don't know anything about business. I'm an ex-politician and an ex-teacher. In other words, completely fucking useless.'

'I've never seen you this down before,' David said, concerned.

'I've never *been* this down before. I've only just begun to realise how much of my strength I've drawn from Maggie. Now her support's been taken away, I'm nobody.'

'Don't do yourself down. You're not nobody now, and you never were.' David chuckled. 'Who was it who came up with the idea of the Secret Camp?'

'It was my idea, but you built it, and Jimmy taught us how to defend it.'

'You've always been the one with the imagination. That's why you could do the job I'm offerin' better than anybody else I know.'

Paul was intrigued, despite himself.

'What in God's name is it?' he asked.

'I need an editor for my magazine.'

'Your *porn* magazine!'

'It's not hard-core,' David said. He was not being defensive, merely factual. David was never defensive about his business operations. 'An' it's not all pictures. There's articles an' letters, too. You've never seen it because it only sells in London at the moment, but I've got plans for it to go national.'

Paul realised that he was grinning. It seemed a long time since he had found anything funny.

'You've always got plans,' he said. ' "Harrison Enterprises International – Paris, New York . . . Buckworth". No, seriously, mate, thanks a lot, but I couldn't do it.'

'You could,' David insisted. 'Why don't you give it a try?'

'Would it mean moving to London?'

'Yes.'

'Maggie'd never go.'

She would have gone, though she wouldn't have wanted to, if Paul had been elected MP for Norton. But not with Paul the porn merchant, the man who scribbled a few words to provide padding for the *feelthy* pictures.

'She doesn't need to go,' David said. 'You'll earn enough money to keep her in comfort here and have a flat yourself in London.'

It sounded very attractive, leaving all this behind. No need to have Maggie around, her very presence a constant reproach to him. Freedom to do what he wanted.

He remembered the morning of his wedding, walking in the rain in his new suit, contemplating doing just what David was suggesting. He had stayed and faced his problems then, and he would do so now. Running away was no answer.

'Sorry, David.'

The big man shrugged his shoulders.

'I'll keep the offer open for a week,' he said, 'and then I'll have to look for somebody else. You've got my London number, but if you change your mind before tomorrow, you can reach me at The Diamond.'

'I won't change my mind,' Paul said.

The bulky businessman and the small ex-teacher hugged each other, and David was gone.

It was an hour before Maggie came home. Her hair was disarranged, her face flushed, and there was a wild look in her eyes.

'I've finally done it,' she said.

Paul didn't speak.

'I've finally had my fourth lover.'

'Your what?'

'My fourth lover. You remember the other three, don't you,

395

Paul? In the corporation park, when I was almost unconscious with the drink your friend Jimmy Bradley MP had forced down me. Well, I wasn't unconscious this time. I knew exactly what I was doing!'

He didn't say anything. What *could* he say?

'Don't you want to know who it was? Don't you want to know the name of the man who had me for the first time with my permission?'

She would not be happy until she told him.

'Who?' he asked.

'He's been after me for years. I used to feel his gaze following me. His eyes undressing me.'

It couldn't be! It just couldn't be!

'That's right,' Maggie said. 'Your dad. My dear father-in-law.'

Paralysis came over Paul. But only in his body. His imagination, not confined to any chair, was moving at a furious rate, producing a large, three-screen film of the event. Maggie and his father. His father and Maggie.

'Well, aren't you going to do anything?' Maggie demanded. 'Aren't you going to hit me?'

He had to force life back into his dead muscles. Had to move, shatter the images which were flashing across his brain. He pushed himself to his feet and lurched awkwardly towards Maggie. He must look threatening to her, he thought, but she held her ground.

As he passed her, his nose was invaded by smells. Her perfume, her sweat, the stink of the coupling – the rutting – which had taken place only minutes earlier. He opened the back door and gulped in fresh air like a drowning man. That was better. Not good, but better. He crossed the yard towards the gate.

'Don't you even want to know if I enjoyed it?' Maggie screamed after him.

He ran down to the phone box in front of the post office and dialled a number he knew by heart. His hands trembled as he fumbled for change, his fingers had difficulty in guiding the coins into the slot.

'David? I've changed my mind about the job.'

He caught the early morning train to London.

Jimmy stood in the large Central Lobby of the Palace of Westminster and watched his visiting constituents walking towards the door. He had done a good job on them, he thought. They would carry back to Norton stories of an MP who was already making himself useful in the House but who could still find time to talk to the folk who'd elected him.

A smoothly-dressed young man, his head held at an arrogant tilt, almost bumped into them. At the last minute he swerved, as if they were too low even to collide with, and headed for the Members' Corridor. Jimmy gave his constituents a final friendly wave and followed.

'I say, Tony,' he said when he had caught the man up, 'this is ridiculous. We've been here for almost six weeks and we never seem to find the time to have a good talk.'

Tony Hawsley, ex-President of the Seahaven University Conservative Association, second-term MP, stopped and looked at him coldly.

'After the *last* time we talked, I shouldn't think we've got much to say to each other.'

Jimmy didn't need to be reminded of the occasion. Sitting in David's living room in Buckworth, calling Hawsley on the phone, threatening him, getting the information on Major Yatton which would have won Paul the '70 election if only he'd used it.

'Look, Tony,' Jimmy said. 'I probably mishandled that. I suppose it's because I've always been a little in awe of you.'

'In awe of me?'

Jimmy laughed.

'You must have realised it, surely. I mean, when I first went to Seahaven you were already a big wheel. I used to dream of taking your place, but at the same time, it frightened me. You were a difficult act to follow and, to be honest, I don't think I fully succeeded.'

'Well . . . I . . .' Hawsley began.

'Let's go and have a drink,' Jimmy suggested.

They went to Annie's Bar. Jimmy thought back to the first time he'd been to Hawsley's rooms, when the other man suggested sneeringly that he might prefer *cream* sherry.

They ordered drinks, and Jimmy paid for them.

'I'm a little out of my depth here,' he confided. 'I mean, it takes a bit of getting used to.'

Hawsley nodded his head sagely.

'Yes. I imagine it does.'

'I could use some help,' Jimmy continued. 'Someone to guide me a little. Like you used to in Seahaven.'

At the end of the meeting, Hawsley was well satisfied. Bradley would be a useful disciple, he decided, someone to do his donkeywork for him, a loyal supporter as he began to rise in the Conservative hierarchy.

Jimmy was pleased, too. Hawsley was just the sort of contact he needed, the perfect representative of the uninspired, unimaginative Conservative MPs over whose backs he intended to climb to the top.

Contrary to general expectation, Edward Heath did not resign as Leader. Labour had formed a minority government with only four more seats than the Tories and it was obvious that there had to be another election soon. Heath wanted to lead the Party into it, and had his Cabinet's backing. Only Keith Joseph let it be known that in any leadership election, he would be a candidate.

'Jolly fine chap,' Hawsley said. 'I've let him know he's got my support now. When he becomes Leader, he'll remember that.'

Jimmy considered Joseph's chances. Sir Keith had strong views on tighter currency controls to combat inflation. Jimmy had no idea whether the policy would work or not. But that didn't really matter because most of the back-bench MPs believed it – and they were the ones with the power of election. Yet even though he held opinions which were right for the time, Jimmy couldn't see him getting the leadership. He was too much of an intellectual gentleman and not enough of a politician to really suit the Conservative Party.

If not Joseph, then who? Someone who shared Sir Keith's vote-winning views. Jimmy thought of the blonde woman with the humourless face, rigid jaw and aura of blazing certainty about her own rightness. Remembered her as Minister of Education, appearing on television to defend her policies, letting the taunts of 'Maggie Thatcher, Milk Snatcher' run off her like water from a duck's back.

A woman? Was the Party ready for a woman? Jimmy rather suspected not – but it could be talked into it.

'You should go and see Joseph yourself,' Hawsley said. 'Do yourself a bit of good as you say "Up North".'

'Thanks for your advice, I'll do that,' Jimmy lied.

Labour called a second election in October. Jimmy increased his share of the vote – many of his colleagues didn't. Wilson gained a majority in the House.

Heath's position began to look shakier and shakier. There were rumblings in the backwoods. One Tory from Ashton-under-Lyme said on television that though he believed that if Wilson

398

took him on a bus to Victoria he would end up in Waterloo, with Heath in charge he would probably never get out of the garage.

'He's not popular with the back-benchers,' Hawsley told Jimmy, as if the novice MP were both blind and deaf. 'Doesn't know how to handle them. There were three of them dining with Jim Prior the other day. In marches Heath, talks to Jim about some policy matter and walks off again. The others might have been invisible. Even Jim himself said, "What am I to do with him?" Have you seen Joseph yet?'

'Not yet,' Jimmy admitted.

He recalled a quote from the *Liverpool Daily Post* the previous summer.

'It will be years before a woman either leads the Party or becomes Prime Minister,' Margaret Thatcher had said. 'I don't see it happening in my time.'

So she didn't see it either. Well, that was all to the good.

'You should go and talk to Joseph,' Hawsley said, slightly miffed that his advice had been ignored for once. 'Go any later, and it'll seem like you're just jumping on the bandwagon.'

The problem of backing favourites, Jimmy thought, was that even if they won you got very short odds. Far better to pick a dark horse and stick everything on it. Joseph might well stand in the end, and if he did, he would probably win. Which would leave Jimmy, if not precisely out in the cold, then at least a long way from the fire. But there were lots of hurdles before the finishing post, and Jimmy was betting that Joseph would fall at one of them.

The hurdle which tripped Sir Keith Joseph was a speech he made on Conservative social policy in October. He was worried, he said, about the poverty of single mothers and divorcees in the lower social classes. They should be encouraged to make more use of contraception.

The newspapers could always recognise a good story when they saw one, and this was a beauty. Joseph was advocating Social Darwinism, they claimed – the survival of the better off. *Private Eye* nicknamed him Sir Sheath, and printed a photograph of him wearing a Viking helmet. In the speech balloon – which only served to emphasise his wide, almost manic grin – were the words, 'If the cap fits, wear it'.

If this was the sort of ridicule he was subjected to while he was only a candidate, what would it be like if he actually became Leader? He could have ridden out the storm, but he was a sensitive man and he chose not to. On the 21st of November, he went to see Margaret Thatcher to say he would not be standing and that she must. He was not the first to put forward the idea – Jimmy Bradley had phoned her up the night before.

The committee which Heath had himself set up to look into election procedures reported back in December. Its recommendations were a slap in the face for the Leader. There should be annual elections, it said. In a contested election, the winner would need at least 15% more votes than his closest rival. If a second ballot was held, new candidates could put themselves forward.

'It's just a way of getting rid of Heath,' Hawsley explained, never ashamed to state the obvious. 'None of his cronies in the Cabinet will stand against him on the first ballot, but if he drops out after that – and he will unless he gets a massive vote of confidence – the way will be open to them on the second ballot.'

'Unless,' Jimmy thought to himself, 'one of the other candidates – my candidate – makes such a convincing showing on the first ballot that she can walk away with the second.'

The problem was not that he couldn't manage Margaret Thatcher's campaign, it was that no one else would *accept* that he could. In time they would come to appreciate that Jimmy Bradley could do anything, but at the moment he was an unknown quantity who had been in the House less than twelve months.

So he would have to work at one remove, like a puppeteer. He looked around for a glove puppet, and found one in Airey Neave.

When it was all over, Jimmy would claim modestly that you simply did not manipulate a man like Neave and his cronies would just laugh and say that they knew better. But Jimmy was being honest, although he was certainly not trying to *sound* honest. Neave was not a man to be manipulated by anyone. Still, it was true that when *he* looked back, he would acknowledge that young Jimmy Bradley had helped him in two very important ways.

The first had been to persuade him to come in at all. Neave had been neglected by Heath and had already tried to get several prominent MPs to stand against the Leader. None of them would.

'So why don't you join Margaret?' Jimmy suggested as they stood on the House terrace one cold afternoon, watching the boats chug by on the river.

It was ridiculous, Neave replied. She hadn't got the stature. She stood very little chance.

'But she does have some chance?' Jimmy asked, and Neave admitted that she did.

'Then she's worth backing,' Jimmy said, 'because you'll get more out of her than you'll get out of anybody else.'

He waited for Neave to ask him why, but the other man just stood silently looking across the water.

'If one of the others gets in,' Jimmy persisted, 'it'll be jobs for the boys, all the old Cabinet, maybe shuffled around a little. But if Thatcher gets in? She can't get rid of all the old Heathites immediately, but she won't trust them. So who can she depend on? Keith Joseph – and any other eminent men who decide to back her now.'

Neave nodded, wheeled and walked back into the House. The next day he offered his services to the Thatcher campaign.

Neave was a superb organiser. Intelligence gathering was his forte and his polls of likely support were far more accurate than those carried out by Heath's men.

The candidate herself was doing very well, too, talking to back-benchers, *listening* to back-benchers in a way that Heath had never done. The Leader tried to emulate this tactic, suddenly dining with members he had snubbed for years, but he didn't have the temperament for it.

One other candidate emerged, Hugh Fraser, but he was strictly lightweight. Everybody knew it would be a battle between the Grocer and the grocer's daughter.

The second occasion on which Jimmy Bradley helped Airey Neave came just before the poll itself. Jimmy didn't meet Neave – the Campaign Manager was far too busy – but he did talk to one of his assistants.

'Airey says it's very tight,' the aide said gloomily. 'Even if Heath hasn't enough support to stay in for the second ballot, Margaret probably won't poll enough votes to make herself a serious contender when the real heavyweights like Whitelaw step in.'

Jimmy pondered the problem.

'Why are people voting for Thatcher?' he asked.

'Some of them like her, but for a lot it's just a vote against Heath.'

'If she doesn't get enough votes, there won't *be* a second ballot,' Jimmy said. 'And then they'll be stuck with Heath.'

'I don't . . .'

'You normally overplay your strength to get people jumping on the bandwagon,' Jimmy said. 'This time you should *underplay* it. Panic people into voting for Thatcher just to make sure there *is* another ballot.'

A look of enlightenment filled the aide's face.

'Bloody good,' he said. '*Bloody* good.'

Some strategies work well, others work brilliantly. On the first ballot, Margaret Thatcher got 130 votes to Edward Heath's 119. Heath resigned in disgust. Thatcher was on a roller. On the second ballot the only serious contender was Whitelaw – and he polled a poor 79 against Thatcher's 146.

The aide came to see Jimmy again.

'Your advice was much appreciated,' he said. 'You're too new to be given a proper reward yet, but you'll find we've got long memories in Parliament. Next time we're in power you can look forward to being a junior minister – that's definite – and if you do all right in that, there's nothing to stop you getting an early seat in the Cabinet.'

'Christ!' Jimmy said, abandoning his poise for once. 'I didn't know Neave had *that* much influence.'

'I'm not here to speak for Airey,' the aide said. 'I've come directly from the Leader.'

Chapter Thirty-Seven

He would soon get used to the porn business, David had said, and David was right. Paul had been working at the job for a year and a half, but he had learned all he needed to know in the first two or three weeks. There was nothing to it really – the product sold itself.

He never saw a naked woman, only the glossy pictures of them which landed on his desk after the photographers had done their work. These he sifted through with the same objectivity and lack of interest as he applied to the articles on vintage cars, World War One fighter planes, drinks and other macho subjects which the readers might care to peruse once they had had their fill of large breasts and spreading thighs.

For the first time in his life, he had some real money in his pocket, even after he had sent home a generous amount to support his wife and son. And he was living in London, a place which had once been only a dream.

He didn't want to be in London, he wanted to be back in Norton. That wasn't true either. What he really wanted to be was three people – or rather a single person with three bodies, one to perform the drudgery on the magazine, one to look after Maggie and spend time with young Paul, one to be with Lucy. But that was impossible. He had only one body and it was not even a huge, muscular machine like David's, nor a slim, elegant masterpiece like Jimmy's. It was nothing more than a perfectly ordinary, slightly puny, affair. So it was his soul which divided, which was torn apart as his imagination dwelt on the various lives he wanted to lead and which he knew could never be reconciled.

He saw the rest of the gang sometimes, but there were other demands on their time. Jimmy had been busy in Parliament ever since his candidate had become Leader of the Tories, David devoted every spare second to the dying Phil.

He saw young Paul, too. Maggie brought him down to London once a month, handed him over to her husband at Euston Station and then went off to stay with a mate of hers who had moved down from Norton. He didn't see her again until he returned their son to her on Sunday night.

It was difficult to explain it all to the child.

'Daddy, why aren't we together any more?'

'Daddy has to work, and his job's in London.'

'But Mummy comes down on the train with me. Why does she go away as soon as we see you?'

Why indeed? Perhaps because she had nothing to say to him these days. And though he had a million questions for her, he had no right to ask them – not after Lucy.

'Mummy has to see her friend.'

'But aren't you her friend?'

No. Not now.

'Of course I'm Mummy's friend. It's just that . . . she wants to see her other friend.'

'But you should be more importin'. You *are* my Daddy.'

Yes, he was. Whoever was the boy's biological creator, whoever's seed had successfully completed the perilous journey that night in the park, he *was* young Paul's father.

He recognised an important truth. Without these monthly visits, without the expression of love and admiration when the child looked at him, he would have killed himself long ago. Without his son there was nothing – life was simply not worth living.

The nights were the worst. Alone in his flat, trapped between the oppressive walls, he sometimes thought he would go insane. He was tempted to pick up the phone and call a whore, but he knew that would be no cure for loneliness. He wouldn't be screwing her, he would be making love to tender little Lucy, he would be comforting his wife.

He needed something to fill his time, and so, one warm Autumn evening, he started to write seriously again as he had always promised himself he would. Night after night he sat at his desk, spilling out words on fresh white paper.

It was meant to be a work of fiction, and in a way, it was. There was no violation in the park, no shot-gun wedding for a brilliant young scholar. Yet when he read the results of his labours, he was astonished to discover that though many of the events were a product of his imagination, the people and their relationships weren't. David, Jimmy, Maggie, Lucy – they were all there, living a story which he had created, *but living it as themselves.*

Jimmy travelled First Class to Crewe, read the papers and

laughed his way through David's – and Paul's! – *Hard Man* magazine, but when he boarded the local train it was as a Second Class passenger, and the material he glanced through all related to his work in the House.

The train rattled across the heavy Victorian arches and gave Jimmy a panoramic view of the town – the old gas works, the council estate, the river and the Drill Hall – and the corporation park. And the house where he lived. Where he *used* to live – he hardly ever went there any more. He hardly ever slept with Claire any more either. He took his pleasure from discreet, high-class prostitutes. Professional. Uninvolved. There would be no Lucy fucking up his life.

Lucy was getting married. Only the day before Paul had received the letter which told him she'd fallen in love and was very happy.

'Well, bully for her!' Jimmy thought angrily.

But where did that leave Paul? Stuck in a grotty office producing wank fodder for frustrated middle-aged men. When he could have been in Parliament, fighting for what he really believed in.

Travelling by bus would have been pushing his affinity with the common man just a little too far, so Jimmy took a taxi from the station. It was mid-afternoon when the cab pulled up outside his expensive detached house.

He didn't ring the bell. Claire would be in her studio and probably wouldn't hear. Even if she did, she was as likely as not to ignore it, as she ignored everything which disturbed her work. He turned the key in the lock and entered the hall.

He wouldn't see her right away. He needed a fortifying shot of whisky to give him the strength to climb those stairs. He headed for his old study.

It was the noises which struck him first. Grunting, gasping, gurgling. Animal panting. Deep throaty cries. And then he saw them. On the floor behind the desk. A collection of limbs thrown together in a crazy, disorganized profusion.

White buttocks, white legs, blue overalls around thick ankles, trunk thrusting and retreating like a steam engine.

Shirt open to reveal black hairy chest, solid muscular shoulders now pressing against the carpet, now heaving upwards, face twisted in a lopsided grin, almost cross-eyed.

Standing up, coated from neck to shoes in blue cloth, no flesh on view but a single pink tube, and most of that vanishing on the regular beat.

Long black hair, high pointed breasts held in thick brutal hands,

405

hips gyrating, mouth sucking and releasing, and sucking and releasing.

One Claire. Three of them!

'Like in the park,' Jimmy thought irrelevantly. 'Except that at least we had the good manners to go one at a time.'

The man who was taking her from behind – 'Fucking her up the arse,' Jimmy thought viciously – noticed him first. His mouth dropped open. His hands, which had been digging into her hips, fell to his sides. His ploughing motion juddered to a halt and he pulled himself free.

The man Claire was straddling saw him next, looking up to see the well-cut pair of trousers, letting his eyes climb over the waistcoat and up to Jimmy's face. He released Claire's breasts and gaped at his hands, as if wondering how they had ever got there.

The third man, still fully dressed, was in the best position to make a rapid escape, except for his single link with Claire – his penis in her mouth, her teeth teasing, her lips tightly wrapped around the shaft.

And finally, even Claire herself noticed that something was wrong. She stopped moving and brushed her hair, sticky with sweat, out of her eyes.

'Hello, Jimmy,' she said casually. 'Sorry, there's no hole left – unless you fancy fucking me in the ear.'

They expected big trouble. The outraged husband catching them – *all* of them – in the act. If he had picked up the heavy desk light and attacked them, they would not have fought back. But he did nothing except stand there as they adjusted their clothing and shuffled past him, muttering their excuses, saying they'd been led on. And never once looking at him.

Claire was still sitting on the floor. Her pubic brush was wet, her breasts and face glistened with spent semen.

Jimmy reached into the cabinet, pulled out the scotch and took a slug straight from the bottle.

'How could you?' he asked.

'What's the matter, our Jimmy?' she replied, in a fair imitation of a Buckworth accent. 'Council workers not good enough for you now we're goin' up in the world?'

'Three of them! For God's sake, why three of them at once?'

'Because I'm good enough,' Claire screamed. 'Because I can handle them. Fucking's the only thing I *am* good at. And it's all your fault!'

'My fault!'

'I could have been a great painter. I would have been. But then you had to introduce me to sex.' She crawled across the room like a demented wild-cat and stopped at his feet. 'I should have been a nun. I should have been a nun and done nothing but paint all day long. But once I'd got the taste for screwing, it was too late! I don't feel with my soul any more, I feel through my cunt.'

She clawed at his trousers and her teeth dug into his flesh. She had the strength of a mad woman. She *was* mad, he thought. She would have to be committed. He grabbed her long, black hair and tugged violently, trying to pull her away, but still the teeth held on, sending shooting pains up his legs, making him giddy. He made a fist and struck her on her cheek as hard as he could. Her neck snapped back. She fell sideways, and was still.

He limped painfully from the study. There was a phone on the desk, but he couldn't use it, couldn't stand where they'd been . . . He picked up the hall phone and dialled.

'Norton General? Could you put me through to the Psychiatric Unit please?'

She was barefoot, so he didn't hear her padding down the hallway towards him, didn't turn and see her raising the whisky bottle, didn't know anything until the glass crashed down on his skull.

He couldn't have been unconscious long. Not more than a minute. He hadn't realised that pain could bring you round again, but that was what happened to him. Yet the pain was not in his head, it was lower down. He forced his neck upwards so that he could see what was going on. He was lying flat on his back. His trousers had been pulled down and his legs spread. He tried to close them, to see if that helped ease the pain, but he couldn't because Claire was kneeling between them. What was she doing? Sucking him off, brutally, hungrily, not caring if it hurt? No, her head wasn't low enough down for that. Besides, he thought hazily, that wasn't where the pain was coming from either.

He saw the shard of broken whisky bottle in her hand. It had cut a deep gash in her palm and she hadn't even noticed. There was a lot of blood, but he knew, without being able to explain how, that it was not all hers.

Suddenly he realised what she was doing. Realised where the pain was coming from.

As she sliced her way through more muscle, he tried to twist free, but she was firmly wedged between his legs. He raised

407

himself on one arm, grabbed her hair and pulled. His head was swimming and he could feel his strength draining away.

'Don't let me faint now,' he prayed. 'Don't let me faint now.'

He was tugging Claire closer to his face, further away from his groin. The burning sensation had stopped, and in its place was a dull, throbbing ache.

'Let go,' Claire screamed. 'I have to have them.'

Her head was level with his chest. Her arms were flailing and the shard of glass kept piercing his jacket, making small, painful punctures in his skin.

'I have to have them. I need them for my one perfect painting. Jimmy Bradley – the complete prick.'

Her head was almost on his. She would start biting soon, or go for him with the glass. He butted her with all his strength, and though it sent fresh ecstasies of agony reverberating through his entire body, it at least made her drop the weapon.

He rolled them over so that she was on the bottom. God, it hurt. Hands came up to scratch him, to claw out his eyes. He forced himself upwards so that he was straddling her, as she had straddled one of her three lovers. Nails reached face, tearing away at tender skin.

With both hands, he seized her head, lifted it and slammed it back down, hard, against the parquet floor. He had to do it five more times before she was still. By then his face was torn and bleeding, and he could hardly see out of one eye.

He eased himself gingerly off his unconscious wife and trousers around his ankles, hand helping what was left of his damaged muscles to keep his testicles in place, he staggered towards the phone.

In the early stages of his illness, Phil tried to carry on as normally as possible. He hadn't the energy for a series of his own but he was still very much in demand, and it was easy to get less exhausting bookings as a guest star.

'Just carving myself out a bit of immortality, sweetheart,' he told David in his camp voice. 'And God knows, we need the money. We'd never keep body and soul together on what you bring in.'

David grinned. Despite the fact that he spent as much time with his lover as Phil would permit, Harrison Enterprises was going from strength to strength. It was like a snowball rolling downhill – David had given it the initial push and now it would grow on its own.

At first, they made love regularly, even though David had protested.

'It's not like I've got the clap,' Phil said, tempering his harsh words with a gentle tone. 'You won't catch anything.'

'I know,' David said awkwardly. 'I don't want to tire you, that's all.'

'I *want* to be tired. It's worth it.'

But as the illness progressed, even the mildest foreplay was too painful.

Phil became almost impossibly thin. And yellow.

'Just like a skelington covered in skin,' he sang in a voice like crackly brown paper.

It was an effort to take even short walks down the street, and because of the strain, and because people stopped and stared at him as if he were already a ghost, he gave up going out at all.

'By rights, he should be dead now,' the doctor confided to David.

He was a brisk, balding man in a thick tweed jacket with leather patches. David knew that he was not being deliberately unkind, that so much death had desensitized him, but he still wished the doctor would show a little more feeling. Poor Phil's true qualities had been so little appreciated in his life, he at least deserved credit for dying courageously.

'God alone knows where he's getting the strength from,' the doctor continued, unable to read the expression on David's face. 'He says he doesn't want to leave *you*. Are you very close?'

'Yes. Very close.'

The doctor noticed the tears in David's eyes. Who would have thought that such a big man – broad as a bear, strong as an ox – would break down like that? The doctor turned away, embarrassed.

'Yes . . . well . . . humph . . . they all say that,' he went on. 'What they really mean is that they're afraid of going themselves. Frightened of the great black void, all that sort of stuff. Try to get him used to the idea that he's going to die, Mr Harrison. It'll be kinder in the long run. Reassure him. If he's religious, talk to him about heaven. Does he believe in heaven, do you know?'

'Yes,' David said.

'And how does he see it?'

'It's a place where people are only laughed at if they want to be.'

'Hmm,' the doctor said musingly. He glanced at his watch. 'I've got to go. I'll call in again tomorrow. Make sure he takes his painkillers. But you must realise that the longer he hangs on, the less effective they'll be. He's got to go soon.'

But Phil refused to die. The doctor was wrong. It wasn't fear of what lay beyond which was keeping him alive, it was the worry of how David would manage without him.

'How *will* I manage?' David asked himself, banging his head again and again against the kitchen wall. 'How, how, how?'

Chapter Thirty-Eight

It was the middle of December. Hoar frost coated the yard in the early mornings and robin red-breasts bobbed around on top of the coal shed. For Maggie, it had always been the rushing season. Finding time for shopping after work. Going from window to window, examining the toys, puzzling out which would give her son most pleasure. Hanging the Christmas decorations. Making the cakes and puddings.

There was no rush that year. She didn't have Paul to look after so she had plenty of time to spare. She had plenty of money, too – her husband at least saw to that.

She wished that things were harder, wished that every day was a battle for the most elementary kind of survival, so that she would be totally absorbed in just getting by, so that she would have no time to think.

She thought now – of the night with Paul's father nearly two years earlier. She'd been walking, not to get anywhere, not so she could reach a decision, just walking blindly. Anything to get out of the house, away from Paul.

She hadn't expected to see his father lounging in the doorway of the pub.

'What you doin' out so late on yer own?' he'd asked. 'Lookin' for somethin'?'

And he'd known that his moment had come. That the years of watching her like a hungry wolf had paid off. That she was finally ready to be his victim.

As they'd headed towards the woods, he'd tried to take her hand, but she'd knocked it angrily aside. She didn't want intimacy, she wanted mindless sex.

And mindless it had been. The hungry wolf had become a raging bull, mounting her and thrusting away with animal urges, animal energy. She didn't see how a man with so much power could fail to excite her, yet fail he did.

She didn't know why she was doing it at all, unless it was to get a response from Paul. Not tenderness, she thought as Wright ploughed in and out of her. Paul had given her a great deal of that over the years, but he would have lavished it just as willingly on a stray cat or an unhappy child. Not the show of sympathy, obligation and responsibility which he felt for all mankind.

The response she wanted was something uniquely for her – from him. Even if it was only hatred.

And when it was all over, when Wright slid off her, already beginning to pull up his trousers, she asked him a question.

'Doesn't it bother you that you've done this with your son's wife?'

He shrugged.

'Well, I'm not the first, am I? Not by a long chalk. There was a time I thought our Paul had some lead in his pencil, but I were wrong.'

'What do you mean?' she demanded.

'Well, that lad of yours. You shouldn't have called him Paul, his proper name's *Jimmy*.'

The sudden knock startled her, vanquishing the memory of Wright's hard body pressing down, of his breath assaulting her cheeks, of the sneer on his face as he spoke about her son. She opened the back door to find Jimmy standing there.

He looked thin and drawn. There were scars on both cheeks from cuts which had only recently healed. And he seemed nervous and uncertain. For the first time since the night in the park, she did not feel threatened by him.

'I've been in hospital,' he said, knowing that some explanation was necessary.

She was surprised that it hadn't been in the newspapers. Maybe he had a reason to hush it up.

'Claire didn't let me know about it,' she said, 'or I'd have told Paul.'

'She's been in hospital, too. She's still there. She'll be there a long time.'

'It's serious then.'

'Not serious, no. She's just . . . not well. Is young Paul here?'

'He's at my mum's,' Maggie said. They were still standing in the doorway. 'Won't you come in?' she asked. 'It'll not take me a minute to make a brew.'

Jimmy shook his head.

'I only came to see young Paul,' he said, and Maggie noticed the boxes under his arm. 'I've brought him a few presents.'

'A few! It looks like you've bought up the toy shop. Jimmy, you shouldn't have!'

'Think of them as early Christmas presents,' Jimmy said.

'No, really!' Maggie protested. 'You'll spoil him.'

'I'm his godfather,' Jimmy said – sadly, Maggie thought – 'I'm entitled to spoil him.'

Young Paul had two Christmases that year. The first was in London, the weekend before the 25th.

'Daddy,' he asked as he sat under the tree and tried to show enthusiasm about opening his presents, 'why can't we all have Christmas together?'

'Because I can't get away.'

No, he couldn't, could he? Life was a helter-skelter, and once you'd made your decision, sat on the slide and given yourself a push, there was no getting away. No escape.

'But everybody goes home for Christmas.'

'Well, I can't!'

Snappy. Irritable.

'Be careful,' Paul warned himself. 'You can't afford a normal parent's temper, because you're not around long enough to make up for it. These weekends have to be all sweetness and light, or you'll lose him.'

The boy went home to spend the real Christmas with his mother and her parents. Paul was left in London, surrounded by festivities and goodwill, by families getting together just as the child had thought *his* should.

Paul sat at his solitary breakfast on Christmas morning, listening to the bells, feeling the loneliness soak through him. Without The Book, he thought, he would probably have lost his mind.

The Book was absorbing him more and more. He was new at the skill – writing a novel wasn't like producing a short piece of prose or delivering a speech – and some of what he wrote was clumsy and awkward. He would work through the night – on one paragraph or even one sentence – until it sounded right. But it wasn't the technical details which interested him, which kept him chained to his desk. The fascination lay in reading a finished page or chapter. Somehow, though the words were his, the thoughts and images were those of an outsider, who had seen the whole thing through clear, unprejudiced eyes and was now using Paul as his instrument to get it down on paper.

He read of himself, not as the socialist hero fit to stand shoulder-to-shoulder with Keir Hardie, nor as the miserable, insignificant failure he imagined himself to be in his blacker moods. He was

413

sometimes weak, sometimes strong. Sometimes sensitive, sometimes crassly self-absorbed. But above all, the picture was of an honest man who had always tried to do his best. And that, he supposed, was at least something.

The others, as they sprang from the page, surprised him too. Though he had always loved Jimmy, he had occasionally been unfair, letting their rivalry – a rivalry that neither had with David – cloud his vision. The clashes between them in the Book were of his invention, but still they forced him to really appreciate for the first time just how much Jimmy had done for him over the years. The sacrifices he had been prepared to make. He had risked his own political career by helping Paul in '70. He would, Paul was sure now, have given up his candidature in '74 if it had been to Paul's advantage. And while it was all very well to say that was easy for Jimmy, because he always had a new angle, another racket waiting in the wings, Paul knew it was never easy to give *anything* up.

He read about Maggie, and she seemed almost a stranger. Could she really have been so courageous? Taking the batterings of life with such good humour, waiting patiently while the boy she had married grew into a man?

He tried to re-write her, but it would not work. Each attempt to knock her down a little only resulted in her being raised even higher. And he realised that in taking over from the observer he was producing a Maggie who was too good to be true, no longer a photograph but an idealised portrait. In the end, he went back to the words which had originally been dictated to him.

David was there, unedited by the intervention of Paul's ego – solid, muscular, dependable . . . and tragic. So were Claire and Paul's father, linked by an animal drive which controlled them like cheap wine grips an alcoholic and which, in much the same way, was denying them something they wanted more. Phil and Barry floated in and out of the narrative, one a ghost, the other inches from becoming one.

And Lucy. Only in Lucy did Paul feel the god-like writer had failed him. She was there, as pretty and loving as she'd always been, as vulnerable as ever. Yet she did not feel real. The emotional bond they'd shared no longer seemed like a bright burning sun illuminating their love – it was more an early morning mist which made everything vague and fuzzy.

At five o'clock on a cold New Year's morning, he came to a sudden halt. The words no longer flowed; the fingers, which had seemed to have a life of their own, stopped typing; the Muse had left him.

He understood why it had happened. He had been chronicling the spiritual-emotional biographies of his characters, and now they were complete. No, not complete – just up-to-date.

Where did he go from there? Books, like life, didn't just stop, all ragged edges. There had to be an ending, a rounding off. A note of optimism, pointing to a better future. Or . . .

David would find a new lover, with the beauty of Barry and the sincerity of Phil. Jimmy would divorce Claire, marry a new wife and raise tall, blond, elegant children. There would be strong indications that both men were assured a brilliant future.

And an ending for Paul himself? Someone in the book would have to give it realism. Someone in the book would have to be sacrificed.

He would lose the most precious thing in his life. His son – and in the Book there was no doubt, absolutely no doubt at all, that the boy was his – would die. After the child's death, he would walk to the old school. The wooden gate would creak as he pushed it open. He'd follow the perimeter fence until it was level with the old infants' classroom, then kneel down and run his finger through the dirt where the ant pit had been.

Him and David, letting an ant climb to the top of the hole then pushing it back down with sticks. Jimmy standing there, watching.

'It's scared. Why don't you let it go?'

'It doesn't matter if it's scared. It shouldn't want to get out. It should want to stay with its pals.'

'Shall we be pals?'

'If we're goin' to be, we've got to be real pals, not like the ants.'

'I won't leave you in no hole. Never. Cross me heart an' hope to die.'

The human ants had tried to stay together, to protect one another, but there had been too many forces working against them. Other ants had poured into the pit, coming between them. Fate, that malevolent giant with a bullying schoolboy's sense of humour, had squatted at the edge, poking them with sticks, forcing them to go in directions not of their choosing.

Enough of reflection! The semi-fictional Paul would scrape a new hole and watch the ants struggle one more time. Then he'd leave the playground for ever. He'd climb the fence, walk to the pond and keep on walking until the water covered the tops of his shoes, his knees, his waist, until it had immersed him completely. The swans would circle around him. They wouldn't mind the disturbance, because they would know it was only temporary, that peace would follow – for all of them.

By the time the sun rose, the ending was clear in his mind. It took less than a week to finish the book and as he dropped it into the post box he felt as if a great weight had been lifted off his shoulders.

Phil was so light that only the sheets seemed to be anchoring him to the bed. His skin was a faded yellow, the colour of demolition notices posted on long abandoned buildings. He had lost control of his bowels and slime ran from the corner of his mouth. The pain was constant now, but he didn't have the strength to wince, to cry out, under its merciless assault.

'Why doesn't he die?' David thought desperately.

The sick man had not said a word for days. He hardly seemed to be aware that there was anyone in the room. But he was *aware*, David knew he was, and he never left his post on the chair opposite Phil's bed, a bed which looked too large, too substantial, for the tiny shrinking frame it contained.

'David . . .'

A sound so slight it could have been his imagination or the whisper of a draught under the door. David moved quickly to Phil's side.

'Are you there?' Phil asked, looking through his yellowed, almost sightless eyes.

'I'm here.'

David wanted to take his lover in his arms and hug him. Or at least stroke his forehead. But even that would cause the dying man more agony.

'I can't . . . I can't hold on much longer,' Phil rasped.

'I know. It doesn't matter.'

'It does. I'm frightened of what you'll do when I'm gone.'

'I'll be all right,' David reassured him.

But how could he be, in a world which no longer had meaning?

Others survived deaths, he told himself. He himself had killed and buried his own father. He had let Barry walk out into the world alone, to a death that he should have foreseen. But he had really tried with Phil, really wanted to make Phil's life better, to alter his destiny. And it had all been futile.

'I'll be all right,' he said. 'I'm tough.'

'I'm the tough one,' pathetic little Phil whispered, 'not you. But people don't understand that. They see this towering giant and they think "David Harrison, the strong man of the Secret Camp Gang". You've always been the most vulnerable of the three of you, David, and nobody ever realised it but me.'

'Get some rest,' David urged him. 'You're tiring yourself out.'

'Without me to protect you, you'll do something stupid,' Phil said. 'Something noble and self-sacrificing. And there's nothing I can do about it.'

Tears appeared in his eyes – David would not have thought he had the strength left to cry – and he died.

Phil was still a big enough name – still had enough friends – to make his funeral a massive affair. Celebrities crowded around the grave, show business executives lined up to throw a handful of earth on the coffin, journalists looked on sombrely while in their minds they composed sensationalist paragraphs.

Paul was there, smiling sadly, encouragingly, at David.

'Where's Jimmy?' David asked, when it was all over, when the final piece of turf had been laid and even the most curious of onlookers had drifted away.

'He couldn't make it,' Paul replied. 'Some important constituency matters back in Norton, he said.'

Yet it was unlike Jimmy to let down one of his friends. Or to exile himself to the sticks when things were *really* happening in Parliament.

'What will you do now?' Paul asked.

'I'm buyin' up some more property in the West End. An' it seems daft to put people on Harrison Tours up in somebody else's hotel, so I'm lookin' into the possibility of expandin' onto the continent.'

'What will you do *now*?' Paul insisted.

'I'm takin' a month off.'

'Somewhere in the sun?'

'No,' David replied. 'I'll give you a number where you can ring me if any urgent business comes up.'

He didn't seem to want to say any more, and Paul didn't push him. They embraced and went their separate ways.

O'Malley stood at the entrance of Harrison Enterprises (Automobile Parts) – David's first scrapyard – and watched the Lamborghini make its way along the rutted road from Buckworth. The boss should have been coaxing his car gently over the dips. Instead, he was driving as if he were on the motorway. O'Malley winced as the vehicle rose and fell, dreading to think what was happening to the chassis.

David slammed on the brakes in front of the big double gates and eased his large frame out of the car. He was still wearing his black mourning suit. And a nice piece of material it looked, too,

O'Malley thought. Savile Row or one of them other fancy London tailors. Then he noticed that David's eyes were red.

'Oi was sorry to hear about your . . . friend, Mr Harrison,' he said.

He was embarrassed talking about the Camp Comedian and found it almost impossible to imagine that this giant of a man before him had ever . . . could ever . . . it didn't seem right. But he respected David more than any other man he had ever met, and he would never wish to work for anyone else.

'You still keep in touch with this operation?' David asked, and O'Malley could tell that he was doing his best to sound crisp.

'Not as much as Oi'd like to, Mr Harrison. What with the other yards, the club, the tours . . .'

'Take me to somebody who does know what's goin' on.'

O'Malley pushed open the gates and David followed him into the yard.

There were rows and rows of cars where once there had been only a couple of battered Morris Minors. A proper brick office had been erected on the site of what had once been Fred Rathbone's old shed.

So many ghosts. So much that had happened in a few short years.

O'Malley signalled a muscular, conscientious-looking middle-aged man to join them.

'This is Mike Hough,' the Irishman said. 'He runs the yard.'

Hough looked worried. As well he might. It was a long time since David had visited the place. The head of Harrison Enterprises had become a legendary figure, someone you read about in the papers.

They shook hands.

'Who's the best worker you've got here?' David asked.

'A feller called Marty Edge,' Hough replied without hesitation.

'And what do you pay him?'

Hough told him and David reached into his pocket, pulled out a thick bank roll, and peeled off some notes.

'Give him this,' he said. 'Tell him to take a month off.'

'The sack, is it, Mr Harrison?' O'Malley asked incredulously.

'It's what I said. A month's paid holiday. We won't be needin' him for a while.' David turned to Hough. 'I want you to put me to work. I want you to give me the dirtiest, toughest jobs you've got, and if I think you're goin' easy on me, *you'll* get the sack. Understood?'

'. . . er . . . yeah, Mr Harrison. When can you . . . when would you like to . . . er . . . start?'

'Right now,' David said.

Hough looked dubiously at the expensive suit, wondering if this was some kind of practical joke. David tore off his jacket and flung it on top of a pile of rusting metal.

'It's cold when you're just standin' around,' he said. 'Let's get started.'

Hough glanced at O'Malley, and O'Malley nodded, finally understanding. Non-Catholics might say the boss was throwing himself into the hardest work possible so that he could lose his mental anguish through physical aches. Possibly that was what the boss believed himself, but it wasn't true. It would take a true follower of the Church of Rome to see it as it really was, the Irishman thought to himself. What Harrison was doing was paying a penance. Not for something he had done – for something he hadn't been able to prevent.

Orders were tentatively issued. David marched purposefully towards his task. History repeating itself.

David's muscles burned, but he didn't slacken off his pace. Hough came across once to see him.

'I know it's not time for the tea-break, Mr Harrison, but you've already done what would have taken the rest of us until tomorrow morning, so if you fancy . . .' He caught the look on David's face. 'I'll . . . uh . . . leave it up to you, then, Mr Harrison.'

The break finally arrived. The men sat on wooden boxes holding mugs of steaming tea in their work-hardened hands. David didn't join them. They were entitled to a bit of peace, and the boss's presence would only inhibit them. Besides, he didn't feel like company.

He walked painfully out of the scrapyard and stood looking around him. To his right was Buckworth, a little smarter than it had once been, but essentially unchanged. Ahead lay the canal. No salt barges any more, no horses straining on the tow ropes. Only the anaemic jug-jug of the occasional pleasure boat.

And to his left, near the woods, he saw two figures. A graceful, tall blond man dressed, uncharacteristically, in jeans and an anorak, and a small, yet equally graceful, blond child. They were walking side by side, holding hands, and they were undoubtedly father and son.

Chapter Thirty-Nine

Paul glanced around Euston Station. There were no commuters heading home, no housewives weighed down with purchases, no migrant Irish workmen rushing to catch the Liverpool boat-train. It was a Saturday morning in early March and Paul, the winos and the shopping-bag ladies had the place pretty much to themselves.

This was his favourite time of the month. In five minutes, the train carrying young Paul and Maggie would be pulling into the station. He would use those precious minutes for anticipation, for savouring what was to come. Because once the lad had arrived, thrown his arms around his father and asked excitedly what they were going to do over the weekend, then the countdown began.

Back to Paul's flat and it was only another twenty-six hours before they had to set out for the station again. Give the boy a glass of milk and some biscuits, and it was only twenty-five hours before he would be handing him back to his mother. Go for a walk, feed the ducks in Hyde Park, and there was less than a day left.

Paul wished that he was allowed to go home sometimes. He had the magazine well under control, he could have done the work on a four-day week, maybe even a three-day week. But Maggie didn't want him at home. It was as much as she could bear to watch until her son ran to his father, then she would quickly turn her back and walk away. Like a hand-over at Checkpoint Charlie.

Paul wasn't quite sure what he'd done wrong. Or rather, he knew what he'd done wrong, but not what Maggie considered wrong. She had let him back into her bed when he had finally broken up with Lucy. Yet after that night with his father she had seemed to want to have no more to do with him. As if *then*, and not earlier, had been when he'd failed her.

The train pulled in. Paul stood a good fifty yards from the barrier. He did this partly so that Maggie wouldn't be forced to get close to him. But he did it for young Paul as well – the child liked to run across the big empty station to his daddy. He seemed to have a flair for the dramatic just like . . . like so many children had.

Paul watched the two figures pass through the gate – mother and child. Lots of working class wives turned into sluts as soon as they got married, he thought – trodden-down carpet slippers, hair in curlers, Embassy Tipped hanging from the corners of their mouths. Not Maggie. She looked as young and as fresh as when he had married her nine years earlier – as when the gang had spotted her that night in the Drill Hall.

He suddenly realised that for once it was his wife, not his son, who had captured his attention. Something was wrong. The boy was not making a mad dash for him. Maggie was leaning over her son and talking earnestly in his ear. Then the child slowly, reluctantly, made his way across to Paul.

The hug had less than its usual warmth. The boy stood scuffing his shoes and looking down at the ground. He was sulking, Paul thought. He had never done that before.

'Daddy, what are we going to do this weekend?'

'Walk round the park. Go to the pictures. Anything you like.'

'We always do those things,' the child said.

'What else do you want to do?'

'I don't know.'

Paul knelt down and cupped his hands around the boy's face so that their eyes met.

'Are you missing your friends?' he asked. 'If you are, you can bring one of them down with you. I'll pay his fare. I don't mind.'

A new look came over the child's face. He was ashamed that he had treated his daddy like this, ashamed of whatever it was he was hiding.

'It's not that,' he said. 'I'll see my pals again in school on Monday.'

'Then what is it?'

Indecision.

'Just that this weekend, I *could* have gone in a helicopter,' he blurted it out. As if it were a confession. He made a twisting motion with his index finger. 'We would have flown very high up, and you can see people as if they were just toy soldiers and all the trees and things look like they're ever so tiny and you can go ever so much faster than a car . . . and . . . and . . . and I could have gone, and now I'll never be able to do it ever again.'

He stopped, breathless.

'Of course you'll be able to go again,' Paul said reassuringly. 'I'll take you.'

But it was guilt, not petulance, which consumed the tiny frame now, and Paul was not even sure that his son had heard him.

'I'm sorry, Daddy,' he said through the tears. 'I did want to see you, really I did. Only I've never been in a helicopter before, and he said it had to be *this* weekend.'

'Who said?' Paul asked, trying to keep his voice level. 'Who told you it could only be this weekend?'

The boy looked surprised, as if the answer were obvious to everyone.

'Uncle Jimmy,' he said.

There was a traffic jam on Euston Road and the taxi, hemmed in on all sides, had no choice but to sit there. Maggie watched the meter click-click and thought back to the days when she and Paul had first moved into their own home. They'd been poor, but they'd been happy. Or at least, she'd *thought* they were happy. She remembered coming home in triumph with tins of cheap paint and slopping it joyfully on the walls in an attempt to disguise the dinginess of their little terraced house. Then, a taxi ride would have seemed an extravagance and she would have fretted every time the meter clicked, notching up another five pence.

Money was no problem now. Paul was being paid five times what he'd earned as a teacher. Still, she wished he'd find some other way of earning a living, even if it meant a drop in salary. She'd seen the magazine. It wasn't terrible or anything like that, it was just pathetic. Paul had so much talent and he was squandering it on something that neither helped nor educated anyone. If it hadn't been for that girl, he would have been MP for Norton now, instead of Jimmy.

The thought of Jimmy sent a wave of guilt through her. She felt uneasy about letting him spend so much time with young Paul. As he'd pointed out, he *was* the child's godfather, but it still seemed unnatural that he should want to see him as often as he did.

He was so intense about it. After years of virtually ignoring his godson, the child had suddenly become important to him. If she and Jimmy were talking and Paul came into the room, Jimmy – calm, confident, controlled Jimmy – immediately lost track of the conversation or fumbled his words. Without even noticing it. And his eyes! They seemed to burn as they fixed on the boy, seemed to feed off him.

Jimmy appeared to have no desire to return to London, even though he was now looking much healthier than the night he had appeared on her doorstep, laden down with presents.

She'd probed, gently.

'Shouldn't you be in Parliament in the middle of the week?'

'I'm paired with one of the Labour MPs.'

She didn't know what that meant.

'It means that when it comes to a vote, he isn't there and neither am I, so it's the same as if we both were.'

It sounded to Maggie like a pretty funny way of running things. There didn't seem to be much point in having an MP at all if that was how they carried on. And it wasn't like Jimmy not to be at the centre of things, in the limelight, taking his opportunities before other people even realised they were up for grabs.

In fact, nothing about Jimmy these days was like the Jimmy she'd known. Maybe it was because of what had happened to Claire. She was in hospital, he'd told her. But she'd heard that Claire wasn't just sick, she'd gone completely round the bend. They kept her in a padded cell and fed her with a plastic spoon.

The taxi was moving again.

'Traffic jams!' the driver complained, turning his head briefly. 'Get worse every day, don't they?'

She felt sorry for Claire, although she couldn't honestly say that she had ever really liked her. It wasn't that the woman virtually snubbed her – Claire treated everybody like that. No, it lay more in the fact that she was always so self-absorbed, had so little time for other people. She'd never got to know Claire because there wasn't really a Claire to know – not in the way she understood the word.

They were clear of the shopping streets and speeding towards Kilburn.

' 'bout another five minutes,' the taxi driver informed her.

The new Jimmy was very confusing, she thought. He was much kinder and more considerate than the old Jimmy.

'You could do with a holiday, Maggie,' he'd said. 'Why don't you take young Paul away at Easter?'

She'd laughed.

'Why get wet away when you can get wet at home?'

'It doesn't rain everywhere, you know.'

'It certainly seems to.'

'Not abroad, it doesn't.'

'Abroad! I've never been abroad.'

'A friend of mine's got a villa in the Canaries. He'd lend it to you if I asked him.'

'I couldn't cope.'

Not alone with a child. Not without Paul. And she wouldn't go *with* Paul.

'You wouldn't have to cope. It'd only be for a week or so. I could come with you.'

She'd seen right through the charm of the old Jimmy, and had known that all she had to do was keep her distance and she would be safe. But this new, uncertain Jimmy was harder to resist. She wasn't sure exactly how she felt about him, only that finally, after all those years, she'd begun to like him, almost to be fond of him.

'We're here, lady,' the cabbie said. 'Lady?'

But Maggie was so deep in thought that she didn't hear him.

'How often does Uncle Jimmy come round to our house?' Paul asked, trying not to sound like an interrogator.

Young Paul mused as he munched on his biscuit. Grown-ups were very difficult to understand. They told you always to be honest, but sometimes when they asked you questions they didn't want to know the real answer, they wanted you to say something else.

'You don't want to play your drum now, do you, pet? Not when Mummy's got a headache?'

'No, Mummy.'

Although he did, he really did.

And he sensed that this was another of those times. Daddy didn't really want to know how often Uncle Jimmy came round to see him and Mummy, *whatever* he said, and while Paul wasn't going to lie, he would do his best to hide the truth.

'Paul?'

'He comes round quite a lot.'

'On the weekends when you don't come to see me?'

'Yes.'

A little too quick!

'Does he come at other times?'

'Well,' the child said grudgingly, 'he didn't come last Thursday because we had a football match against Ashton Primary.' A chance of escape! 'Would you like to know the score?'

'Not now. What do you do when Uncle Jimmy visits you?'

This was safe anyway. He could say what he did with Uncle Jimmy without saying how *often* he did it.

'We go to the woods. He showed me this place in a big eldiberry . . . elbaberry . . .'

'Elderberry.'

'. . . elderberry bush where he said you had a secret camp when you were little. He said he'd build me a secret camp when the weather gets warmer.'

'Doesn't he have to come back to London? To work? Like Daddy?'

The boy shook his head.

'He says he'll be around nearly all the time. Whenever I need him. Can I have another chocolate biscuit, please, Daddy.'

'Yes. What's Mummy like when Uncle Jimmy's there?'

'Like Mummy.'

'What I mean is, does she go very quiet?'

The child giggled.

'Mummy doesn't go quiet. Ever. Uncle Jimmy and her – she – laugh a lot. She likes Uncle Jimmy.' A frown crossed the small boy's forehead. '*We* like Uncle Jimmy, don't we, Daddy?'

'Yes, we like Uncle Jimmy,' Paul said.

But that doesn't mean we have to be fooled by him, have to believe everything he says.

He remembered a warm summer's day nearly twenty years earlier. *David holding the boy who had wrecked the Secret Camp. Jimmy brandishing a kitchen knife, shouting 'I'm going to cut your willie off,' the boy in tears, utterly humiliated, and Paul almost crying himself. Jimmy putting his arm around Paul's thin shoulder.*

'You've got to fight for what's yours, Paul. Any way you can.'

Young Paul looked down at the table, the fresh biscuit in his hand untouched.

'I've got a secret,' he mumbled. 'I'm not supposed to tell anybody, but you *are* my Daddy.'

'And you're so like me in so many ways,' Paul thought. 'Burdened with guilt and responsibility, always trying to do the right thing and never sure that you have.'

'What's the secret?' he asked.

'Uncle Jimmy said we could go away for a holiday. Across the sea to a place where they have lots of lakes and big mountains. He said we'd be like spies. Not *really* like spies, I mean we wouldn't do anything naughty. We'd just be playing a game.'

Paul's stomach churned, his head swam and his mouth was suddenly very dry.

'What kind of game?' he croaked.

'We'd pretend that he was my daddy. He said it would be easy because I look just like him.'

Paul's hand shook as he reached for the telephone.

'You're a big boy now,' he said, 'and I'm going to ask you to do something for me. I'm calling you a taxi and sending you back to Mummy. And you must promise to sit very quietly in the back until you get there. Will you do that?'

'I only just came, Daddy.'

'I know. I'll see you again tomorrow,' Paul said, so unconvincingly that the child knew he didn't mean it.

*

425

David was working in the yard when the phone call came through.

'He just put young Paul in a taxi and sent him right back to me,' Maggie said hysterically. 'I don't know where he is now, but I'm sure he's heading back to Norton.'

'Why?'

'I think he's jealous of Jimmy. The boy must have told him that Jimmy promised him a helicopter ride this weekend. I told him not to. At the station I told him. But you know what children are. Oh David, I'm so frightened he'll do something terrible.'

'When did all this happen?'

'About twenty minutes ago.'

'Then Paul won't be up here for at least another couple of hours. I'll go and see Jimmy myself.'

The sign outside Jimmy's house said 'For Sale'. David knocked on the door and Jimmy opened it.

'Hello, old chap,' he said. 'Nice to see you. Come on in.'

It was all wrong. The voice, the gesture, as Jimmy invited him into the house. This jovial smoothness was the face Jimmy reserved for the outside world, not the one he showed to his best mates.

'We need to have a serious talk,' David said in the hallway. 'Shall we go into your study?'

'No, I . . . I don't use it any more.'

They went into the living room instead. The three piece suite was still in place but everything else was either gone or packed up in boxes.

'So you're movin',' David said, sitting on the sofa.

'Yes. This house holds too many unhappy memories for me.'

'An' where are you movin' to?'

'Haven't decided yet,' Jimmy said evasively. He walked to the other end of the room, opened a box and took out a bottle of Bell's whisky. 'Drink? I'm afraid I haven't got any glasses.'

'It's a bit early in the day for me.'

'Don't mind if I have one, do you?' Jimmy asked, but he had already uncapped the bottle and was lifting it to his lips.

There'd been a boxing machine in the amusement arcade they'd visited as children – model figures in a glass case who could be made to punch one another by moving the right handles. And that was what this conversation was like, David thought – two wooden men sparring. It was time to end the pretence.

'Paul's on his way up,' he said bluntly.

'Oh yes? That'll be nice. We must go out for a pint. Like in the old days.'

'He's not coming to see *us*. He's coming to see *you*.'

Jimmy feigned mild curiosity.

'Really? Why?'

'He thinks you're trying to steal young Paul from him.'

'Wherever did he get that idea from?'

'Come on, Jimmy, for Christ's sake!' David said angrily. 'You haven't been to London for months and now you're sellin' your house in the constituency without any plans to buy another.'

Jimmy laughed unconvincingly.

'Parliament's not like school, you know. They don't take a register, And there's no rule that says an MP has to have a house in the area which elects him.'

David remembered the night of the '70 election. His fear of what Paul would do if he ever found out that it was Jimmy who'd told Major Yatton about Maggie's child. He glanced at his watch. Paul would be well on his way to Norton by now. This thing had to be resolved before he arrived.

'I've seen you two in the woods together,' he said. 'Seen the way you hold his hand, the way you talk to him. You want him, Jimmy.'

The masked dropped from Jimmy's face. The effortless grace which had carried him through life deserted him. He was suddenly tense and coiled – a wild animal cornered and ready to spring.

'He's my son.'

'No,' David said. 'He's Paul's son.'

'For God's sake, David, you've only got to look at him.'

'I'm not sayin' he's not – what's the phrase – the seed of your loins, but he's not your son. You gave up any rights on that when Paul married Maggie.'

'Paul can have more children. His own. All I want is mine.'

'Maggie can't have any more. You know that.'

'Then he can dump Maggie and get somebody else.'

'You could dump Claire.'

Jimmy's shoulders slumped for the first time in David's memory.

'It wouldn't make any difference,' he said wearily. 'Claire . . . injured me. I can perform – just about – but I can't have any more children. Young Paul's the only one I've got.'

'He's not yours,' David said firmly. 'You've lost this one, Jimmy, like Paul lost the strike at Blackthorne's. It won't be easy, but you'll have to accept it – just like he did.'

'It's not the same thing, David,' Jimmy said. He was almost screaming. 'Surely even a thick bastard like you can see that.'

'It is,' David insisted. 'We're the Secret Camp Gang. There's certain things we can do, and certain things we can't. If you take the kid off his dad – and you could, Jimmy, you've got charm enough to win over any eight-year-old – then you'll destroy Paul. We've all hurt each other, and sometimes we've meant to. But we've never betrayed one another, an' we're not going to start now.'

'The Secret Camp Gang,' Jimmy sneered. 'We're not kids any more.' He took another slug of Bell's. 'When young Paul comes back on Monday, I'm going to tell him I'm his real father. And we'll soon see which of his two daddies he prefers.'

'I can't let you do that,' David said gravely.

'Then you'll have to kill me.'

'You don't mean it.'

'Don't I?' Jimmy asked.

His face was pale but his eyes blazed with determination. And the eyes said, 'There are some things worse than death. Hell doesn't have to be a hot burning cavern. It can be here on earth – cold and lonely.'

'Please, Jimmy,' David said. Tears flooded his eyes. Tears like those he had cried for Barry, those he had cried for Phil. 'Please, Jimmy, don't make me do it.'

'I'll tell him on Monday. I'll meet him at the station.'

David rose heavily to his feet. Jimmy was only yards away, but there was still time for him to say something to stop this happening.

Silence!

David started to walk across the room. His giant frame, a masterpiece of muscle and bone, moved stiffly – unwillingly.

A smile came to Jimmy's lips and for a moment he was the old Jimmy again, the one who had enjoyed the risk of the Odd Man Out.

'Be careful, David,' he warned. 'A whisky bottle can do a lot of damage. Claire showed me that.'

But he made no effort to use it as David's massive hands went around his throat. The broad thumbs pressed the jaw upwards and the head back. Death came with a slight click.

. . . The school yard, the ant pit, all that followed – everything they'd done for each other, everything they were to each other – had been leading up to this. A sad funeral on a freezing March morning. They reached the lych-gate and turned to wait for the policemen.

The rest of the mourners still stood around the grave. Mrs Bradley, grey-haired now, staring into the hole. Unable to believe that anything had happened – could ever happen – to her wonderful golden boy. Mr Bradley putting his arm around her, for once needed for more than his pay packet, for once making his presence felt.

Paul's parents were there – his mother had never liked Jimmy, but she knew what was right. And the Harrisons, all grown-up, but still clustering around their mother as they had at their dad's funeral.

Other faces. Stan Blackthorne, Jimmy's first boss, shoulders slumped, head bowed. Robert Macintosh, his normal dour expression shrouded in a look of conventional piety. Major and Mrs Peel, who had travelled by over-night train – second class – to see their son-in-law buried. The politicians who nightly invaded the television screen and were on show even here . . .

Chief Inspector Cooke drew level with the lych-gate.

'David Harrison?'

'Yes.'

'I arrest you for the murder of James Philip Bradley. You are not obliged to say anything, but anything you do say will be taken down and may be used in evidence against you.'

David had never been a man for wasting words.

'Yes, I did it,' he said, and held out his arms for the handcuffs.

It would have been hard to miss seeing such a big man being bundled into the police car right outside the church. Within half an hour Norton Central Police Station was besieged by a pack of hungry reporters and more were already setting out from London.

In contrast to the hysteria outside, Interview Room Two exuded an air of calm. Chief Inspector Cooke flicked the ash from his cigarette into an old tobacco tin and looked across at David.

'We thought at first Mr Bradley'd fallen and broken his neck,' he said in the matey voice he had often found more effective than the aggressive approach. 'After all, there he was, lying at the foot of the stairs, stinking of alcohol. And then we got the results of the PM. Most of the whisky wasn't inside him at all, just splashed over his clothes. And his injuries weren't consistent with a fall.'

'It was stupid of me to try an' cover it up,' David admitted.

He was full of surprises, this one, Cooke thought. He'd been completely open in the graveyard. Why then, did Cooke get the feeling that he was lying now? And *what* was he lying about? It *had* been bloody stupid to try and cover it up.

'We'd have got on to you sooner,' the Chief Inspector continued, 'if we'd been able to find the neighbour. He saw you enter the house, heard the row, noticed you rushing out again, then buggered off for a few days to his cottage on some God-forsaken Welsh hillside. In March! No running water, no electricity – and no newspapers. Didn't know a thing about it until he got back.'

'I always expected to be punished in the end. I just wanted to stay free long enough to see Jimmy properly buried.'

'Anything more you want to add? Any extenuating circumstances?'

'No.'

'All right, son. I'll have your statement drawn up and you can sign it.' He moved closer to the tape recorder on the table, to make sure that his voice came out clearly and distinctly. 'You have made this statement voluntarily and refused a solicitor even though one has been offered to you. I ask you again, do you wish to see a solicitor?'

A hesitation.

'Not a solicitor, but there is somebody I'd like to see.'

Cooke exchanged glances with the sergeant sitting opposite.

'A relation?'

'A friend.'

'The one who's been waiting outside? What's-his-name? Wright? Used to be a Labour candidate?'

'Yes.'

Cooke shrugged.

'Why not?' he said, almost to himself.

Paul stood in the doorway and looked across the interview room with tired eyes. Walls brown to waist height, green above. Small window near the ceiling. Table in the middle with two chairs on opposite sides. David sitting on one of the chairs.

He advanced across the room towards his old mate. David started to rise, but when the sergeant placed a warning hand on his shoulder he sank back into his seat. And so instead of hugging each other, they were forced to settle for an awkward handshake across the table.

'How are you, David?'

'Bearin' up.'

God, how conventional, how false, the whole thing was.

'Could you leave us alone for a while?' Paul asked.

'I'm going anyway, but my sergeant'll have to stay,' Cooke replied sharply. Then he remembered that despite his fall from grace Paul still had influence in the town. 'He'll stand by the door. He won't listen.'

The Chief Inspector left, the sergeant took up his assigned position. The two friends sat looking at each other, separated by a table – and a death.

'Why did you do it?' David asked in an angry whisper. 'Why did you try to make it look like an accident? Didn't you know you could have gone to jail for that?'

Paul had known, but he hadn't cared. He'd arrived at the house and found Jimmy on the carpet, his neck bent at an inelegant angle. The whisky bottle was by his side, almost as if Fate had left it there to point the way. He'd picked it up and tried to pour the liquid down his dead friend's throat.

'Why?' David asked again.

'Because I'd have done anything – anything – to protect you.'

They had always protected each other, the three of them, and that would not change now there were only two. So he had done what he had to do with the body.

The body! It hadn't mattered that the head banged on each stair as Paul pulled and strained. It hadn't mattered that the trunk bounced first against the banister and then against the wall when he threw it down again. It wasn't Jimmy any more, it was just a lifeless slab of meat.

'An' you were sure that it was me who'd killed him.'

Yes, immediately, but it hadn't been until he was dragging the corpse upstairs that he'd realised how he could be *so* sure.

'It *had* to be you,' Paul said, his voice cracking, 'because it wasn't me. And we were the only ones who cared enough about him to kill him.'

David nodded sadly.

While he was faking the accident, Paul hadn't stopped to ask himself *why* David had killed Jimmy. It was enough that he had and must be saved from the consequences. Punishing the one would not bring back the other. He would have felt the same, done the same, if it had been David lying there instead of Jimmy.

But since then – since he had taken a final look at his dead friend and left the house for ever – he had been racked by guilt.

'I've got to know *why* you did it,' he pleaded. 'Was it for me? Was it because he was trying to steal my son?'

'I did it because you both needed the same thing,' David said heavily, 'an' Jimmy couldn't have found a balance this time. Somebody had to lose out an' it was Jimmy who was goin' to break the rules.'

The rules of the Secret Camp, a hollowed out elderberry bush which had come to mean so much more.

'I think I did it for Jimmy, too.'

'For Jimmy?'

'I asked him at your weddin' if he'd have married Maggie if the coins had turned up different. He said he would, because it was the right thing to do.'

Paul had always wondered. And finally, when Jimmy was dead, he had his answer.

'Why are you telling me this now?' he asked.

'Because there's more. He'd have given the child his name, taken out a big insurance in its favour, an' then done away with himself. He said he couldn't settle for just bein' content. With him, it was all or nothin'. An' that's how he felt when young Paul started to matter to him. He couldn't share him. He couldn't play the godfather any longer.'

'I still don't . . .'

'Jimmy never *wanted* to take Paul off you. He never wanted to hurt you. But bein' Jimmy, he *had* to have it all . . .'

'. . . or nothing,' Paul said, understanding at last.

'He'd only to say he'd give up Paul to stop me killin' him. It would have been a lie, an' I'd have known it was a lie, but I couldn't have gone through with it. But he didn't lie. Because he could see that I was offerin' him a way out.'

'Oh, Jimmy, Jimmy,' Paul thought. 'What made you like you were? You'd do anything to get on. Sleep with girls you didn't fancy, charm men you despised. But when it came to something you really wanted, you wouldn't give an inch.'

'If anybody had to kill him, it should have been me,' he said. 'I should be in here, not you.'

David shook his head.

'You've got a future. A son. After Phil died, I'd got nothin' left to lose.'

'You'll be a lonely old queen like me one day,' Archie had said outside the recording studio in London a million years ago.

The sergeant at the door coughed discreetly.

'Time to leave, sir.'

Paul stood up but made no move to go.

'Get yourself off,' David encouraged. 'And don't worry about me. Remember how I built a business with only fifty quid. Remember how I saved The Diamond. I've never yet dug myself a hole I couldn't find my way out of.'

People didn't knock on front doors in Buckton, not unless there was a wedding – or a funeral. Paul groped sleepily for the alarm clock. Seven a.m. He opened a window and stuck his head out. Christ, it was cold.

A grim-faced policeman stood in the street below, next to a patrol car.

'What do you want?' Paul demanded.

'Chief Inspector Cooke would like to see you down at Norton Central, sir.'

'Now?'

'Now.'

'Am I under arrest?'

'No, sir, but he said to tell you it's very important.'

There was black ice on the road, and the car moved at a crawl. The driver was silent, and Paul filled his worried mind by looking out of the window. Frost clung to the panes of the phone box. Salt workers pedalled up the street, breaths frozen, eyes red and watering. At the edge of the village a scraggy stray dog huddled against the wall, getting what shelter it could from the biting wind.

Just outside Norton, they saw a crashed car, its bonnet concertinaed into a lamp-post. The windscreen was smashed and the pavement stained red. Paul's driver pulled up and wound down his window, letting the cold air stream in.

'Anything I can do?' he asked the constable standing by the wrecked vehicle.

'Not a lot anybody can do for the poor bastard that was drivin' this.'

433

They moved off again, even more cautiously.

It was half past seven by the time they reached Norton Central. Cooke was already down in the cells, but his sergeant briefed Paul on what had happened. A constable was detailed to show him where to go. Paul followed him like a zombie along the echoing corridors, down the stone steps.

The Chief Inspector was waiting for him at the entrance to the holding complex.

'Where's David?' Paul asked in a voice that was little more than a croak.

'In there.'

Paul opened the door and looked up at David's huge head and broad shoulders. And at his trunk-like legs – hovering six inches off the ground.

He flung his arms around his hanging friend. His fingertips only just met and his head reached no higher than David's rib cage. He tensed and lifted, so that the neck was no longer stretched. Even though he knew it was pointless because the body was already cold and stiff.

Cooke, who hadn't let him hold David in life, in the interview room, did not interfere now. Paul stood there for a full five minutes until the weight – the dead weight – became too much and he gently lowered David down again.

'Why is he still hanging there?' he demanded angrily.

'Can't cut him down until the experts have had a look at him,' Cooke said.

'And why did you have *me* brought here? So you could gloat?'

'No, sir, not so we can gloat. So that you could see for yourself how it happened.'

He was Paul Wright and he still had political pull. The Chief Inspector didn't want him stirring up trouble.

'We take all the precautions we can,' Cooke said, 'but if a man really wants to kill himself, you'll not stop him.'

No, it would take a better man than Cooke to stop David doing what he wanted.

'Any idea *why* he did it, sir?'

Because life was meaningless without Phil?

Because David, who thought best when he was striding along the canal bank or through the woods, would have hated the restriction of short walks in a walled enclosure?

Yes, that was part of it. But not all. He *had* gone on living after Phil's death and he *had* worked for years in Fred Rathbone's junkyard prison. What finally pushed him over the edge must have been the thought of the trial.

The prosecution would have searched for a motive, even though David had confessed. They would have talked to witnesses who'd noticed a resemblance between the murdered man and Paul Wright's son. They would have remembered the reports of Paul's debate with Major Yatton. They would have uncovered the story piece by piece, until they had an almost complete picture. It would all have come out in court.

And in later years, when he was old enough to understand, young Paul would hear all about it.

'I said, have you any idea why he hung himself, sir?' Cooke persisted.

'He did it so that Jimmy wouldn't have died for nothing.'

'I don't follow your meaning,' Cooke said.

Of course he didn't! How could he? It would take a lifetime together to really understand. Paul turned and marched towards the stairs, leaving the Chief Inspector to puzzle it out as best he could.

After the shock and the anger came the numbness. Paul sat in the police canteen drinking mug after mug of hot, sweet tea, hardly tasting it, hardly even aware where he was. His mind replayed scenes from the past – when there had been three of them. And now there was only one.

Slowly, the paralysis wore off. By half-past nine, two hours after he had abandoned his friend's body to the police, he felt ready to move again.

There were no reporters outside as there had been the day before, just a pretty blonde woman waiting on the corner. How long had she been standing there in the cold? Half an hour? An hour? Longer than that. He had made her wait in the cold for him for years.

He saw that she was crying.

'You've heard,' he said.

'Yes. Have you seen him?'

Paul nodded.

'It's all my fault,' she said.

Because she had made the phone call which had led David to Jimmy's house? That had only been the last link in a long chain of events.

'It's nobody's fault,' he assured her. 'Least of all yours.'

'Do you want to go home?' she asked.

'Not yet.'

David was everywhere – the Drill Hall, in the woods, but most of all in the little palace he had built for Barry, a few doors down from Paul's house.

'Let's go for a walk, then,' Maggie said. 'It's cold just standing here.'

'Where do you want to go? Down by the river?'

He had walked there while Maggie struggled to give birth to young Paul. He had met Lucy there and told her that their relationship had to end.

'The park,' Maggie said.

The park! Yes, it had to be faced. The park was the place it had all started. Without the carnival night, they would all have led very different lives. Maggie would have married someone else, someone who could have brought her the happiness she deserved. Paul would have gone to Oxford, David would not be hanging in a police cell. Jimmy would not now be lying in a cold grave. If Maggie was brave enough, then so was he.

Arms linked, though through the thick cloth of their coats it was hardly like touching at all, they walked through the ornamental gates. The frost covered the paving stones with an icy sheen. The pond was frozen over, the flower beds a moonscape of petrified soil. Stark trees stood like crucified messiahs against the pale sun.

'I've written a book,' Paul said. 'It's about us . . . all of us.'

'Oh yes.'

Neutral. Cautious. Not touching.

'It's going to be published. I got the letter yesterday morning. Just before I set off for the funeral.'

'You should have started writing a long time ago.'

He had. The stories he had written in secondary school! The notebooks he'd filled! The novel he was going to write when he got to Oxford! Then there had been the night in this park, and it had all come to an end.

'Will you be able to live off your writing?' Maggie asked.

'Not at first, but maybe eventually.'

'That's good, then.'

This wasn't them talking, he thought. They'd never talked like this.

They reached the crown of the hill and gazed across the flat expanse of land which led to the northern boundary of the park. The ground was rutted with tyre marks, and the edges of the ruts, frozen now, seemed razor sharp.

This was where the funfair had been. Over there was the booth

436

where the Everton Kid had pounded hell out of David and then taken a dive himself so that he wouldn't have to hurt his opponent any more.

'He was the gentlest man I've ever met,' David had said.

David, with hands like spades and a trunk as hard as oak. David, who could lift a hundredweight of scrap or break a human neck as if it were nothing.

'And you were the gentlest man *I've* ever met,' Paul said silently to his dead friend.

Maggie wheeled him round and led him through the skeletal trees to a clearing – to *the* clearing.

It all came back to him.

Maggie lying on the ground, the flashing lights of the fairground – the music.

I . . . wond . . . er if one day that . . . you'll say that . . . you care,
If you say you love me mad . . . ly, I'll glad . . . ly be there,
Like a pupp . . . et on a string,
Like a pupp . . . et on a . . . string.

Himself, a puppet on a string, thrusting away in time to the music, feeling no lust, wanting only not to be left out.

Jimmy, smiling that ruthless smile of his, the smile he kept for people outside the gang.

'I don't care what happens later, Paul. All I want now is a bloody good shag!'

Ah, but would you have cared if you'd known where it would all lead, Jimmy? Cold and stiff at the age of twenty-seven.

He saw it as clearly now as he had that first time they had made love on their honeymoon. Jimmy thrusting elegantly, David ploughing away. Into Maggie. The two of them, always coming between him and the woman he had married. They wouldn't come between them any more. They *couldn't* come between them any more.

Maggie suddenly pulled herself free of him and knelt down at the base of a tree.

'Look!' she said.

In the middle of the hard, tangled root system had sprouted a clump of snowdrops.

'Aren't they beautiful?'

'Yes,' Paul agreed. 'But they won't survive the frost.'

Maggie laughed. It had been a long time since he'd heard her laugh.

'They're not meant to survive,' she said. 'They're messengers

437

from nature. They say, "Keep your chin up. Won't be much longer until everything's green again." They give hope, and when they've done their job, they die.'

She rose to her feet and he cupped her face in his hands. Her skin felt cold even through his gloves.

'The important thing about my book isn't that it's going to be published,' he said. 'The important thing is what I've learned from writing it. About me. About you.'

She made an effort to pull away, but he held her firm.

'When young Paul told me about Jimmy spending all that time at the house, about how you seemed so happy when he was there, I thought you were planning to run away together.'

'I never . . .'

'And when I caught the train last Saturday, I wasn't only doing it to save my son. I was fighting for you as well.'

'That's all I ever wanted,' she said. 'Not your protection, not your concern. Just to be important enough to fight for. I think that's why I slept with your father.'

'So that I'd fight him? Or so that I'd say I loved you?'

She was silent, but her eyes challenged him on to the total honesty he had once promised her.

'I never said it, did I? All those years and I never once told you I loved you.'

'I . . . used to think it would come in time, but it never did.'

'I didn't love you. I could have lied, but I'd never have fooled you, would I?'

'No,' she admitted. 'I'm not easy to fool.'

'And if I told you that I love you now – finally – would you believe me?'

'Yes.'

'But is it too late? Have I left it too late?'

Maggie looked down at the ground and nibbled her lip.

'Is it?' Paul shouted. 'Is it too late?'

And the stark black trees echoed back at him, 'Too late. Too late.'

She lifted her eyes and looked into his.

'Maybe,' she said. 'I don't know.'

He wrapped his arms around her, hugging her body to his, and felt her hands pressing against his back.

They stood there for a long time. Around them the soil cracked and groaned as the icy fingers of frost bit into it. Above them, the watery sun shed its sickly light on the dead park. They did not move, they did not speak. They were two little people, surrounded by a hostile universe, keeping each other warm.

A Picnic in Eden

SALLY SPENCER

ORION

Puppet on a String. Words and music by Bill Martin and
Phil Coulter © 1967, reproduced by kind permission
of Peter Maurice Music Co Ltd, London WC2H 0EA.

The right of Sally Spencer to be identified as the author of this work
has been asserted by her in accordance with the
Copyright, Designs and Patents Act 1988.

First published in Great Britain in 1995 by
Orion
An imprint of Orion Books Ltd
Orion House, 5 Upper St Martin's Lane, London WC2H 9EA

A CIP catalogue record for this book is available
from the British Library

ISBN 1 85797 686 X

Typeset by Deltatype Limited, Ellesmere Port, Cheshire

Printed in Great Britain by
Butler & Tanner Ltd, Frome and London